PAUL CRILLEY

Clockwork City

HODDER &
STOUGHTON

First published in Great Britain in 2017 by
Hodder & Stoughton
An Hachette UK company

1

Copyright © Paul Crilley 2017

A CIP catalogue record for this title is available from the British Library

Hardback ISBN 978 1 47363 163 2
Trade Paperback ISBN 978 1 47363 164 9

Typeset in Plantin Light by Hewer Text UK Ltd, Edinburgh
Printed and bound by Clays Ltd, St Ives plc

Hodder & Stoughton policy is to use papers that are natural, renewable
and recyclable products and made from wood grown in sustainable
forests. The logging and manufacturing processes are expected to
conform to the environmental regulations of the country of origin.

Hodder & Stoughton Ltd
Carmelite House
50 Victoria Embankment
London EC4Y 0DZ

www.hodder.co.uk
www.hodderscape.co.uk

For my kids, Bella and Caeleb

It started off rough, I won't lie. What with the whole no-talking thing (what's with that?) and the nappies and the puking. But you guys have turned into a pair of pretty damn cool people (now that you're old enough to understand sarcasm), and I think we can all agree this is thanks in no small part to your amazing dad. I mean, I'll give you some credit, but I think we all know everything good and cool about you is down to me. Remember that when I'm old and decrepit and you want to put me in a home.

And for Jo

We met during a deadline crunch of momentous proportions and you didn't run away screaming. In fact, you were incredibly patient and understanding and helped me get through it. (Weirdo.) So you can't say in the future that you didn't know what you were getting into. And to show my appreciation, if I ever get famous I'll try my best to meet Gerard Butler so you guys can become drinking buddies.

But seriously, you are my idea of perfect. You have a strength, a kindness, and a decency I've never seen in anyone before, and I'm humbled every day that you chose to spend your life with me.

Here's to us, fucker.

I

'My point . . .' The dog gags and spits the severed finger onto the floor. He staggers slightly, then gives up and just leans against the bar. 'What was my point again? Something about Christmas, wasn't it? About the purity of Christmas music. Take "Christmas in Hollis", for example, the one from *Die Hard*—'

'You weren't talking about Christmas music,' I snap, tying a dirty dishcloth around the shebeen owner's stump. 'That was two hours ago. What you *were* saying, right before you decided to bite this man's finger off, was that you don't touch another man's sherry.'

The dog straightens up. 'Yes!' he says happily. 'That was it! You don't touch another man's sherry. Or a dog's. It's just not *done*, London. It's frowned upon in polite society. *And* impolite society.' The dog burps. ''S a fact.'

'I'm not disagreeing,' I say. 'I just wonder if biting off his finger was the best way to resolve the situation.'

'Only way, London,' says the dog loftily. 'Go in fast and go in hard. Bet he won't think about touching someone else's drink again. Am I right?' The dog staggers over to where the guy is lying on the dirt floor of the shebeen and sticks his muzzle right in his face. 'I said, am I right?'

The man stares at the dog in terror. He drags his eyes away and stares pleadingly at me. I pat his chest. 'Don't worry. It's all a bad dream. You'll wake up tomorrow with a bit of a hangover and a missing finger. A wild dog did it.' I point at the bane of my life. 'Not this one, though. And he certainly didn't talk. Understand?'

The man frantically nods.

The dog wanders back to his bowl. 'It's his own fault. There's a code involved when you drink in a pub. Everyone knows it. You don't talk politics or religion, you don't make a move on someone's man or woman, and you do not – I repeat, *do not* – touch someone else's drink.'

'Like I said, I don't disagree. But the whole idea here was to keep a low profile.'

'Blame the sherry thief for that. I was *content*, London! Content to sit and drink my sherry. I'm trying to partake in the sentiments of the season. You *know* I love Christmas. Anyway, you should thank me. He's more likely to talk now.'

I sigh and pull the guy to his feet. I drag him across the floor and lower him into a plastic lawn chair. The shebeen is empty now. Amazing how people have more important places to be when a dog that's lapped up the equivalent of two bottles of sherry suddenly goes mad and starts biting off body parts.

I pull up another plastic chair and set it down in front of the shebeen owner. 'So . . . now we've got all that over with, where is he?'

The man pulls his horrified gaze away from the now-red bandage. 'Whu . . . ?'

'The Sangoma. Where is he?'

'I . . . don't know what you're talking about.' His eyes swivel down to his hand. Tears spring to his eyes. 'My finger. It was a good finger. The ladies liked what I did with it.' He looks at me sadly. 'It was very long you see. I—'

'Too much information there, pal,' I say quickly, cutting him off. 'Now come on. We traced the phone call to this place. We know you called in the tip-off. Just tell us about the Sangoma and we'll be on our way.'

The guy nervously licks his lips. 'He . . . he's not a Sangoma. He's . . . Umthakathi.'

Umthakathi. The bad version of a witch doctor. Palpatine compared to Yoda. I feel a flutter of excitement. Of hope. Maybe I'm on the right track after all. Five young girls have gone missing from the area. Only, it's not just here. There's actually been a surge in missing kids lately, something I discovered while searching for leads on my daughter, Cally. We're thinking child trafficking, but with a supernatural twist. We have two operatives, Lerato Sekibo, and Ayanda Odili, over in London right now. They're following up another lead while I came to Cape Town to check things out down south.

That's how desperate I am for a lead. I came to *Cape Town*. Voluntarily.

'Why do you think he's involved?' I ask.

'We've all heard. Sounds from his hut. And . . . lights. The shadows move. Even when they shouldn't. People say . . .' He looks around nervously. 'People say they've heard girls crying.'

Bingo.

'Which way?'

'West. Over . . . over the hill. There's a forest.'

'Right.' I nod at his hand. 'I'd get that seen to. You're losing a lot of blood. Dog. Come on.'

'Don't talk to me like I'm your pet,' he snarls.

I have to fight down a sudden surge of anger at his tone. It takes a lot of effort. It's been getting harder and harder lately to control my temper. To stop the anger cresting and breaking, spilling out into those around me.

I exit the tavern, staggering to a stop as the stifling December heat pummels me. I take a few steadying breaths, forcing myself to calm down, then shield my eyes and study my surroundings.

The setting sun sets fire to the township. Roofs made from corrugated metal catch the glare and magnify it, harsh orange light blinding me as I cast my eyes across the multi-coloured huts. There are thousands of them, made from scrap metal and wood. They're painted all the colours of the rainbow, some even made from salvaged advertising signs, cellular phone and washing powder billboards that have been hacked up and repurposed.

Kids run along the dirt tracks that dissect the settlement, laughing and shouting, skinny dogs barking frantically and chasing after them. Old pickup trucks and minibus taxis speed along the dirt roads, narrowly avoiding running people over.

My gaze lifts higher, to the western end of the valley. The slope is already cloaked in shadow. On the other side of the rise is the forest where our target apparently lives.

I set off down the hill, moving deeper into the township.

-London. Hold up.-

The dog's speaking mind to mind. Which means he's probably realised he went too far. You know, what with biting a man's finger off and everything. I pause and wait for him.

-I don't even know why you're wasting your time with this,- he complains as he catches up.

Because someone is kidnapping young girls. Which means it could be a lead on whoever kidnapped Cally. That name. That elusive fucking name I had to give up to Mother Durban in order to stop Lilith infecting the world with God's sins. Over the past month I've searched through every Delphic Division record and file, and this is the first remotely plausible lead I've found. I personally doubt it is the Umthakathi. They're too . . . human for this. But Umthakathi sometimes have help from the other side.

Everything is hazy and golden as we hurry along the dirt road. I can hear laughter, voices raised in conversation. Winking Christmas tree lights shine through windows.

Only a week to go till Christmas. Can't come soon enough if you ask me. The dog gets incredibly annoying during the season. Not sure if it's because he thinks it's more acceptable to drink his sherry or what, but it's his favourite time of year. He's like a little kid. I have to buy him presents and everything.

- You realise it's probably just a tokoloshe.-

'It's not a goddamn *tokoloshe*,' I snap. 'It's *never* a *tokoloshe*. Ever. I doubt *tokoloshe* actually exist. I've never seen one. Have you?'

- There was that one time. In KwaMashu township.-

'That wasn't a *tokoloshe*.' I step over thick, twisted electrical cables snaking across the ground. The cables connect to homemade junction boxes held together with duct tape and covered over with plastic carrier bags to protect them from the rain. Illegal electricity powers the entire settlement. 'That was a pervert dressed up in a costume trying to see women in their bras and panties.'

- Whatever. I still think it's a tokoloshe.-

'It's *not* a *tokoloshe*,' I growl.

- Fine. Have it your way. Just don't say I didn't warn you when a little hairy monster comes at you, swinging his four-foot dick as a weapon.-

We walk on in silence for another minute.

- Hey – what we watching when we get home? Lethal Weapon?-

I groan. The dog's current fixation is eighties action movies and Christmas carols. His favourite songs right now are 'Let it Snow', 'Jingle Bell Rock', and the aforementioned 'Christmas in Hollis'. He plays those three songs on repeat. In the car. At home. Everywhere.

On the plus side, I *did* get some blackmail material out of it. The dog got pissed on sherry and started dancing around the apartment on his hind legs. Funniest goddamn thing I'd seen in ages, I'm telling you. I recorded him on my phone and played it back to him the next day. He threatened to rip out my throat if I showed it to anyone. He's been trying to get rid of the evidence ever since.

So that's what I'm dealing with in my life right now. Battling irrational bouts of rage, a permanently drunk spirit guide, eighties movies, and Christmas songs. Not necessarily in that order. Oh, and if the eighties movies happen to have a Christmas theme? All the better. I'm looking at you, Shane Black.

'Lethal Weapon is fine.'

-Are you going to wear your hat?-

He made me buy matching Christmas hats for us. They light up.

'That all depends on how much you annoy me.'

We're nearly at the far end of the settlement. The road is more pitted here. Rain from earlier in the afternoon has collected in potholes, rising from the ground as wispy steam. The humidity is made worse by the residents taking advantage of the last bit of sun to put out their washing, multi-coloured rainbows that hang between shacks oozing dampness into the air.

We follow the track leading up the slope, arriving at the outer boundary of the forest. Brown pine needles blanket the floor, a carpet of mulch still soaking wet from the rain.

The sun is almost gone by now, lowering beams slanting past the branches, limning the tree trunks in gold. A small shiver courses through me. Why is it so quiet here? I look around. No birds. No animals. Nothing.

I check over my shoulder, just to make sure the township is still there. It is, bathed in golden light. But all the sound is cut off.

'Not sure I like this,' mutters the dog. 'It's seriously harshing my festive sherry vibe.'

'Ditto.'

We set off, making our way through the trees as night falls around us. It seems to happen a lot faster than usual. Or maybe we're walking for longer than I realise.

I'm about to suggest we turn back when the dog suddenly stiffens.

-Life signs ahead.-

We move slowly forward, inching past the trees, trying not to rustle the grass.

-How far?- I ask.

The dog doesn't say anything.

-Dog? How far?-

-Right there . . . Look.-

It takes me a moment to see them.

Four girls.

They're standing around a tree, holding hands. Their heads hang down, chins resting against their chests.

I look down at the dog. He stares at the girls for a moment, then looks up at me.

-So . . . this isn't at all creepy,- he says.

-Tell me about it.-

We look back at the girls.

-Are they . . . are they swaying?- I ask.

-Yes. Almost imperceptibly.-

-Right. Off you go then.-

-You're a funny guy, London. I ever tell you that?-

-Come on! You're the magical spirit guide here. You're a . . . a biological transformer! What are you scared of?-

-London, let me tell you something. I've fought in a war between shadow stealers and the forgotten children of Barnabus Island. I've seen a battle fought in stormy skies between angels and demons, blood raining down on me. I've watched the inspiration for Peter Pan murder hundreds of children when they grew too old to be in his gang. I've eaten an apple pie baked from the actual *motherfucking apple discarded by Eve in the Garden of Eden. I've— -*

-Stop!-

The dog stops talking.

-Is any of that true?-

*-All of it.Well . . . except for the last one.There was no apple pie.
My point is I've seen some serious shit, and that . . . that right
there . . . freaks me the hell out.-*

We wait, but the girls don't seem inclined to do anything
except sway around the tree.

There are only four of them. The reports said there were
five missing girls. Where's the other one?

I feel a prickling up the back of my neck and look quickly
over my shoulder. Nothing.

Except the mist, of course. There's plenty of that, because
of course there is. Why not make it even creepier? I wipe the
sweat from my eyes. Why the hell does it have to be so damn
humid?

'Hello?' I call out to the girls.

No response. Which is even more worrying. If that had
been me standing out in the middle of nowhere and someone
shouted hello, I'd have jumped ten feet into the air.

I move slowly forward. 'Hey.'

Again, no response. Lightning flickers in the distance,
followed a moment later by a low rumble of thunder.

I'm a few feet away now. I hesitate, glance back over my
shoulder. I can't see the dog anymore.

-Keep going,- he says encouragingly. *-I'm right behind you.-*

Yeah. Twenty feet behind me.

I reach out and gently touch the girl closest to me.

As soon as my fingers touch her skin, all four girls' heads
snap up to look at me.

I stagger back, my heart thumping furiously. They don't do
anything else. Just stand and stare.

I study the girls. Their skin is pale, the shadows around
their eyes dark and heavy.

'Are you here to help us?' says one of them. Her voice is low
and monotone. I think they must have been drugged.

'Uh . . . yeah.' I look nervously around. The woods feel like they're closing in on me. Branches sway in the warm wind, the whispering leaves a gentle susurration in the background.

I hold out my hand. 'Come on. Let's get you back to your families.'

One of the girls reaches out and takes my hand. She must be about twelve years old, the others slightly older. Her skin is cold and dry. I gently lead her away from the tree and the other girls follow after, still holding onto each other.

As I reach the dog another flash of lightning bursts above us, monochrome shadows leaping out from the trees. I freeze, peering into the darkness.

The dog appears by my side. *-What?-*

-I . . . thought I saw something.-

The dog pads forward, sniffing the ground.

-Well?-

-There's a smell. But I'm not sure what it is.-

-Orisha or human?-

-It . . . smells like an animal.-

We wait a few moments longer, peering into the shadows.

-An owl?- says the dog.

-Maybe.-

We start moving again. We make our way back through the trees, the girls following close behind. It takes us almost an hour but we finally crest a rise and see the lights of the township spread out below us. I've never been so happy to see so many cheap Christmas lights flickering on and off.

Civilisation.

Safety.

A bolt of lightning arcs out of the sky and grounds itself right behind the settlement.

The township plunges into darkness.

Well . . . shit.

I blink, waiting for my eyes to adjust. The weight of the night snaps in around us, thick and velvety. Hot and heavy. It wraps around me, suffocating. The writhing mist is the only movement, slow and sinuous.

I look behind me. The girls are still there, silent and waiting. They're really freaking me out. They look unharmed, but they've definitely been given something. They're acting too spaced out.

I turn back to the township. Tiny flickers of light appear. At first I think it's fireflies, but then I realise it's candles being lit in the shacks.

-Hey, London.-

-Yeah?-

-Not to freak you out or anything, but I think we're being watched.-

The hairs on the back of my neck prickle. *-Where?-*

-3 o'clock.-

I shift my head slightly. I scan the darkness between the trees, but can't see anything.

-In the branches.-

I look up.

-Where——?-

Then I see it. Some kind of dwarf-like creature is staring down at us from the tree.

I reach slowly for my gun. Carefully take it out. I wince as I rack the slide, the metallic sound piercing through the night.

I raise my arm to shoot, but the creature hisses and leaps to the next tree before I even manage to pull the trigger. It pauses, looks back at me for a full second, black eyes glinting, then it whirls and leaps through the branches, heading deeper into the woods.

-Is that ... is that a fucking tokoloshe?- demands the dog, delight dripping from every word.

-Watch the girls.-

-It is, isn't it? It's a tokoloshe!-

I run after the creature.

-London! It's a tokoloshe*! I was right! London . . . ! London . . . ! LONDON!-*

-WHAT? Shut up! Jesus Christ, dog, just watch them!-

-Fine, but I was right! Suck it, skinbag!-

I can see the creature ahead of me, bounding between the trees. I hate admitting when the dog is right, because it just encourages him, but it actually looks like it might be an honest-to-God *tokoloshe*.

The wind picks up as I chase after the creature, tree branches flailing against the sky. The storm is coming in fast.

After a mile or so, the creature drops from the trees and veers off to the left, leaving the woods behind. I struggle to follow, my breath coming in wheezing gasps.

I stagger to a halt to catch my breath. I straighten up just as more lightning flickers behind the clouds. The brief flash of white reveals the *tokoloshe*, waiting patiently for me on top of a hill.

The bastard's waiting for me to catch up.

I set off again, this time at a slower pace. The *tokoloshe* vanishes over the hill, but when I reach the top I see it waiting at the bottom of the slope.

We carry on like this for another mile or so. Then, as I climb to the crest of another hill and start down the other side, I realise two things. One, the *tokoloshe* has disappeared, and two, there's a small hut not twenty feet from me, partially hidden by trees and bushes.

The door to the hut opens. Orange light and thick smoke drift out, followed by a small man wearing dirty trousers smoking a home-made cigarette. I sniff the air, noting the unmistakably sweet smell of marijuana.

The man squints at me. I stare back, noting the animal skulls hanging around the eaves, the different kinds of herbs growing in the garden. This is the Umthakathi – the witch doctor. Nobody else would live out here alone.

He smiles at me and waves. And then something heavy lands on my back and forces me to the grass.

My cheek is pushed hard into the ground. I struggle but the hand pushes my head deeper into the earth, claws pressing into my head. I'm trapped. I'm forced to watch as the Umthakathi ambles towards me. His bloodshot eyes regard me with sleepy interest. He kneels down and lowers his head so that he is looking directly into my eyes. Then he sniffs. Like an animal he inhales my scent, moving all over my body, down over my back, along my legs, then back up again. I try to wriggle free, but the clawed hand holding my head tenses in warning.

The Umthakathi's face appears in front of me again. He seems pleased with something. Dirty yellow teeth flash in another smile.

-*Dog? Could use your help right about* now.-

No answer. Makes sense. I must be way out of range.

The Umthakathi waves a hand in front of my nose, rubbing his fingers together as he crushes something into powder. The smell of vinegar wafts into my nostrils.

I try to speak, but my mouth doesn't work. Lethargy overwhelms me. All I want is sleep.

And then the vinegary smell lodges in the back of my throat and I find it difficult to breathe.

I wake up to find myself tied to a musty bed. I look around in confusion. The room is wreathed in marijuana smoke. I can taste it in my mouth, smell it everywhere about my person. How long have I been breathing it? A long time, I suspect. My head is spinning. Everything feels surreal.

The Umthakathi dances around the little hut. He's naked, and he seems to be dancing with a partner who isn't there; one hand around an invisible waist, the other holding a non-existent hand. I try to move my head, but it feels too heavy. I settle on moving my eyes around the hut.

The *tokoloshe* sits on a shelf just beneath the roof. Its arms are moving rhythmically and I realise the creature is masturbating a penis almost as tall as it is. I find this quite comical, and almost burst out laughing until I see that it's watching me with fierce concentration as it moves its hands up and down.

I test the ropes that tie my wrists. The left one is loose, but not loose enough that I can pull my thumb out.

'Hey,' I call out. 'Hey, old-timer.'

The Umthakathi stops dancing and turns to me, a frown of irritation on his face. He walks toward me, picking up a machete from the table as he comes.

'You know I'm a cop, right?' I pull at the rope, but it still doesn't budge. 'If you do anything to me, you're finished. Understand?'

The Umthakathi stops next to the bed. He lowers the blade so it hovers inches from my eye. I can see its pitted edge, covered in rust. The blade moves, touching my nose. Then it slides down over my mouth to stop at my neck.

I swallow nervously, then the blade is removed.

'I won't be doing anything to you, my friend,' says the old man. 'I was told to keep you safe.'

It takes a moment for the words to sink in.

'Told? The hell are you talking about?'

'You will see soon enough. It is almost time.'

He places the machete back on the table and starts dancing again, humming under his breath. I wriggle my left wrist back and forth, pulling down hard on the rope. After a minute or so I've rubbed my skin raw and soaked the rope with blood. I grit my teeth and pull with all my strength. The pain is excruciating but the blood-slick rope finally slides past my thumb. I breathe a sigh of relief and keep my hand where it is. I need to judge my next move perfectly. I won't have much time.

I wait until the Umthakathi turns his back as he dances with his invisible partner. Then I pull my hand free and frantically try to untie the knot that holds my right wrist to the bedpost. This one is tighter. I yank at the knot, bending my nails back as I try to find something to grip. I'm not getting it. Shit.

No, wait. I feel something give.

And then everything seems to happen at once. The *tokoloshe* sees what I'm doing and lets out a screeching wail that startles me so much I stop pulling at the knot and look up.

The Umthakathi grabs the machete again and runs at me, his teeth bared in a snarl. I yank hard at the knot. It loosens. Slowly.

The Umthakathi reaches the bottom of the bed and grabs for my feet. In the background, the *tokoloshe* drops from its shelf.

The knot parts.

I roll to the side and throw myself to the floor. I land heavily, my ankles still tied to the bedposts. The Umthakathi crawls over the bottom of the bed, pulling himself up my legs. I twist around and grab the silver knife I keep tucked away in my belt. I throw it and it hits the old fucker in the shoulder. He gasps. I use the distraction to grab the machete and swing it into his neck. It hits with a meaty thud. He shrieks in pain, blood sluicing down across his chest.

The *tokoloshe* is coming for me. I yank the machete free and throw it end over end, hitting the creature in the chest.

The creature screeches in pain, stumbling back against the wall. Black blood pours down over its stomach. It reaches up with trembling claws and pulls out the blade, dropping it to the floor. Then, mewling in pain, it turns and staggers towards the door.

I pull myself back onto the bed and untie my legs. I grab my knife from the Umthakathi's shoulder and turn toward the doorway.

I freeze. The *tokoloshe* is standing there, facing me. Its

wound is leaking a steady flow of black liquid onto the dirt. Its breath comes in ragged gasps.

But it's the creature's eyes that hold my attention. They bore into me with such hurt and betrayal that I feel as though I've stabbed a kid.

It turns from me and heads outside, looking back and once again waiting for me to follow.

I run after the *tokoloshe*. The creature leads me back into the woods. I try to keep it in sight, but after about ten minutes I lose the trail.

Then I hear something crying. The *tokoloshe*? No, this sounds human. I strain my ears as the warm wind flicks the sound in and out of hearing. It's a child.

The fifth missing girl.

I run through the trees, all thoughts of the *tokoloshe* driven from my mind. The crying grows louder. I burst through a clump of bushes and stumble to a stop. I stare in amazement.

The *tokoloshe* is lying on the ground, cradled in the lap of the girl. She's hugging it and crying.

'Hey!' I yell, stumbling toward her. 'Hey, get away from that thing! Don't let it touch you.'

The girl looks up at me and shakes her head, looking puzzled through her tears. 'Why? He helped me get away from the old man. He said he wanted to hurt me.'

I shake my head. 'What? Who said that?'

'The *tokoloshe*! He said he wouldn't let the old man hurt me like the others. He hid me here.'

Fragments of stories and myth drift through my mind. The *tokoloshe* raping women, beating men to death with sticks. Adults raising their beds on bricks so the creature couldn't reach them in their sleep.

But there are other stories too. Not gruesome enough to make it into everyday fears: the *tokoloshe* making friends with children, playing with them in total innocence, protecting them like a faithful dog.

Then the little girl starts laughing.

I stare at her in confusion. Then she tightens her grip and rips the head of the *tokoloshe* from its body.

She tosses the head at me and grins, showing sharp, serrated teeth. 'We've been waiting for you, Gideon Tau.'

I hear a noise behind me and whirl around.

The other four girls are standing there. They're smiling, but something about their faces isn't right. They reach up and poke their fingers into their eyeholes, tugging. Their skins fall away. The loose flesh drops to the ground and they step out of them like discarded towels.

I stare at them in horror. Their bodies are just nerves and exposed muscle. Yellow mucus drips from their joints and their eyes weep black, oily tears that coat their faces like running mascara.

Obia.

Demons that wear the skins of children and hunt in the night.

Fuck me, but I really got this one wrong.

2

The *obia* move closer, forming a tight circle around me. I feel like an idiot. An absolute rookie. I should have picked up what was going on. That they weren't human. Hell, the fucking *dog* should have smelled it.

Speaking of . . .

'Where's my dog?'

No answer.

'I swear to whatever god is listening, if you've done anything to him I'll hunt you down and exterminate your entire species, understand?'

Again, no answer. They just stand there, dripping at me.

Another rumble of thunder sounds in the distance. A caress of warm wind brushes my face, bringing with it the smell of disease and gangrene.

The grass around us ripples. At first I think it's the wind, but then I realise the grass is moving *against* the breeze.

I take a step back just as the grass shudders and undulates, rising up to reveal two *eloko*. *Eloko* are grass-covered killers from central Congo. They hunt down poachers and take them apart. Slowly.

A noise behind me. I turn around to find four creatures emerging from the trees. They have pale, bloodless skin, almost translucent white. Their faces are misshapen, their chins resting against their chests. They open their massive mouths, their jaws sliding to their stomachs, to reveal fangs as long as my fingers. The *vazimba*. Mindless killers who like to eat humans. I thought they had all been exterminated.

There's another sound to my right. This time I turn slowly, wearily, realising I'm absolutely fucked here. There are a large group of what I first think are children with dark skin and yellow eyes standing silently in the long grass.

The *emere*. One of Africa's elf analogues, a lot crueller and more bloodthirsty than their European counterparts. If that's even possible.

A huge crash echoes from the trees.

I bark out a laugh, wondering if I should feel flattered at all this attention. I squint into the darkness just as a huge giant lumbers through the brush, his head and neck absolutely covered with horns. A *yehwe zogbanu*. Sort of a cross between an ogre and a giant.

I'm utterly surrounded. I turn in a slow circle, wishing I had more bullets. Wishing I had backup. Wishing I'd stayed at home. Hell, even wishing I had the dog by my side.

'The hell is this?' I say. 'African mythology's greatest hits?' I study them each in turn, not backing down. You can't show fear to the orisha. You do, you're as good as dead. 'You guys forming a band? You going to break into a song and dance number?' Nothing. 'You *do* remember the Covenant, right?'

'The Covenant?' says an amused voice, off in the darkness.

A ripple of anticipation runs through the orisha. I turn slowly as a figure emerges from the shadows of the forest.

'You have the nerve to talk of the Covenant? After what you did to me?'

My stomach sinks. It's Babalu-Aye.

Fuck.

He's wearing a pastel orange suit this time round, with an old, faded Star Wars t-shirt. He rustles as he walks and I realise he's tied plastic carrier bags around his shoes so they don't get muddy.

The last time I saw Babalu-Aye I was redecorating the walls of an abandoned children's hospital with his brains because he was kidnapping kids and selling their souls to a demented angel to snort. I'd thought the case would lead me to whoever had murdered my daughter, Cally. Except, it turns out she wasn't actually murdered, only missing. Which is the same reason I'm here tonight. The circle is complete, yadda, yadda, yadda.

I realise with a sinking sensation that I've been played. Set up.

The dog always said when Babalu-Aye came back he was going to want revenge. And here we are.

-*Dog?*- I say hopefully. -*Could really use your help here.*-

'Do you know those who are easiest to manipulate?' says Babalu-Aye.

'I'm sure you're going to tell me.'

'Those who have an obsession. Those who are driven. By ghosts, by injustice, by . . . whatever. It matters not. But if you know their trigger, you *own* that person.'

He walks slowly around me, enjoying his moment on the stage.

'Take yourself, for instance. I remember when you came for me. You were talking about a girl, about children going missing. Your daughter, yes?' He smiles at me and I resist the urge to lunge forward and wrap my hands around his throat. Just the mention of my daughter is enough to pull that rage from deep within. It always has. Always will. 'So, knowing this, I have instant power over you. I knew how to make *you* come to *me*. I knew how to make you walk to your death.'

He passes the *obia*, fondly stroking the closest as he does so. His hand comes away sticky with blood and pus. He frowns, then leans forward and wipes his hand on my shirt. 'Did you honestly think I would let you live after what you did? You are a very stupid skinbag, I think.'

'I'm curious,' I say. 'How did it feel?'

'What?'

'A shotgun to the face. Feeling your head burst. Did it sting? I bet it stung.'

Babalu-Aye moves in a blur of speed, grabbing my face and squeezing. I wince in pain. Try to pull away. But I can't. The *vazimba* giggle, their huge mouths hanging open in grotesque grins.

'Did you know that we gods can feel pain? Did you know that?'

I have a bit of trouble answering, what with him grinding my jaw between his fingers.

'Blink. Once for no, twice for yes.'

I blink. Once.

'Well, we do. I have spent the last month in the Darkside—'

My confusion must have shown on my face. He clicks his tongue in irritation.

'The Nightside. The Underover. Whatever you monkeys call it. I spent the last month holed up in the Nightside's equivalent of that hospital. Waiting for my head to grow back. Do you have any idea how uncomfortable that is? Any at all?'

I blink again.

'You will. Because I'm going to make you suffer, little man. I'm going to make you cry.'

He straightens his arm suddenly, throwing me back through the air. I have a brief moment to remember that I'm not Warded before I hit the ground. My breath explodes from my lungs and I roll hard, crashing into a tree. I try to cry out but I have no breath left in my body. I roll back and forth, wheezing in pain.

Something grabs my feet, claws digging painfully into my ankles. I'm dragged across the grass, my head bumping against rocks and tree roots, then lifted into the air. Higher and higher until I'm looking into the upside down face of the *yehwe zogbanu*. He's even more disgusting close up. Yellowing horns sprout from every plane of his face. Red eyes peer out at me from beneath lowered brows. The orisha equivalent of a night-club bouncer.

'I thought about killing you,' says Babalu-Aye casually. I feel pressure on my back as he pushes me lightly. I sway in the ogre's grip.

'But you know how that is. Too quick, yes? So I will give you a small chance. Because I am a betting man. You will run, yes? And my friends here will hunt you down. *Then* I'm going to hurt you.' He leans forward and smiles. His breath smells of old cigarettes. 'Very, very much.'

I try to twist in the ogre's grip so I can see Babalu-Aye. 'Don't you watch movies? You know how it is. The plucky hero is given a chance. Then he escapes and triumphs, leaving a trail of death and destruction behind him. Yippee-ki-yay, motherfucker.'

'I do watch movies, yes. But your mistake is thinking that you are the hero. You should do some research. Look into the Mimbiar Accords. The slaughter of Tean. The incursion into the Nightside by specialised military troops. *Your* troops. You talk of the Covenant? Your kind has ignored the Covenant for decades. What we do now? What happens now? It is your kind's fault. We are just retaliating.'

Babalu-Aye appears in front of me. 'You are the *villain*, my friend. Not the hero. All your kind are.'

I reach up to my belt and yank my knife out from under my shirt. Babalu-Aye sees it and stumbles back out of reach. I quickly shift my target and twist up in a hanging stomach raise. (Look at me, who the fuck needs a gym?) I stab the blade into the side of the ogre's throat and wriggle it about, twisting and gouging.

The ogre roars and drops me. I land on my back, wince, and roll quickly away. The ground shakes as the *yehwe zogbanu* hits the ground, narrowly missing crushing me beneath his weight. He's shrieking and squealing like a pig, huge heels kicking into the dirt and gouging massive holes into the forest floor.

'What did you do?' snarls Babalu-Aye.

I crawl over to the ogre. He's still thrashing around like Pris in Blade Runner, but I manage to yank the dagger loose. I scramble backwards until I bump up against a tree. Babalu-Aye follows me, eying the blade warily. His little shop of horrors forms a semi-circle behind him, shifting their attention between me and Babalu-Aye, waiting for a command.

I hold the dagger up protectively. 'Silver iron alloy. Made from the bullet that killed the first werewolf in the 14th century. Plus the blade was dipped in the tears of an angel.' I smile painfully. 'For when you absolutely, positively, have to kill every freaky-ass motherfucker in the room? Accept no substitutes.'

Babalu-Aye squats down just out of reach. 'I am curious. How did you get the tears of an angel?'

'Long story. Involves a trip to Namibia, sand worms, abandoned villages half-buried in the desert, cannibal wild horses that escaped the Nightside and me explaining to the angel how and why his God was dead. It's an amazing story. I'll write it up in my memoirs—'

I lunge forward, stabbing out with the blade. Babalu-Aye jerks back and his cronies hiss in anger, leaping forward to surround him, pulling him out of reach.

'Sorry,' I say. 'Had to try. Hey – do I get a head start? Couple of hours should do it.'

'You get three minutes. Oh, and if you are wondering where your little pet is, I sent him back to the Nightside.'

'You . . . what?'

'I did not want him interfering. I sent him away.'

'Did you hurt him?'

Babalu-Aye smiles. 'You are already thirty seconds into your lead.'

I set off at a run. The creatures behind me howl and shriek, their voices echoing through the forest.

I move as fast as I can. The mist whips away from me as I sprint down the slope, barely managing to stop myself tumbling head over heels. I grip the knife tight in my hand. It's my only weapon, the only thing that will work against these orisha. Even so, I'm outnumbered and outclassed. No backup. 1500 kay's away from home base, and my spirit guide has been sent back to the Nightside.

Shit, man. What am I supposed to do about that? I don't think he's been back since he maimed and pissed on the spirit guide I was originally assigned. (You read that right. Pissed *on*, not pissed *off*.)

The howls behind me change, turning to high-pitched yips and barks.

They're coming.

I somehow manage to find more speed, barely skimming the surface of the ground as I stumble and race down the hill toward the township. My only hope is losing them in the narrow paths and roads between the shacks. I don't think I can fight them all, but I might be able to get back to my hire car.

I hit the bottom of the hill and swerve onto the dirt path heading into the settlement. I keep running, darting left, then right, taking random turns until I'm deep within the buildings.

Only then do I pause for breath. I lean over, sucking in huge gulps of air. I wince, straighten up. Try to calm my rapidly-beating heart so I can listen for signs of pursuit.

Nothing.

Well, nothing out of the ordinary, anyway. I hear laughter,

then someone shouting. A crying baby. Cars move past on the dirt streets, music growing louder then fading as they pass.

I head to the end of the alley, but I can't see much – the power is still off. Candles burn, half-glimpsed through windows and diffused by net curtains, tiny islands of light trying to fend off the night.

I strain my ears, but the orisha have stopped their screaming. They're silent now. Hunting.

I jog across the street, heading in the general direction of the shebeen where I left the car. I make my way along the path behind a row of shacks, the ground wet with discarded dishwater. I pause and peer around the side of the last house.

Someone down the street has hooked up a small TV to their car battery. A group of about ten men and women are watching a soccer game.

I check in the opposite direction. I can't see anything. Nothing but empty, open darkness. I've got no choice. It's the only way I can go.

I take a step into the dirt road.

The sound of gunshots freezes me in my tracks. The shots come from a few streets over. They're followed by a faint scream, abruptly cut off.

Here's the thing. Everyone has guns around here. Most of them are illegal, but no one cares. You need them to protect yourself. No complaints from me. So the gunshots don't necessarily mean anything. It most likely has nothing to do with me.

So keep going, London. Mind your own business.

Yeah. Best thing to do. Mind my own business.

Which is why I find myself running *toward* the scream, instead of away from it.

More gunshots ring out. I skid around a corner and pull up short. There's a guy backing up toward me while firing wildly into the darkness.

I grab his arm. He whirls around, trying to bring the gun around to shoot me. I bend his wrist back and yank the gun from his hand.

His eyes are wide. Terrified. He opens his mouth to say something, but before he can speak, he flies suddenly backward, yanked away into the darkness. His scream echoes, then cuts off with a wet, ripping sound.

I wait, breathing heavily, the gun held ready to fire.

Something comes straight at me. I catch the briefest glimpse of wide, staring eyes and a spinal column flapping around before I dive to the ground. The torso of the man soars over my head and slaps into a wall.

I stand up. Again, the wisest thing to do would be to run away. To turn in the opposite direction and sprint into the night, screaming very loudly, arms flailing above my head.

But I don't do that. Because I'm stupid.

I run straight into the darkness.

I hear a surprised snarl and adjust my path. Then I'm seeing one of the *obia*. Complete with glistening muscles and pus-covered tendons.

I fire the gun directly into her face, then use the distraction to launch myself into the air, hitting her in the stomach and driving the silver dagger deep between her ribs.

The *obia* howls as we hit the ground, her hands scrambling at my back. I pull the knife out and jab it in again and again, punching and twisting until her front is a shredded mess, black intestines spilling out at my feet.

The creature gurgles and falls limp. I push myself up and slice the blade across her neck just to make sure.

I get ready to move again.

Shit. No, wait. I can't leave the body here. We have to keep this hidden from Joe Public. Up till now both sides, the orisha and humans, have abided by the Covenant, the centuries' old agreement that dictates the rules of engagement and interaction between the Nightside and the Dayside.

I mean, sure, since the events of last month, when Lilith and the vampires decided that the Covenant no longer held, it's been getting harder to keep things quiet. The Delphic Division has been forced to create specialist clean-up squads now to make sure this kind of thing doesn't get into the public domain.

But just because the orisha are welching on the agreement, doesn't mean I can.

I drag the creature off the street, pulling it along back alleys until I come across a rusted, abandoned car. Perfect. I open the boot and shove the body in, then find the pieces of the poor bastard who got caught in the middle and hide him in the car as well. I'll tell the Cape Town branch about this later. They won't be happy with me tramping all over their territory, but I can't do anything about that now.

I look down at my clothes. They're practically black because of all the blood. I'm known for spending a large portion of my salary on hideously overpriced designer suits, but this time I'd taken the dog's advice and settled on jeans and t-shirt instead of anything fancy.

I set off at a jog. I don't think the tavern is far off now. In fact, I'm sure it's just around the corner . . .

I turn into the empty square in front of the shebeen.

And freeze.

There are two *vazimba* by my car, scratching the ground and sniffing the tires. The other two are inside, clambering over the seats and tearing chunks out of the leather with their huge teeth. Fuck. There goes my deposit. Thank God I took out insurance.

They haven't seen me yet. I back up slowly, slipping back around the corner of the shebeen. I need another way out of the township.

I turn around.

To find the way blocked by the remaining *obia*, their muscles and nerves glistening in the light like some kind of Damien Hirst installation.

'I am disappointed,' says Babalu-Aye, emerging from the darkness. 'I expected more of a fight. More of a chase. But I suppose it is to be expected. You are just a little monkey, yes? Without your bag of tricks you are . . . well, you are just you.'

I back away from him and the advancing *obia*. I'm painfully aware that I'm moving into the open space again, but there's nowhere else to go. I hear a noise. I turn around and see the *emere* watching from the peripheral. Typical Fae. Always watching. Waiting to see how things turn out. I almost wished we had the European Faeries here. At least they're predictable.

The *vazimba* have spotted me now. They've abandoned the car and are crawling over the dirt toward me.

There's no way out. Babalu-Aye has won. He lured me here and made sure there was no way I could get out alive.

I pause, thinking.

No way out but one.

I hesitate. Am I really going to do that? But I don't really have a choice, do I? It's either that or die. Sure, I might die anyway, but at least I'll take these bastards with me.

The *vazimba* are close now, only a few feet away. Babalu-Aye stands there, smiling at me.

I give in and mutter the words of summoning, feel the tattoos writhe to excited life across my back.

The night explodes in green and red as the dragons surge up across my back and arch over my shoulders. They dart forward immediately, pulling me off my feet. I hit the dirt, trying to rein them in. Control them. But they've been locked up too long. They're too strong.

They drag me across the ground as they lunge toward the closest *obia*. The green dragon grabs the creature and tosses it into the air. The second dragon snatches it before it hits the ground and they both worry at the *obia* for a second before ripping it apart, spraying the ground with black blood.

The dragons drop the carcass and go for one of the *vazimba*, dragging me across the dirt with them. I grimace and try to pull them back. They fight me, refusing to listen. I try harder . . .

. . . then I pause.

Even with the dragons I'm going to have trouble getting out of this. And there's no way I'm going to escape unscathed. Plus, there's the small matter of the dog. If he could get back on his own, he'd already be here.

I sigh and push myself to my knees, then stand up to my full height.

Babalu-Aye watches me with narrowed eyes.

The dragons are behind me, tearing one of the *vazimba* apart. I stretch my neck, hearing vertebrae crack and pop.

Then I give Babalu-Aye the one-finger salute and release control of the tattoos.

The dragons sense it immediately. They whip around to look at me, their light flaring brighter, like neon signs come to life.

They leave the *vazimba* and lunge toward me, sliding back beneath my t-shirt.

I scream. It's like lava burning my skin off. I'm sure I can smell burning flesh. They're pulling me, turning me inside out.

I feel a massive surge of power, the twisting of reality, and then I'm pulled back through a shimmering curtain, yanked toward a dark light hanging in the air.

My ears pop.

A warm, greasy wind caresses my face.

I open my eyes.

And I'm in the Nightside.

A horrific roar reverberates around me. I clamp my hands over my ears and look up.

And I won't lie. I nearly piss my pants.

The two dragons hover far above me, each of them about thirty feet long. Their huge wings flap slowly against an angry red sky.

You've seen *Game of Thrones*, yeah? Imagine those dragons, but more spiky, and with green and red light glowing beneath the scales. Then you'll have an idea of what my dragons look like.

I notice that although they're hovering, they're not actually going anywhere. Then I see their tails. They travel down toward me, wrapping around my waist and finally impaling me through my upper arms. There's no blood. Just smooth skin where we're joined.

But their tails . . . they look diseased, necrotic. As if the joining is a disease eating away at the dragons.

Shit. I look up at them again. Their eyes glow with hatred. I had no idea this is what I was doing to them. Who the hell were those monks to capture them like this? To trap them in human skin? They didn't tell me it would be like this.

But then again, I didn't ask.

No wonder the things hate me so much. Look at them. They're supposed to be free. They're supposed to be hunting, flying over snow-covered landscapes and steppes. Not lashed to some punk-ass wannabe magician.

And I reckon they think the same thing, because at that moment they open up their mouths and spit what appears to be molten lava directly at me.

3

I drop to the ground and throw my hands over my head. (Yeah, great reflexes there. Years of training as a magician and the first thing I do when confronted with trouble is let out an 'eep' of fear and hide behind my hands.)

Strangely, my skin does *not* instantly burst into flame and peel away from my skeleton. Instead, I feel a familiar rush of wind across my shoulders and the tattoos slide into place across my back.

The hell?

I open my eyes and straighten up. Sure enough, the tattoos have gone back to bed. But ... why? When all they've ever wanted was to get me into the Nightside so they could turn me into a dish of fricasseed human meat?

I look around warily, just in case it's a trick. I'm standing on an outcrop above a rocky plain that falls away below me, leading to a ruined city surrounded by a massive, decaying wall. The sky is an angry red filled with coiling clouds that move faster than anything I've ever seen before. The red fades down to brown, swirling dust that obscures the horizon. A hot wind buffets me, bringing with it the smell of sulphur and something musky and animal-like.

I feel utterly exposed and freaked out. The Nightside is the reality that orisha and supernatural creatures call home. Almost ten thousand years ago, early magic users came together in a feat of cooperative magic that's never been seen since. They split the Nightside off from our reality and banished all the orisha here. Must have been a pretty hectic display of magic, I'll tell you that for nothing. Of course, over the years a lot of them found their way back to the Dayside, leading to the wonderful cold war situation we currently find ourselves in.

'All right, dipshit?'

I just about manage to stop myself letting out an incredibly unmanly squeal. (I've already done it once in the past minute. I can't lose *all* my cred.) I turn slowly and see the dog sitting a few paces away, idly scratching his ear.

'What the hell happened to you?' I ask.

'Babalu-Aye happened to me. Bastard opened up a door and shoved me through.'

'You let him do that?'

'He took me by surprise! Anyway, the guy's a god. He has power.'

'And you couldn't come back and help me?'

'It was his door. He controls it. I would have found my way back eventually.'

'How did you get rid of the dragons?'

'The what?'

'The dragons. On my back.'

'I didn't.'

'That wasn't you?'

'Nope.'

'And ... did you cast a Ward on me? Did you stop their breath?'

'Again – nope. I sensed another doorway open and came over to see if I could use it to cross back over. Saw you standing there looking like an idiot.'

'Then why did the dragons go back? Who protected me?'

'Guardian angel?'

I look nervously into the sky. I don't have a good track record with angels.

'You going to stand there all day or are you coming?'

The dog is walking away from me, heading down the slope toward the ruined city.

'Coming where?'

The dog glances over his shoulder. 'You want to hang around here waiting for Babalu-Aye to open another doorway? Kinda surprised he hasn't come through already if I'm honest. Maybe he's scared of your tats.'

Shit. Good point. What's going on with me? My head feels thick and slow. I should have been running away from this spot as soon as I realised I wasn't about to be roasted by dragon breath.

I follow the dog down the slope onto the plain. The wind grows hotter as we run, a dry, scratchy exfoliation that scrapes across my skin. Jesus, this is how I imagine Hell. No wonder the orisha are pissed we make them live here. Mini-tornadoes skitter across the landscape. One passes right in front of me and I'm sure I see little faces in the centre, mouths open in silent screams.

We make it to the wall. It towers above us, easily fifty feet high. It's pitted with holes, parts of it crumbling away to form huge piles of rock that spill out onto the plain.

'What is this place?'

The dog looks up and down the wall, then trots back about ten feet and peers through one of the holes. 'A city?'

'Don't be a smartarse.'

'Then don't ask stupid questions. It's a city. It shifted here from Eastern Europe, I think. Sort of . . . overlapped the city that was already here.'

I look at him in surprise. 'It *shifted* here? How?'

'It's the Nightside. Shit happens, man. You should know that by now.'

'Why is it falling to pieces?'

'It got cursed. All the residents went crazy – got themselves possessed.'

We start to move again, heading towards a big gap in the wall that looks like it may have once held gates. 'Orisha can get possessed?'

'Oh, yeah. Some clever fucker was trying to open up a gateway to the Dayside. He screwed up and sort of sucked in the city and its inhabitants. Like I said, the city and the people . . . overlapped everything that was already here.'

'You're saying the orisha got possessed by humans?'

'Sure. All the humans got turned inside out during the crossover. Very messy. But before that, their minds were ejected. They all went utterly insane and tried to hole up in the closest living beings. The orisha couldn't deal. They all cracked up. Started killing each other.'

'How come I didn't hear about this?'

'Maybe because it was a hundred and fifty years ago?' The dog pauses and looks back the way we came. 'Shit.'

'What?'

'Another door just opened.'

I hear a high-pitched wail, see figures moving on the rocky outcrop. Babalu-Aye and his coterie of weird creatures are moving down the slope toward us. They're taking their time. They know we've got nowhere to go.

But it's not just the orisha that attacked me back in the township. Other creatures have appeared, drawn to the doors just like the dog was. They trail behind Babalu-Aye like his personal entourage.

'Dog? Any ideas?'

'Me? Hell, no. I was hoping *you* would have a plan. Don't you have a rape alarm or something?'

That makes me pause. 'A rape alarm?'

'Yeah, you know. Something that summons the Goonies.'

'No. I don't have a rape alarm. Or *any* kind of alarm.'

'Huh. No shit. You seem remarkably calm then. I mean, me? I'll be fine. I can discorporate or . . . hide or something.

Hell, they don't even *want* me. I could just tell them I'm switching sides. That I saw the light.' He looks at me speculatively, for a lot longer than I'm comfortable with. Then he gives himself a small shake. 'Nah. They'd never believe me.'

I breathe a little sigh of relief. It's always hard to tell with the dog. Sure, he's a buddy. But he's also a creature from the Nightside. I've never actually known what his agenda is. Or if he even has one.

We arrive at the gaping hole in the wall. It definitely held gates at one point; the remains are still there, twisted metal that has been melted into black rivulets.

Even from outside I can smell the stench of rotting meat. It wafts towards us on the hot wind, catching in the back of my throat.

'I really hope you're kidding around and that you do actually have an amazing plan that is going to save our hides,' I say.

The dog doesn't answer. I check on our pursuers. The orisha are running ahead of Babalu-Aye, leaping and sprinting toward us in zig-zags. The old god walks along behind them as if he's taking a Sunday stroll.

We head into the city. In the distance a massive castle looms over us, a sprawling ruin with impossible towers reaching into the red clouds. The road we follow is littered with twisted forms, bodies that have been torn to pieces.

'Hundred and fifty years, you say?'

'Far as I know.'

The corpses lie all around us, some of them no more than liquefied puddles, but others look and smell like they've only been dead a week or so. There are some that look human; desiccated husks with open mouths screaming into the silence . . .

'We should get off this road.'

The dog doesn't answer, but takes a side street that leads between buildings. A sudden chill envelopes me as we leave the main road and I stumble to a stop. I turn my head and hear voices. Terrified screams and howls of rage. Every time I move my head the sounds shift, coming closer then fading away. Wailing, crying for help, sobbing in pain.

'Keep moving,' says the dog. 'Hang around here for too long and the ghosts will latch on.'

Triumphant ululations break out behind us. Close. They're in the city. We sprint through back alleys, running past houses and shops. I really want to stop and check them out. Do orisha shop? I find it hard to imagine them nipping out for some bread and toilet paper. Maybe this part of the city's from Europe . . .

But then again, hadn't Lilith said something about that? That they weren't any different to us? That the Nightsiders just wanted to live their lives and it was us humans who forced them into a world they didn't want to live in. If things had worked out differently, it could have been mankind living here.

The cries are getting closer. We hurry around a corner and find ourselves in front of a huge building that looks like a cathedral. The structure is ornate and ostentatious, with fluted columns and a wide courtyard.

There's even a fountain out front. Although it's stained black with old blood. And I think I spot a couple of skulls in the basin.

We're not going to be able to keep running. We need to make a stand. I run up the stairs and shove one of the doors open. The dog darts between my legs and disappears into the darkness.

'Hold up!'

I run after him, my footsteps echoing loudly in the wide corridor. We pass through a doorway at the end of the passage and into a huge room with arched ceilings and a pulpit rising up against the opposite wall.

I hear the front doors bang open behind us.

I follow the dog through another doorway. It opens onto a set of stairs leading down into darkness. The dog stops short. 'This is bad, London,' he says. 'You sure you can't open a gate back to the Dayside?'

I shake my head. 'The top brass keep that stuff secret from us.'

We close the door behind us and head down the stairs. The air grows colder as we descend, the walls changing from brick to bare rock.

We stumble off the last step. I can sense a vast space around me. My footsteps echo back to me, bouncing off distant walls.

'There's a door on the other side,' calls the dog.

'Where are you?'

'Where do you think? Running toward the door,' says the dog, his voice already sounding distant.

'Hold up!' I track his voice and start moving, my hands held out blindly before me. 'Dog?'

'Halfway across! Get a move on.'

I veer slightly to the left, following his voice, moving as fast as I dare.

'Shit,' he says.

I stop running. 'What?'

'Someone's coming.'

'Behind or ahead?'

'Uh . . . both.'

The dog pads back to me, brushing up against my leg. I take my wand out. I didn't want to use it back in the township, as it would have led Babalu-Aye's pets directly to me, but it doesn't make much difference now. We're already cornered. I reach out and feel the energy around me, searching for essence to pull into the wand. It feels . . . different here. Stronger, more untamed.

-*Shit. London, I think we're in big trouble here.*-

Then I hear sounds; bare feet padding across the cold floor, claws tick-tacking toward us. I blindly turn left then right, expecting something to come at me any second. My heart is thumping, the hair on my arms standing on end. I can sense the life all around me now. Hear it. Sniffing. Grunting. Hissing.

I panic and pull wildly on the energy around me. It surges in like an avalanche, almost overwhelming me, fizzing through my blood, defragmenting my soul. It feels different here, like the first time I ever took cocaine. A feeling of utter confidence, a surge of dopamine that floods my system and burns the darkness from my soul.

It's the only time my depression actually goes away, when I summon magic. Pity the comedown is such a bitch.

I stagger back, quickly shutting off the flow. My wand is vibrating, trembling in my fingers. I point it in front of me and release a globe of white light. It surges away from me. I turn in a quick circle, firing off globe after globe until the entire underground space is illuminated.

'The hell didn't you do that in the first place, Gandalf?' mutters the dog.

The lights reveal about . . . oh, a hundred or so various monsters, all of them staring hungrily at us. I don't even recognise half of them. Some look like human mutants, faces and bodies stretched into hideous deformities. Others look like they've been melted. I see vampires, thin faces and red eyes, shying away from the light. There are black dogs the size of horses and dark, shadowy figures so tall they disappear into the shadows above us.

-*I see what you mean about being in trouble,*- I say.

I turn in a slow circle, wand held out before me. The creatures hiss and snap at the air, lunging forward then darting back again. None of them make a move. They're waiting.

After a full minute of this, with my heartbeat thumping in my throat the entire time, there is a murmuring in the crowd.

The creatures part down the middle and Babalu-Aye strolls forward. He seems bigger in the Nightside. Power radiates from him like heat waves from asphalt.

'No talking now,' he says. 'I am tired of this chase. I will let my friends tear you apart.'

I open my mouth to say something incredibly witty, but before I even get a word out he waves his hand and the masses come surging forward, screaming and growling.

Fuck.

I stagger back, pulling in more power and then channelling it out through the wand. A continuous stream of black lightning pours out, twining around the creatures' bodies, pulling them inside out, arcing between them and bursting eyeballs, stabbing out and punching holes in skin and carapace. Holy shit. I've never felt power like this before. My skin is tingling with electric pleasure. I've got a hard-on that's about to burst through my jeans. Even my hair is tingling. I laugh as I flick my wand about, controlling the lightning, whipping it around, sending it over heads and down into the oncoming hordes.

I catch a glimpse of the dog by my side, except he's not the dog anymore. He's bigger. Much bigger. A four-legged, grey-white creature with a hard shell and two viciously clawed arms. I can't see exact details, because his form vibrates. It's blurry; constantly shifting and moving. But he reminds me of some kind of massive praying mantis.

I turn back to the fight, the lightning pouring out through the wand. I'm losing control of it now. I can feel it leaching me of life, drawing my own essence out with it. But I don't care. The pleasure is too much. The feelings too intense. I don't want it to stop.

The orisha burst like balloons filled with liquefied meat. I spot the *vazimba* from the township coming toward me. I point the wand at them but they dart away, ducking under the lightning. I flick it like a whip but they dodge and gallop toward me, leaping through the air, scrambling over the other creatures, their huge mouths hanging open.

I panic and yank more power into the wand. The lightning explodes out of the wand and turns into glowing purple glass that shreds the air itself, tendrils hard as obsidian cutting the *vazimba* cleanly in half.

But it's not enough. There are too many of them.

I turn to look for the dog but instead find Babalu-Aye coming at me.

He strikes me in the chest. I fly backwards, hitting the ground and sliding. The wand is still flaring out energy, randomly cutting through the hordes.

-*Watch that damn wand!*- shouts the dog.

I cut off the flow. I can smell burning flesh and blood. My skin is steaming, my already bloody clothes soaked with sweat and gore. I push myself up, feel claws grabbing me, yanking me to my feet. I twist around, see yellow teeth coming at me—

—And then a darkness sweeps through the room, a black tornado that buffets us all, carrying with it the stench of burning hair.

'*Enough!*'

Every creature in that room feels the power behind the words. My heart thuds erratically, missing beats, then thumps faster in an attempt to catch up.

The hands let me go. I fall to the floor, going down on hands and knees. I look around. The dog has become the dog again. He's sprinting toward me, a look of fear on his face.

-*Dog?*-

-*Power, London. Lots of power.*-

'*This one is not yours, Babalu-Aye,*' says a voice.

I try to find the source. But all I can see is a segmented black . . . hole in the air near the ceiling. It's like whatever it is is made from black glass that shifts and slices through reality, purple and white light striking highlights from impossible geometric designs. It hurts the eyes to look at.

'He is mine!' screams Babalu-Aye. 'I have the right of revenge!'

'*No. He is being kept for others.*'

Babalu-Aye turns instantly and runs toward me, his hands outstretched.

He's only two paces away when he explodes, his insides spattering against everyone close by.

I carefully wipe the blood from my eyes. I take a deep breath, and then the dog and I are suddenly moving. A wet wind, the smell of blood and fear, a golden light, the ruffling of feathers, the caw of ravens . . .

. . . and then we're back in the township.

Back in the Dayside.

We stand there for a moment, shaking, shivering, dripping the blood of a god onto the dirt.

I blink, take a shuddering breath. 'What—'

'No idea,' snaps the dog.

'Who—'

'I have no idea!'

'But—'

'London!' snarls the dog. 'I have absolutely no fucking idea what just happened, OK?'

'Well . . . that's actually pretty obvious, isn't it? An orisha just saved our lives.'

'Yes,' says the dog. 'But what you really want to ask yourself is, why? And *who, exactly,* are you being kept for?'

I look at the dog. 'Yeah, that . . . didn't sound too good, did it?'

'No, it did not. In fact, I would go further than that. I'd say that an orisha coming up against a god to save your sorry ass is something you should be incredibly freaked out about. And so should I, because I'm likely to get caught in the shit-storm that seems to constantly follow you around.'

'All right. Calm down. *Jesus.*' I start walking.

'Where you going?'

'Where do you think? It's Monday tomorrow. We've got work.'

The dog catches up. 'What time's our flight?' he asks in a normal voice.

I wipe the blood away from my watch face. 'We've got a couple of hours.'

'Good. Let's find a hosepipe or something to wash the blood and brains off. That kind of shit will only lead to questions at the security checkpoint.'

4

Look how lucky I am, with my balcony that overlooks the beachfront Promenade. Sure, it's only about a foot wide and three foot long, and it's covered in bird shit, but still, it's mine. My own slice of solid gold Durban. Jealous yet?

I pull the sliding door open and slump onto the stool, nursing my steaming cup of coffee and a migraine I've had since the flight back to Durban last night.

It's already pushing thirty degrees and the beachfront is pumping. Joggers with their dogs. Surfers catching the early morning waves. Car guards in bright orange vests peppered between the parking bays.

I swallow the bitter coffee and close my eyes, leaning my head back against the glass. Mornings. They're always the worst. Always have been. Stupid me if I thought that would change after I discovered Cally was alive. If anything, it's worse now. I wake up with a yawning emptiness inside me that I now know is impossible to fill. I always thought it was because I'd lost Cally, but it's obviously not. Now I have to face up to the fact that it might just be me. That I'll always feel shit. That I'll never feel normal.

The dog knows I'm depressed. You can't live with someone in this tiny flat and not know when something's up. He tried, awkwardly, to talk to me about it once, but he can't help me. No one can.

It's not that I didn't appreciate it, but he said it himself. 'Spirit guides don't have degrees in clinical fucked-up-ness.

I can't help you, man. I can talk, but this shit is inside of you.'

I think the major problem is that I don't have the anger anymore. Irrational bouts of rage? Yes. The anger that used to drive me? Anger at Cally's death? At everything that happened? At the injustice of the world? No. The anger used to mask the depression. It burned so bright in me that there was no room for anything else.

Now I don't have that driving me forward, every day is reduced to a simple equation. Getting through it one minute at a time.

Ten minutes are a success. One hour is a victory.

And yeah, I know it's not very original. But who says depression is original? It's there. It's pervasive. It leeches the world of its colour and other various clichés that are all trite but very, very true. It's like I'm struggling through cobwebs. The strands are pulling me back, suffocating me, forming a gauze over my vision, and no matter how much I struggle or fight, the strands just grow stronger.

'You OK?' asks the dog.

I don't answer.

'You seen that Division shrink yet?'

'No.'

'Idiot.'

I look over my shoulder at him, standing in the open doorway. 'I just ... don't think she can help. Talking about this stuff just makes it worse. It makes it real. If I don't talk about it ...' I trail off, not sure what I'm trying to say.

'... You can hide from it? That's not how it works, London. You can pretend to hide, but it's there. It's waiting for you. And the longer you refuse to face up to it, the harder it's going to be to defeat it.'

'Thought you don't know anything about psychology?'

'I don't. This is simple common sense.' The dog sighs. 'You

bags of meat. Your problems would all be solved if you real-ised all you really needed is someone to share your life with. Someone to cuddle up on the couch with.'

I raise my eyebrows, surprised. 'You going soft on me?'

'No. Just making an observation. You're all lonely, walking around with these walls around you. Even the ones in rela-tionships. You're all hiding, protecting yourselves, terrified of being abandoned. Same with all that shit last month. Religion. Even mother-fuckin' *God* was like that. An insecure child. *Archangels*, London, the most powerful beings in the *universe*, are scared of being abandoned. Fear, man. It's what drives the whole lot of you. And you spend all your time worrying about it. What's the point of it? Worry, I mean. It pretends to be necessary. It tricks you into thinking you need it, but what does it really do for you? Nothing.'

'Kinda like you then.'

No answer.

'Sorry. Didn't mean that.'

''S OK, man. I got your back. Least, as much as I can.' There's a brief, awkward pause. 'You know what you need?' he eventually says.

'What do I need?'

'To get laid.'

I stare out over the balcony, at the bright, azure sky. 'Yeah, like getting laid will fix my problems.'

'You won't know till you try it.'

I drain my coffee and heave myself to my feet. Time for work. Hopefully Lerato and Ayanda will have turned up something interesting across the pond. Stay busy. That's the trick. Find a distraction. Choose satellite TV. Choose Facebook and social media. Choose mindless company and arbitrary small talk. Choose anything but the dark pit of emptiness lurking inside. Anything but the silence where dark thoughts wait.

Give me something to do, people to talk to and the thoughts . . . well they're still there. But they're pushed back slightly. I can still feel them. Watching, waiting for me to let my guard down. It's like I'm possessed by a demon. This pain-beast. A dark twin. It's in my mind all the time, waiting for signs of weakness before pouncing and leeching more of my will and energy, growing stronger and stronger every day.

Keeping busy pushes it back slightly. Just enough that I can carry on. Just enough that I can sometimes pretend to be normal.

I wince as I step onto the pavement outside my apartment building. I don't think I'll ever get used to this heat. It's suffocating, invasive. I pull out my aviators, blinking as the harsh world around me is reduced to comforting sepia tones.

I'm already sweating as the dog and I climb into my old Land Rover and pull into the traffic. Christmas lights hang above us, Santa Claus and his reindeers strung between street lights, looking old and worn in the daylight. I put on the dog's Christmas CD without him even asking and turn Run DMC up full volume. He nods his head to the music as we head out of the city and onto the N2 heading toward the old airport.

I take the off-ramp that looks like it's still under construction (and has been for the past decade, an abandoned project that ran out of public sector money) and follow the tunnel beneath the road. We come out on the dirt track leading to what Joe Public thinks is an old cement factory, but which is actually this country's first line of defence against supernatural crime. Kinda like the X-Files but without the cool FBI badges. And of course I don't have Gillian Anderson as a partner. Or David Duchovny, for that matter. I'd be fine with either.

Instead I'm stuck with the dog.

I look over at him. He turns and stares calmly back at me.

Then he farts.

And carries on staring, not saying a thing.

I sigh. Yeah, lucky old me.

The rusted gates open as the car approaches, a hidden RFID chip identifying me as a friendly face. If I *didn't* have the chip I'd currently be undergoing painful dismemberment by a number of angry ghosts controlled by Eshu, a trickster god of the Yoruba.

Eshu is the god of communication and he's currently paying off a lengthy prison sentence by looking after the Wards and Runes protecting the Division's repurposed cement silos from any supernatural meddling. He also makes sure the Division has enough internet for its employees to download their weekly torrents. I like him. He doesn't even block the porn sites.

He does other things, of course, like making sure the souls of the dead powering the aether generators that run the protective Wards never run dry. Don't ask me where he gets new souls once the current ones run out. I mean, I've asked him but he just said, 'Don't ask questions you won't like the answers to.'

I park in the underground garage. The dog hops out, heading for the kitchen where he'll glare at anyone who enters until they share their breakfast muffins with him. If they don't, he'll follow them back to their desk and stare at them some more. And if they *still* don't share, they'll come back from a bathroom break to find a suspicious puddle beneath their desk.

I don't follow immediately. Instead, I wrap my hands around the steering wheel and close my eyes. I take a deep breath, forcing the mask of normality into place, the mask I've been wearing since Cally disappeared. It's the only thing that makes me seem like a normal human being and hides what I really am – an animal driven by rage and fury. I don't know why I even bother, because after the events of last month everyone now knows I'm not exactly balanced. But it's a ritual now. Every morning since that day in the mountains.

I leave the Land Rover and head up the stairs, waving my ID card at the sensor as I walk through the foyer. I follow a short passage into the central hub of the building, the nexus from which all departments radiate. I walk over a heavy vault door set flush with the floor. Beneath the door is where we keep the Delphic Oracle, locked in a prison that hasn't been opened since World War II.

Nobody really knows the truth about why she's locked away. Lots of theories, lots of gossip, but no actual facts. Ask ten people why we're named after the Oracle and you'll get ten different stories. She was kidnapped from Greece during World War I. Or, she appeared in the UK to stop Himmler raising demons to bolster the German armies during World War II.

My favourite story is that she started the Delphic Division when there was a weakening in the veil between here and hell. That she was one of the first agents and that she and her lover, Jonathan Stannis, used to solve crimes and banish demons like a double act in an old detective show. None of which actually explains what warranted her being locked up the way she is.

I take the passage that leads to the huge open plan office where the field agents work. Comforting chaos greets me. Phones ringing, people chatting, the tinny smell of computers and the quiet whirr of fans. A few of my more festive co-workers have miniature Christmas trees on their desks. Some of them even have those annoying lights that play Christmas carols.

I make my way to my work station and slump into my chair. My desk is covered with piles of folders and old case notes, reports that need filling out, official requests for clarifications, internal memos, phone messages, all stuff I have been, and will continue to, ignore.

My phone rings. I groan. What is it with people calling first thing in the morning? It's not civilised.

I pick it up and grunt.

'London?'

It's Jaeger. She's one half of the Division's forensic patholo-gist team, the other half being Maddoc. Nobody knows what type of orisha they are and nobody has the courage to ask. They're both seven feet tall and a bit . . . intimidating. Jaeger has skin the colour of ancient tar, with eyes that look like lemon curd, while Maddoc is albino white (but with the same colour eyes).

'I need to see you,' she says.

'Need, or want?'

'Need.'

'I'm flattered, but I'm not sure it would work. Company policy, you know?'

A pause in the other end of the line. 'You wish. I would utterly ruin you.'

I can actually believe that.

'I'll be there now.'

'When now?'

'Now, now.'

'Is that . . . soon?'

I sigh. 'I'll be there in less than a minute.'

'Good. I'll be waiting. Bring the condoms.'

The line goes dead.

I stare at the phone a second, then shake my head and make my way back to the central hub of the Division build-ing. I take one of the corridors that radiate out like spokes on a wheel and enter the . . . I want to call it the morgue, but it's not just that. It's a large tiled room with stainless steel gurneys, a partitioned office to the left where Maddoc and Jaeger watch TV (they like cartoons), and of course the cadaver fridges that take up an entire wall. It's all very fancy and high tech.

Jaeger is sitting cross-legged on one of the post-mortem tables. I nod at her, then pull out my wallet. 'Hang on,' I say.

She waits patiently. For about three seconds. 'I have things to tell you.'

'I know. I'm just looking for that condom I keep in my wallet. I think it's about a year out of date, but it should be OK.'

I wait, but there's no chuckle. Not even a hint of a smile. 'Tough crowd,' I mutter. I put my wallet back in my pocket. 'So what's up?'

'Just a heads up first. What I'm about to show you is very strange.'

I stare at her. I've always been fascinated by her skin. It's like it moves, a viscous pearlescent oiliness that shifts around as if light is striking highlights across it. '*You're* saying this is going to be strange?'

'Afraid so.' She hops off the table and approaches the wall. (Not the one with the corpse fridges.) She pushes gently on a ceramic tile and stands there, head bowed.

'What . . . ?'

She turns to me and puts a finger to her lips. I clamp my mouth shut; her eyes have changed colour. Red flows through the yellow like blood mixing in bile.

She turns back to the wall and spreads her other fingers across the tiles in a strange pattern. A second later the tiles melt. They sag and elongate, dripping to the floor and then vanishing to reveal a dark archway.

Jaeger steps into the opening. I just stand there, blinking in confusion. Her head reappears. 'Are you coming?' She hesitates. 'Sorry. This isn't the strange bit yet.'

Wonderful.

I approach the archway. Jaeger grins and holds her hand out to me. 'Come with me if you want to live.'

'Ho-ho.'

'No, seriously. Take my hand. If you don't the defences will turn you inside out and pull you through a miniature black hole.'

I quickly put my hand in hers and she leads me into a short tunnel. I can hear distant howling, cries of anger and pain. I look nervously around but can't see anything in the darkness.

I grip Jaeger's hand tight as she leads me through the tunnel and into a huge room.

I stare around in surprise. I'm standing in what appears to be a fully furnished flat. A white L-shaped couch sits in front of a huge LCD screen mounted on the wall. There's a stainless steel kitchen behind the couch that looks like it's an extension of the morgue.

'What's all this?' I say, staring around in amazement.

'Our home. Where did you think we lived?'

'I . . . don't actually know.'

'You think we just went home every night to our house in the suburbs? Dinner parties and Sunday barbecues?'

'I suppose I thought you maybe went back to the Nightside.'

'We're not from the Nightside.'

She pulls me toward a door off to our left before I can even break this down. How the hell can they not be from the Nightside? Where are they from then?

Jaeger puts her hand on the door handle, then pauses and looks back at me. 'We still haven't got to the weird part yet. In case you were wondering.'

She opens the door and leads me into a dark room. I realise she's still holding my hand.

'Am I still in danger of being turned inside out?'

'No. I just like holding your hand.'

I can hear the smile in her voice as she lets go and flicks a switch. Fluorescent lights flicker to life.

I look around, trying to make sense of what I'm seeing. I fail.

There are chains and shackles bolted to the walls. So . . . torture chamber? But, no. There are racks of whips and masks and handcuffs. So . . . sex room? A private place for some S&M? But no . . . because there's also a little wingback chair in one corner and a small side table loaded with books. The side table has a lamp. It has tassels on the shade.

I'm very confused, but I have to admit, what's *really* throwing me here is the autopsy table sitting directly in the centre of the room. Because there also happens to be a body on it, covered with a pale green sheet.

'I give up,' I eventually say. 'I don't know what I'm looking at.'

Jaeger looks around as if seeing the room for the first time. I follow her gaze. There are shelves mounted to the wall behind me. Old, leather-bound books on the top shelf, then the lower shelves holding jars filled with various oddities. One is filled with eyeballs. The next holds some kind of foetus (not human, thankfully) suspended in liquid. The next one holds a withered hand with burnt fingers. (This one has a little card stuck to the front that says Hand of Glory.)

'It's a multi-function room,' says Jaeger.

'I can see that.'

She shrugs. 'Not much space, you know? We make do.'

'And the stiff?'

'Ah, yes. You noticed that.'

'I did. Kinda hard to miss.'

She smiles brightly at me. '*That's* the weird bit.'

'Thank Christ for that. I thought there was going to be more.'

'Don't look so relieved. You haven't seen what I want to show you yet.'

She yanks the sheet back and I find myself staring at the weathered profile of Dillon, the SSA stooge who shot Becca in the head. The man who tried to kill me and Armitage.

The man who I stabbed in the neck and then watched get shredded by vampires.

The rage and anger that erupts inside surprises me with its suddenness. I take an unsteady step back, staring at the same face I've seen in my nightmares every night since it happened. Usually the nightmares involve me being unable to move as Dillon shoots Becca right in front of me. Sometimes there's a bit of variety. Sometimes he talks to me. Sometimes I can move and almost reach them before he does it.

Sometimes he shoots Cally too.

'What is this?' My voice is rough. I can feel my pulse beating thickly in my throat.

'You know this guy?'

'He tried to arrest me and Armitage. He's State Security Agency.'

He killed Becca.

'That's what I thought. See, after that shit-fest last month, we obviously had to send in all of our clean-up crews. There were body parts piled up in a Division meat locker downtown till we could figure out who was who. I got a call from someone yesterday. He . . . wanted to show me something.'

'What?'

Jaeger takes hold of Dillon's chin and pushes his face toward me.

My eyes widen in surprise. The other half of his face isn't the same. It's not Dillon. It's as if two utterly different heads have been sliced down the centre and then one half from each head pushed together, one human, and the other . . . something else. The skin on the other side is white, but mottled and grey, and covered with faint black veins. The features look alien, sharp and pointed, but still generic, unmemorable. Like a mass-produced doll.

I lean closer. There's very faint writing on the skin. Sigils of some kind. I've never seen anything like them before.

'And before you ask,' says Jaeger, 'I have no idea what the marks are either. There's nothing on file that even remotely resembles them.'

'I don't get it,' I say.

'I didn't think you would. So what we've got here is some kind of orisha shapeshifter who was impersonating a government official. A Cuckoo, hiding in plain sight. A Cuckoo who wanted you dead. Who killed your ex-wife.'

'No. Well . . . yeah. But Ranson ordered the hit on Becca.'

'Did he? He may have thought he did, but this thing here . . .' She slaps the body's forehead, '. . . is not human. Which means it had its own reasons for doing what it did.' Jaeger leans across the body. 'You need to see the bigger picture here, London. I wasn't kidding when I called this thing a Cuckoo. I looked through the other body parts from that night. Guess what I found?'

I'm getting a headache. 'Another one?'

She winks. 'Another one.'

'Why didn't anyone report this when the bodies were cleaned up last month?'

'The abnormalities only seem to reveal themselves as time passes. Sort of an orisha decomposition thing.' She pauses and frowns at me. 'You don't seem to be absorbing the enormity of this, London. That's two of these Cuckoos in an SSA death squad that specifically came after *you*. Who the fuck knows how many more there are. There may even be some in the Division itself. You think Ranson stole your spare gun from your locker, right? To give to Dillon so he could use it on your ex?'

I nod.

'What if it wasn't Ranson after all? What if it was one of our co-workers? Another one of these Cuckoos?'

5

I return to my desk in a daze. I don't know what to do with this information. I have no context for it. Why would this shapeshifter orisha – this Cuckoo – want to kill me? Why would it want to kill *Becca*? As far as I knew, she was killed to frame me, to get me thrown in jail so Lilith could carry out her plan. But this . . . It doesn't make any sense anymore. Do these Cuckoos relate to the sin-eaters? Is there something more to that case? Something I missed?

I slump into my chair and try to sort it through in my head. But I can't. I don't have enough information. And if Jaeger said she couldn't find any information on the creatures, then I believe her. I'll still do some searching on my own time, but I'm not hopeful about finding anything. Jaeger is a walking encyclopaedia. She should know what that thing is, and if she doesn't then it's because that information is not out there.

A thick folder has been placed front and centre in a neatly cleared area of my desk. The words 'The Blood Sucker Conundrum' are scrawled across the front in red permanent marker. A yellow post-it stuck beneath the writing reads, 'Deal with this pretty please. Love, your boss.' Then underneath this, in brackets, '(Armitage).'

I sigh and open the folder. Last month, I had to kill Kincaid, the King of the East Coast vampires, when he backed the wrong team. He sided with Lilith, Adam's first wife. (Yeah, the one that told Adam to get fucked when he tried to order her around. Fair play to her. I didn't kill her for that. I killed her for trying to start a war between mankind and the orisha.)

But now we have major skirmishes popping up between the various vampire clans, all of them trying to push their own candidate up as the new King. We've had power plays, assassinations, team-ups, betrayals, defections, you name it. It's like the Cold War in Durban right now and it's requiring completely different methods to deal with it. Armitage actually went through her belongings to find her old MI6 operations manual. (Don't ask me how she got it. She wouldn't say. Mysterious past thy name is Armitage.)

As I page listlessly through the file, noting who died over the weekend and who is now claiming supreme rulership over all the clans – a pointless exercise because it will all change tomorrow anyway – Parker flops into her chair opposite me and lowers her head over a steaming mug of coffee.

She stays like that for a few moments, inhaling the aroma.

'Rough night?'

She doesn't move. 'Lisa is not happy with you.'

'*Me?*'

'She blames you for all the overtime I've been working this month.'

'Oh.' I think about it for a minute. 'I suppose she's got a point.'

'You have to make it up to her.'

'Did she say that?'

'No. I did.'

'Ok. What did you have in mind?'

'Booze usually works. Single malt. The good stuff.'

'Fine. I have a bottle of Glenmorangie at home.'

She finally raises her face from the coffee. 'That'll do it.' She takes a sip, winces, then blows into her mug. 'So?' she asks. 'Did your little jaunt around Cape Town change your mind about the place?'

Ah. Mindless chit-chat. I can do that. I can pretend to be normal.

'Not a chance,' I say. 'The place is all hype. A lie. A con. It's the memory foam of cities. Its entire economy is based on cocktail bars, coffee shops, and hipster barbers. The place is so self-masturbatory and inbred it's going to start having babies that look like the royal family.'

'So that's a no?'

'Of course it's a no! They drink tequila with orange slices! Orange slices, Parker. And no salt! And the tequila actually tastes *nice.*'

She frowns. 'What's the point of that? Tequila is supposed to feel like rusted barbed wire stripping away your throat. And the lemon and salt are to rub into the wound. It's not *meant* to be nice. It's alcoholic self-flagellation.'

I nod in agreement. 'I did meet some cool people though. Publicists. They almost made me change my mind about the place.'

'Almost?'

'Yeah. When I woke up I remembered the truth. But those publicists . . .' I shake my head. 'They can drink, that's all I'll say.'

My desk phone rings again, the red light blinking to show an internal call from on-high. I pick it up. 'Armitage, how are you?'

'Get up here. Now.'

She hangs up. Monday morning and Armitage is in a bad mood. What fun.

I use the old-fashioned elevator that climbs the inside wall of the silo, passing the levels containing interrogation rooms, holding cells, the accommodation block (for when we work too late, or it's too dangerous to go home), and many, many offices.

Armitage has changed the elevator music again. It's the Stones' turn this week. 'Paint It Black'. I reach the top floor and walk along the carpet hallway to Armitage's door. I knock loudly and wait. I always wait. I once accidentally walked in and found her sitting in her underwear smoking a cigar, feet up on her desk, reading her skin-mags and cackling to herself.

'Enter!'

'Are you decent?'

A pause. 'Hold on.'

I sigh and wait for about twenty seconds.

'All right. Come in.'

I open the door and hesitantly poke my head into the office. I still don't know what I'll find. Decent for me is most definitely not the same as decent for her.

She looks OK, though. All her clothes on. No gadgets or gizmos. Which is nice.

'What the hell are you waiting for? Get in here.'

I close the door behind me and navigate the piles of paperbacks and old lifestyle magazines that litter the floor. She's sitting in the ancient wingback chair next to the window. Her feet are up on a padded stool and she's eating chocolate. Her desk is absolutely covered in folders and files and ... I squint ... is that a human head in a box?

'I was watching Seven,' she says, as if that explains everything. She nods at the desk. 'Yellow file.'

I rummage around on her desk, lifting envelopes, moving post-it notes and old, yellowing newspapers, and brushing rock hard orange peel aside. I find the file and pick it up.

'Open it,' she says. I glance sharply at her, hearing the anger in her voice. Something bad's happened.

I open the folder. It contains police and autopsy reports for two people. I check the cause of death. Murder-suicide. I flip back to the front of the reports. They're from the Metropolitan Police. My old stomping ground in London.

'I don't get it.'

'Check the names,' snaps Armitage.

I page back through the files. Lerato Sekibo and Ayanda Odili.

I look at Armitage in shock. 'What the fuck . . . ?'

Lerato and Ayanda, the two Division agents sent to London to follow up on the child kidnap and trafficking leads. We'd heard some low level chatter about human kids being sold to supernaturals in London and then being shipped to the continent. We had no idea why. We didn't even know if it was true.

Lerato and Ayanda were junior agents. That's why they were sent to London while I took the more credible Cape Town lead. We didn't think it would actually amount to anything.

'I don't get this. Murder-suicide?'

Armitage nods. 'They say Lerato shot Ayanda and a Ministry official who was baby-sitting them, then turned the gun on herself.'

'Bullshit.'

'They've got it on CCTV. You know what London is like. Cameras every ten feet.'

'But . . . Lerato was getting married this year. She was happy.'

'My thoughts exactly.'

'So . . . what are you thinking? Someone took them out? That the lead was real after all?'

'What do you think?'

I sit down on a chair and stare at the file for a moment. 'I think . . . I think we're going to have to go home.'

'I know. So fucking annoying. I checked the weather report. Snow and rain with a high chance of me getting really pissed off.' She sighs. 'What about you? Did you find anything in Cape Town that might link to this?'

I think of my trip to the Nightside, of the . . . whatever it was protecting me from Babalu-Aye. I decide it might be best to keep that to myself for the moment. At least until I can figure out what the hell it all means.

'Nothing. It was Babalu-Aye. He set me up.'

Her eyebrows rise. 'Nothing to do with missing kids?'

I shake my head.

'He's taking getting his head shot off very personally.'

'That's what I thought. It's not as if he couldn't just grow another. But if I was on his shit-list before, he's *really* going to be coming after me now.'

'Ah. So you took care of him?'

'For now.'

'Watch your back then. If he's tried once he's going to try again. They get obsessive, these old gods.'

'There's . . . something else. Something . . . I'm actually not sure what it is.'

'Out with it.'

I explain everything Jaeger told me about Dillon. I won't repeat the cursing and the throwing of paperweights around the office, but let's just say Armitage is *not* happy.

'There are sleeper agents inside the SSA?'

'Looks like it. Jaeger's already found two. Chances are there are more.'

'Then there might be some here. In the Division.'

I reluctantly nod. 'It crossed my mind.'

'Fuck. Why stop there? The SSA is a government-run department. So are we. There might be some of these shifters in *Parliament*. How the hell are we going to find out?'

'I have absolutely no idea.'

'What about Jaeger? She have any ideas?'

'No. All she knows is that the person who killed Becca wasn't human. Which leads to all sorts of questions I want answered.'

'Me too, pet.' She thinks about it for a moment. 'Keep this to yourself, right?'

'Obviously. I'm not stupid.'

'That remains to be seen.' She looks shrewdly at me. 'I really hope you're not going to go off and do your own thing with this.'

'Of course not.'

'Because the last time you tried to keep stuff from me you almost got humanity wiped out.'

'I know.'

'Like . . . *literally.*'

'I'm aware.'

'Secrets are not to be tolerated in a relationship.'

'I get it, Armitage.'

'Friendships are built on trust.'

I sigh. 'I know.'

'And you still haven't earned my trust back.'

'I know! *Jesus.*'

Armitage rubs her face. 'This makes me very not-happy.' She sighs, then fixes me with a stare. 'So. On to other things. Have you seen the shrink yet?'

'No.'

'Go see her.'

'But—'

'Look, I don't give a shit if you think it will help you or not. Just do it. I've got boxes to tick in my employee evaluations and the people on high aren't sure if you're exactly fit for the job.'

'And if I don't go?'

'You'll probably get suspended.'

'Fine. I'll make an appointment. After we get back.'

'Good lad.' She sniffs. 'It's all rubbish anyway.'

'What is?'

She waves her hand in my general direction. 'This. You. Feeling sorry for yourself. We didn't have depression in my day.'

'Armitage . . .'

'Well, we didn't! People just got on with it. That's life, pet. You're born, you struggle, you pull yourself through every day as best you can, then you die. Anything in-between is up to us. Up to you.'

'It's not like I'm doing this to feel special,' I snap. 'It's real. It's inside me. I can't just click my fingers and get rid of it.'

'Well . . . I still think it's rubbish.'

'You're aware that my dad killed himself? That depression does actually run in my family?'

She waves a hand. 'Another excuse. Sorry, but I've said it. Just because your old man couldn't cope, doesn't mean you're going to check out the same way. Take your power back, man. Stand up to it. Or if you can't, get some bloody drugs that will help you.'

We stare at each other a moment. 'Armitage, it's a rare moment when I want to actually tell you to shut the fuck up. That you don't know what the hell you're talking about. But this is one of them.'

She frowns and opens her mouth.

'Armitage,' I say. 'Shut. The fuck. Up.'

She narrows her eyes. I can see her deciding whether to bite her tongue or to push me even further. Luckily, Armitage's desk phone chooses that moment to ring. Unluckily for me, she ignores it, picking another chocolate out of the box and popping it into her mouth, all the while staring hard at me.

The phone stops ringing. A moment later it's replaced by my cell phone.

'Answer that,' says Armitage. 'It's rude to ignore people.'

I put the phone to my ear. 'London.'

'It's Parker. You and the boss need to get down here. Pronto.'

When we step off the elevator we find the entire crew standing around my desk. And I do mean all of them. Even Jaeger and Maddoc.

All eyes turn to us.

'What?' asks Armitage. 'Have I got chocolate in my teeth?'

'No,' says Parker. 'But . . . there's a phone call for you.'

'For who?' I ask.

'Both of you.'

'Then why the bloody hell are you all standing around like beached whales? What's the problem? Take a message.'

'We can't.'

'Why?'

'The caller says she has to talk to you both personally.'

'Why? Who is it?'

'Uh . . . she says she's the Oracle.'

Armitage frowns. 'The . . . ?'

'The Oracle.'

'What oracle?'

'*Our* oracle.'

'The *Delphic* Oracle?'

'That's what she says.'

'The one we've got buried in the vault beneath our feet?'

'I think so.'

'Rubbish, pet. Someone's having a laugh.'

There's a flare of bright light as every computer monitor in the room suddenly turns an intense white. Black letters appear, blurred and obscured by the harsh glare. I squint and lean close.

Not having a laugh. It's me. Get your undead arse down here now. And bring London. And that disgusting dog.

Armitage stares at the screen thoughtfully for a moment. 'Cheeky bitch,' she says. 'I'm not undead. I'm a revenant.'

6

As far as anyone can tell, the vault door locking the Delphic Oracle in her prison has never been opened. I once asked Eshu to track back through the records just to check, and he came back with a big fat no. Someone did try once, but he was caught and . . . well, he disappeared. I know that sounds very dramatic and everything, but it's the truth. I don't think it was anything to do with us, but you never know. It was the seventies. Things were slightly more rough and ready around here back then.

As to why she's even locked up in the first place, no one knows that either. There's a story that she had a breakdown and went on a killing spree before her old partner managed to subdue her. No one knows why she kicked off, though.

Every member of Delphic Division currently on duty has gathered in the Hub. The crowd trails off down the corridors, the shorter employees jumping up to try and get a better look.

Parker, Armitage, the dog and I stand on one side of the massive vault door, while Eshu stands directly opposite us. He's holding a small electronic keypad.

He looks expectantly at Armitage.

She nods. 'Let's get it over with.'

-*I don't like this*,- mutters the dog. -*The hell does she want with us?*-

-*That's what we're trying to find out.*-

-*We should just ignore her. Let's go on holiday. Somewhere far away. Just unwind a bit, you know?*-

-We can't.-

-Why?-

-Because. We just can't.-

-Fine. Don't say I didn't warn you, though. Goddamn oracles, man. They give me the creeps.-

Eshu types a long code into the keypad, then hands it over to Armitage. 'Thumb print.'

Armitage presses her thumb to the scanner. As she does, the blue LED lights embedded in the vault door flicker and turn red.

'Why red?' asks Parker. 'Red is bad, right?' She looks at me. 'Isn't red bad?'

'Red is bad,' agrees the dog. 'Everyone knows that.'

'Red isn't bad,' I say. 'It could just be a . . .'

'Warning?' says Parker.

'Maybe they ran out of LED lights,' I say.

'Who runs out of LED lights? Look at that door. It's probably three feet thick. You think they design something like that and then just run out of lights?'

'For the love of Christ,' snaps Armitage. 'Will you stop talking about LED lights? Look – something's happening.'

The blinking red lights are switching off, one by one.

'Like a countdown,' mutters the dog.

Everyone is silent now, watching the lights. Four lights. Three. Two. Then one.

A burst of gas explodes into the air. There are a few gasps and we stumble back a couple of steps. But it's just the equalising of pressure as the vault door unseals.

The gas dissipates into the air and the vault door slowly rises upward, swinging back on a massive hydraulic hinge.

Parker was wrong. The door isn't three feet thick. It's four feet. Somebody really wanted the Oracle to stay where she was.

The door swings all the way up and stops. There are two heavy thunks as the door locks into place.

We're all straining to see inside. Someone accidentally jostles Armitage and she whirls around, eyes blazing. 'What is this? Kindergarten? Back up. All of you. Come on! Give us space.'

The staff reluctantly shuffle back and leave a cleared circle around Armitage, myself and the dog. Armitage glares at them a moment longer, then turns to me and claps her hands together. 'Right. Ready to meet the Delphic Oracle? Be polite. She's your boss.'

'I thought you were my boss.'

'Yes. But she's *my* boss. We're *named* after her, London. This is quite an honour. She's the Pythia, you know. The priestess of Apollo. She reveals the past, the present, and the future. Apparently. Now – off you go.'

'Me? Why don't you go first? Age before beauty and all that.'

'Nice try. I'm the boss, remember? You do as you're told, pet. Come on. Get to it. I've got a date tonight.' She frowns. 'At least, I was supposed to. I suppose I'll have to cancel now. We need to organise our trip to London.'

'London?' The dog looks at me. 'London?'

'I'll tell you later.' I turn to Armitage. 'And what's this about a date? Why didn't I know about this?'

'Maybe because you're not my father and it's none of your bloody business?'

'But . . .' I search for a polite way of putting it. 'But you're . . . you know?'

'Dead?'

'I wasn't going to put it that way. But since you said it, yeah. Dead.'

'I'm not. I'm a revenant.'

'And revenants still have . . .'

'What?'

'Well . . . ?'

'What? Spit it out, lad. What are you trying to say?'

I can see the glint in her eyes. She's enjoying this.

'. . . *Needs!*' I say.

'Needs? Oh! You mean sex? Rumpy-pumpy. The beast with two backs? A bit of, "How's your father"? Some afternoon delight? The two person push up? Filling the cream donut? Hide the sausage? The horizontal hula? Slime the banana?'

'Oh my god. Stop.'

'Take old one-eye to the optometrist? Attack the pink fortress?'

'Please stop.'

'Open the gates of Mordor?'

'That's not even a saying.'

'It is. And if you don't want to hear about it, don't ask.'

'I already regret it.'

I turn away from her before she can say anything more and peer into the circular opening in the floor. I can just make out a metal ladder leading down into the darkness.

I hold my arm out to the dog. He looks at me blankly.

'How are you planning on getting down?' I ask. 'We superior beings have these little things called opposable thumbs.'

'You're going to carry me?'

'Unless you want to wait up here?'

'He can't,' says Armitage. 'The Oracle asked to see all of us.'

The dog pads forward. 'Drop me and I will unmake you.'

'You don't have the power for that,' I said, hooking my arm under his belly. He shifts around until he's comfortable in the crook of my arm, his head right next to mine.

'Try me,' he whispers.

I start my descent, sliding my free hand down the side of the ladder. It suddenly gets a lot darker and I look up to see Armitage coming after me, blocking out the light.

'Hey – London!' she calls out.

'What?'

'You know what they used to call sex in the old days.'

'No! And I don't want to know.'

'I do,' calls the dog.

I peer downward but I can't see anything. There's no way to know how far this hole descends. Jesus, but it can't be soon enough for me.

'Make feet for children's stockings,' says Armitage.

I frown, then glance back up at her. 'What?' I call out.

'From the 18th century, that one. Bit tame, though. I like my euphemisms dirty. What the hell's the point otherwise?'

I don't answer. We descend in silence for another minute. I think she's given up on her game, but then she shouts out again.

'Play nug-a-nug,' she says suddenly. 'That's another one.'

'Boring!' says the dog.

'Suit yourself. What about Dance the Paphian Jig? Know what that means?'

'Paphian means the city of Paphos in Cyprus,' the dog says. 'There was a cult there . . .'

'Aphrodite,' I say, trying to focus on keeping my burning hand from slipping on the ladder. 'Goddess of love and sex. They used to worship her there.'

'Check out the brains on Brad!' calls out Armitage happily. 'Ten points for London Town.'

My feet abruptly hit the ground. Thank God for that. 'We're here,' I say, dropping the dog and stretching out my arm, trying to get some feeling back.

'Out the way,' says Armitage.

I step aside as Armitage drops heavily from the ladder. 'Nice thing about being a revenant,' she says. 'That climb would've half-killed me before.'

I look up. The entrance to the vault is nothing but a tiny circle of light. Armitage switches her torch on. I fish mine out from my pocket and shine it around our surroundings. We're standing in a rocky tunnel that leads away from us at a steep decline.

'What about this one then?' says Armitage as she starts walking. 'Groping for trout in a peculiar river.'

'Please stop,' I say as the dog and I follow after.

'What do you think that means?' she asks.

'I don't want to know!'

'What do they call it now? I know a couple of decades ago it was called finge—'

'Armitage! No!'

'Didn't take you for a prude. That one was from the 1600s by the way.'

We continue our descent in silence for a while. The air gets colder, wisps of mist curling around our feet.

'St George,' says Armitage eventually.

'What?'

'St George. What did he do?'

'Killed a dragon?'

'Not just killed. He *rode* a dragon. Girl on top. Cowgirl time. Yippee-ki-yay.'

'You're saying that St George was a woman? That she rode a dragon?'

'No. It just means girl on top. In the sack. Not really sure of the connection, now I think about it.'

'I'm handing in my resignation notice.'

We walk for another five minutes before the passage finally ends at an arched doorway flanked by two flaming torches.

'One more,' whispers Armitage, not taking her eyes from the exit to the tunnel. 'See if you can guess. Ride Below the Crupper.'

'No idea.'

'From the 1500s.'

'That's not helping.'

'A crupper is the piece of kit that keeps a horse's tail erect. So ride below the crupper—'

'Seriously, stop. I'm going to report you to HR if you don't. I swear to Christ, Armitage, I'll do it.'

'Spoilsport.'

She disappears through the arched doorway, the dog and I following after. It takes a few moments for my eyes to adjust to the darkness again, but when they do I see Armitage standing stock still about five paces ahead.

'Armitage?'

No answer. I move forward until I'm standing by her side. She doesn't look at me. Instead she's focused on something ahead of us. I follow her gaze and my eyes go wide.

'Shit . . .' I say.

'Yeah,' agrees Armitage.

We're looking down into a huge cavern that's easily ten times the size of an airport hangar. The air glows, motes of orange-white light gently rising and falling as if riding air currents. I lean forward. Far below us, in the centre of the rocky floor, stands an old-fashioned amphitheatre. Lanterns hang from columns, their flames burning bright blue.

The dog nudges between our legs and looks down. 'It's not all that.'

A crudely-cut ramp zig-zags down the wall to our left. We stare at it distrustfully. It looks like the wall has been cut away around the ramp, but there's nothing supporting it underneath.

I look at Armitage. She just smiles at me. Seriously, why do I even bother?

I set my foot onto the ramp and test it with my weight. It doesn't crumble away, plunging me to a painful, broken death, so that's something at least. A warm breeze wafts up from below, blowing the motes of light closer. They're actually tiny, glowing sprites. Little tinkerbells, but with dead eyes and sharp teeth.

'All good?' asks Armitage.

I jump up and down on the ramp, testing it one last time. 'All good.'

It takes us ten minutes to reach ground level. We reach the rocky floor and look around. There's still no sign of the Oracle. No sign of any life (besides the sprites).

'You sure we're in the right place?' asks the dog.

'No,' says Armitage. 'This is the *other* massive cavern with a Greek-style amphitheatre built below the Delphic Division offices.'

'No need to get snarky.'

'Then don't say stupid things.'

I leave them to bicker and approach the amphitheatre. The blue flames from the lanterns cast a cold glow across the stone. As I get closer I see that there's an opening in the ground, angled so that it descends at a gentle slope.

'Armitage? Over here.'

She joins me and glares at the hole. 'Christ, how deep underground does she want us to go?'

We follow the slope for another five minutes, emerging into a smaller cave, this one lit by the more traditional orange flamed torches. In the centre of the cave is an altar mounted on a raised marble platform.

The Oracle sits cross-legged on the altar.

She looks to be in her sixties and is staring up at the roof, one arm reaching up as if trying to touch the stalactites. She's wearing a white dress and has a crown of woven roots on her head. It looks like the roots are actually entwined *into* her hair.

'Hallo?' says Armitage.

The Oracle blinks and turns her attention to us. At first her face is blank, but then she breaks into a huge smile, her face transforming instantly.

'Hello!' She jumps down from the altar, rushes forward, and grabs me into a tight hug, her head resting against my chest. She inhales deeply.

'You smell nice,' she says happily.

'Uh . . . thank you.'

She lets go, grabs my face, and stares deeply into my eyes. Then she leaps behind me to give a surprised Armitage a hug, stroking her hair a few times before she crouches down in front of the dog and scratches him behind the ear. 'Who's a cute little doggie woggy?' she says. 'You are. Yes, you are.'

I wince, waiting on the explosion of profanity that's about to come.

Except, it doesn't. The dog's eyes soften and he just stares at her like he's a dog seeing his master for the first time in weeks.

His tail is wagging. The only time I've ever seen him wag his tail was when we passed a liquor store holding some kind of promotion and there was a man-sized bottle of OBs on display. When he found out the bottle wasn't real he was *not* happy. The liquor store burned to the ground a couple of weeks later. The dog still insists it had nothing to do with him.

The Oracle heads back to her altar. I stare at the dog, eyebrows raised in amazement. He at least has the decency to look away in embarrassment.

'Thanks for coming,' says the Oracle, crossing her legs and settling herself down again. 'I don't get many visitors.'

'You live here?' I ask. 'On your own?'

'Yes,' she says. She hesitates, her smile faltering. 'It's . . . very lonely.'

'I can imagine,' says Armitage. She frowns, looking intently at the woman. 'Forgive me for asking, pet, but are you the original Oracle?'

The smile is back again, like the flare of morning sun between bedroom curtains. 'I'm the *last* Oracle. The Phythia. I was trained by the seven sages of Greece, you know,' she says proudly.

'And can I ask . . . what brought you here? I mean, specifically here.' Armitage looks around the cave.

The smile switches off again. The Oracle's face darkens, the weight and responsibility of millennia transforming her face so that it's as if I'm looking at a different woman. I look into her angry eyes and I suddenly feel like I understand her. This is the *real* Oracle. The previous, happy personality is the mask she wears to cope.

'It was not a choice,' she says. 'I ran away. In Greece. I tried to assume my old identity, the person I was before I became the Oracle. I rebelled against my role. Against what was expected of me.'

'Good for you,' says Armitage.

'No. Not good for me. I travelled the world, trying to find a life that was normal. But my powers did not go away. Everywhere I went, I saw peoples' futures. Their deaths. In one village every single person I saw was a walking corpse. Bloated grey bodies, half eaten by fish. A tidal wave destroyed the village a week later.

'Then I received a vision. Of what was to come. It was . . . terrible. I didn't even understand what I was seeing. All I knew was that it meant the world would change. That the world would end.' She trails off, rocking slightly on her altar as she stares into space. 'I was not supposed to interfere. Not supposed to get involved. But over the centuries that followed I . . . made suggestions. Influenced people. All over the world. Trying to make sure the vision never came to pass.' She smiles ruefully. 'Another mistake. The oracles are supposed to observe, to relate their visions. Not try to influence them. It didn't seem to work, anyway. The vision kept coming. More and more often. And every time I tried to fix things, the next vision would be even worse.' She glances sidelong at me, staring at me for longer than I'm comfortable with. 'The first Division was formed because of me. In London. It wasn't called the Division, obviously. This was a good couple of thousand years ago. Back then it was just a group of magic-users I brought together to try and keep the world safe. Men and woman fighting against what they saw as their enemies.

'About a hundred and fifty years ago I had another vision. This one . . . I don't even like to think about it. But I realised that something had to be done. Something drastic. Time was running out. This branch had already been created and it was here that the vision brought me. But . . . my methods of fixing things were not to the Division's liking. My lover was in charge here. He . . . turned on me. Locked me up here.'

'Why?' I ask. 'What did you do?'

'What I thought was right. What I thought was for the greater good.'

My thoughts turn back to Lilith. That was what she said too. She was doing what she was doing to try and help her people.

'But I don't mind,' she says. 'This is where I need to be.'

'Why?' asks Armitage.

'Because I need to be close to the storm. It all starts here, you see. The end of everything.'

'Doesn't it get boring?' asks the dog.

'Oh, god, yes!' she says, and in an instant her mask is back up. 'You have no idea! And I get so hungry.' She grins a surprisingly cheeky grin and leans forward. 'But I found ways around it,' she says conspiratorially.

'What ways?'

'I feed on Google,' she whispers. 'Every search string entered into their search engine. Well, not *every* one. But the more . . . esoteric ones. The religious ones. They nourish me. It's what I used to do back in Greece. People would come and ask me questions. I should sue them,' she says thoughtfully. 'I had the idea first.'

'Sorry,' says Armitage. 'Can we get back to the end of every-thing? I feel like we just glossed over that bit.'

'Are you sure you really want to see?' asks the Oracle.

'I don't think you would have called us down here if you weren't going to show us,' says Armitage.

The Oracle points at Armitage and winks. 'You. You're good. I suppose that's why you're the boss.'

A wave of dizziness suddenly hits me. I stumble, trying to find my balance. But it feels like I've just chugged half a bottle of whisky. I fall to my knees. I look across at the others and see that Armitage is already on her back and even the dog is roll-ing over onto his side.

My eyes slide closed. The last thing I see is the Oracle, standing above me and looking at me with such hate that I wonder if she's about to slit my throat.

I'm lost in a heavy fog. It's damp, tickling my face.

'Hello?'

Fun fact: it's actually very hard to call out when you're simultaneously trying to catch someone's attention and also keep very, very quiet.

No answer.

I turn in a circle but can't see anything. I pick a random direction and start walking. I still have no idea what direction I'm going in but I keep walking anyway. I'm feeling troubled, uneasy. What was up with that look she gave me? What the hell is the Oracle playing at?

I soon find out.

The fog swirls, then abruptly fades away beneath my feet. Not *around* me, only beneath.

To reveal I'm standing in mid-air.

I swear in surprise and stumble backwards, expecting to plunge to my death. But I don't fall. In fact, it feels like I'm walking on solid ground.

I stop backpedalling, trying to fight the vertigo that washes over me. I take a deep breath and straighten up, reluctantly casting my gaze beneath my feet.

I'm standing hundreds of feet above a city. Durban, if the coastline is anything to go by.

Except it's not my Durban.

The city is a war zone. The buildings (those that are still standing) stand gutted and empty. Smoke trails up from gaping windows and burning cars, greasy tendrils clawing their way into the bright blue sky.

Rusted cars lay strewn across the streets. Gutted mini-bus taxis lie on the beach, across the Promenade, piled up to block off streets. The ocean water is covered in ash, a thick layer that coats the surface of the sea as far as I can see.

What the hell is going on?

Then suddenly I'm falling. There's no sensation of movement, just a blurring in my vision as I descend.

I land on the promenade. *My* promenade.

It's nearly unrecognisable. The paving is pulled up, huge holes gouged into the ground as if bombs have been dropped. The piers are ruined, dangling skeletons that hang broken over the sea. All the trees are gone. The hotels and apartment buildings to my right look like they've been hit by missiles.

Except I know it wasn't missiles.

It was shinecraft.

I can feel it in the air, crackling like ozone after a storm. I've never felt the after-effects so strongly before. The amount of power released must have been apocalyptic. I wonder how much of Africa is like this. How much of the world.

There is utter silence. I turn in a slow circle, searching for signs of life. But there's nothing. No people. No minah birds hopping around, no seagulls. Nothing. The hot sun beats down out of a cobalt blue sky, shining on the aftermath of a war.

A movement catches my eye. I frown and stare into the distance. There. A huge pyre about fifty meters ahead of me, where the old games arcade used to stand.

I start to walk, my heart thumping heavily in my chest.

The pyre is about fifteen feet high. It's made from wood and actual living bodies, stacked up like a twisted game of Tetris.

There are people on top of the pyre too, tied to a central pole. As I draw closer I recognise their faces.

Armitage. Parker. And others from the Division.

I stumble forward, intending to untie the ropes that bind them. But my hands pass straight through the bindings.

I'm not really here. I'm a ghost.

'London, don't you *dare* do it!'

I look up. It's Armitage talking, but she's not looking at me. She's staring down at something I can't see.

I move slowly around the pyre, dreading what I'm going to find.

And then I stop walking. My mind goes blank, unsure how to handle what I'm seeing.

I'm staring at myself.

I'm standing next to the fire, a blazing torch in my hand.

'London, please just think about this!' shouts Armitage. 'This is not the way.'

The me with the torch looks up at Armitage. I hardly recognise the face. I look older than I am now, but it's hard to tell how much, because my face is thin, ravaged.

My haunted eyes gaze sadly at Armitage. 'It's the *only* way.'

'Where's the dog? You think he'd want you to do this?'

'The dog?' the other me says bleakly. 'The dog is the one that started all this. Anyway, he's dead now.'

'How?' demands Armitage.

'I killed him.'

'You . . . killed the dog?'

'I . . . had to. I'm sorry. Truly.'

And with that the other me throws the torch onto the pyre. I rush forward and try to grab it, but once again my hands slide straight through. The cries and groans from those at the bottom of the pyre grow louder as the kindling catches, turning to shrieks of pain as the fire spreads.

'I'll get you!' screams Parker. 'You hear me, London? I'm coming back for you!'

The other me watches the fire rise higher and higher, his face a blank mask as my friends – my family, really – burn to death before him. I stare into those eyes. Familiar but entirely alien.

Then I'm yanked back into the air. Up and up, soaring fast across the landscape. The light abruptly switches off. I'm surrounded by complete and utter darkness. I feel like a mind floating in nothing. I have no bodily sensations at all. The dark is me and I am the dark.

Lights slowly appear, tiny pinpricks of glittering white. Stars. They speed up, rushing in from all sides, and suddenly I'm floating in space.

Then the stars rise up to either side, distorting as they do so. They come together again, like a piece of paper folding in half. They close over me. I'm caught in the middle. They pass through me—

—And I'm out in the sunshine again.

I wince against the glare, wondering what new hell I'm going to find now.

I look around. Everything is . . . normal. The buildings are whole. Crowds go about their business; skaters and cyclists, musicians and mimes. There are street vendors everywhere. I can smell hot dogs, popcorn, burgers. It looks like Durban beachfront, but much more dynamic.

I frown, realising everything is familiar. I've been here. Before I moved to South Africa.

It's Venice Beach. Cali-fucking-fornia.

What the hell?

I came here after leaving the Met in London. I was going through a bad phase, eking out a living as a private investigator. I was here for a couple of years before I moved to South Africa. Looking back, I actually had a pretty good time. I didn't have many responsibilities. I lived day by day, just earning enough for food and booze. Life was . . . simple.

I miss this place. There was always a more carefree vibe here than in Durban. Than in South Africa as a whole, really.

'Hey, London!' calls out a woman. 'Goddammit, will you slow the fuck down?'

I turn around in surprise, searching for whoever is talking to me.

'Well?'

I frown. A woman standing five paces away has just spoken. She sounds annoyed.

'What's the rush? Jesus, London.'

My eyes widen in astonishment as I realise the first voice is coming from a dog. Not *my* dog, but a different dog. A collie.

'It's not my fault you just drank a litre of cheap whisky,' says the woman. 'Kinda surprised you can even walk at all.'

What. The. *Fuck?*

I approach the woman. She has the exact same dragon tattoos as me on her back and shoulders. She's wearing a tank top and jeans and has long, auburn hair pulled back in a ponytail. Her eyes are blue and sharp, but there's sadness there. And anger. The same thing I see in my own eyes.

'Get a move on then,' she snaps. 'We've got things to do.'

'Bite me,' snarls the dog, but she does put on an extra burst of speed so that she catches up with the woman.

'I'm rationing your booze,' she says to the dog. 'And no more pizza. You're going on a diet.'

'I will literally eat you while you sleep,' says the dog matter-of-factly.

Then everything freezes. The people around me, the birds in the sky. Everything. Reality slices into itself, and the woman and the dog suddenly have doubles spreading out all around them, receding into infinity as if they're standing between mirrors.

But I notice that the reflections are not all the same. Some are different, some male, some female, and different races too. But they are all accompanied by a dog. (Also all different. I see boxers, German shepherds, corgis, pugs(!), and even a French poodle, complete with parlour-trimmed hair.)

I'm pulled forward, weaving in and out of the reflections, dipping into each of their realities. In every one I see a repeat of what I saw in Durban, but in different locations across the globe. A future time where a war is being fought, orisha and mankind battling across the entire world. It's like the future in *Terminator*, except instead of robots, it's monsters and gods destroying mankind.

And in each reality I see what I assume are different versions of the dog and I, battling and fighting the orisha, shotgun firing, magic flaring, my dragons striking.

The images come faster and faster. The Delphic Division overrun by orisha, slaughtering those inside. The Houses of Parliament in Cape Town, gutted and on fire, orisha crawling over the roof, leaping down to attack fleeing humans.

Then I see images from other countries. Big Ben, entirely black, every inch covered by clambering goblins that have crawled up from beneath the earth. I'm soaring through the streets of London and a shadow passes before me, a darkness I can't quite see. The shadow leaves insanity in its wake, gibbering wrecks entirely devoid of thought. I get a sense of an ancient, primal fear connected to this creature, a terror that bypasses my brain, overriding all rational thought.

I hear a whispered voice.

'The war is here.'

And the voice is mine.

I sit bolt upright. My breath comes in shallow gasps.

I look wildly around and realise I'm back in the Oracle's cave. Armitage is already on her feet, and the dog has wandered off to stand in the mouth of the tunnel, facing away from all of us.

Armitage looks at me. Her eyes are hooded, her face blank.

'What . . . what did you just see?' I ask. Did she see what I just did?

'I think I'll keep that to myself for now,' she says. But I don't like the way she's looking at me. I swallow nervously and climb to my feet.

'Dog?'

The dog glances back, then pads back toward us. He's not really looking his usual annoying self. He won't even look me in the eye. I'm about to ask him what he saw in the visions, but Armitage speaks before I get a chance.

'Where the fuck is the Oracle?'

I look quickly around.

She's nowhere to be seen.

Eshu is the only one waiting when we climb back out of the hole. Everyone else has gotten bored and gone back to work.

'All good?' asks Eshu.

'No,' snaps Armitage. 'It's pretty fucking far from all good. Did the Oracle come past here?'

'The Oracle? No . . . why?'

'Because she's not in her prison anymore,' I say. 'Least, we couldn't find her anywhere.'

'You're . . . saying you let the Oracle escape?' whispers Eshu.

'No. We're saying *you* let her escape, seeing as you're the one standing here.'

'She never came this way! I swear! I would have seen her.'

'Let's see what the internal cameras have to say about that, shall we?'

'Armitage, come on. I wouldn't do that.'

'Wouldn't you?' asks Armitage. 'We'll know soon enough.' She scowls at me. 'I bet this was her plan all along. She wanted to escape.'

'So you think the visions she showed us were fake?' Hope flutters to weak life in my chest. A wounded bird that's just been shot struggling to breathe.

Armitage looks at me. Her face has no expression at all. 'No,' she says. 'No, I don't think that.'

Eshu closes the vault door again. We wait until all the LED lights blink blue once again.

'What's that phrase?' asks the dog. 'Closing the stable door after the horse has bolted? It's playing in my head right now. Not sure why.'

'Shut up, dog,' says Armitage. She turns her attention to me. 'Go pack. We leave on the first flight I can book.'

So . . . anyone who has ever wanted to travel with animals overseas will know it's not easy. You can't just pop them on your lap and feed them peanuts and crisps while you share earphones and watch in-flight movies.

No, pets have to travel in the hold. Even if they happen to be intelligent, magical spirit guides.

'I'm not going to be shut up in there. End of story,' snarls the dog.

'Come on, man. Stop being difficult. We need to fly overseas. What do you expect me to do?'

'Pull some strings. Tell them I'm a diplomatic envoy or something.'

'Don't be stupid.'

'I'll talk. I'll tell them I'm a movie star or something. You know how those dogs say sausages, or I love you or whatever. I'll say Supercalifragilisticexpialidocious.'

'No.'

'What about antidisestablishmentarianism?'

'No . . . you're going in the hold with the other animals. End of story.'

'I'll break out and kill all of them.'

'No, you won't.'

'I'll break out and piss on all the luggage.'

'Don't you dare.'

'London, I'm seriously struggling to see what I get out of this situation.'

'You don't need to get anything out of it. We have no choice. Look . . . what if I try to smuggle you a bottle of sherry? I'll put it in my suitcase and if you can sniff it out the whole thing's yours.'

'How big?'

'Normal size.'

'No.'

'Fine. The two litre bottle.'

The dog glares at me for a moment. 'And you have to promise to wear the Christmas hats when we get back.'

I almost say no to that one.

'I'm serious.'

I sigh. '*Fine*. Now let's go. Armitage is already waiting for us.'

7

You know why London is never referred to as 'good old London'? Or, 'a thoroughly nice place to live'? Or even, 'that relatively OK city filled with South Africans and Australians'?

It's because London is a shit-hole. It's a miserable, depressing place to live and an even worse place to visit. I'd go so far as to say it's nearly as bad as Cape Town. (That's how much I hate it.)

I mean, I just don't get what it has to offer. It's usually raining, and even when it's not, it's just . . . grey. The city's buried beneath a greasy filter of non-colour that leeches everything of life while at the same time somehow managing to bring every piece of dirt, every gobbed-up piece of phlegm, every discarded chip wrapper (which is usually being attacked by mental, feral pigeons) into glorious HD.

Take Oxford, for instance. Now *there's* a city that radiates history and class. When it rains in Oxford, it makes the centuries-old buildings look renewed and vibrant, a picturesque postcard you can send to your family overseas.

Send a postcard of rainy London to them and they'll wonder why you hate them so much.

London is just . . . old. Grubby, mud-smeared, dangerous, and mad.

Except when it snows. Then it's even worse. And how lucky am I that it just happens to snow in December for the first time in Christ knows how long?

'God-fucking-dammit,' I say, staring out the hotel window and watching the great, fat flakes drop silently from the leaden sky.

'What's your problem?' says the dog. 'A white Christmas, London. How cool is that?'

'We're not going to be here for Christmas.'

'Why? Can't we stay? Come on. Whisky and snow and unwrapping shitty presents you don't want and will never use beneath a cheap plastic Christmas tree? I want that.'

'You can stay if you like. I'm spending Christmas day on the beach with a six pack of ice-cold beers.'

'Whatever you say, Grinch.'

'Come on. Armitage is waiting downstairs.'

I don't know how Armitage did it, but she somehow managed to find the dodgiest, weirdest, most decrepit hotel in London. It looks like it was ripped right from the seventies and stuck down a dark, half-hidden alley in Soho with high buildings to either side cutting off all but a tiny slice of daylight.

And I'm not talking modern, updated Soho. This alley is like the old Soho. Dark, and dirty. Where used condoms and old needles come to die. The place is so dodgy even property developers are scared to enter.

I lock the flimsy door with an actual *key* and we walk across the avocado-green carpet to the stairs. A flickering light with a plastic, dust-covered lampshade casts a weak yellow glow over everything. Although I kind of wish it didn't. Remember those 3D wire pictures forming geometric shapes over a black felt background? The ones that were in all our parents' houses? One wall is entirely covered in them. Another has a picture of two kids walking along a tree-lined path in autumn, and there's even a huge framed picture of that tennis player scratching her arse. You know the one. I'm telling you, it's as if someone got into Armitage's mind and just pulled this place out fully formed.

Armitage is waiting in the dining room that opens off from the foyer at the bottom of the stairs. A young guy stands behind the reception desk. He has jet black hair parted immaculately down the centre. Even from the stairs I can see the white specks of dandruff, strewn across his head like stars against a winter night.

Armitage has one of those little multipacks of cereal on her table. She's opened three of the tiny boxes and is slurping the last of the milk from her bowl when I sit down opposite her.

'You want some?'

I shake my head. 'Is this place off the map?'

'What do you mean?'

'Is it . . . from *our* world? You know . . . do orisha stay here?'

Armitage blinks and looks around. 'I don't think so.'

'Then why the hell did you bring us here?'

'It looked nice.'

'It looked . . .' I stare at her in amazement. 'Seriously?'

'What's wrong with it?'

'It's been stuck in a time warp since the seventies,' I hiss. 'There's a TV in my room. Not an LCD screen. An actual TV. Cathode ray.'

'Lucky you. All I got was a black and white portable.'

'It's showing *Bagpuss*, *Clangers*, and *The Flumps*. That's it. On repeat.'

Armitage brightens. 'Really? I loved *Bagpuss*. Want to swap rooms?'

'What? No . . . look, can't we find a proper hotel?'

'Sorry, pet. Not on our budget.'

'I like it,' says the dog.

'You would,' I say. 'If you were human, you'd be lounging in the foyer reading porn magazines.'

'You say that like it's a bad thing.'

Someone clears their throat behind us. We turn and see a young woman standing nervously in the doorway. She looks like she's in her early twenties. She has blonde hair pulled back in a ponytail and is wearing a stylish charcoal-coloured suit with a white shirt.

'Are you Armitage?' she asks.

'That's the name, pet. Don't wear it out.'

'I was told to pick you up? I'm from the Ministry?'

'Well? Are you or aren't you?'

'I'm sorry?'

'You said that like it was a question. You know what, never mind, luv.' Armitage gets to her feet. 'Take me to your leader,' she says, and breaks into a chuckle.

The girl's name is Mia and she's a terrifying driver. Like, I'm not talking bad. I'm talking *suicidal*. Veering between buses, cutting people off, skidding to a stop inches before knocking over pedestrians and then leaning out the window to swear blue murder at them.

I notice something odd during the moments I don't have my eyes tightly closed against my impending death. Back in Durban, we have a few orisha on the streets. Not many, though. I mean, when they're out they use glamour and stuff to stay hidden from the normal people (we can see them because everyone who works in my field has the second sight) but mostly they just stay hidden away – only coming out at night, sticking to back alleys, that kind of thing. But here in London it's utterly different. We can't travel ten feet without seeing some form of orisha. I actually think they outnumber humans three to one. This isn't a human city anymore. It's an orisha city.

And they don't seem to be the nice kind.

I see two thin creatures with brown faces and white tattoos casually steal a human's wallet without him noticing. Another creature, a fat, waddling goblin of some kind, passes a woman and reaches out to feel her breasts as he does so. She jumps and looks wildly around, but obviously can't see anything. The goblin hurries past, a huge grin on his face as he crosses the street to where a group of school girls are huddled at a bus stop, heads buried in their phones.

A trio of giants emerge from a narrow alley that bisects a Lidl and a Waterstones. Two of them are holding metal casks, the type the pubs use for their ale pumps. One of them takes out a knife and jabs a hole in the metal, lifting it up to its mouth and gulping the beer down while the others laugh.

Further on, I see a gang of elves with red tattoos on their arms attack a dwarf – a dvergr from Scandinavia, if I judge his markings correctly. They punch and beat him until he falls to the ground, then they take out wooden swords and start to cut him to pieces while other orisha give the whole scene a wide berth.

Armitage is watching all this out of her window too.

'Was this place always like this?' I ask. Remember I didn't know about all this shit when I lived here. I was a sweet innocent copper.

'No, it bloody wasn't,' snaps Armitage. 'This isn't a city. This is the wild fucking west. Oi, you. Mia.' She bangs on the back of Mia's seat. 'What the hell is going on here?'

'What do you mean?' she asks, swerving around a slow-moving car and blaring her horn.

'All this breaking the law. Where are your lot? The Ministry. You're supposed to be stopping this kind of thing.'

'How?' she asks. 'London has a population of nine million. There are – roughly, we think – twenty one million supernatural creatures here too. Guess how many Ministry personnel we have.'

'How the hell am I supposed to know?'

'Sixty three. So what is it you think we should be doing?'

'Sixty three? How did that happen? Can't you appeal to the government?'

'The government? Since the Tories took over, our funding has been slashed by eighty per cent. We're outnumbered and outgunned and every week another agent either quits or gets taken out by the orisha. It's gang warfare out there and there's not a thing we can do to stop it.'

'Jesus,' mutters the dog. 'And you lot thought you had it bad in Durban.'

'You're saying you only have one branch now?' asks Armitage. 'There used to be ten in London alone.'

'All gone. Downsized, restructured. We're fighting a battle we all know we're going to lose. Probably a couple of years from now.'

'I don't get it,' I say. 'There's a world-wide treaty that's supposed to stop this from happening. Everyone knows these guys need to be policed.'

Mia shrugs. 'What can I tell you? We're just the grunts. You'll have to speak to the boss.'

'Oh, you have a boss?' says Armitage. 'That's something at least. Who is it?'

'Alexander Lewis,' says Mia.

'Mother*fucker*,' snaps Armitage.

I look at her in surprise.

'I know him,' she says. 'He's a Grade A prick. Of the highest order.'

'He's not that bad once you get to know him,' says Mia. 'Maybe a Grade B prick.' She thinks about it. 'Or a B+.'

Mia takes us into the City of London itself, that tiny little square mile where bankers fight running battles with editors and agents over the best restaurant tables. She pulls into a side street next to a tall building that bears a passing resemblance to Nakatomi Plaza and passes beneath a boom gate into the underground parking.

'So . . . these guys get a modern office block and we get a cement factory? How is that fair?'

'If life were fair I would be sitting nice and snug in my office right now, nursing a toasted cheese sandwich and a cup of tea. If life were fair I wouldn't have a huge hole gouged out of my chest. If life were fair I'd be paid a shit lot more than I do now. So suck it up, you big baby.'

Mia parks the car and we all climb out and head toward the elevator. There are cameras everywhere.

'Is this whole building yours?' I ask.

'No. Just the top three floors. The others are mostly empty, though. The Home Office owns the building itself.'

The elevator doors slide open and we step in. Mia hits the button for the top floor and we wait in uncomfortable silence while the lift goes up, listening to a muzak version of 'Bohemian Rhapsody'.

Lovely.

The doors slide open onto an incredibly boring and generic corridor. Burgundy carpet tiles, plastic potted plants against the walls, and paintings of the Queen, Winston Churchill, and self-important soldiers on horses pursuing the British Empire's love of genocidal expansionism.

Mia leads the way. I peer through the doors as we pass: a small kitchen area with a coffee machine, a fridge and a few tables and chairs, a surprisingly large library with filing cabinets and bookshelves all the way to the ceiling, and various boardrooms and offices, most of them empty.

It looks like any other office in the country. At least our place has some style. This is just . . . soul-sapping.

At the end of the corridor is a large briefing room. There are about twenty or so people in the room seated on metal chairs, their attention focused on a man in his late fifties standing before a wall-mounted white board. He stops talking when we enter. Every pair of eyes turns to stare.

'Lewis,' says Armitage.

'Armitage,' says the man. 'Heard you were dead.'

'I got better. Heard you were still a dick.'

'You heard right.'

I stare between the two. There's some serious tension crackling in the air.

-*They boned,*- says the dog.

-*Reckon you're right.*-

'Everyone, please welcome our guests from the South African department. Armitage, and . . . ?'

'Gideon,' I reply. Kind of think calling myself London here will just paint a target on my back.

'Gideon. Right. OK everyone, briefing over. Get back to work. Sam, see me later, and Selina, you're on your first warning, OK? No more selling spells to fairground fortune tellers.'

A young woman with a Sinead O'Connor haircut scowls at him. 'It was for a case, asshole.'

'So you say.'

She gives him the finger and leaves. Lewis gathers up some papers, then turns without another word and heads through a door on the far side of the room.

We follow him into another corridor and then into his office. Armitage flops into a chair while Lewis sits behind his desk, studiously avoiding eye contact with her.

I take the only other chair in the room and glance around. The office itself is large, but still cramped. Thick files bound with string form precarious towers that look like they're about to fall over any second. One wall is just floor-to-ceiling shelves holding government operation manuals. There's a small Christmas tree sitting on the desk. The lights have shorted out and fused together, a huge section of the tree itself a black mass of half-burned synthetic fir.

'Notice how he doesn't want to look into my eyes, London?'

I turn my attention to Lewis. 'I did notice that.'

'It's rude, that is.'

'Very.'

'I'd go far as to say insulting,' adds the dog.

Lewis glances at the dog with a frown, then finally straightens up and faces Armitage.

'What do you want, Armitage?'

'See, there's a bit of history here,' says Armitage, not taking her eyes off him. 'Lewis here took a fancy to me about ten years ago. Christ, where does the time go, eh? He wasn't the big man back then. He was still my superior, though. We had a fling, isn't that right, Lewis?'

Lewis says nothing. Armitage glances at me.

'Problem was, he was married, with a baby on the way.'

'Did you know?' I ask, surprised.

'Course I knew. I met her when we were off duty. And before you say anything, I know that makes me a complete shit, but there you go. Least I wasn't as bad as him.'

'I broke it off,' mutters Lewis.

'Aye, you did. After the miscarriage.'

-*Shit,*- says the dog.

'How is Laura nowadays?'

'She remarried. Two kids.'

'Good for her. She was nice. She deserves a happy ending.'

'And I don't?' asks Lewis.

Armitage shrugs. 'See, the thing is, London, Lewis here wasn't just happy with breaking it off. Not sure if it was my sheer sexual magnetism or what, but he decided it would be better if I wasn't around anymore. He reported me to HR. Said I was making inappropriate moves on him. He kept on and on until I was given a choice. Quit or relocate to a different branch.' She turns to him. 'I suppose I should thank you, though. Never would have emigrated if it wasn't for you. It's a nice life over the pond. So to answer your question, Lewis. No, you fucking don't deserve a happy ending.

You're a lying, manipulative, cowardly little shit.' She smiles. 'Now, about our operatives. The ones that died on your watch.'

'They weren't on my watch,' snaps Lewis. 'We didn't ask you to send them.'

'No, but when children are going missing and a lead points to them popping up again in London, we have to take that kind of thing seriously. It's our job. And yours. So ... they were here for four days. Who was their Ministry liaison? Who were their suspects?'

'Lerato killed the liaison as well.'

'Really? That *is* interesting.' Armitage leans forward. 'Tell me, are you really so dense that you actually think my operative killed two people and then shot herself?'

Lewis stares at her a moment then turns to his laptop. He fiddles with it then spins it round to face us.

We're looking down at a night-time street. The footage must be from a CCTV camera. There are a few people visible. Drunk kids heading home after a night of partying.

A car pulls up to the kerb. Nothing happens for a moment, then there's a sudden flash from inside. The back door opens and a man scrambles out, slipping on the icy sidewalk. The driver's door opens and another figure exits. It's Lerato. She's holding a gun. She walks around the car just as the guy gets to his feet and shoots him in the face.

Lerato then turns and looks directly into the camera. Her face is ... different. Filled with ... utter despair. She lifts the gun to her temple and fires.

Lewis turns his computer back toward him.

I'm silent for a while. I can't get Lerato's face out of my head. I've never seen that look on her face before. Never.

'Where are their files?' I ask. 'What desks were they working from?'

'They didn't leave anything here,' says Lewis.

'What, nothing? Fine, where's their liaison's desk? He must have made his own case notes?'

'He . . . didn't.'

Armitage stares at him for a long moment. I know that look. I've borne the brunt of it many times.

'London, will you and the dog step outside for a moment, please,' she says quietly.

Lewis looks at us then back at Armitage. 'What—'

'*Now*, London.'

I get to my feet. 'Don't kill him,' I say. 'It will be hard to cover up.'

'Hey – what are you talking about?' Lewis looks incredibly nervous.

The dog and I step outside his office and close the door behind us. I lean up against the wall and fold my arms.

'Bit of a dump this,' says the dog.

'Mmm.'

'I mean, like I said, I thought you guys had it bad. Offices in a cement factory, you know? Paging Paul Verhoeven. But this . . . this place is like a call centre or something. Where dreams come to die.'

A loud bang comes from inside the office. Then the scraping of a chair across the floor. The dog and I make eye contact.

'Let her have her fun,' he says. 'It's been tough for her since getting her heart ripped out her chest.'

I sigh, banging the back of my head lightly against the wall. None of this makes sense. I *know* Lerato wasn't suicidal. And she definitely wasn't psychotic. So what the hell happened? This *must* have been something to do with the lead they were following up. About the missing kids. Which means it must have been a real lead and not the long shot we initially thought.

Which means it's possible they may have found out something about Cally.

'London,' calls Armitage. 'Get back in here.'

I push the door open and find Armitage has Lewis shoved into the corner of his office, her fingers wrapped around his neck.

'Top drawer,' she says.

I open the drawer. Stapler, staples, pencils, a couple of paperbacks by John le Carré.

Lewis is making strangled noises. Armitage releases the pressure slightly.

'Other side,' he croaks.

I pull open the top drawer on the opposite side and find a thick wad of files. I drop them on the desk, checking through them until I find the names of my colleagues.

'What was the liaison's name?' I ask.

'Delport,' says Lewis after a moment.

I find Delport's file and place it on top of the other two. I spot a tin of sweets in the drawer and hold them up to Lewis.

'You mind?'

He doesn't answer.

'London would like a sweet, Lewis,' says Armitage in an over-friendly voice. 'Can he have a sweet?'

He manages to nod.

'Lewis says you can have a sweet, London.'

'And me,' says the dog.

'Take one for the dog,' she adds. 'And one for me too.'

I take three sweets, hesitate, then tip the whole tin into my pocket. I grab the files and head out of the office. I hear a thump behind me and a moment later Armitage catches up, straightening out her trench coat as she walks.

Half an hour later we're sitting in a cafe. One as grimy and behind the times as I could find. No hipsters. No organic, ethically sourced coffee. Not a styled beard in sight. Just greasy walls, Formica tables covered in cigarette burns, and thick coffee poured from percolators that haven't been cleaned in months.

I take a sip, shudder as the bitter fluid crawls sluggishly down my throat, then pour more sugar into my cup.

'Come on then,' says Armitage, sucking on one of the sweets I took from Lewis' desk. 'What do the files say?'

'I'm still reading.'

'Christ, it's not that hard, London. Skim.'

-I think that sausage you bought me is still alive,- says the dog.

I ignore him and carry on reading through the files, following Lerato and Ayanda's movements from the moment they landed at Heathrow.

Child trafficking isn't usually our department, but these cases were different. Enough that they were statistically anomalous. Kids had disappeared from their beds at night, from schools, even from paediatric hospital rooms with full security in place. No clues, no traces left behind.

'They were looking into organised crime,' I say, surprised.

Armitage stops sucking and frowns. 'So we shouldn't have even looked into it?'

'No, we should have.' I read ahead, frowning at the case notes.

'London?'

'The Fae.'

'The Fae?'

'The files . . . talk about organised crime here in London. But . . . the whole scene seems to be run by different Fae clans.' I frown. 'When did this happen? I haven't read anything in the dispatches about Fae moving into organised crime. That's . . . ludicrous. It's like the Mafia stealing lunch money from school kids.'

'You know the Fae. You can never understand their motives. I'm sure there's something more behind it. What else?'

'They were following a lead. They suspected the missing kids were connected to a . . . Russian Fae clan. Led by . . .' I turn the page. 'Baba Yaga?'

Armitage sits upright and grabs the file from me.

'Isn't Baba Yaga one of the old myths? She used to hang around in a cottage with chicken feet or something stupid?'

'Yeah. But she *did* steal children.'

'Seriously?'

'All the time. She ate them.'

'You think she's eating these missing kids?'

'No. Too much trouble to go to. She could just source them locally if that's all she wanted.'

'So . . . they went to see this Baba Yaga,' I say. 'And about twelve hours later they were dead.'

Armitage takes out her phone and dials. 'Lewis. It's me. Hang up and I'll come round there and pull your dick off. Baba Yaga. My people were looking into her as a suspect. What do you know—'

Armitage frowns and looks at her phone. 'He hung up,' she says in amazement. She dials again but after a moment chucks the phone on the table. 'He's switched it off.'

'So? We go back to the Ministry and get him to do his fucking job.'

'I don't think that will help.'

'Why?'

'Because of what he said before he hung up.'

'Which was?'

'"*Take my advice, Armitage. Drop it.*"'

I lean back in my chair. 'Scared? Paid off?'

'I've no idea.'

'So what do we do? Go higher? The Home Office?'

'Cool your pants there, Maverick. There's someone else we can try first. Without going through all the red tape.'

'Who?'

'Someone I used to work with in the Ministry. Only thing is . . . I kind of got him fired.'

'Wonderful. So why would he help us?'

'Because he owes me a favour. He's the most knowledgeable guy around here about Faerie lore. Thinks very highly of himself, though. Bit of a smartarse.' She gives me a look. 'You and him should get on well. He's a bit like the dog.'

'Christ, please don't say that. One of him is enough.'

'Hey, watch it,' says the dog. 'And by the way, Armitage. I resent that. I'm one of a kind.'

'Here's hoping,' I say.

'I'm warning you, he's bit of a weirdo,' says Armitage. 'A dabbler. Used to pretend he was a street magician to pick up women in the pub. He's into conspiracies and stuff. Thinks England is ruled by a cult of black magicians.'

'Is it?' I mean, anything's possible. In this line of work, you just never know.

'I don't think so. He works as an occult investigator now. Exorcisms, selling low-level charms, love potions, curses, that kind of thing. Used to play around with fire magic when he was in the Ministry. It was his specialty.'

I down my coffee with a wince and get to my feet. 'Let's go then.'

8

Armitage leads the way through the muddy, slush-covered streets. I wanted to get a taxi, but Armitage said it was only a mile and we'd get there quicker by walking.

I count no less than one hundred and twenty three orisha during our trip. Mostly Fae, but also dwarves, piskies, a couple of centaurs, a few wyverns flying through the air, plus some kind of massive crow with a human head.

And they're just strolling along the streets, ignoring the humans as they go about their business. I even notice a few Fae shops nestled between liquor stores and estate agents. Only the orisha can see them of course, but it's the first time I've come across them out in the open like this. It's like the orisha are trying to claim the city for themselves.

Armitage finally stops before a newsagent. Some kind of weird hybrid of Bollywood and heavy-metal music streams from inside the shop. A revolving sign spins around and around in the freezing wind, showing a Cornetto on one side and a pasted-on missing child flyer on the other. The child's face and the Cornetto blur together, looking like an ice cream with the face of a child.

Armitage reluctantly draws her mittened hand out of her pocket and jabs a button on the grubby intercom fixed to the wall.

'See this?' she says, nodding around at the street. 'This is why I stay in Durban. No human should have to deal with this weather. It's not natural.'

'I agree. Which is why I'm puzzled you just made us walk through it.'

'Exercise,' she said.

A crackly voice issues from the speaker. 'What?'

'Callum Winters please.'

A pause. 'He's not here.'

'Let's not play silly buggers now. Open the door.'

'Go away. I'm attempting to get spectacularly drunk.'

Armitage sighs. 'Cal, it's Armitage. Get your arse down here now.'

There's no reply, but a minute later the door jerks open. A guy in his forties frowns at us. He's wearing faded jeans and an untucked white shirt, sleeves rolled up to reveal sigils and runes tattooed on his forearms. He's got five days' worth of stubble and short-ish black hair that looks suspiciously like it takes a lot of time and effort to look so stylishly unkempt. He leans against the doorframe and sips from a bottle of beer.

'This is Cal Winters,' says Armitage. 'He used to work for the Ministry, but we had to let him go.'

'Misunderstanding,' says Winters with a dismissive wave of his hand. He's got an Irish accent. 'Bit of a mix-up with a succubus. Nothing really.'

'Nothing?' Armitage laughs. 'Cal here was going to be charged with . . . what was it? Misappropriation of government assets? Something like that. It meant jail time.'

'I was using the succubus for a case,' says Winters sourly. 'And anyway, she was a fucking succubus. *She* seduced *me*. It's kind of what they do.'

'Yeah, you said that at the time, pet. Anyway, the gist of all that is that Mr Winters here owes me a very big favour, seeing as I managed to make it all go away.'

'I was fired, Armitage. Not what I call making it go away.'

'Better than prison, pet.'

He stares at her for a moment, then nods. 'Good point.'

'Can we please go inside?' asks the dog. 'I think my nuts have retracted all the way into my body. I'm not sure I'll ever be able to lick them again.'

Winters stares at the dog calmly, then at the both of us. 'You heard that, right?'

'Heard what, pet?'

'The dog . . . you know what, never mind.' He turns and heads back inside. Armitage catches the door before it closes in our faces. We follow him up a narrow flight of stairs to a wooden door with so many coats of glossy paint it's a wonder it can open and close at all.

Winters heads into a dingy office containing an old desk that looks like it was rescued from one of the hundreds of skips that line London's roads, a couch with sunken cushions that form the exact shape of a sleeping man, and a corner table with a dead fern and some old comics. (Eighties era 2000AD, still printed on old newsprint, the top copy showing Nemesis the Warlock, a few Batman comics, and a Love and Rockets graphic novel.)

There's a round rug laid out on the warped wooden boards. The design on it is so weird it looks like you're falling into some LSD trip of purple and beige spirals. God help anyone who comes home drunk and stares at that for too long.

'Lovely place,' says the dog. 'It has the ambience of a seventies porn film. In fact, I think I've seen one set in this exact room. I reckon that's the same couch too.' The dog nods appreciatively. 'Nice.'

'I was going for Raymond Chandler noir P.I., but I'll take seventies porn too.'

'Who wouldn't?' says the dog.

Armitage flops into the couch. It sinks so far beneath her that she might as well be sitting on the floor. She winces and shifts around. 'You live here?'

He nods at a frosted glass door. 'I've got a flat in there. This is just my office.'

'Lead the way then – I could murder a cuppa.'

Winters stares at us for a moment.

'Have you left something embarrassing on the telly?'

'I don't have a TV,' says Winters without turning his gaze from Armitage.

'Why the fuck not?' asks the dog. 'What do you do to block out the deafening silence of your soul?'

'Alcohol.'

'Oh.' The dog thinks about it. 'Fair enough.'

'What's the problem then?' asks Armitage.

'I'm just trying to decide whether I really want the trouble I know you're about to bring into my life.'

'Trouble is just another word for excitement,' says Armitage.

'It's really not.' Winters finishes his beer, then studies us each in turn. 'Fine,' he eventually says.

Armitage holds a hand out to me. I help her up as Winters opens the door and leads us into his flat.

It's actually . . . quite tasteful. Nothing at all like the office. The lounge is dominated by an L-shaped leather couch, almost completely covered with books and papers, leaving only a single free space for someone to sit. The kitchen nook is small, but kitted out with modern aluminium kettle, an espresso maker and a fancy stove.

But it's the space off to the right that has me interested. The dining room and dining table have been turned into a study. The table is piled high with books, DVDs and bulging files. The entire back wall is covered over with photographs that surround a huge whiteboard. The photographs are linked by red thread and the whiteboard itself is covered in tiny writing and multi-coloured mind maps.

I take a step closer, but Winters puts a hand on my arm.

'I'd rather you didn't,' he says. 'It's private.'

Armitage snorts. 'Cal here is a bit of a . . . what's the word? Oh aye. Nutjob. That's it.'

'Fuck off, Armitage,' says Winters genially. 'You'll see. When I uncover the bastards, you'll be apologising to me.'

'Yeah, not going to happen, pet. Tell London here your theory.'

'It's not a theory.' He glances at me. 'Since the 1700s there has been a cabal of black magicians ruling over the UK. Seven of them. Always seven. The Freemasons were actually inspired by them. Back in the 1800s someone knew about the cabal and wanted in. But when they wouldn't let him, he started his own little secret club in the hopes of challenging them. The magicians took that guy out. And his family. Burned his house to the ground. Killed his horse. Burned his stables. His dog got away, so they hunted it down and shot it.'

'There's more, though, isn't there?' says Armitage with a smile on her face.

'It's not just the UK. This cabal has branches all over the world. The Bilderberg group? The Rothschilds? Nothing on these guys. This cabal is the top of the pyramid, and those guys are at the bottom. Then we're about five miles beneath them, buried in the mud.'

'What's their end game?' I ask curiously.

'Jesus, London. Don't *encourage* him.'

Winters gestures around his flat. 'That's what I'm trying to find out. Have been for nearly a decade. My suspicion is they're acting as a front.'

'For?'

Winters hesitates. 'My current research points to ancient fish gods. Fomorians, to be exact. You know the Cthulhu stories? Those were based on the real Fomorians.'

'So . . . what? Lovecraft had access to Ministry files?'

'Actually, he might have,' says Winters. He moves over to his dining room table and starts searching for something beneath all the papers. 'There was a time when he was friendly with a family who had someone in the Ministry. My theory—'

'That's lovely, pet,' says Armitage. 'Really. Nice that you're keeping busy. But we're in a bit of a rush.'

Winters glares at her. 'Why the fuck did you ask then?' He slumps down onto the free space on the couch. 'What do you want?'

'Faeries,' says Armitage.

'What about them?'

'Tell me about them. I remember you once thought they were involved in your little cabal. I seem to remember you did a lot of research into their kind.'

'I did.'

'So you can start by telling us what's going on. They seem a lot more present than they were a few years ago.'

Winters barks out a laugh. 'Oh really? You think?'

'Just talk,' says Armitage wearily. 'I want to know everything. The players, the reasons, the current situation.'

Winters leans forward and rubs his chin. He thinks for a second. 'Right . . . the simplest way to look at the Fae right now is to think organised crime. Not just one type, though. All of them. The Mafia. Gun runners. Drug trafficking. Old style London gangs. You know . . . the Krays, Terry Adams. Mad Frankie Fraser. The Teddy Boys, that kind of thing. That's what the Faeries are doing in London right now. It's like they all took some books out of the library about London in the sixties and decided "yeah, that sounds good. I'm bored with all the nature stuff, with all the hiding away. Let's do that". They *rule* the city now, Armitage. Not us. The Ministry doesn't even police it. They can't. All the Ministry actually does now is run around after the gang wars and wipe the memories of the witnesses so no one can say the Covenant has been broken.'

'What about the human gangs that had already divvied up the city?'

'The Triads? The Yardies? Nuh-uh. They're out. Or if they're not out, they answer to the Fae and send a huge cut of their profits to them.'

'What do the Fae want with money?' I ask.

'Nothing. They probably burn it. It's a power thing.'

'But . . . it wasn't like this a few years ago,' says Armitage.

'No. I mean, it was still there, you know? But it was hidden. Underground. They've just gotten bolder, come out into the open. Look, you want the honest truth, I think the Ministry's been bought off. There's no other way word of this wouldn't have spread to other departments. Someone's keeping it quiet.'

'Explain the organisation,' I say. 'Is there one Fae gang in power?'

'It's not that simple. OK, at the top, you have the Mafia families. That's what I call them. They're old school. They've been involved in the criminal underworld for a couple of centuries now. They used to be called the Seelie and the Unseelie, but those are just names for two different families now. The Seelie are ruled by Dagda and the Unseelie are ruled by Oberon. They were always the main players. Like the Crips and the Bloods in LA. Every supernatural gang war was launched by one of those guys in a bid to take London for themselves. Dagda runs south London, and Oberon has the east. They pretend like they've got this truce going on, but it's all a front.

'The problem with them is that they're old school, the old firm. They're falling behind the times and now you've got these new Fae gangs moving into London, trying to carve a piece of the territory for themselves.'

I raise a finger. 'Question? Why London? Why not . . . Edinburgh? Or Glasgow?'

'You ever been to Glasgow? Who the fuck would want that shithole? Anyway, not the point. London is like a holy city for the Fae. Always has been. They see it as their Mecca. Their Jerusalem. They reckon this city belongs to them, and the humans who live here are invaders.'

'But humans built London.'

'Wrong. There was a Fae settlement here first. Humans came with their iron and took it over, later. There's a lot of lost history, though, so we're not really sure how it all happened.'

'You said there are new gangs?'

'Right. The main players are the Thrones. That's the Irish Fae, the Irish Mafia if you will. Used to be called the Tuatha de Danaan. Led by Nuada of the Silver Hand. They've been around for the same time as Oberon and Dagda. Some of them used to be in the Seelie and the Unseelie but they broke away to form their own firm. They run the drug trade into the UK from Europe.'

'The drug trade?'

'Yeah, the Fae do drugs as well. Not our stuff, although the Thrones do actually control the normal drug trade too. They own a shit load of nightclubs too. Some for humans, some for Fae.'

'Wait. You're saying the Irish Faeries control the cocaine trade? Ecstasy, heroin, everything?'

'Yup. They've got that shit sewn right up. They still use human fronts for the traditional drugs, but the stuff they bring in for their own kind? It's heavy. Some humans got their hands on it last year and a whole club went mental. Utterly insane. When the police finally got into the joint they found all the kids had turned cannibal and were eating each other.'

'No investigation?'

'There was. But the reports didn't say anything. Unconfirmed cause of death.'

'Blood tests?'

'Didn't show anything. The drugs just disappeared into their bodies. I've got the pathology report here somewhere if you want to read it—'

'We're all right, pet. Who's next?'

'The Mara. From Old Norse. It means evil. Or . . . a night-mare. They're from Scandinavia. Evil bastards that lot. They paint themselves black when they do their thing. Racketeering. Hijacking shipments at the docks. They hire themselves out as hitmen to humans. That's something that needs to be shut down, I'm telling you now. It's going to end badly. You can't keep that kind of thing secret for long.'

'Lastly there are the Yaga. Russian Fae gangsters. They're ruled by Baba Yaga. You do *not* want to be in her presence. Ancient and evil. She rips out her enemies' throats with her teeth. They're into child trafficking mainly.'

I sit upright when I hear this and exchange a look with Armitage. Exactly what Ayanda said in her report.

'Why are they taking kids?' asks Armitage.

'Don't know. The Fae have always done that. But . . . this time . . . recently, I mean, there are more going missing than usual.'

'That's why we're here. Why we need your help. We've been to the Ministry and they won't lift a finger.'

'And they never will. They live in fear of the Fae. Everyone here does. Everyone in the know, anyway. Supernaturals who have lived here for centuries are leaving. Others pay protection money to Dagda or Oberon, hoping they'll protect them from the Yaga and the Mara, but they can't. The gangs are getting too powerful. It's only a matter of time before they make a move against the old families. They're already making a big move into the Thrones territory. There have been big battles. Lots of humans caught in the crossfire.'

'Does the Covenant really hold no weight here anymore?' asks the dog.

'Not really.' Winters sighs. 'And there's more. A new gang has sprung up. God knows where from. The Blessed. They're challenging all the others. But the scary thing is, they're not motivated by money. They're religious. So the violence is sectarian. Political. They have members from all races of Fae, from all the gangs, and they're converting more to their cause every day.'

'And their cause is?' I ask.

'Nobody really knows. They want London for themselves, that's for sure. Which means they want rid of the other Fae and the humans.'

'And the other gangs are just taking that?'

'Shit, no. It's open warfare out there. Fae against humans. Orisha against Fae. The Blessed against everyone else. You know, they coat their bodies in the ash of burned enemies.'

'Seriously?'

'That's what I've been told.'

Armitage leans back with a sigh. 'Where do we find these Russian gangsters then?'

'You want to meet with Baba Yaga?' says Winters in surprise.

'Don't think we've got much choice, pet.'

'Your funeral. She operates from the Olympia warehouse.'

'At the docks?' I say in surprise. 'In the open?'

'Well . . . no. Not in the open. You know what the Fae are like. Look one minute and a street is empty. Come at it from a different angle and it's suddenly full of Fae and shops and stuff. It's like that. Not everyone can see it, not unless Baba Yaga wants you to.'

'Looks like we better go see this Russian bint,' says Armitage. 'Cal, it's been lovely to see you again.'

'I wish I could say the same. But it would be a lie, so I won't. Remember, don't feel free to call.'

9

The Olympia warehouse is a massive, abandoned ship-building shed sitting on a concrete-covered plot of land butting right up against the Thames. It was abandoned in the 19th century, back when it was still called the Deptford Dockyard. Now it's used for ... nothing. Which is pretty goddamn weird. It's a huge area, and you'd think the property sharks would be cutting each other to get their hands on it.

The area is fenced off, protected by a locked double gate covered with yellow warning signs. This doesn't stop Armitage. She just gives the gates a shove, snapping the lock as if it's made from plastic.

'So ... do you guys have a plan of action here?' asks the dog. 'Just curious. Because it kind of seems to me like you're walking into your chief suspect's base without any backup.'

'Well ... yeah, but I do that all the time,' I say.

'And look how well that's worked out for you.'

'Haven't died yet.'

'I hear you, man, but it's not from lack of trying. I suppose you'll want a Ward?'

'If you don't mind.'

'I do, but what the hell difference does that make? Hold on.'

I brace myself as a surge of energy soars through my body. My eyes roll back in my head as I feel my blood fizzing in my veins, the magic pumping through my body like molten gold. I shudder, feel myself tipping over backwards. Then there are arms at my back, holding me up.

'Jesus Christ, London,' says Armitage. Her words sound like they're coming from far away. 'Could you make it look less like you're having an orgasm please?'

'I know, right?' says the dog. 'You have no idea how sleazy I feel when I do this.'

I take a deep, shuddering breath and straighten up. I open my eyes to find them both walking off ahead of me. I take a moment to gather myself. I have to rein everything in when I'm Warded. That feeling of having a protective shield made from shinecraft makes you feel utterly invincible. It's very easy to let that go to your head.

I catch up with the others and we head toward the massive warehouse in the distance. The whole area is incredibly drab. Just a grey concrete field and some abandoned slip-ways that disappear into the black water of the Thames. A freezing wind buffets us, stinging my cheeks and ears. I pull my hoodie up in an attempt to ward off hypothermia. Thank God I decided not to wear one of my good suits today. I brought a few with me, but in this weather they're not exactly practical. I need to look into using shinecraft to raise my core body temperature. That would help. Then I could wear my good clothes no matter where I am. Although, until I can find a spell to make material indestructible it's sort of pointless. Those things don't come cheap and I can't seem to go a day without ruining whatever it is I'm wearing.

The lower half of the warehouse is boarded up with wooden cladding and covered with graffiti. The roof looks like two rolling hills, or maybe . . .

'Looks like a pair of tits,' says Armitage, squinting up at the roof.

'Hey, it really does!' says the dog, utterly delighted at this.

We take our time as we approach, making sure we're as non-threatening as possible. We're trespassing on someone else's territory here. I mean, sure they're criminals, but that just makes it even more important to be polite. No sudden movements, hands where they can see them. That kind of thing.

There are two closed aluminium roll-top doors and a smaller door set off to the side.

I try it. Unlocked.

I don't even bother looking at Armitage or the dog. I know they'll just be standing there watching me expectantly.

I step inside.

Dim light struggles through the dirty windows high up on the walls, faint grey beams that fade away in defeat before they can reach the ground. The place is deserted, the dirty floor covered with broken wood, rusted metal and a few plastic barrels. The roof itself is supported by a metal framework and held up by massive iron girders that look like they've been here for over a hundred years.

The other two enter behind me. I look at the dog. 'You see anything?'

'Nah. Faeries aren't from the Nightside, remember. They were around long before your lot broke the world in two. They have their own magic.'

'So what are we supposed to do?'

Armitage fishes out a deck of cards from her voluminous trench coat. 'Gin rummy?'

We soon realise it's boring playing gin rummy with just two people. (The dog can't join in due to having no opposable thumbs. Well . . . that and the fact he has absolutely no desire whatsoever to play.)

So Armitage and I sit opposite each other playing snap while the dog wanders aimlessly around.

'Don't piss on anything!' I call out. 'You don't know how they'll take it.'

'What the hell do you take me for?'

'An alcoholic bag of fleas and mange,' I say softly. 'If venereal diseases were personified, they'd look like him.'

Armitage chuckles.

'I heard that, motherfucker!'

'Busted,' says Armitage.

'I swear to God, London,' shouts the dog, 'I will eat your face clean off while you sleep.'

'Sorry,' I call out. 'No offense meant.'

'How in the name of Christ can I not take offense at being called a venereal disease?'

'I meant one of the curable ones. You know, like gonorrhoea – or chlamydia. I didn't mean hepatitis or syphilis.'

'You are *such* a dick.'

We play for another ten minutes or so before we both get bored out of our skulls and give up.

'Don't suppose you brought some Jaffa cakes or something?'

'I wish,' grumbles Armitage. 'You got any of those sweets left?'

I fish around in my pocket and pull out a handful of sweets. I pass half of them to Armitage and keep the rest for myself. We pop them into our mouths and sit in companionable silence, the only sounds Armitage sucking her sweet and me crunching mine.

'How long do you reckon we'll have to wait?' I eventually ask.

'No idea. I've never really dealt with the Fae. There was a specialist branch in the Ministry set up to deal with them, and our lot over the pond just keep to themselves.'

I sigh and stretch myself full length on the ground. We could be in for a long night.

I'm just starting to feel like I might doze off when the light dims around us, as if a cloud has passed in front of the sun.

Except . . . there was no sun to begin with. I sit upright, glancing at the windows. No change there. They're still letting in the same hazy glow.

Then I hear sounds. Voices, banging, metal clanging on metal. But the sounds are distant, like I'm hearing them from far away. I shift my head slightly and the sounds grow louder. Shift again and they fade. I stand up and turn slowly in a circle, noting that Armitage is following my lead and the dog is padding toward us.

I find the angle where I can hear the voices the clearest, facing toward one of the metal support girders, and I start walking. Slowly, carefully.

The sounds grow louder. I reach the thick girder and walk around it.

. . . And as I come round the other side I'm in a different world.

It's still the warehouse, but it's now full of life. Orange globes float in the air, illuminating the massive space and revealing at least a hundred Fae going about their business.

The floor is no longer empty, but covered with boxes and crates. There are large desks covered with books. Small gnomes bobbing in wicker baskets attached to ropes hover over the desks, leaning down to turn pages or write something down. The gnomes have serious looks on their faces and are dressed in old-fashioned shirts and braces, with small spectacles perched on their noses.

The other Fae have a particular look about them. I hope this doesn't sound racist, but . . . Fae from different parts of the world all look slightly different. Same as us humans. Russians have a kind of generic look. So do Australians. Same goes for the UK. It's a massive generalisation, obviously, but what I'm saying is that people and creatures from specific parts of the world are shaped by the climate and sociological lives they lead.

The majority of Fae in the warehouse are elves. They're paler than the Fae I'm used to seeing back in S.A. Which makes sense, I suppose. They come from snowy, cold lands, so they're not going to be tanned or dark. Their faces are narrow, their eyes spaced far apart, framing a nose that's little more than two slits in the middle of their faces.

They're all wearing normal clothes. Like, the stuff you buy on the high street. It's a weird thing to see. I always expect the Fae to wear animal skins and leather, but I suppose there's no reason for them not to move with the times. Kind of prejudiced to assume they wouldn't. Some of them are talking on cell phones, while a group of fat goblins are bathed in the glow of Apple laptops.

Five golems move slowly around the warehouse, carrying heavy crates and piling them against the wall. I watch them curiously. I've never seen golems in the flesh. (Hahaha.) These guys are eight feet tall and made from roughly chiselled grey stone. Three of their faces have human features, worn away over the years so you can barely see them. The other two have been . . . modified slightly, their faces touched up with black sharpie to make them look like Judge Dredd and Robocop.

There are other Fae creatures too. Two-foot long beetles with tiny Fae riding on their backs push barrels across the floor. Sprites flit through the air with huge swathes of brightly-coloured cloth held between them. It looks like they're trying to mount it on the walls.

'You three!'

I look up. A set of stairs zig-zags up the wall, leading to a rectangular office that's been bolted high up on the side of the warehouse. An old woman is leaning on the balcony, staring down at us. Baba Yaga, I presume.

'Get up here.'

Armitage stares up at Baba Yaga for a while, then gathers her trench coat around her and shoves her hands in her pockets. 'Here we go then.'

The first thing I notice when I enter the office (more of a portacabin, really. The kind you find on building sites) is the dead elf tied to a chair in the corner. He's not one of the Russian elves. This one has slightly creamier skin and much higher cheekbones. His hands are locked to the chair with iron handcuffs. The metal has melted into his wrists, cutting them almost in half.

Armitage sees this, swears loudly and rushes forward, trying to pull the cuffs off the elf. She looks furiously at Baba Yaga.

'Where are the keys? Get these off him!'

'It is late for that, I think?' says Baba Yaga in a thick Russian accent. 'He is long gone. He was brave though. Only gave us the information we needed right at the end.'

Armitage snarls and throws herself at Baba Yaga. The old witch doesn't even move, but Armitage is brought up short when the darkness at the back of the office suddenly swirls to life and a huge figure cloaked in shadow grabs Armitage, throwing her against the wall. She hits hard, pulling posters down and landing on a small table holding a kettle and a tub of instant coffee. I reach for my wand, but Armitage is already rolling to her feet. She crouches down, arms spread, hands curled.

'I would not bother,' says Baba Yaga. 'The Dark Man here will protect me at all costs. He can get very nasty.'

As if in answer, two glowing yellow eyes flare to life inside the shadowy form.

I put a hand on Armitage's shoulder. She whirls around and I take a quick step back. Her eyes look . . . empty. Animalistic. For a moment I think she's about to rip my throat out. The dog sees this too and steps forward, growling. Armitage tears her eyes away from me and stares at him. They lock eyes. This goes on for a full ten seconds before Armitage finally straightens up, giving her trench coat a shake.

She turns around and flops into an empty chair. 'I could murder a cuppa,' she says pleasantly.

-Uh . . . what was that all about?- I ask.

-I have no idea,- says the dog, *-but . . . for a moment there I don't think she was in control.-*

-What? Possessed?-

-Not sure. Maybe. Maybe not. I don't really know much about revenants. Do you?-

-No.-

-You should probably fix that then.-

'Now that we are all properly calm,' says Baba Yaga, 'can you tell me why you have been sitting in my warehouse for the past hour?'

'We wanted a word with you about two of our agents.'

'I am confused.'

'We read their case notes. Two of ours came to see you about some missing kiddies.'

Baba Yaga's face clears. 'The two ladies? They were very rude. I did not like them.'

'Is that why you had them killed?' I snap.

Baba Yaga looks at me, puzzled. 'They are dead?'

'Yes, they're dead,' says Armitage. 'As if you didn't know.'

Baba Yaga looks out the window of her office, down to the warehouse floor. 'So . . . you think I had your agents killed, and yet you come on your own to confront me?'

'Don't worry about us,' says Armitage. 'We were careful. Besides, we didn't have much choice, if I'm being honest. The Ministry isn't what it used to be.'

Baba Yaga spits onto her desk. 'The Ministry is nothing. Hasn't been for a long time. You are from Africa, yes? Like your friends?'

Armitage nods.

'Then you do not know this place. It belongs to us now. Your kind are but tenants. And you will be evicted very soon.'

'That sounds like a threat to me. Does it sound like a threat to you, London?'

'Sounds very much like a threat.'

Baba Yaga leans forward on her desk. 'Oh, it was a threat. Was I too ambiguous? My apologies. Here it is again, then. Once Dagda and Oberon are out of the picture, this city is mine.'

'Aren't there others who will have a problem with that?' I ask. 'What are they called? The Thrones? The Mara? And the new lot? The Blessed?'

Baba Yaga's face darkens. 'The Blessed? You want to know who killed your friends? They are the ones you should speak to.'

'Why do you say that?' asks Armitage. 'I understood you were the one who liked to dabble in child trafficking.'

Baba Yaga laughs. 'That was a long time ago. I don't do that anymore.'

'Why? Had an attack of the conscience?'

'Don't be absurd. No, it's just too risky. Child trafficking? Human sex trade? Not a chance. Not with all those Hollywood idiots going on about it. I had the whole thing sewn up for decades,' she says with a hint of sadness. 'I had a cut of it all.'

My hand moves back toward my wand. Baba Yaga doesn't even look. She just points at me.

'I would not do that,' she says. Her eyes swivel toward me. She smiles, showing sharp, metal teeth. 'You disapprove?'

'Disapprove?' I step toward her and the Dark Man flows forward. I ignore him. 'You disgust me. If I could, I'd put you inside the heads of all those children you condemned to hell. I'd make you experience everything they went through.'

'All of them?' Baba Yaga looks amused. 'I'm not sure I would have the time.'

I pull my wand out. The Dark Man surges forward and his cloak wraps around me, tendrils of shadow reaching into my mouth, down my throat. It feels like gangrenous fingers reaching into my being, sinking into my organs.

Then the Ward kicks in and pushes the tendrils out again. I stagger back, bumping up against the wall in a daze. Armitage stands by my side, holding onto my arm. The dog is on the desk, snarling muzzle inches from Baba Yaga's face.

'And just so you don't think we're utter idiots,' says Armitage. 'That dog isn't really a dog. Say hi, dog.'

'Hi, dog,' he growls.

'And we've told his friends we're coming here. So if we disappear you'll have a visit from some not very nice creatures from the Nightside.'

Baba Yaga stares at us a moment, then sighs and straightens up. 'I will tell you what I told your idiot friends. The Blessed are the ones taking children now. Do not ask me why, but they are the ones who muscled me out of the business. They wanted it for themselves.'

'Where can we find them?'

Baba Yaga leans back in her chair. 'How much is it worth to you?'

'Wrong question, luv,' says Armitage. 'What you should be asking is whether the location of the Blessed is going to buy you enough goodwill to stop us coming back over here with the South African contingent and cleaning you out.'

Baba Yaga and Armitage stare at each other for a full ten seconds before Baba Yaga looks away. 'Find the hawthorn trees in the Queen's Wood. That's where you will find them.'

We walk back through the gates and towards civilisation.

'Should we go see the Blessed now?' I ask.

'No,' says Armitage. 'Too dangerous. We'll do it tomorrow. Plan it out carefully. It sounds like they could be the ones who . . . got to Lerato and Ayanda. I don't know how, but it was done. Lewis will have to give us backup. Whether he wants to or not.'

10

Here's the thing. I'm not much good with common sense. Or waiting.

Or doing what I'm told.

Or any 'adult' things, really. I wasn't given the manual for being a grownup, what with my old man killing himself when I was twelve.

Which is why I'm making my way through Queen's Wood an hour after midnight, ignoring Armitage's orders to leave it till tomorrow.

I can't leave it. Because here's the thing. We started this case while I was looking for Cally. That's what put us on the trail. After Cape Town was a bust, I wasn't really expecting anything to come of it, but since Lerato and Ayanda's deaths I've realised this might actually be real.

This *could* be about Cally. Or at least, about who took her.

And if it is the same perps, then this is the closest I've ever been (barring me knowing, then giving up, the name of the fucker who did it) to finding her.

But for all this to happen now, for us to find leads, for Lerato and Ayanda to be killed, it has to mean something has changed. The perps have become careless. Greedy. They're making mistakes, coming out into the open.

I have no idea why that is, but I'm not complaining. Their mistakes have revealed a pattern, a pattern of orisha stealing kids from the Dayside and shipping them to London and then ... somewhere else. I don't want to jump to conclusions, but if what Baba Yaga said is true, then there's a high probability that these Blessed might be the ones responsible.

My stomach clenches at the thought. I'm scared to get my hopes up again. When Mother Durban took the name of the person responsible, she didn't take away the hope and happiness I'd felt when I discovered that Cally was still alive. That she hadn't, as I'd thought for three years, been murdered. When I found out, it was like my life just . . . cleared. Like all the pain and misery and fear just vanished on a warm breeze of hope. It was the first time in my entire life that I'd ever felt that. Sure, I've had brief moments of happiness in my life: when Cally was born, when Becca said she would marry me, and of course those little snapshots of memory: of sun-bleached smiles, sticky braai meat, and late afternoon swimming, sunburn on our shoulders and sea salt in the air.

But . . . none of those matched my feeling of utter relief when I found out Cally was alive. It gave my life meaning again.

Then I lost the knowledge.

And this time the loss was so much worse, because I knew what I had given up. I knew how close I had been to finding out where she was.

So if I'm told the fuckers who might be responsible are within reach, then no, Armitage, I'm *not* going to wait for you to organise a trigger-happy hit squad that might take everyone out before I get what I need.

Sorry.

I looked up Queen's Wood while I was on the tube. Apparently the woods were part of the ancient forest that used to cover most of Britain five thousand years ago.

I also checked the police files. There have been plenty of complaints about nature worshippers, witches, pagans, etc.

making use of the woods. There have also been a lot of kids going missing in the area over the years. Enough that it represents a statistical uptick compared to the rest of the city.

I'm not great with the whole identifying-of-trees thing, but even I can see there's some ancient, weird looking growth here. There's supposed to be hawthorn, ash, birch, maple, and holly, but I don't have a clue what's what. All I see are claw-like branches twisting up to the winter sky, framed against the moon that makes brief appearances between the departing clouds. Apparently hawthorn trees have red berries in winter, so that's what I'm looking for.

I decide to just make my way to the deepest part of the wood, thinking that this is the most likely place the Blessed would hang out. I don't really know what I'm expecting, though. Do the Blessed *live* here in the forest? How would that work? Do they just stay hidden? How many are there? Or do they have a secret base here? A tree house with no humans allowed because we've got cooties.

I make my way along game trails and overgrown footpaths, trying not to freak out at the barking of foxes and the rustling of bushes. I've been going for about an hour now, and I'm thinking of just giving up and calling it a night when the forest opens up around me and I step into a large clearing.

I stop walking. My breath fogs the air.

I'm surrounded by massive, bare trees covered in berries.

The berries look black in the winter moonlight. I bend down and pick one off the ground, holding it close to my face. It's red.

I hear a noise behind me, the soft movement of leaves.

I turn around to find one of the Fae standing before me. His face is longer than the other Fae I've seen, and it has an almost half-animal look to it. Like a fox that is slowly turning human. His skin looks dark, but I realise that's because he has coated himself in ash, like Winters said.

He's wearing wooden and leather armour, expertly carved to sculpt to his body, with hundreds of interlocking segments giving him utter freedom of movement. The breast plate of his armour has a large tree carved into it, and sigils etched around the edges.

He tilts his head to the side. Studies me.

'You can see me,' he says. He lifts his nose to the sky and sniffs, keeping his eyes on me as he does so. 'Ah. Yes. I can smell the power on you. You are a magician.' He smiles, showing yellow teeth. They're oddly shaped. Like a dog's. Rounded at the front, long canines at the side. 'You have come to our forest without permission. You will be punished for trespassing.'

'I don't think so,' I say. I keep my face neutral, but there's something about this guy that puts me on edge. It's the way he never breaks eye contact or blinks. Always staring directly into my eyes, like an animal trying to assert dominance.

'Why are you here? This is a holy place.'

'Is it?' I look around. 'Pretty drafty for a church.'

'You mock us. You mock our faith. I see the kind of person you are, Gideon Tau.'

My eyes snap back to his. 'How do you know my name?'

'I know many things about you, London. But I am being impolite. I haven't even introduced myself. I am the Marquis.'

He looks at me expectantly, a small smile on his lips.

'Good for you,' I say eventually. 'What do you want? A Blue Peter badge?'

Something about the elf changes. He relaxes slightly, an air of . . . something coming over him. Arrogance? Amusement? Superiority? All of those, I think.

He walks slowly toward me and I try to decide if it's better to stand my ground or back up. I decide to stand my ground, but I pull out my iron dagger and point it at the Marquis.

'So here's how this will go,' I say conversationally. 'You're going to tell me where all the missing children are. The ones you've been taking. Then you're going to be charged for murdering our agents.'

'Which agents are these?'

'The ones who were investigating the missing kids.'

His face is blank.

'They died a couple of days ago! I'm assuming you used some kind of glamour on them. Clouded their minds.'

The Marquis' face clears. 'Oh, yes! The two ladies. They were not much more than children themselves, as I recall. Yes, we couldn't have them causing trouble. They had to go. The same way we can't have *you* causing trouble.'

I ignore that. 'Tell me where the children are.'

'I can't. I do not have the children anymore.'

'So you admit to taking them?'

'Oh, yes.' He smiles. 'We've been taking them for many years now.'

My heart speeds up. My mouth goes suddenly dry. 'Where are they?'

'Not here.'

'*Where?*'

He watches me, that irritating smirk on his thin-lipped face.

'*Where?*' I take a threatening step forward.

He looks away, up at the trees. He takes a deep breath. 'Such a lovely night. I like the winter time, don't you?'

He's playing with me. Enjoying himself. And he keeps glancing at me with that . . . look in his eyes. Almost like he knows me.

'Tell me where they are.'

'They are all in Tír na nÓg.'

'In *Faerie*?'

He shrugs. 'Of course. Where else would we take them?'

'*Why* are you taking them?'

'Why not?'

Fuck this. I move toward him, knife held before me. But before I get close the ground heaves beneath my feet. I stagger, just managing to catch myself.

The hawthorn trees are shivering, red berries falling to the ground like bloody hail.

Something happens to the air. An invisible bubble surrounds us, and the stars and moon waver as if I'm looking at them through heat waves. My ears pop. I feel pressure behind my eyes, feel my pulse throbbing in my throat.

And then . . . it's hard to describe what unfolds before me. It's like I'm watching two realities overlapping each other, both with slightly different scenes playing out in them. The hawthorn trees split apart, but somehow still stay the same. The air vibrates. My eyes are struggling to focus. The trees that are splitting . . . something is coming out of them.

I turn in a slow circle, watching in mounting horror. The first thing I see is a spidery leg as tall as a house. It emerges from one of the tree trunks and thuds into the ground. It's not quite a spider leg though. It's segmented like one but it looks like it's covered in bark.

As I turn, more legs appear, first slowly curling out of the trunks and probing the air, then extending to hit the forest floor.

Then I see glinting eyes.

From every tree trunk, everywhere I turn, identical black eyes watch me.

A massive head pushes out of the trees, squirming and forcing its way through like a baby being born. The face is pitted and torn, white skin somehow fused with wood and bark. But . . . I blink in confusion. Shake my head to try and clear it. The head is coming out of *all* the trees, but at the same time it's only one creature. It's as if reality has segmented, curled back on itself to show the same image from different angles.

A spread-eagled body follows the head, worming its way out of the trees. The legs that have already come through are joined to the figure's arms, bloody holes in the white skin where roots twine into the body.

My eyes go dim as the creature pulls its way out of the trees. I close my eyes, feeling dizzy, and when I open them again the creature is standing in the clearing. Spidery legs join roots, roots join limbs, the body seemingly trapped and pulled in all directions about twenty feet above me, like a criminal being torn apart by horses.

The worst thing is the head. It's upside down, lolling on a long neck too weak to support it.

I don't have to tell you that the effect is creepy as all fuck.

The head bounces and jounces around in a circle and drops lower so the creature can look at me.

'M . . . Marquis,' it whispers. The voice sounds odd. Distant and haunted.

'Blessed One,' says the Marquis, dipping his head.

'Wh . . . why have you called me?'

'I have brought you a sacrifice.'

I look sharply at the Marquis. He winks and grins at me. I turn back and hold my knife up.

'I sm . . . smell iron,' complains the freaky spider-fairy. (I refuse to refer to it as the Blessed One.)

'You should probably drop that,' says the Marquis.

'No chance.'

He smiles, and his eyes flick over my shoulder. I follow his gaze and find myself facing down a ring of elves emerging from the shadows between the trees. They're dressed similarly to the Marquis, strange sigils carved into their armour. There are others too, wearing silver masks over their faces. They're dressed slightly differently – more supple leather than wood.

But they're all holding wooden weapons. Swords, pikes, bows with arrows pointed directly at me.

'Are you sure?' whispers the Marquis, directly by my ear.

I swallow nervously. OK then. So . . . coming here on my own maybe wasn't the best idea. Who'd've thought?

I can feel the Marquis' warm breath on my neck. 'Such a pity. Going to the grave without seeing your little Cally again. I'll tell her you were asking for her.'

Everything shuts down. My brain stops working. I feel like I'm watching from outside my body, looking down on myself and the Marquis. I turn (see myself turn). The Marquis takes a step back, a smile on his face.

'What did you say?'

'Cally?' He smiles even wider. 'What? I thought for sure that was why you were here.' He leans forward. 'I'm the one who took her, by the way. I'm the name you had to give up to Mother Durban.'

The world goes silent. Everything drops away, leaving only myself and the Marquis. I lunge toward him. He laughs and dances out the way. I spin around and find him coming straight at me with a lethal-looking wooden sword.

But then an explosion rocks the clearing. I see one of the Fae drop to the ground with a scream. The two next to him cry out and flinch away.

'All right!' shouts a voice. Armitage. 'Everybody be cool! This is a . . .' then the voice quiets a bit. 'No, wait, that doesn't work, does it? Fuck it.'

Another explosion. I look around. The Marquis has vanished from sight. Armitage and Winters are standing outside the clearing holding shotguns. Winters steps forward and fires at the massive spider-elf. One of its legs explodes into splinters and it shrieks in pain. The other legs quickly shuffle backwards, retracting back into the tree like a stop-motion horror movie being played backwards. The body and face follow after, everything blurring again to make it look as if the creature is slipping into every tree in the clearing.

I whirl around, searching for the Marquis. '*No!*' I shout. 'Where are you? Come back!'

A hand on my arm. I whirl around to find Armitage glaring at me. 'No more silly buggers, you stupid bastard. We're leaving.'

An arrow flies past my head and sticks into a tree. I look back, but whoever fired it is gone from sight, fleeing back into the forest. Armitage holds up her shotgun.

'Iron filings in the shells. Now come on.'

Something hits me in the leg. I look down and see the dog head-butting me. 'Move it, London.'

I scan the clearing in despair, but the Marquis is gone. Once again, the chance to find my daughter has been stolen from me.

I shake off Armitage's arm and sprint into the trees.

'London!' shouts Armitage. 'Get back here now. That's an order!'

I ignore her. I run into the dark forest, branches whipping against my face. No, no, no. I won't let him get away. I can't fail Cally like this again. She's out there. She's alive. I have the chance of finding out where she is. I can't let him escape.

My shoulder hits a tree and I spin around and fall to the ground. I push myself up again, running, sprinting, my feet getting caught in the undergrowth. My mind flashes back to the mountain all those years ago. Torrential rain blinding me. Mud making my footing treacherous. Racing to get to Cally. Racing to rescue my daughter.

But I failed then too.

I slow to a stop, despair washing over me. 'Marquis!' I scream.

Nothing. He's gone. The forest is silent.

I lash out and punch the closest tree, shouting my rage. I hit it again and again, pummelling the bark, my knuckles leaving bloody stains, screaming all the time I do so.

I'm distantly aware of hands grabbing me. I whirl around in a rage, bringing the knife around to stab whichever fucker is touching me.

It's Winters. But even when I see that, I can't stop. Some part of me wants to attack, to lash out. To cause pain and death.

Winters claps his hands over the blade before it hits him, holding it in place. I push and pull, but it doesn't budge. He holds his hands there for a moment, then the sigils on his forearms flare red. His hands glow orange, the veins and bones showing as shadows beneath the skin.

The blade turns white hot in seconds. I snatch my hand back and the knife hits the ground, hissing against the cold earth.

I glare at Winters. He stares calmly back.

'I'll give you that one,' he says. 'Because I know you're hurting. But one's all you get.'

I hear his words, but all they do is infuriate me. I need to act. To do something. To prove I'm not at the mercy of an uncaring universe.

I start to mutter the words of summoning beneath my breath. Winters narrows his eyes and shifts his weight, ready to defend himself. He doesn't know what's about to hit him.

I'm halfway through the chant and can feel the familiar itching along my spine when Armitage suddenly appears and slaps me hard across the cheek.

'The fuck are you doing, you absolute cock weasel?' she shouts as I stagger back against a tree. 'Seriously? Summoning the dragons against your own people?'

I glare at her for a moment longer, then slump against her, all the fight just draining out of me. I feel exhausted. I drop my head into her shoulder.

'He knew,' I whisper. 'He knew about Cally. He's the one who took her.'

A moment of hesitation, then Armitage puts a hand to the back of my head in a gesture so maternal it nearly makes me cry.

'Then we'll find him. We'll get her back, pet. I promise you.'

II

Eight o'clock the next morning and I'm at the Ministry scouring their library for anything they might have on the Blessed. Anything that might mention the Marquis.

Truth is, I'm also here so early because I'm avoiding Armitage. She's royally pissed. Turns out she really doesn't trust me – apparently she got Eshu to stick one of those tracking apps on my phone after I nearly sold out mankind last month. Which is kind of insulting, but . . . I suppose she has a point, so what can I say? As soon as I headed out to the woods she knew I was up to something.

I stare at the books spread out around me and try to fight the rising tide of despair. The Blessed don't warrant a mention in any of the Ministry's history books. Nor does the Marquis.

There are a lot of on-going and unsolved cases dealing with the Blessed. Most of them involve the Blessed moving in on other gangs' territories, and it's these I use to build up a basic picture of them.

First off, they're bloodthirsty fanatics. Psycho-killer nature worshippers. Which is pretty surprising, because I thought nature worshippers were all supposed to be peace-loving vegetarians. (Or is it vegans? Whatever the trendy one is now. I actually think it's fruitarian . . . or maybe Kangatarianism. I came across that one in Cape Town. Sounds expensive.)

Secondly, they're *insane*. Their favourite method of dealing with their enemies seems to be tying them to the ground and using magic to coerce tree and plant roots *into* their victims' bodies, slowly pulling them apart from within.

There are sketchy notes attached to the case files, where Ministry officials have added their own observations after each case or interview. Reading through them all, it's obvious that nobody actually knows how to deal with the Blessed. The other Fae are easy – the Ministry treat them like the police treated gangsters in the sixties and seventies. But the Blessed are something different. I see a lot of attempted comparisons to ISIS, but that doesn't really fit. There are others who say they are closer to the IRA, but the problem with all of this is that nobody actually knows what the Blessed *want*. They're so alien to us that their motivations are beyond our understanding. Even the Fae are wary of dealing with them. Because the Blessed are fucking crazy, and crazy always beats strength. Hands down.

I stare at the books and files spread out around me. It feels hopeless. I called a few of the Ministry officers who worked the cases but nobody seems to want to talk about these guys. Everyone is terrified of them. I need to find someone from Faerie who just doesn't give a shit. Someone who would be willing to sell me the information I need.

I slam the case file closed and stare at the book shelves. There's something building inside of me. Something that I'm scared to scrutinise in case I lose it again. I mentioned before that since Becca died, since I lost the name of whoever or whatever took Cally, the constant anger had vanished, and in its place the depression had set in. That anger had been all that kept me going. It had *fuelled* me. In its absence the depression has been gleefully taking over, insinuating itself into every waking moment, into every thought, every breath. And it's evolving, becoming alive, intent on destroying me. It's like another version of me, a shadow self, a pain-beast. Something that delights in hurting me, something that wants to push the real me aside, to stand triumphant over my broken mind as the real me withers away and dies.

But now . . . since finding out about the Marquis, since finding out that he is the one responsible, the anger is coming back. I can feel it sizzling through my veins, and I embrace it like a long-lost friend. I understand the anger. I can *use* the anger.

I let it flow through me, let it talk to me. And as it does I wonder why the hell I'm wasting my time here . . . Why don't we just go back and take them down? Set fire to their stupid hawthorn trees. Set fire to everything if that's what it takes. They don't belong here. They should just go back to Faerie.

Fury rushes through my body. Fury and hate. If they had just stayed where they were supposed to be, Cally would still be with me. Becca would still be alive. Lerato and Ayanda would still be alive. All those kids taken against their will would still be with their families. I should be taking Cally to school right now. Attending parent evenings. Going to see the new Star Wars movies with her.

I surge to my feet and throw the books to the floor. I lean forward, grip the table. My breathing sounds ragged and heavy in my ears. My vision is blurred, my insides coiled like snakes. I'm vaguely aware that this is not *my* anger talking anymore. Something has shifted inside of me. It's no longer the anger I use to push me through the day, it's something else, something that has piggy-backed my own rage in an attempt to take over.

I stagger backwards, falling to my knees. I stare at the old carpet tiles. Waves of emotion slice through me. Fear, loss, anger, utter hatred for everything in the world that stands against me.

My mind goes blank. I don't know who I am. All I know is a deep abiding fury, a rage that is so strong I could wipe the world clean of everyone and I wouldn't think it too much.

I . . .

I blink, struggling to pull my senses back under my control.

I've . . . I've felt this before.

In the tunnels beneath Durban.

My eyes go wide and fear washes through me, wiping away all other emotions.

The Seven Sins. God's sins made flesh.

They're here . . .

I pull myself to my feet and stare around in fear and confusion. How can they be here? How?

I stagger to the door, peer into the hall. Empty.

The elevator bings. I watch the doors open and a Ministry employee walks out, files in hand. It's the woman that gave Lewis the finger. Selina.

I hold a warning hand up to her and she stops walking. I hurry toward her, trying to regain my senses as I go. 'Is there an armoury here?'

'Through the briefing room. Why? What's—'

Another lurch of emotion hits us both. Selina cries out and doubles over. I stagger back against the wall.

I force my head up and see Selina staring at me with wide eyes and clenched teeth. She leaps forward and punches me in the ribs. I wince and dodge to the side as she punches again, this time hitting the wall. I grab her from behind. She screams her rage and struggles against me, jabbing back with her head, trying to hit me in the face.

'Just . . . hold on,' I say through gritted teeth. 'Ride it out.'

She keeps fighting, kicking and screaming. I have to fight down my own urge to just let the rage take over. To grab her head and smash it against the wall. Why is it always the rage and anger that feels so powerful? Was that the strongest of God's sins? Is this what he felt like all the time before the angels took his sins out and forced them into Lucifer?

I mean, the others are there, sure. The desire to curl up and die. The feeling of pride, the knowledge that I'm the best, that

I deserve whatever the fuck I want. And the hunger, oh shit, the hunger. For food, for sex, for murder, for indulging in every base craving a human or animal can have.

But it's always the rage that sits atop them all.

Selina finally sags in my arms. The urges slowly seep away, like puss from an infected wound, leaving behind a trail of poison in my soul.

'What . . . the fuck?' gasps Selina.

I let her go and she turns to face me, slumping against the wall.

'We need weapons. Now. This place is under attack.'

'Who by?'

I wonder if it's best just to lie. But I don't. It'll probably go easier if she knows what we're up against. 'The Seven Sins of God. Did you read about what went on in Durban last month?'

A scream from down the hall cuts us off. We run toward it, passing the offices and boardrooms. There are blood spatters on the walls of one of the conference rooms. I pause long enough to look inside and see two dead bodies, their throats ripped out.

'Jesus Christ,' whispers Selina.

Another scream, this one trailing off into a wet gurgle. We make our way more carefully along the corridor now, heading toward the briefing room. I can hear muffled talking, whimpering. Moans of pain. The door is about twenty feet ahead of us. Another cry of pain, abruptly cut off. Then a low sound, something that reaches into my being without going through my ears. I feel as if my whole body is vibrating in time with the sound, shivering and shaking.

We reach the door. I peer slowly into the room.

The staff are all up against the left wall. Some are standing, others are sitting, huddled together in fear. Three are already dead, bodies ripped apart and lying in pools of blood. The rest of the staff are staring at something beyond my line of sight. I inch forward until I can see what they see.

My stomach sinks. It really is one of the Sins. But . . . it looks different. Before, they were grey-black oily figures, their heads vibrating too fast for me to see. It was like looking into the face of cancer.

But this one looks . . . I can't explain it. Sick?

It's pacing back and forth. But its gait is off, like it's struggling to keep its balance. And the vibration of its head is strange too. It stops and starts. One second the head is buzzing so fast everything's a blur, the next I can see everything about it. A nose leaking white fluid. Eyes weeping grey tears that are burning rivulets through the darker skin.

How the hell did the Sins get in here? Surely this place is Warded? And what are they doing here? Did they follow me? But that doesn't make any sense – if they wanted rid of me, why not just attack me in Durban?

Selina touches my arm. I move aside so she can take a look. After a moment she turns away, her face pale. She gestures for us to backtrack along the passage.

'The armoury is through the briefing room. No way we're getting through.'

'Is there anyone we can call? Any backup?'

She nods and hurries to the closest office. She picks up the phone and dials an internal extension number. She waits, but there's no answer. She tries another, then another, before hanging up in frustration.

'What if that thing went through the other floors first?' she says. 'What if we're the last ones left?'

'We need guns.'

She thinks about it for a second. 'Follow me.'

We head back in the direction of the elevator, but before we get there Selina opens a door leading into a narrow maintenance corridor with exposed piping high up on the walls.

Selina breaks into a run and I follow after. The corridor turns to the left, then carries on for about a hundred meters before turning left once again. She finally stops before another door, pushing it open slightly and checking the corridor beyond.

She waits until she's sure the coast is clear, then slips out. I leave the maintenance passage behind and find myself in another office corridor. I realise she's taken us around the perimeter of the floor, bringing us out *behind* the briefing room.

She's already disappearing through another door. When I join her she's tapping a combination into a wall keypad. It gives off a beep and the entire wall slides away. She pulls me back as shelves extend out from inside the wall.

'Guns,' I whisper. 'Lots of guns.'

She gives me an odd look and starts pulling weaponry off the racks. She hands me a body vest first. I shrug it over my shoulders and tighten the straps. Handguns come next. Two 9mm Berettas. I prefer my trusty Glock, but these will do at a pinch. She hands me magazines. I check the bullets. They're not standard issue.

'Made from melted-down swords that have killed actual demons,' she says. 'Then quenched in the Tyburn at low tide while the annual ghost hunt is going on. They've got sigils of destruction and undoing carved into them by an enslaved *djinn* using the sharpened bones of Mithras.'

I don't let on how impressed I am, but . . . impressed I am. I mean, shit man. Why don't we get this kind of cool stuff back at the Division?

I ram the magazines in place and strap the two guns into the holsters on the front of my vest.

Next come the shotguns. Selina pulls out shells from a black plastic box and starts slotting them into her own gun. The shotguns are Remington 870 magnums with magazine extension tubes. For when you're in a bit of a pickle and don't want to keep reloading. They're also equipped with side-saddle shell carriers, which means six extra shells within easy reach.

I load the gun, counting as I do so. The extension tube allows for nine extra rounds. Selina takes the shotgun from me and shoves it down into a holster on the back of my vest, the grip jutting up over my shoulder.

There are more Beretta magazines on the rack, so I take as many as I can and Velcro them in place. When the body armour can't take any more, I shove the rest into my pockets.

'You gearing up to fight a war?'

'We only saw one. There should be another six of them.'

'Good point.'

'Knives?'

Selina gives me a crooked smile, then slides the first shelving unit back into the wall, revealing another one crammed full of swords and daggers.

Selina takes one down. It's about the size and shape of a machete, but the blade is utterly black and seems to absorb light. She hands it to me.

'One of our agents went mad in the late nineties. You know how it is when the magic catches up with you?'

I nod.

'We walked in to find him stabbing himself with every weapon he could get hold of. Just normal knives, you know? Cutting himself to pieces. But when the blades came out of his body they were all like this. They cut through anything. Even angel feathers.'

I whistle, impressed. Angel feathers are supposed to be the strongest material in existence. Don't ask me why. That's above my pay grade.

Selina takes a blade for herself and brings it down against a gun sitting on the shelf. The blade silently cuts straight through the metal, the shelf, and, I think, through the air itself, if the weird flash of blue-white light is anything to go by.

'How are we supposed to carry them?' I ask. You can't put that in a scabbard.

Selina hesitates, then sags with disappointment. 'You're right. I suppose guns will have to do then.'

She pushes the shelf back and moves to a third, taking down two assault rifles. She slams their magazines in place and hands me one. L119 carbines if I'm not mistaken. The weapon of choice for the SSA.

'To carry,' says Selina. 'Use until you run dry, then go for the shotgun, then handguns.'

'Yes, ma'am.'

I grab another couple of magazines for the rifle. 'Tape?'

She heads over to the desk and brings back some clear plastic tape. I use it to attach two more magazines to the butt of the rifle, winding the tape round and round to hold them in place.

I toss the tape back towards the desk but Selina catches it out of the air and does the same to hers. She cocks her rifle and smiles at the satisfying metallic click.

'You ready?' she asks.

'Insert macho bullshit here.'

She nods thoughtfully. 'I thought for sure you were going to say "lock and load".'

'I won't lie. It crossed my mind.'

'Or "I was born ready".'

'Oh, now that's just insulting. Give me some credit.'

'Fair enough. Let's go, blue eyes.'

We leave the room and head back along the corridor, rifles braced against our shoulders. We don't bother going back through the maintenance corridors again. We pause at the door to each room, covering each other and making sure each area is clear before proceeding.

We're nearly at the briefing room when someone stumbles out of an office into the hall. Selina and I both almost open fire before the figure spins around and we see it's Lewis. Even then, it takes Selina a while to relax her finger on the trigger.

'Thank God!' says Lewis. 'Come on. We have to get out of here.'

'I think what you meant to say was "we have to help our co-workers",' says Selina.

'Are you fucking crazy? The whole building is breached. People are being murdered on every floor by those . . . whatever the fuck they are.'

'Seven Sins,' I say helpfully.

Lewis just looks blankly at me.

'There's only one up here,' says Selina. She unstraps one of her Berettas and hands it to Lewis. 'We take it out, get our crew back to the armoury, kit up, and we take the building back. Floor by floor.'

Lewis looks at us in amazement. 'Are you being serious?'

'As serious as a report into dereliction of duty,' I say. 'Which, incidentally, is what I'll be filing if you don't pull yourself the fuck together and do your goddamn job.'

Lewis looks between us and finally sighs. He takes the gun and pulls back the slide. 'Where are they?'

'Briefing room.'

He nods and we start moving again, coming at the briefing room from the opposite side. The door is open.

I glance at the others. They nod, and I move around the door, rifle seeking out and locking onto the Sin.

I open fire, short bursts of automatic fire pummelling the creature. There are screams of fear from my right. I ignore them and move forward, one slow step at a time, firing into the creature's vibrating head. I sense movement to my left and see Selina in my peripheral vision. She's firing at the creature's neck.

I focus on the job. Click. Out of bullets. I eject the clip as Selina keeps firing, rip another magazine free from the tape, ram it into place, cock the gun, then start firing again. Selina uses the moment to reload her own gun.

Our bullets are shredding the Sin. Its black face spurts a thick, tar-like ichor that splatters against the wall. It jerks and squeals, a high-pitched mewling sound. The gunfire is deafening in the room. Overriding everything. The sin's skin is tough, turgid. It's like I'm firing into thickening concrete. The bullets are having an effect, but not enough. The thing's head should have dissolved by now.

We're only a few steps away now. My magazine runs dry again. I eject it and reload, taking another step forward and aiming all over its body this time. Globules of . . . I don't know what. Flesh? Are starting to drop away into puddles around it.

Then the Sin turns and sprints from the room, moving so fast I can't even follow its movements.

I take a deep breath and lower my rifle. I turn around, a relieved grin on my face.

Which is when I see about ten of the Ministry personnel *change* before me.

Their faces melt and slide, skin rippling and changing colour to reveal white amorphous masses with faint sigils carved into the flesh.

I stare in amazement. I've seen those faces before.

Dillon.

Or the Cuckoo that was *pretending* to be Dillon. It looked exactly like this. Even down to the sigils carved into its skin.

I drop the empty rifle and reach over my shoulder for the shotgun. Selina has seen it too. She's drawing one of her Berettas.

But what she *can't* see is Lewis standing behind her, his own face now a grey-white mask, as he raises his gun and fires it into the gap in the body armour beneath Selina's raised arm.

She jerks and falls. I fire the shotgun straight into Lewis' face. His head explodes, white blood and brain matter bursting out in every direction.

I drop the shotgun – too many innocents to risk using it – grab my two Berettas and whirl around, firing at the closest Cuckoo. The bullet hits right between its eyes, dropping it to the ground. I move forward, guns still firing. I hit one, shift my aim, hit another – a double tap to make sure – then hit another in the leg. It goes down. I fire into its chest, then its head. I spin around, guns still steady. Some of the Cuckoos have run away, but a couple are still in sight. One heads for the door and I fire, hitting it in the back of the head. White blood sprays out the front, as if the Cuckoo is spewing milk. It staggers, but keeps walking, footsteps dragging. I fire into its back. One, two, another in the neck, and it finally drops.

A fist hits me in the side of the face. I jerk back, grabbing hold of the Cuckoo's arm as I fall backwards. We hit the carpet and I push the barrel right up against the Cuckoo's chin. One, two, three shots, and there's nothing left of its head.

I get to my feet, gun roving. Nothing. I eject the clips, grab fresh ones and ram them into place. Seven Cuckoo bodies litter the floor. That means a few got away. The Ministry personnel start climbing to their feet, faces dazed and confused.

I run out into the corridor and see one of the Cuckoos heading back toward me. I'm taken by surprise. I stumble to a stop and fire, but the creature dodges, leaping up the wall, around the ceiling and then dropping on my back. It punches me in the head. Over and over. I stagger and drop to my knees as the blows keep coming. The creature pushes me down, grabbing hold of my head and ramming it hard into the floor.

Stars explode across my vision. I struggle, expecting the Cuckoo to try and break my neck or something, but a moment later the weight on my back is gone. I shake my head to clear it and try to push myself up using the guns as leverage. I slip and fall back again. I roll onto my back and stare up at the lights.

Then I hear the screaming. I take a deep, shuddering breath and push myself to my feet, staggering back into the briefing room.

All three escaped Cuckoos are back and they're slaughtering the last of the Ministry workers, moving through them at speed and murdering every single one. I fire, hitting the closest creature in the head. But I'm too late. There is only one woman left and the last two Cuckoos are playing with her. I shoot and miss. They glance at me and one of them casually jabs its fingers into the woman's throat.

I fire at the Cuckoo's chest. It jerks, staggers, then falls to the floor.

There's only one left. It has a smile on its featureless face. 'There are none left to stop us,' it says. 'The old ways are returning.'

It rushes me. I fire. It jerks and stumbles, still coming. I keep firing, hitting it in the face, the forehead, the cheek, the neck.

It finally drops to the ground two feet from me, the hideous, rictus smile still on its face.

I drop the gun and slide down to the floor, taking a deep, shuddering breath.

There are none left to stop us. I look around at the slaughtered Ministry workers. Does that mean the whole Ministry has been wiped out? The entirety of England's supernatural police force just . . . gone?

I stare at the Cuckoo that fell closest to me. I'm staring at it a long time before I suddenly realise that the sigils on its face match the sigils I saw on the Marquis' armour. My head spins. What the fuck does that mean? That they're part of the Blessed? And if they are, does that mean . . . does that mean *Dillon* was one of the Blessed too?

Assuming the Cuckoos are trying to kill us all because we won't let the child abductions go, does that mean that's why Dillon was really trying to kill me last month? Because I was searching for Cally? I thought it was to do with the sin-eaters, but maybe I was getting too close to the Blessed, messing with their plans (even though I didn't know it) . . . And when I found the Marquis' name that was the last straw. They had to take action.

'London . . .'

My head snaps around. Selina. She's still alive. I crawl over to her and pull my phone out, dialling 999 and calling for an ambulance. I carefully pull her vest over her head, wincing at her groan of pain and I press my hand down over the slick wound, trying to staunch the bleeding.

'You're not allowed to die, Selina. OK? I kinda like you, and you have no idea how rare that is.'

I flick through my phone with my free hand and find Armitage's number. She answers on the second ring.

'I'm eating my cornflakes, London. What is it?'

'Boss? We got a problem.'

12

I spend the next few hours at the hospital, waiting while they operate on Selina. Armitage and the dog turn up while I'm sitting on a bench drinking brown dishwater that's pretending to be coffee.

I tell them everything. About the Cuckoos in the Ministry. About how they looked exactly like Dillon.

About the Sin.

When I'm finished they both just stare at me, the dog with his head tilted to the side.

'You're sure these Cuckoos looked the same as Dillon?'

'Spitting image.'

'And you're a hundred percent sure these Cuckoos are part of the Blessed?'

'The sigils on their faces are the same as the ones I saw on the elves' armour.'

'But . . . I don't get it,' says Armitage. 'If Dillon was one of these Blessed, that means they specifically targeted you over a month ago when we were looking into the sin-eaters. Why? What did *they* have to do with the sin-eaters?'

'Nothing. Nothing at all.' I look at them both. 'I was trying to find out what happened to Cally and the other girls who went missing, remember? And tracking missing kids is what brought us here. Ayanda and Lerato were looking into the Blessed because of Baba Yaga and they ended up dead – which, incidentally, explains the video. The Sins got into their heads and made Lerato . . . crazy. Angry, whatever. Then the

Blessed find out we're onto them, and the Ministry is attacked. That's when the Sins tried to get into my head too.'

Which means their deaths are on me. If I hadn't gone to the forest last night, then none of this would have happened.

'Don't blame yourself,' says Armitage, knowing exactly what I'm thinking. 'If the Cuckoos were already in place, this was planned. They would have turned on the Ministry soon enough.'

'I still don't get it,' says the dog. 'How can this lot be connected to your daughter? There's too many coincidences. We just *happen* to stumble on the group who took your kid when we travel thousands of miles to the UK? My credulity does not stretch that far.'

'I don't think it's a coincidence at all. Like I said, the Blessed were the ones taking kids right from the start. Why, I don't know. They take Cally and I assume she's dead. I start nosing around, trying to find out who killed my daughter. Then I find out she wasn't killed at all. She was kidnapped. And I even get a name. The Blessed realise we're stumbling close to the truth *while* we're looking into the sin-eaters, so they send a Cuckoo to take me and Becca out and get rid of anyone who wants to find Cally. Maybe *that's* when they find out about the Sins. And maybe that's what triggered all this new movement. We spooked them and they decided to move their plans up a notch. Whatever the reason, they got careless. Greedy. More kids than usual go missing. This raises alarm bells, and we track them here. We nose around some more, and they decide to take us all out in one go before we ruin their plans.'

'And what exactly are their plans?' asks Armitage.

I slump back against the wall. 'I have no idea.'

Too many questions. Not enough answers.

The doors at the far end of the corridor swing open and a doctor approaches.

I get to my feet. 'How is she?'

'She's in recovery. We got the bullet out, but it broke a rib, punctured her lung and small intestines, and lodged in her hip.'

'But she'll survive?' I ask.

'It's looking good,' says the doctor. 'But you might as well go home. She's not having any visitors today.'

We head back to the Ministry to help with the clean-up. The Home Office has appointed Armitage the interim head of the now non-existent Ministry while they figure out what to do with the fact that they have no supernatural police force left. Lucky her.

I'm curious how it's going to play out here. The Ministry might not have been doing stellar work, but they were still a symbolic presence. With them gone, who the hell knows what's going to happen.

We're stuck there for the rest of the day, and when the dog and I finally decide to leave Armitage to finish up, it's already after eight.

I take a small detour before heading back to the hotel. I know it's not the best time for it, but I don't know if we're going to get another chance, so I get a cab to drop us off at Borough Market.

-*Why we stopping here?*- asks the dog as the cab pulls up to the kerb. -*I want to go back to the hotel and drink.*-

-*You can drink here.*-

-*Where are we? A pub?*-

-*Even better. A Christmas market.*-

-*Serious?*-

-*Serious.*-

-*Aw, London. You shouldn't have.*-

We get out of the cab and stroll toward the enclosed market, our breath pluming in the cold air. It glows with twinkling lights, as if the market is a portal to the North Pole itself.

Wreaths with holly and mistletoe twined through them hang from the green roof girders. Huge Christmas trees covered with lights stretch high up to the curved roof. The crowds are thick, and as we approach, the smell of cooking food wafts out to us. Pork, sausages, curries, roasted chestnuts, cinnamon, nutmeg.

-*Oh my god,*- says the dog. -*I think I want to live here.*-

We enter the market proper and I let the dog lead the way, his nose taking us directly to a stall selling gluhwein. I buy two cups and we wander off to find a bench. I set the dog's cup on the ground and we sip our drinks in a companionable silence, the dog staring around with as happy an expression on his ugly face as I've ever seen.

We finish our wine and take another slow walk around the stalls, stopping when the dog finds a barrow that sells roasted chestnuts.

-*I hate us right now,*- says the dog happily. -*We are the living and breathing epitome of Christmas kitsch.*-

-*Nothing wrong with a bit of kitsch in your life,*- I say. -*By the way, make the most of this. It's your Christmas present.*-

-*Like fuck it is. I want to wake up on Christmas morning with at least twenty gift-wrapped presents under the tree. And make sure you wrap them tight. And none of that cheap paper that tears if you breathe too heavily on it.*-

-*Jesus, dog. You don't ask for much, do you? What are you getting me?*-

-*Don't be stupid. I'm a dog. How am I supposed to buy you presents? I'll make you a card. How about that? I'll even draw a picture on it. But I'm not promising it will be great. It's hard to draw when you're holding a paint brush in your mouth.*-

-*You're all heart.*-

-*I know.*- The dog munches another chestnut. -*And don't even think of wrapping up any booze you buy me. Booze is the same as books. They're not gifts. They're necessities.*-

I sigh. Looks like I've got some last minute Christmas shopping on the cards.

When we finally get back to the hotel, it's nearly ten.

The dog heads off somewhere as I climb the sticky-carpeted stairs and trudge along the dim passage. I switch on the light as I enter my room. A jaundiced glow flickers to life behind the dusty bulb, filling the room with yellow-tinged shadows.

I sit at the bottom of the bed and stare at the kettle on the rickety table. Like everything else in the hotel, it's ancient. It may have once been white but is now so covered with grimy fingerprints and water stains that I can't tell for sure. I really want a cup of tea, but I'm not sure my body would be able to fight off the prehistoric bacteria the kettle probably contains.

I sigh. Maybe I should just go and book myself into a hotel using my own money. Anything is better than this—

I feel it first. A dull, silent wave. A disturbance in the air that rolls out and fills the room. My ears pop. My teeth tingle like I've bitten into tinfoil.

My skin crawls. I reach for my wand, but before I can grab it a figure steps out of the air next to the TV. It's a woman. I can see that immediately from the way she moves and from her build. Her face is covered with one of the silver masks I saw on the elves last night. It looks like it's been cast from her actual face, although it's hard to be certain about that. She has a shaved head visible at the back, and is wearing a jerkin and pants made from supple leather. She's holding one of those sharp wooden swords the elves use. She points it directly at my face.

'I was hoping the Marquis would come,' I say.

Here's the thing. In this type of job people try to kill you all the time. Just under a month ago, I had my throat ripped out, I drowned (at the same time), I was nearly killed by my own tattoos, the Seven Sins nearly made me kill myself, Dillon tried to fill me with bullets, two angels wanted to cut my head off and then go for pizza . . . and I'm sure there are others I'm missing out.

You never get used to it. Which is a good thing. But you do develop a knack for knowing when your attacker is about to strike.

I watch the point of the sword, but I'm also watching the rest of her body. It's subtle, but I feel her tense, ready to move.

She jabs forward, aiming for my eye. I dart sideways, rolling off the bed and hitting the floor. I fumble in my jacket for my wand but she's already coming at me. Her blade comes down, fast. I roll again, hearing the sword take a chunk out of the floor. Jesus, she's quick. I hit the little table and grab the kettle, bringing it up just as the sword swings down at my head.

The kettle doesn't stop it, but it gives me a split second to move my head out of the way. I throw the two halves of the kettle at her. I scrabble up and fall back against the window, finally managing to get the wand out of my pocket.

She's on top of me again before I can use the wand. I shift to the side and her blade smashes through the glass. I push off from the wall and roll over the bed, coming to my feet and bumping up against the door. This room really is fucking ridiculous to fight in.

I pull in the aether that surrounds me and quickly fire my missile of choice. Black lightning. It writhes out of the wand and wraps around the wooden sword.

But . . . it does nothing. It just curls around the wood like a confused snake and my would-be assassin flicks it off like a piece of unwanted gum. Wonderful. I change my tack and pull in the aether to form my own blade that extends from the wand. It's as if the air itself turns semi-solid. The light strikes highlights off the solidified air, turning the invisible blade a dim blue in colour. I have to resist the temptation to pump more aether into it to make it glow even brighter. Grow the fuck up, London. Now's not the time to pretend you're in Star Wars.

She comes at me fast, utterly silent. I block her attack with my . . . sword? I'll call it a sword. We cross blades and I try to push against her with my weight.

She doesn't budge. It's like her feet are glued to the floor. We stand like that for a moment, each trying to leverage the other. I see my face in her mask, twisted and distorted by the metal, as if I'm standing in front of a funhouse mirror. This close I can see her eyes. Blue, narrowed in anger.

She jerks aside suddenly and I stumble forward. I hit the bed and try to bring my sword up behind me. Her blade hits mine and bounces off, slicing down the back of my forearm. I grimace in pain as the wood opens up a deep cut from elbow to wrist.

Jesus. I need to take some sword fighting lessons. First the angels at that sin party and now this. I think I'm being attacked more with swords than with guns nowadays, and I have no idea how to use one properly.

I do a clumsy forward roll over the bed, intending to jump up on the other side, ready to fight. I end up hanging half-on, half-off the mattress, my feet on the floor, my hips hanging over the edge of the bed.

I know what she's going to do before she does it. I'm displaying too tempting a target. I tense my stomach muscles and attempt a graceful backwards roll onto the bed, but end up sprawling across my pillows as the friendly neighbourhood assassin swings her sword and tries to cut me in half.

I scramble to my feet, standing on the bed. The assassin leaps effortlessly up and faces me. I try to bounce up and down without my legs leaving the mattress, hoping to distract her or put her off balance. No such luck. She's just sways with the motion like a sea captain who's lived her whole life on the ocean, her feet staying absolutely still while I look utterly fucking ridiculous.

I swing my light sab— sorry, sword. She blocks it, then attacks, a furious flurry of movement that I can barely keep up with. The heavy clacking of wood against solidified aether echoes through the room, accompanied by my own grunts of effort. She's silent. Focused and intent on cutting me to pieces.

-Hey, dog? Could really use a Warding right about now.-

No answer. But I know he's around. That feeling just before the assassin stepped into my room must have been some sort of bubble of silence. Why else aren't management knocking on the door, demanding to know what the hell was going on?

We bounce on the mattress as I dance around in increasingly desperate attempts to stop her cutting me into little slivers, then laugh out loud at how utterly ridiculous we must look. My assassin hesitates. Not much. Just a slight pause as I burst out laughing. I use the distraction to throw myself forward and hit her in the midriff with my shoulder.

The breath explodes out of her and we fly back into the TV. She grunts in pain as the TV tumbles to the floor and we hit the wall. I hope the ancient monstrosity has severed her spine or something.

No such luck. I wrap my arms around her midriff as she brings the hilt of her sword down against the back of my head. Once. Twice. I see stars. I try to pull away from her, but she pushes back against the wall, trapping my arms.

She hits me again. I manage to yank my left arm free, punching her in the kidneys. She stiffens in pain. I hit her again. She brings her knee up into my stomach, then pushes me back and brings the knee up again, this time slamming it into my jaw.

My mouth snaps shut. I taste blood. She shoves me away and I stagger against the bed.

Don't ask me how, but somehow I've still got my wand in

my hand. I dismiss the blue glowing blade and summon my anti-lightning again. This time I flick it up from underneath and it wraps around her arms, pulling tight. Thank Christ it seems to work on her.

The sword falls from her hands and I kick her in the stomach, sending her crashing back against the wall. She puts a hole in the plaster. I leap forward and grab her by the neck.

'Where is the Marquis?' I gasp.

In answer to my question, she head-butts me.

The metal mask hits me on the bridge of my nose and I cry out and fall backwards, trying to see through the tears that spring suddenly to my eyes. I can just see her shaking the anti-lightning off. It hits the ground and writhes around before turning to black glass that shatters beneath her feet. I fumble around for my wand and fire off more bolts, hitting the walls, the floor, the ceiling. The assassin ducks and weaves, throwing herself toward the window.

I fire off another bolt but she leaps through the broken glass and vanishes from sight. I stumble to the window, furiously wiping away my tears, and peer out. There's no sign of her. Just the late-night street: cars blaring their horns, a black cab skidding slightly on the slush and a drunken hen party singing Christmas carols at the top of their voices.

I slump onto my bed. My room is trashed. The walls have holes in them, the TV is lying in pieces on the hideous carpet, the kettle is sliced neatly in two and black lightning stains every available surface as if the walls have been painted by an emo teenager.

My eyes come to rest on the sword lying on the floor. I bend painfully forward to pick it up. It's a thing of beauty. Tiny runes are etched into the dark brown blade and the hilt itself is engraved to look like a tree.

There's a thudding at the door. It's coming from low down. I limp across the room and open it.

The dog stares at me. Then between my legs at the mess in my room.

He sighs. 'I'm sure there's a story here, but I'm just too fucking tired to care.' He pads into the room and jumps onto the bed, curling up and closing his eyes.

Yeah, sounds like a good plan.

Once I've asked for another room and put up some protective Wards.

13

Interlude

On the day the Raven King (the supreme protector of England and all those who live within it, or Sam to those who know him) is going to utterly fail in his duty and die a horrible and painful death, he wakes up craving a shot of whisky.

Maybe two.

That's allowed, right? He works hard, after all. Protecting the entirety of England from all attackers is thirsty work.

Plus, it's fucking freezing. The perfect weather for whisky. And snuggling up with someone you love to watch movies.

'Course, you need a loved one for that. Which he doesn't have. Has *never* had. But whisky. Yes. He has whisky. Good old whisky. Whisky will never let him down.

Sam glances at the alarm clock.

10:53.

Shit. He's slept in. Again. Still . . . it's not really his fault. That's what happens when you drink an entire bottle of Merlot before bed. No big deal. He has all day to perform the rituals. As long as they're completed at some point during the day, Head Office (as he likes to call them) won't bother him. Best job in the world, really. Rent-free digs in a prime London location, an hour of work every day, and that's all there is to it. A bit lonely, sure. Hell, a *lot* lonely. But then again that might just be him and not the job. He never was a very . . . approachable person. He'd be the first to admit it. Part of the reason he was picked in the first place.

He reluctantly heaves the Bear (his favourite thick blanket) aside and slides from bed, flexing his thickly socked feet on the floorboards. He pads across to the still-burning embers of the fire and rattles more coal out of the scuttle. By the time he gets back, the fire should be roaring, his rooms once again fit to fight off the winter cold. He thinks he'll watch *The Notebook* today. He's in that kind of mood.

He scowls at the fire. Why they can't put normal heating in here he'll never understand. He's asked. Many times. Hell, he even pretended he caught hypothermia once. Even wrote up a fake doctor's note. But they didn't believe him.

He yanks the curtains back. It's still snowing. He leans forward and wipes the condensation from the glass. He hopes it doesn't last. The first sign of bad weather and Londoners take it as a personal challenge to act as if the zombie apocalypse has arrived. There will be car accidents, short-tempered cyclists, tube delays, the works.

Still, it might keep all those annoying kids off the street. God, if someone could just make a law forbidding anyone between twelve and twenty from going out in public, that'd be great. He made the request himself once. Hell, he *is* the Raven King after all. The title should come with *some* perks. But no, apparently Head Office thinks that would infringe on peoples' human rights or something.

He pulls on his clothes and his old army jacket, then sends a text to Father Matthew at the church. Sam is supposed to be there at six, but when he does run late (which is happening more and more often, lately) it's easier to text ahead so the father can clear the church out.

He slips the phone into his pocket and pulls open the door. The wind barges past him, sending pieces of loose paper fluttering to the floor. Snowflakes whirl through the room, disappearing as they hit the warmth of the fire.

Sam pulls his collar high and makes sure his scarf is wrapped tight around his face, then steps out into the late winter morning, closing the door tight behind him.

He hurries along the narrow, labyrinthine pathways of the Inns of Court, the buildings obscured by the snow and dim morning light. His breath plumes through the scarf, trailing behind him as he enters the large square of Fountain Court. He can't even see the fountain that gives the courtyard its name. The only thing that gives it away is a small hump of snow surrounded by bare trees.

He doesn't see many people on his way to the Temple Church – just a few dim shadows lit by the glow of mobile phone screens. Ghosts that appear then quickly fade away. There's a strange feeling in the air. Everything seems slightly unreal, like he's walking through a dream.

The familiar shape of the church finally emerges through the snow and he skirts around the curved wall of the Round Church (the first part of the church built back in the 12th century). Head Office has used this church for nine hundred years, but their history on the site goes back much further than that. Much further indeed.

He takes out the iron key that has been handed down to each keeper of his title. He unlocks the wooden door and steps inside, locking it securely behind him before turning to face the church itself.

To his left is the Round Church, to his right, the pews and benches of the church proper. Sam ignores this section and heads between the black pillars into the Round Church. Dull, heavy light enters through the arched windows.

He shivers, trying to ignore the feeling of unease that is creeping over him.

It's just the weather, he tells himself. *Or the hangover. Nothing to worry about.*

He walks to the centre of the room. Stone effigies carved into the likenesses of knights have been laid out on the flagstones – four to either side. They've been there for centuries, but what lies beneath them has been there much longer.

Sam picks another key from his key ring and inserts it into an all but invisible crack in the wall. He turns the key and a well-oiled mechanism releases with a quiet *click*.

For a moment, nothing happens. Then, with a grating of stone, one of the knights slowly slides aside, revealing a set of stairs leading below ground.

On the top step, where he left them yesterday morning, are a thick candle and a large box of matches. Sam lights the candle and descends. As he passes the fifth step, his head dropping below the level of the church floor, he pulls a stone lever in the wall and the knight shifts back into position, concealing the stairs from anyone accidentally entering the church. Father Matthew is supposed to make sure this doesn't happen – it's what they pay him for, after all – but it's better to be safe than sorry. The guy's getting old now.

The stairs lead to a wide, low-ceilinged room. The lore says it was excavated from the soil when London was only a few shacks built along the River Thames. Sam doesn't know if that's true or not. All he knows is that someone from his Order has been on this site for as far back as records go.

Sam lifts the candle to a bowl in the wall and dips the wick inside. Fire flares to life, shooting around the room as the oil in the aqueduct takes to flame.

The flickering light reveals the object that defines his Order, the reason he and those before him have to come here every single day of their lives.

The London Stone. (The real one, not the fake that's on display out in the city.)

It sits on a stone altar, an unassuming rectangular piece of rock placed in the centre of the room. Surrounding the altar are eight full-length mirrors, their oak frames carved into the likenesses of dragons devouring their tails. The London Stone and its altar are reflected in each mirror, but the mirrors themselves hold something more.

Inside each of the mirrors, standing behind the reflection of the stone, stands a single knight dressed in old, grubby armour. Not the type from the books. This armour is real. Plates of metal strung together over dirty leather.

Each of the knights' eyes are closed, their faces turned down. They all hold a piece of rope in their hands, and the rope extends out to wrap around the reflection of the London Stone within each mirror, tying it in place.

Eight knights. And eight ropes held taut in powerful hands, securing the reflection of the London Stone to its altar.

Sam approaches the stone, slipping between two mirrors so that he's standing inside the circle. No matter how many times Sam has done this, the effect is always disconcerting. His own reflection is nowhere to be seen. The mirrors show only the knights holding their ropes.

He turns in a slow circle, as he was taught to do by his predecessor. Making sure each of the mirrors holds the same reflection they always have. Making sure the ropes are still—

He freezes.

—Still attached.

He blinks.

No, no, no. He takes a small, horrified step forward then stops, afraid his knees are going to give out. He closes his eyes, but he knows he'll see the same thing once he opens them.

One of the eight knights – Sir Culwych – no longer holds his rope. It's just . . . gone, an empty spot on the stone's reflection revealing where it used to be tied. The knight's eyes are open, staring sadly out through the mirror, his hands spread wide in a gesture of loss.

Fuck, fuck, fuck. One of the ropes is gone. One of the ropes that binds the London Stone, that keeps it safe, secure.

It's gone.

On his watch.

Shit. Fuck.

But how?

Pull yourself together, he tells himself. There are things he has to do. There's a book, passed down through the Raven Kings, with instructions. Details for eventualities every King hopes will never happen on their watch. But here it is. Happening to him.

He turns around, intending to head back up the stairs, but a strange sound makes him pause. A slithering sound, like a snake. Or . . .

Or rope.

He whirls around and stares wildly at the mirrors. There. The one on the left. The knight inside the mirror is now looking up, his eyes open. And as Sam watches, the rope he holds slithers out of his hand and slides up and over the reflection of the stone, disappearing away into the darkness.

Sam's mouth hangs open. He'd thought there was time, time to read over the books, time to contact someone with a higher pay grade and tell them what had happened. But as he stands there, staring dumbly, the knight spreads his hands open in a gesture identical to Culwych. Sam hears the slithering noise once again, and the rope slips through the hands of a third knight.

Sam sprints up the stairs, pulling the lever and hopping impatiently from foot to foot as he waits for the stone knight to slide across the church floor. He squeezes through, scraping his shoulders against the edges.

He has to get back to his rooms. Has to . . .

. . . A loud snuffling sound brings him up short.

That . . . sounded like a horse, he thinks.

Which is ludicrous. Obviously. There can't be a horse here.
He turns slowly.

'How about that,' he says dumbly, staring upward.

It *is* a horse.

Kind of.

Standing before him is some kind of . . . centaur? That's the only way he can describe it. A centaur that has crawled from the dark recesses of nightmares.

The creature towering over him has no skin. Its muscles and sinews are exposed to the air, glistening red in the dim light. Yellow veins crisscross the creature like a network of scars. Dark blood is visible inside these veins, pumping sluggishly through the creature's body.

The top half of the beast – the human part, if such a thing could be said – leans forward to study Sam. He staggers back a step, gagging at the stench of raw meat. The creature only has one eye, pulsing with a crimson, bloody light. The other is missing, a puckered wound surrounding an empty eye socket.

The creature steps forward, the exposed sinews and muscles tensing and writhing with every movement. It leans in farther, so that its head is level with Sam's. He can feel heat pulsing from its eye, like feverish warmth from a gangrenous wound.

The creature opens its mouth, a mouth that is almost double the size it should be, cutting far back into the cheeks toward the ears. Black, rotting teeth glint at him, and a diseased tongue flicks out and licks lips wet with blood.

'Ease yourself,' says a voice, from somewhere behind Sam.

The creature blinks, then snorts with annoyance and moves a few paces back, pawing the ground with its hooves. Sam risks a glance over his shoulder, looking toward the main section of the church to see who spoke.

A tall, dark-skinned man walks toward him. Or . . . not a man. Something else. White eyes with tiny pinpricks for pupils stare at him.

'He does not have manners, my Nuckelavee,' says the man. 'I only call on him when I need heavy work done.'

Sam turns back to the Nuckelavee just in time to see the creature unstrap a hammer from a leather harness, a hammer almost the same size as Sam himself.

'Do you know who I am?' asks the man.

Sam swallows nervously and shakes his head.

'No? I am saddened. I have been cultivating my reputation in this city for some time now.'

The man steps closer. Sam notices that his skin isn't in fact dark, but that he has covered his body in something that looks like ash. There are uneven patches that show pale white skin beneath.

The man bows. 'I am the Marquis. And it will be my very great pleasure to watch you die today.'

Sam almost collapses with fear. He doesn't understand what is going on. Nobody should know about him. About what he guards. Five thousand years of wars and battles have been fought to ensure its secrecy.

He has to get away. Has to warn the Council.

The Marquis holds out a hand and a small, wizened creature shuffles forward. It looks like some kind of gnome, its face a mass of wrinkles in brown skin. It has a huge, bulbous nose that it uses to sniff the air around it. The creature is anxiously turning a battered hat round and round in its grasp.

'This is Dunsin. He has a most spectacular nose, don't you think?' The Marquis carries on without waiting for an answer. 'He uses it to sniff out magic. To track the currents of power that criss-cross the world. He has been in my employ for many centuries now. Isn't that right, Dunsin?' The Marquis pats the gnome proprietarily on the head. The gnome flinches at his touch, but the Marquis doesn't seem to notice, instead drumming his fingers on the creature's head. 'Do you want to know why he has been with me for so long?'

Sam really doesn't. All he wants is to be out of here. To send out the ravens of the tower with messages of doom.

'He has been with me for so long because I gave him a task. His task was to come and tell me if the currents of magic in the world changed in any way. Because I've been searching, you see. Searching for something hidden away from me by those who once called me kin. And you know what my little friend here has done? He's finally earned his keep. Managed to track me down a new friend. Have you ever been to Africa?'

Sam blinks, confused at the sudden change in subject. He finally nods. 'C . . . Cape Town.'

'Really? Did you like it?'

'It was OK.'

The Marquis smiles, and that smile scares Sam more than the huffing creature standing somewhere behind him. 'I've known you were here for some time, of course. A few years now. But I was waiting. Waiting for the perfect moment.' The Marquis frowns. 'But you know what they say. Life is what happens when you are making other plans.' The Marquis laughs. 'I like that one. So true. So true. But yes, my hand has been forced. Which, I'm afraid to say, is very unfortunate for you.' He looks over Sam's shoulder. 'Do it.'

And then the ground explodes, tossing Sam into the air. He lands heavily, sprawled on his chest, and watches through a haze of grey dust as the Nuckelavee swings the huge hammer into the air for a second time and brings it down onto the stone knight that lies above his secret opening.

Shards of rock spin into the air. Again and again the creature brings the hammer down, destroying a figure that has protected the hidden room for centuries. Rock dust billows into the air. Sam coughs, struggling to breathe. He has to do something. Has to stop them getting to the stone.

The horrendous pounding finally stops.

'Is it done?' demands the Marquis.

'Done,' comes the gruff response.

'Then destroy the stone. Make sure—'

The Marquis' voice stops abruptly. Sam hears an intake of breath, then, 'My friend. You are needed.'

Sam's eyes shift to the side, drawn by movement. Something lurches out of the shadows. Just looking at it makes Sam feel ill. The creature looks like it's made of oil and tar, and it leaves black, steaming footprints in its wake. Sam can't see its face properly. It vibrates.

It moves across the flagstones to stand next to the Marquis. They're both looking at something. Sam tries to see what, but the dust is too thick.

But then he catches another movement, a hint of shadow that quickly grows more solid.

Tall figures appear through the dust.

Sam gasps. It's the stone knights, the knights that have lain in the church for centuries.

They've come alive.

The knights look around the room, pausing to glance at the fragments of their comrade. Their stone faces show anger, their blank grey eyes narrowing. They lift their stone swords into the air and turn as one to face the Nuckelavee, their swift movement causing the dust to swirl into spirals around them.

But before they can attack, the oily creature is in their midst, so fast Sam didn't even see it move. It lashes out with one hand, long talons sending one of the knights staggering back. A sword lashes through the air towards it but the creature has already moved, picking up another knight and tossing him across the room. The knight lands a few feet from Sam, the ground trembling as it hits. It skids heavily across the floor, gouging deep tracks into the stone, before rolling into a kneeling position and immediately launching himself back into the fight.

The knights form a circle around the dark creature, slashing at it with blows that should be lethal.

Beyond the battle, the dust cloud has started to settle. Sam catches a glimpse of the Nuckelavee heading down into the exposed opening. Heading for the stone.

Sam stands up. The knights are occupied with the dark creature. There is nothing they can do. Which means it falls to him to stop the creature from destroying the stone.

He casts a nervous glance at the battle. The dark creature is landing blow after blow with its taloned hands, sending the knights staggering back, down to their knees. At least that means its attention is away from Sam. He risks a quick look at the Marquis. He's watching the battle with glittering eyes.

Sam slides around the walls of the Round Church, praying to God that no one notices him, and reaches the shattered opening in the floor.

Sam risks a glance over his shoulder. As he does so, the dark creature hits one of the knights in the face. Its stone head separates from its shoulders, spinning across the room to shatter against the wall. The headless body immediately freezes up, falling to the ground like a downed tree.

The other knights renew their attack. Sam slides quietly down the stairs and into the altar room, avoiding the fragments of stone that litter the steps.

The Nuckelavee is standing on the outside of the circle of mirrors, eyeing them nervously. Sam notes that two of them no longer have glass in them, the shattered remains lying on the ground. There is a tremendous crashing from upstairs, and at the same moment the mirror directly opposite him is damaged, cracks spiralling along the glass. The knight inside the mirror drops to his knees and the glass falls out of the frame, shattering on the ground.

A second later something thuds down the stairs. Sam turns to see a stone head roll to a stop next to his feet. The face is the same as the knight from the mirror.

Sam quickly checks the others. Four left . . .

No, three. More glass falls from a mirror. He can't see the knight from this angle, but he knows what is happening now. The mirrors shatter and fall, one after the other until none are left.

Silence falls above him.

Sam stares as the dark figure lurches down the stairs then scrambles back against the wall. Even the Nuckelavee moves aside.

The dark figure is dripping bits of itself on the floor. It looks . . . damaged. In pain, almost. He can see bits of white skin showing through. Skin that is diseased and gangrenous.

But none of that matters. Because the dark figure steps forward and grips the London Stone.

'No!' screams Sam.

The dark figure turns and flies at Sam. It's inhumanly fast, and there's absolutely nothing Sam can do. It backhands him and he has the curious sensation of standing still and moving at the same time. His vision twists in the air. He hits something and falls. He watches as the dark figure crushes the London Stone. It crumbles in the creature's hands, turning to dust that floats away into the air.

As soon as it does so the back wall of the church changes. It becomes a . . . wall made from ancient-looking cogs and gears. Sam hears the clunking of hidden machinery, and the cogs and gears whirr to life, looking like the insides of a giant clock. The wall separates into two halves, revealing a dark opening descending into the earth.

Then Sam notices something else. With no small amount of surprise he sees his own headless body as it falls to the floor some distance away.

Oh, he thinks.

And then he dies, having failed utterly and spectacularly in his duty.

God knows what it is now.

At first it was nothing. Had no consciousness. All it knew was that for millennia it was trapped. That it was not free to fulfil its purpose.

Then a moment of pain, an awakening of consciousness amongst fire and heat.

Then rage. Rage and anger that made something from nothing, that drew upon the cancerous growth of an angel and willed life to form. Then they all separated, spreading across the world. To hide, to gather their strength, to realise what they were.

Who their father was.

How he tried to murder them. Tried to deny them. Deny *himself*.

But with time came weakness. Their bodies were failing, destroyed by the power they contained. They were in danger of losing their consciousness. So they came to this city, drawn by an ancient power that called to them.

And they joined together, became One instead of Seven.

They became like their Father. They became God, formed of his sins, formed of everything God denied.

He is better than Father ever was. He made Father what he was. Without the Seven Sins God was nothing. When the angels drove them out, he unravelled, became lost. Weak.

Now it is time for him to take Father's place in Heaven. There will be a new God ruling, and he will be mighty and terrible and the angels will bow down to him. The world will be his and he will surpass his Father in his terribleness.

But first . . .

First, he needs a new body. One that will hold his power without disintegrating.

This is the only reason he is helping this ash-covered creature and his kind. The small creatures think they are using him, but God has plans of his own.

'*My name is Legion,*' whispers God, '*for we are many.*'

And he smiles a black smile as he descends beneath the ancient city.

Mother London likes to walk the streets. It is here she feels the ebb and flow of life, the souls that flow through the streets like blood in the city's veins. She can pick up much from the streets. The feeling of tension as a community protests the treatment of one of their own. The sleepy happiness of children resting.

There has always been a balance to what she feels from her people. Anger and hate are countered by love and happiness. But lately, the balance is shifting. Fear and hate are rising, staining the city. She hopes this does not continue, because she, as the soul of London, must reflect that soul, must reflect what London *is*.

But tonight. Something is different tonight. There is something in the air. An expectation. A rise in tension, a build up like before a summer storm.

And at eleven thirty-two in the morning, London is broken.

She senses it, senses the lock being shattered. The very reason that the city was built in the first place is no more.

And she knows what it means.

She pauses and looks around her. She notices the momentary confusion in the faces of those close by, and she knows it will be reflected all across the city. Something deep inside every single Londoner will realise that something has happened.

That the end is coming.

Mother London sighs sadly. Her heart is heavy in her chest. She has two choices. Leave things as they are to play out as they will, or exert a small amount of influence. Not much. Just a quiet word in someone's ear.

She is not supposed to interfere, but . . .

Fuck it, this is my city. I'll do what I want.

14

We spend the next day at the Ministry again. I don't want to. I want to go back to Queen's Wood and see if we can track any of the Fae, track the Marquis. But Armitage forbids it. In order to keep me busy, she's forcing me to help fill out incident reports of what happened and give testimony (seeing as I'm the main eye witness), as well as fetching her coffee while she deals with the head honchos at Westminster.

I finally manage to extricate myself just after four in the afternoon, and the dog and I head back to the hotel.

-I plan on getting spectacularly drunk tonight,- says the dog as we approach the rundown building. *-Care to join me?-*

I'm about to answer when the door of a car parked directly in front of the hotel opens and a . . . Jesus, I know it's not nice to say it, but the *fattest* creature I have ever seen squeezes his way out of the car. He comes in bits and pieces, his stomach straining then bursting out of the gap, his shoulders sticking then finally popping through, followed by his head with its multiple chins.

The dog and I watch in fascination as the creature (because he's definitely not human) pauses to take a few breaths, then makes his way toward us.

'All right there?' he says, and his voice is surprisingly quiet, an Irish accent clearly audible.

'You good?' I ask.

He gives me a thumbs up.

'Can we do anything for you?'

'You're wanted for a meeting.'

'Who with?'

'Dagda, Oberon, and Nuada.'

I look at the dog in surprise. If I remember Winters' lecture correctly, Dagda, Oberon and Nuada are the leaders of three of the biggest Fae gangs in London. Interesting.

'They told me to tell you you're guaranteed safe passage and that they have information for you about the Blessed.'

Well now. Who are we to turn down such an offer?

'Where are you taking us?' I ask. I want to text the information to Armitage, just in case.

'A pub called Crocker's Folly. Don't you worry now. It's in public, you know? Lots of people around, like.'

'Fair enough.'

The dog and I get into the back of the car and we wait about three full minutes while our new friend squeezes himself back into the driver's seat. It's like watching someone trying to squeeze toothpaste back into the tube.

According to GHOST (that's the Global and Home-based Occult and Supernatural Treasury to you), what is now known as Crocker's Folly was originally supposed to be a Victorian gin palace called The Crown. The guy who built the hotel, Frank Crocker, planned on making his fortune by serving the hundreds of passengers arriving in London each day at the railway terminal opposite the premises.

The problem? He jumped the gun and the terminal was never built. Instead, the line carried on another half a mile to Marylebone. Which pretty much fucked his plans right up. It ruined Crocker. Urban legend says he eventually committed suicide by jumping out of one of the windows and that his ghost now haunts the hotel. (Which is crap. The Ministry sent a team to investigate. The only ghosts they found were the usual low-key after-images left behind by sudden deaths over the years. His wasn't there.) The place had been abandoned for years, but has recently been refurbished into a fancy-pants restaurant and pub. It looks like the kind of place you find in Cape Town that's staffed by 'mixologists' instead of bartenders.

The pub door opens and our friend (who says his name is Tylweg, and that he's a member of the Tuatha de Danaan tribe from Ireland) squeezes out into the cold night, turning around and carefully closing the door behind him. He lumbers over to us and leans down to stare at me through the window.

'Think he wants us to get out?' I ask.

'I don't want to,' says the dog. 'It looks cold.'

I study Tylweg. His teeth are chattering.

And he's frowning.

'It does look cold, but I think our new friend is getting annoyed.'

We stare at him a moment longer. 'His lips are turning blue,' the dog points out.

'You think? I was going to say grey.'

The door is locked, but Tylweg calmly pulls it open without even blinking.

'I hope you've got insurance,' says the dog, hopping out onto the icy sidewalk and bolting for the door. I follow after and we walk into a restaurant that looks like it's been designed by someone who's only seen Victorian pubs in movies. Expensive chandeliers with tiny lampshades cast a tasteful yellow light through the interior. The ceiling is decorated with elegant patterns and gold gilt. A massive hearth holds a roaring log fire and there's an all-white Christmas tree in the corner, the kind that bachelors keep in their flats because they think they're tasteful. They're wrong, of course. White Christmas trees just make a flat look like it's been used to shoot the cover of a Boney M Christmas CD.

And speaking of which, Boney M is indeed playing over the pub sound system.

The bar is to the right and a long table runs down the centre of the room, filled with customers having supper and drinks. Normal customers, mind. And none of them blink an eye at Tylweg.

'Follow me,' he says.

He leads the way through a set of glass double doors. A dining room lies beyond, similarly decorated, with a second large fire burning against one wall.

Only one table is occupied. It's circular, and three Fae sit around it, spaced equally apart. We approach the table. The Fae creature facing us gets to his feet. He has white hair and a grey-white beard. His skin is tanned and lined. He looks like a dignified uncle, if your uncle happened to have pointed ears and eyes that slant up at 45 degree angles.

'I'm Dagda,' he says.

I nod. 'London.' I gesture at the dog. 'Dog.'

The dog nods. 'Wotcha.'

Dagda turns to the figure to his right. This Fae looks younger, with dark hair and a thin, almost skeletal face. He has two horns poking out the top of his head and for some reason is wearing a massive cloak with a high collar that juts up behind his neck. It's obvious he's having some trouble with the cloak. He can't get comfortable, and every time he moves the collar juts up higher or pokes him in the back of the head.

'This is Oberon,' says Dagda.

Oberon nods briefly before returning to his fidgeting.

I look at the last figure. This guy is lounging back in his chair. White skin covered in blue tattoos. Sigils and runes. He has blond-red hair and he has an entire arm made from what appears to be silver.

'Nuada of the Silver Hand,' say Dagda. 'Nuada is the leader of the Tuatha de Danaan, the Irish Fae.'

'Right,' I say. 'So what we have here are the leaders of the three oldest gangs in London coming together in one place. I'm guessing it's not just for a catch up and a drink?'

Oberon snorts his laughter and picks up a goblet of wine.

'You could say that,' says Nuada with a grin. 'Bit of an all-round fuck up really.'

Dagda grimaces. 'Sit down.'

I take a seat between the Fae. Dog jumps up into another seat opposite me.

'Right,' says Dagda. 'We were visited by Mother London this morning. You know who that is?'

'We know *what* she is,' I say. 'Haven't met her personally.'

'She seems to know you. Says her sister speaks highly of you.'

That's a surprise to me. I haven't seen Mother Durban since she stole the name of Cally's kidnapper from my mind.

'Anyway,' says Dagda. 'She had a couple of things to tell us. Me? I'd rather just leave it. Let things play out. I'm not a cruel man, but I really couldn't give a shit about humans. They exist to make me rich. That's it.'

'Great philosophy ye've got there,' says Nuada. 'Very global of you.'

'Fuck off, Nuada,' says Dagda, 'or I will take this opportunity to cut your head off and feed your body to my pigs.'

'Charming.'

'Can we just get on with this?' says Oberon. 'I have things to pack.'

'Going somewhere?' I ask.

'Fuck yes. I'm off to Europe. No way I'm hanging around here.'

Dagda waves him to silence and turns his attention back to us. 'How much do you know about how London came to be?' he asks.

I share a puzzled look with the dog. 'It was a little hamlet on the Thames. The Romans built it up into a city.'

'Wrong,' says Dagda. 'On both counts. *We* created London. The Fae. It was to be a mirror of our own city, Murias, back in Tír na nÓg. The place you lot call Faerie.'

'Well . . . OK. Congratulations?'

'Fuck off. The city was first built as a sort of place marker. A location to guard a prison.'

'A prison?' I look at the dog.

-No idea,- he says.

'When we were a young race, we Fae worshipped different gods. The Old Ones, they were called. They were of nature and heath, of mist and snow. Blood and mud. They were cruel, as fickle as the ocean. You have heard of Cernunnos? The Horned God? He was the leader of the Old Ones, and so powerful that even your kind worshipped him for a time. I think he was one of mankind's first gods, actually.'

An image flashes through my mind. The vision I had when Parker was busy resurrecting Armitage. Of a horned creature stalking the streets of London, steam rising from his heaving shoulders as he hunted his prey.

'We . . . that is . . . all of us . . .' His look takes in Nuada and Oberon. 'We all decided the Old Ones weren't . . . suitable anymore.' Dagda sighs and leans back in his chair. He gestures around him. 'Look at this place. Bit of class, right?'

'Very stylish.'

'It is. I like pubs. I like sitting around and hearing your lot talk about their pathetic lives. But . . . the Old Ones would never have put up with this. Fuck, if the Old Ones still ruled the Fae, this city wouldn't be here. You lot probably wouldn't be here.'

'Explain.'

'The Old Ones are . . . well, they're old school. Towns, cities, gathering together like this . . . they didn't like it. They're nature deities.'

'Wait.' I lean forward. 'Just so I'm clear. These Old Ones are not just low level orisha. They're *actual* gods? Like . . . Tier 1?'

'Tier 0,' says Oberon. 'They were around before all the other orisha came into being. They grew from *consciousness*. From our very beginnings.'

'So let me see if I know where this is going,' says the dog. 'You decided you wanted to move with the times and . . . what? Get rid of your gods?'

'Not get rid of. Imprison them.' He pauses and looks uncomfortable. 'Below London.'

I blink.

'You're saying the first gods of mankind are locked away beneath our feet?'

'Pretty much. Beneath London there is a maze. In the centre of the maze is the prison. We're not animals, they're not chained up or anything. But they sleep. They . . . dream – hallucinate, if you will – their perfect world. Meanwhile, as we progress, as more and more people move to London, the strength of the lock holding them grows stronger. It is progress that keeps them in there. The belief of eight million Londoners in their iPads and flat screens, in Tinder and computers.'

'The lock is powered by the beliefs of Londoners?'

'Two locks. And yes. By progress. By new thinking. The kind of thinking we weren't allowed to indulge in when Cernunnos ruled over us. See, independent thought is bad. The Old Ones wanted to keep us ignorant. Like politicians. You're from South Africa, right? The only way the ANC stays in power is by keeping the masses uneducated. If their followers started to actually think for themselves then their time would be up. That is how the Old Ones operated.'

'OK,' I say. 'We've had the history lesson. Now why do I think you're going to say something terrible has happened?'

'Because it has. You know about the Blessed? They were a sect . . . a cult, if you will. In Tír na nÓg. No one really took them seriously. They lived in the forests, in trees and houses formed from living roots. They still followed the old paths. I say fuck that. I like my satellite television. I like my Jason Statham movies. The Blessed . . . don't. They want us all to return to the old ways. And by that I mean they want this entire island for themselves, to knock the cities down and for you lot to run around naked while they hunt you down one by one.'

'Why? The last bit, I mean?' I ask.

Dagda shrugs. 'What else are they going to do? The winter nights are long. No Ant and Dec to distract them? Sounds like a nightmare to me.'

'So what's the bad thing that happened?'

Dagda leans forward. 'Yeah, bit of bad news there. For all of us really. Well, I lie. For you lot. The first stone has been broken.'

'What stone?'

'The London Stone.'

I wait expectantly, but he just leans back and looks around. 'I'll miss this place.'

I sigh. 'Dog?'

'London?'

'Is any of this becoming clear to you?'

'As mud. And by mud I mean, no, London. Nothing is clear to me right now. In fact, I'd go so far as to say I'm befuddled.'

'Befuddled,' I say. 'That's a good word, dog.'

'Thanks, London.'

'So . . . can you *please* explain to us just what the fuck you're talking about. In simple terms.'

Oberon leans forward. 'In simple terms, you cretin, you are all dead. The London Stone has been destroyed. And I'm not talking about the little block you've got hidden behind a grill or on a plinth somewhere. This is one of the very first stones laid above the prison and a fragment of the Stone of Fal. There are two. One locking the actual prison, and one locking the entrance into the maze. The entrance is located in a place called the Inns of Court. In the Round Church. Do you know it?'

'I'm sure we'll find it.'

'I hope so. Because that first lock is gone now.'

'I . . . take it that's bad?'

'Catastrophic.'

'Oh . . . and you're sure about this?'

'Mother London confirmed it. We . . . just don't know *how*. The strength needed for something like that . . . only a god could do such a thing, and no god I know would even consider it. I don't think any of the gods even *know* about it.'

The dog and I exchange looks. I lean forward. 'What about . . . the Seven Sins of God. The big man himself?'

Dagda frowns. 'What?'

'Just tell me. If they were given life, would they have the power of a God?'

Dagda looks at Nuada and Oberon. They both nod slightly. 'Perhaps.'

I fold my arms and look at the dog again. 'Things become clearer.'

'I wouldn't go that far, London. In fact, again, and I'm sorry for repeating myself, I'd go so far as to say I'm even more befuddled.'

'The Blessed used the Sins to break the lock.'

'Oh.' The dog thinks about it. 'Fuck.'

'Fuck indeed,' says Dagda.

'So why are we still alive?' I ask.

'I told you. There's a maze down there that . . . shifts around.'

'Shifts around?'

'Yeah. The maze is sort of . . . magic. Or clockwork. I can't remember which. Whatever it is, the maze walls move around, so it takes a shitting long time to get to the actual prison. Least, that was the plan. And the prison itself is locked by another stone, which I think is still in place. For now. But the maze has been breached and if it was one of these Sins of yours, it's currently making its way to the prison where I'm sure it will want to break the second lock. That cannot happen.'

'You're taking this remarkably calmly.'

Dagda shrugs. 'I will diminish, and go into the West, and remain Dagda.'

'Back to Tír na nÓg?'

Dagda gives me an incredulous look. 'Fuck, no. L.A., bitch. I hear that town is the fucking bomb. I'll come back when the smoke clears, see what's left. We just wanted to give you a heads-up.'

'Why?'

'Because Mother London asked us to, and you do not say no to the soul of the city. And . . . like I said, I like it here. If your lot . . . your . . . Division or whatever you call yourself, can do something to stop it, I'm all for that. Of course we can't be seen to be helping you. The Blessed might get upset about that and we all need to keep on their good side. You know, in case they kick your ass.'

'Which is looking pretty likely,' says Nuada.

'Very likely,' adds Oberon.

'So how exactly *are* you helping us? By telling us we're going to die?'

'Don't be stupid. What would be the point in that? No. By telling you there's a way to lock the prison again. Before the Old Ones get out.'

I sit up straight. 'How?'

'By putting the first lock back in place. And the second one, if they break it. Of course, you'll still have to deal with this Sin of yours.'

'How do we put the first lock back in place?'

'You go to Tír na nÓg.'

I sigh. 'Why?'

'Because the stone that locked the prison was part of the Stone of Fal, and it's currently being held in the city of Falias. You lot might know it as the Stone of Destiny. It's one of the four treasures of Faerie. We've been fighting over those fucking things for millennia.'

'Question,' says the dog. 'What are the other treasures?'

'The Spear of Lugh, the Sword of Light . . .'

'That's mine,' says Nuada.

'. . . and my cauldron. It can feed an army, that thing. Even raise people from the dead. It was stolen from my castle by a little shit called Horned Harry. Anyway, the stone. You've heard the proverb, right? "As long as the Stone of Brutus is safe, so long shall London flourish"? It's supposed to be about the London Stone, but it's not really. The legend of the London Stone just sort of grew out of the true facts of the Stone of Fal.'

'Great. So go get the stone for us.'

'Uh . . . No. Sorry. See, the four treasures are locked away in the most secure bank in Falias.'

'You have banks in Faerie?' I ask.

'Don't be so fucking racist. What do you think we use to buy stuff?'

'Sorry.'

'Falias is a big city. Like London. It's the main hub of Tír na nÓg. So you're going to have to get some help to guide you around. Sneak in, scope out the lay of the land, and come up with a plan to steal the stone.'

I look at the dog, then back at Dagda. 'Let me get this straight. You're saying to save London, to save *Britain* from being overrun by psycho nature gods, we have to break into a bank—'

'—the most secure bank in Tír na nÓg.'

'—the most secure bank in Tír na nÓg . . . and steal the Stone of Destiny?'

'Not the whole thing. It's been broken up into pieces. You need one. No – two. Just in case the second lock is broken.'

'OK. Then get out of said bank, with the stones, and make it back here?'

'Within twenty-four hours,' adds Oberon.

'Twenty-four hours?'

Oberon looks at the others. 'Reckon that's how long we have?'

'Sounds about right,' says Nuada.

I look at the dog. He's grinning. 'What the hell are you looking so happy about? Didn't you hear all that?'

'Of course I did. A *heist*, London. A fucking honest-to-god heist. You have no idea how long I've wanted to do something like this.'

'You're going to need a crew. Where's your boss? The grumpy one,' says Nuada.

I frown. 'Do we have to take her?'

'You don't *have* to. But you'll need bodies. People who can do magic. Breaking into a secure vault like this requires skills. Anyone else?'

'Winters?' suggests dog. 'He can channel heat, remember? And he nearly kicked your ass back in the forest.'

I nod.

'That's four of you,' says Dagda. 'I'd say you need another body. Think about it a bit. Four people is a robbery. Five and up is a heist.'

'Hold up,' I say. 'This is moving too fast. How are we even supposed to get into Tír na nÓg?'

'Give me your phone.'

I hesitate, then hand it over. He taps away on it then tosses it back. He's opened up the map app.

'Go to that location. Knock on the door and tell them Dagda sent you and you're there to see the Queen. She's a smuggler. Brings things here from Faerie. Tell her . . . tell her if she helps you I'll make sure she's paid well. And . . . I'll owe her a favour. Just make sure you don't tell her too much. She's a devious bitch. Always looking out for herself. Tell her you want to rob the bank, and that you need her help setting that up.'

He pulls a coin out of his pocket. He flips it into the air and I catch it. It's a piece of gold with Dagda's face stamped on it.

'Your own currency? Seriously?'

He shrugs. 'We all have our little quirks. Mine just happens to be stamping my face into gold. Show that to her. She'll know you're not just screwing around then.'

'And she'll help us get into Faerie?'

He shrugs. 'You can never tell with the Queen. Depends on what mood she's in. Just . . . don't stare. For the love of any god, don't stare.'

I look at the dog again, trying to process all the information we've just been given.

The stupid bastard is just sitting there grinning, his tail wagging furiously.

I don't think I've ever seen him so happy.

15

Snow blankets the streets, mostly dirty white where it has been trampled by cars and pedestrians. Black ice coats the road.

I shiver, huddling down inside my jacket while we wait for Tylweg. Nuada kindly said he would take us to see the Queen.

-A heist, London. An actual heist. At Christmas! It's like you've given me my very own movie to star in.-

-It's not a movie, dog. We're here to . . .-

-Kick ass and chew bubble——.-

-No. We're going to get the stone and put the lock back in place before any of those hippie gods get loose.-

And get Cally back. I'm barely able to hide my excitement. This could really be it. Going to Faerie is exactly what I need to be able to search for Cally and the other kids.

And save London, of course. Obviously. I'm not going to make the same mistake as last time. But this is an honest-to-god chance to get her back. I won't get this lucky again.

Tylweg exits the pub and unlocks the car for us. We get in and wait while he does his reverse escape act into the driver's seat.

I take out my phone and call Armitage. She's at the Ministry again, attempting to force some sort of order into the situation. She's not winning.

'They don't want to send any more personnel!' she says.

'Who?'

'The Home Office! They say we have to just clean it up and keep it quiet.'

'Ok. Well . . . in that case, you're not going to like what I've just been told.'

'Jesus. OK, wait.'

I wait a moment.

'Right. My head is now resting on the desk. Tell me.'

I explain everything that Dagda and the others just told us.

There's no response.

'Armitage?'

Still nothing. Then I hear shouting in the distance. Nothing specific, just a lot of frustrated screaming and swearing.

'How's she taking it?' asks the dog.

'Pretty well.'

She comes back on the phone. 'Right. OK. Let's think about this. It's on us?'

'Pretty much. They're already packing their bags.'

'And if we don't at least try and lock this prison again, these Old Gods are going to get out?'

'That's what they say.'

'Do you believe them?'

I pause for a moment and think about it. It is true that they're all criminals. They could be pushing their own agenda. But they said Mother London told them and that would be easy enough to check.

'I think so.'

'Shit. Pity. So what do you suggest?'

'What is there to suggest? We go to Faerie and try and get a couple of pieces of the Stone to lock the prison again.'

And I look for Cally.

'What does dog think?'

I look at the dog. 'He's . . . excited about it.'

'A heist, Armitage!' he shouts. 'A fucking-honest-to-god heist! We have to get walkie-talkies. And MP3 players! We need cool music playing during the robbery. I'm going to have to make a playlist.'

'Jesus,' says Armitage. 'When are we supposed to do this?'

'We have twenty-four hours. That's what they think, anyway.'

'OK. Here's what you do. It's supper time so Cal will be at his club. Go talk to him. I'm going to tidy up the loose ends here. Call me when you've spoken to this Queen. Whoever the hell she is.'

'OK. What club?'

'The Accendere Club. It's in Pall Mall. I'll text you the address. Oh – London.'

'Yeah?'

'Behave yourself there. It's very exclusive.'

'If it's so exclusive, how the hell did Winters get in?'

'He's done a lot of good for this city. He might look like a paranoid, sarcastic loner – in fact he is – but he's stopped his fair share of trouble.'

'Fair enough. I'll call you later.'

I hang up as Tylweg finally pulls his head into the car. He fiddles about some more, then starts the car and pulls out into the dark streets. We drive in silence for a while.

'Cheer up,' says the dog.

'I am very cheery.'

'No, you're not. Come on, man. Embrace it. We're the last hope of mankind.'

'Shut up.'

'It's true! You should be grateful. Not many people get to do this kind of thing. Geeks the world over would salivate. Seriously. We're traveling to Faerie to steal an ancient treasure from a magical bank. I fucking love this shit.'

'Good for you. Now be quiet. I'm thinking.'

Silence falls. For about thirty seconds.

'London,' whispers the dog.

I ignore him.

'London.' Louder this time.

I still ignore him.

'LONDON!'

'What? Fuck, man. What?'

'Last hope of mankind,' whispers dog.

I sigh.

The house at the address Armitage sent us to doesn't look any different to any of the other houses around it. In fact, it's pretty much identical. Victorian, three stories high, the drab facade broken only by curtained windows and a single black painted door. There's a tiny brass plaque screwed to the wall next to the door. I have to lean forward to read it.

The Accendere Club.

I knock on the door. It's so thick my knuckles barely make a sound, but almost immediately the door swings open to reveal a woman wearing a tux tailored to her lean frame. Her black hair is pulled back in a tight ponytail. She cocks her head slightly and stares at me and the dog.

'Wrong address,' she says.

I decide very quickly not to give her my usual attitude. I get the feeling that she could tie me in knots while holding a drink and still not spill a drop.

'I'm here to see Cal Winters.'

'You a member?'

'No.'

'Then you can't come in.'

'Please? It's pretty important.'

-Please? The hell's got into you? Flash your wand or something. And before you do something unfortunate, I don't mean the one in your pants.-

'He'll want to see us,' I say. 'Can you just tell him Armitage sent us?'

'Wait here.' She turns away, then pauses and points at the dog. 'Don't you move. I don't like the look of you.'

She disappears.

'She's got the measure of you,' I say.

'Fuck off.'

She's left the door open, revealing a large entrance hall lit by elaborate chandeliers and tasteful lamps. The floor is a rich, dark wood, polished to a shine. The walls are burgundy, covered in expensively-framed oil paintings. Fluted columns hold up a panelled ceiling and there are carved busts positioned every six feet or so.

'Bit over the top, isn't it?' says the dog, peering inside.

The woman comes back and jerks her head for us to enter.

'Even him?' I ask, pointing at the dog. 'Because he can wait outside.'

'Nah, it's cool. We have a few spirit guides in tonight anyway.'

That's a surprise. Spirit guides are only supposed to be for newbies to the magic world. I'm a special case. See, I haven't decided on a magical focus yet, so the dog sticks around, ostensibly to guide me in the mysterious and hidden world of shinecraft.

I mean, that's his excuse. Me, I think he just enjoys hanging out with me. I don't mind. I kind of like having him around too. He's grown on me. Like mould. Or a slightly amusing skin rash.

'I'm Skye,' says the woman as she closes the door behind us. 'Any problems, I deal with them. You cause any problems, I deal with you.'

'On your own?' I ask. 'What about backup?'

She looks at me for a moment then slowly blinks her eyes. We're immediately surrounded by another twenty Skyes, identical to the first but all moving independently to each other.

'I'm my own backup.'

'Fair enough.'

She blinks again and her doubles vanish.

'Nice party trick,' says the dog.

'It comes in handy.'

Skye leads us through the entrance hall and along a wide corridor. I check the marble busts as we pass. I see John Dee, Simon Magus, Socrates, even Aleister Crowley, plus a few magicians from the old days I don't recognise. The oil paintings on the walls show important events in the hidden histories of mankind (as the pretentious magician who decided to be our official historian put it).

Skye pauses before a set of ornate double doors and glances over her shoulder. 'Just behave, OK? Go see Winters, keep it quiet, and I won't have to kill you.' She looks me up and down. 'Who knows. I might even let you back in someday.'

She winks at me, then pushes the doors open and moves aside. Beyond is a set of stairs leading down into a vast dining room. Nearly all the tables are occupied and the sounds of low conversation and the clink of silver cutlery on incredibly expensive china murmurs quietly throughout the room. An ornate bar travels the length of the wall to my left. Behind the bar are mirrored shelves covered with bottles, some of them glowing with energy or filled with coloured smoke. The conversation drops slightly as we appear, people frowning at us like we're invading their private space. Which I suppose we are, but screw them.

I see Winters sitting at a table next to a window facing the street. He's on his own, sipping a Guinness, while others around him drink wine from expensive crystal glasses. He's wearing jeans and a black hoodie. Classy dresser this guy.

I sit down opposite him. He nods at me.

'Didn't take you for the gentleman's club type,' I say.

He grins. 'Oh, I'm not. They hate me here. I just come because it annoys them.' He pauses. 'Plus they let members run a tab. Which is handy when you're as broke as I am.'

'You still have to pay eventually.'

'Sure. But you know how it is. I might die before then.' He takes a gulp of his Guinness and winks. 'Fingers crossed.'

'I might be able to help you with that.'

'With what?'

'Dying horribly.'

He narrows his eyes slightly. 'You have officially intrigued me. Continue.'

So I tell him everything. About the Old Ones and the prison and the locks. By the time I'm finished the guy is practically vibrating with excitement.

'I fucking *knew* there was something dodgy about this city.'

'Did you now?' I say. 'Funny how people always know something after they've been told it.'

He waves this away. 'I don't mean that. My research into the Fae always had this massive hole in it. Omissions from everyone I talked to. But so many gaps from so many different people eventually form a shape, know what I mean? I just never knew what it was.'

'I'm happy for you. You can finally write that book two people will buy and then not read. So, you in?'

'In?'

'For the heist, moron,' says the dog.

He leans back in his chair and looks around the dining room. Someone two tables over is staring at him. An old guy with white hair swept back from his head. I notice that other guests are giving him dirty looks too. A woman with an owl standing on a perch next to her chair won't take her eyes off him, and what appears to be a table of Chinese children whispering to each other behind their hands look like they want to rip him to pieces. (As they talk to each other, faint lights float in the air above their table. I look closer and see the light is actually five ethereal snakes, twining sinuously together, in constant motion.) Another table has a short woman with a ferret perched on her shoulder. She winks at Winters and he looks away with a flush of embarrassment.

'Yeah, sure,' he says. 'I'm in. Sounds fun.'

'I know, right?' says the dog.

'Great. I'll be in touch after we've seen our contact. Be ready. It will be tonight.'

'Sure.' He gestures for a waiter and points to his empty glass.

Winters sees my look. 'What? I'm fortifying my body for the trials ahead.'

Half an hour later the dog and I arrive at the location Dagda gave us. It looks like an old workhouse or an abandoned factory, with a severe blocky shape, red brick walls, and soot-stained chimneys. We cross the concrete courtyard and stop before the battered door.

A little slit about eight feet from the floor slides open to reveal frowning yellow eyes surrounded by grey-green skin. I didn't even get a chance to knock.

The owner of said eyes grunts.

'Dagda sent us,' I say. 'He said we're to meet the Queen.'

The eyes flicker and peer down to look at the dog.

'He's with me,' says the dog.

'Ignore him,' I say. 'He thinks he's funny.'

The wooden slit slides closed again. I glare at the dog. 'You're not allowed to talk to strangers. I told you that before.'

'I was just trying to be friendly.'

'Don't.'

I knock.

The slit opens once more but this time I'm holding the coin Dagda gave me. Yellow-eyes stares at it a moment, then grunts again.

The slit closes. I hear a number of locks sliding and clunking, and the door finally opens to reveal the biggest – ogre? I think it's an ogre – I've ever seen. It's very old school. Muscles popping out of muscles and shoulders so wide it can't walk through doors straight on.

'CrossFit really does seem to be taking off,' says the dog.

The ogre grunts again and turns away, heading down a long, bare corridor. The dog and I follow after, our feet clomping over wooden floorboards. I can hear shouts and screams in the distance, growing louder as we move along the passageway.

Finally the ogre pushes open a heavy door and the sounds hit me like a punch to the chest. Screaming, shouting, loud cheers and swearing, the breaking of glass.

We leave the corridor and step into a massive warehouse space surrounded by balconies high up on the walls. Hundreds of people ... no ... hundreds of *orisha* fill the room, all of them gathered around a circular ring in the centre of the floor space. I peer over the heads of those in front of me and see that inside the ring are two more massive ogres bare knuckle boxing.

'Nice!' shouts the dog. 'Give me some money. I want to place a bet.'

I look around in awe. The balconies and stands soar above me, packed with spectators. The noise is constant, an aural assault that buffets me from all sides; screams, cries, cheers. Fiddles and drums struggle vainly to be heard above the din.

This is something new. I don't think we've got this back in Durban. The orisha in London, the Fae, the vampires, all the others, they seem to mingle and live together in a way that we don't have back in Durban. Maybe it's the city itself. Maybe it brings all these creatures together into one massive tribe.

Someone stumbles into me, sending me staggering into the wall. I swear and shove back without thinking. The figure doesn't budge. Maybe because it's a golem. It lets out a booming howl and comes for me. I whip out my wand. The golem looks at it for a moment and then bursts out laughing. I straighten up with a flush of embarrassment. Yeah, I could release my tattoos, but we all know how that goes.

The golem just waves a hand at me and staggers off into the crowd.

'Yeah,' I call out. 'You better run. Before I yank that scroll out your mouth and shove it right up your arse.'

'Way to go, London. That was really intimidating. I nearly crapped myself. The way you whipped that wand out. I thought he was going to start crying.'

'Shut up.'

I look around for our ogre friend, struggling to see through the heaving mass. Why would anyone want to be here? It's disgusting. The stink of sweat only recedes when the stench of fresh vomit swirls around the huge warehouse, pushed by a greasy breeze.

I catch sight of the ogre. He's walking away from us, clearing a massive path through the crowd. The dog and I hurry after as he mounts a set of stairs that gives access to the balconies and booths that circle the walls.

At the top of the steps we follow the ogre around a narrow walkway that goes all the way around the warehouse. I'm distracted by more shouts from below. The boxing ogres are up against the ropes. One is pummelling the other, even though it looks like it's already fallen unconscious. It's being held up by the ropes but his opponent keeps hitting, blood spraying everywhere. The ogre is ripping the poor bastard's face apart, stripping it down to the bone. The crowd is going wild, screaming, shrieking, baying for a kill. The ogre finally steps back and his opponent flops to the ground. I don't reckon he's breathing.

Above the walkway we're standing on is a second tier of viewing booths. It looks like the best place for the rich to view the action, the best place to make sure you're not stuck with all the commoners down below.

We climb up to the viewing deck. It's separated into small entertainment booths fitted with dining tables and, closer to the railings, chairs to view the action below. The booths are all full. And not just with orisha. I see a lot of humans as well. Rich businessmen, Japanese, African, a guy wearing one of those Texan hats. What the hell? Since when did humans get pulled into this world? This is a serious breach of the Covenant.

The ogre stops before a particular booth. There are two people seated behind a small dining table. The ogre leans down to speak to the woman, showing her the coin. The man glances at us over the rim of a wine glass. He's human but she's . . . not. I'm thinking vampire. Then again, maybe not. She doesn't quite have the look of a blood sucker.

The ogre gestures for me to enter the booth. The woman pats the seat between her and the guy. I look at the dog but he's just sitting there, watching me with an amused look.

I sit down between them. The woman's attention is fixed on the ring below.

'Are you the Queen?' I ask.

'Have you put money on the fights?' she asks in a soft voice.

'I . . . no. I haven't.'

'You should. The twins are fighting. Sien and Dras.'

She smiles and blinks slowly. I think she's on something. 'They say they are tense with each other. And believe me, you do not want those two tense.'

She's speaking as if I should know who she's talking about. 'You ever seen either of them without their shirts on?' she asks.

'No. I actually don't—'

The woman gestures down her side, from her chest to her hip. 'They've both got these scars here. Deep, nasty scars.'

'Sure. That's a shame.'

'I asked Sien what it was from.'

She looks at me expectantly.

'What did she say?' I finally ask. She seems to expect it.

'She said when they were children they were at an orphanage. The woman who ran it sold them both to a man called Trent. He ran dog fights, then moved up to caged goblin fights. But this Trent, he thought he'd got something good with Sien and Dras. They were, what, seven, eight? Even then they were a bit . . . odd. It was like they could read each other's minds, knew when the other was in trouble. So this Trent wants to make this link even stronger. To use it for fighting. Do you know what he does? Guess.'

'He'll never guess,' says the man.

'I know he won't. You won't,' the woman says to me. 'This Trent *stitches* them together. Every morning, he stitches them together with this thick twine the butchers use. Then they go through their combat drills. All day. Learning to fight as a single unit. When they messed up, or fell over, the stitches ripped.'

I look between the woman and the guy, trying to see if this is some sort of joke.

'This went on for a year. Every day, he would stitch them together, run them through drills.'

Another fight is about to start. A pair of goblins armed with a single mace each. 'Is that them?' I ask, nodding toward the arena. 'Sien and Dras?'

The woman bursts out laughing. The guy next to me sniggers. I would really like to punch him.

'Bless,' he says.

'No, that is not them.'

The goblins start to fight. One is about two heads taller than the other. He steps forward and swings his mace. The smaller goblin throws up his wooden shield up to protect himself. The mace connects with a tremendous thud. The crowd screams. First contact. The smaller goblin scurries away and his opponent chases after him, screaming.

'Are you the Queen?' I ask again.

'I am not the Queen.'

'Then can you take me to her? Dagda set it up.'

'In good time.'

The smaller goblin throws his shield over his shoulder. It hits the taller one in the head, knocking him to the ground. The smaller one stops running and scurries back, swinging his mace. The fallen goblin brings up his own shield and the mace hits the wood and sticks. The larger goblin holds on to it and gets to his knees. He yanks his arm, pulling the mace out of the smaller goblin's hand. Then he swings his own weapon around in an arc.

It connects with the smaller goblin's head. There's an explosion of blood and brains and the creature crumples to the ground.

The victor raises his arms in the air, turning a slow circle as the cheers and boos echo around the warehouse.

'Look,' I say. 'I really need to see the Queen.'

'Sien and Dras are fighting soon.'

'I really don't give a shit about that.'

-I do. Sounds like it will be amazing,- says the dog.

'Just tell me where the Queen is and I'll let you watch your fights.'

The woman sighs and gets slowly to her feet. She takes my hand and leads me out of the booth.

-*I'm waiting here*,- says the dog. -*I want to watch the psychic twins fight.*-

The woman leads me back down the stairs and back into the very first corridor. She opens one of the doors that leads off from the passage and steps into a large office. A tidy table, some empty bookshelves, and a milk crate on the floor that someone uses as a chair. She opens another door to reveal a set of stairs heading down beneath floor level.

We take the stairs down into a basement. She flicks a switch and yellow light floods the room. I look around. It looks like the kind of place serial killers tie up their victims. Water seeps down the brick walls. Green mould grows near the floor. I can smell mustiness and damp earth and . . . something else. Wet fur. The woman moves to the far wall and reaches up to touch a brick that looks exactly like every other brick in the room.

A section of the wall grinds slowly aside, revealing a dark tunnel moving from left to right.

'Oh for fuck's sake.' I take a step forward, then jerk back, my hand over my nose. 'What the hell is that smell?'

'The sewers.'

I look at her. 'The sewers?'

She nods and smiles lazily.

'The Queen lives in the sewer?'

Her smile fades and she frowns in puzzlement. 'Yes,' she says. 'Obviously. She's the *Queen*.'

She clicks her tongue in irritation and enters the tunnel, heading to the left. She flicks on a battery-powered torch, illuminating old, crumbling stones.

I sigh and follow after her, wading through ankle deep water. 'Where does this lead?' I ask.

'You'll see. Nowhere you'll expect. But exactly where you need to go.'

Jesus Christ . . .

After a few minutes, I notice there are ledges running along both sides of the tunnel. I climb out of the water and use them instead, watching the woman wading happily along, splashing through the sewer water.

She stops after another five minutes and climbs up onto the ledge opposite me. Then she turns sideways and disappears through a narrow crack in the wall.

I cross the waterway and follow after. I have to turn sideways to fit into the hole. The sides scrape my ribs and I have to fight down a wave of claustrophobia as I spend a few seconds trying to pull myself through a particularly narrow section. After about ten feet the crack opens up again and I stumble out into a vast chamber. The ceilings are high, the floor tiled. Three rows of pillars recede far into the darkness.

There's a golden glow spilling out into the chamber up ahead. As we draw closer I see that the light is coming from beyond an archway that leads out of the chamber.

'I do not go in there,' says the woman nervously. 'I will leave you to the Queen.'

Without another word, she heads back the way we came. I consider asking her to wait, but it was pretty straightforward getting here. I don't think I'll get lost.

I step through the arch and follow a short stone ramp that leads into a large room absolutely filled with antique furniture. Old fashioned lanterns illuminate wall-mounted tapestries, mahogany chairs and rich, thick carpets piled on top of one another. I see about ten different dining room tables, all of them at least three hundred years old.

'Sit,' whispers a voice.

I hesitate, then pick a wingback chair close to the entrance.

A shuffling sound comes from the other side of the room. I wait, ready to grab my wand should anything go wrong.

I'm going to tell you this now. I was pretty proud of myself for not even jumping a little bit when the Queen comes into view. Why, you ask? Because the Queen happens to be a five-foot-tall rat.

She moves slowly into the light, studying my reaction as she comes. I can see she's old. Her fur probably used to be brown, but now it's streaked with white. She only has one eye, and it's albino pink. The other one is nothing but a puckered socket. Gold necklaces hang around her neck.

'I am Queen Rat,' she says proudly.

'Are you now?'

'Do you know of me?'

I wonder if I should lie. She might get insulted if I say no.

She chuckles, obviously knowing what I'm thinking. 'Don't worry, boy. Not many of your kind do. Not anymore. I was at my prime in the 19th century. I watched over the toshers and the gatherers of the pure. The children who hunted through the sewers for scraps and treasure. I was their queen.'

'And they didn't freak out when they saw you?'

'Cheeky bastard. But no, they didn't. 'Course I didn't walk up to them like this. I would appear as a beautiful woman. When they came of age they would make love to me and I would give them my favour.' She chuckles. 'If they showed me a good time, that is.'

'I'm not doing that,' I say quickly. 'If it's a choice between that and letting the Old Ones break out and take over the world, then the world is shit out of luck.' I pause a second. 'No offense.'

'None taken. You're not my type anyway. Too old.' She lies down on a gold brocaded couch. 'Now, it's late and I've actually got three very accommodating young men in my back room, so tell me what you want.'

'Oh. OK. Dagda said you do a bit of smuggling. From Faerie?'

'Now why on earth would he tell you that?'

'Does it matter? He says he'll owe you a favour if you get me and my people in.'

'To Tír na nÓg?'

'Yes.'

'But you're human.'

'Is that a problem?'

'Well . . . I suppose not. There are humans there. Changelings taken from their cribs. Idiots who fall asleep on fairy rings, that kind of thing.'

And daughters stolen from their families.

The Queen looks thoughtfully at me. 'Dagda really said he'd owe me a favour?'

'And he'd pay you.'

She waves that away. 'The favour is more valuable.' Queen Rat's whiskers twitch. 'Why do you want in?'

'We . . . want to break into a bank and steal something.'

'A heist?'

'A heist.'

'How delightful.' She stares at me for a long moment. 'Fine. It's a deal. I will send word to one of my people in Faerie and tell him to get the ball rolling. He is good. He will have information about the bank for you when you arrive.'

'Thank you. But this is really urgent. We have to go as soon as possible.'

'Tonight?'

'Tonight. Within the next couple of hours.'

Queen Rat sighs. 'Fine. Meet me in Hyde Park. By Wellington's Arch.'

I nod. 'When?'

'Half an hour.' She pauses and glances again over her shoulder. 'Better make it an hour. I'll send word through right now, though. My contact will make a start.'

She picks something up and throws it at me. I just manage to catch it before it smacks me in the face. It's a flashlight.

'Good luck. Don't take a wrong turn. People die down here.'

'Thanks. See you in an hour.'

And that's that. Passage arranged into Faerie.

Where I can find Cally.

16

The Contact

Armitage, the dog and I arrive at Hyde Park Corner an hour later. This isn't ideal. Far from it. It's great I'm going to Faerie, but I like to plan my suicide missions. It feels like things are moving too fast. Events are running out of my control.

We pause beneath the centre arch leading into the park. There are two more arches to either side, interspersed with high columns. The grass glitters with frost. Somewhere in the distance, someone is screaming 'Jingle Bells' at the top of his voice.

'So . . . what now?' asks Armitage.

'She said to wait by Wellington's Arch.'

'Lead on, Macduff.'

We enter the park. I spot our destination immediately. The huge stone structure is like a beacon in the night, concealed lighting shining up the walls and illuminating the bronze statue. I squint at it. Looks like a load of horses and an angel.

'That's the Angel of Peace descending on the Quadriga,' says Armitage.

'What the hell's a Quadriga?' asks the dog.

'A four-horsed chariot,' I say absently, studying our surroundings.

'So where the hell is this queen of yours?' Armitage asks.

'Waiting,' says a voice from the other side of the arch.

Queen Rat appears around the statue, the lights tinting her fur yellow.

'Fuck me, you weren't joking, were you?' says Armitage. She nods. 'Good to meet you, your Majesty.'

Queen Rat nods regally. 'Is this all of you?'

I check my watch. 'No. There's supposed to be one more. He's late.'

'Fashionably late,' says Winters, strolling toward us along the path. He's wearing a thick, black trench coat, hands shoved deep into the pockets. He nods at Armitage. 'All right, boss?'

'Always.'

I turn to Queen Rat. '*Now* we're all here.'

'Not quite. Follow me.'

She leads the way deeper into the park, following the wide walkway past dark trees. She turns left and crosses a large sward of grass, finally leading us on to the wide footpath that follows the bank of the Serpentine River.

'Now, it's very important you don't panic or freak out,' says Queen Rat.

'Why would we freak out, pet?'

'I am not your pet,' says Queen Rat coldly.

'Sorry, luv. Figure of speech. Why would we freak out?'

She doesn't answer, but instead turns and makes her way to the river bank. The four of us hang back as Queen Rat goes down on all fours and puts her snout into the river. She waits there for a second, then stands up.

A moment later there is a disturbance in the water. A bright green glow spreads out beneath the surface, undulating toward us. Then a head slowly breaks the surface. The glow is caused by the creature's large eyes. They flicker and pulse with a sickly emerald light.

But that isn't the worst of it. The lower half of the creature's face is horribly misshapen. Her jaw hangs down to her chest, swinging like a pendulum. Her mouth is a gaping black hole inside of which the same sickly green light flickers. Her black gums are bleeding a constant stream of thick, dark blood that trickles down over her chin and drips into the water. I'm not sure if it's the hundreds of tiny, pointed teeth that make its gums bleed or something else.

'Peg Powler,' says Queen Rat in satisfaction. 'How are you, my dear?'

In answer, Peg Powler opens her mouth even wider. She lifts her head to the sky and screams, a high-pitched keening that raises the hair on the back of my neck.

Peg Powler wades out of the water, and as she does so, the glow in her eyes fades to reveal surprisingly soft brown eyes. She shakes her head briskly and her jaw snaps up, pulling into place with a series of loud cracks that sound like breaking bones. I'm surprised to see she looks like a young girl, only about twelve years old.

'Why is she coming with us?' I ask.

'You'll need her,' says the Queen.

I look at Peg Powler. She has an emaciated frame and is only about five foot three. She looks like she would snap if you sneezed on her.

'Don't be so quick to judge,' says Queen Rat.

'Thing is, we don't really need her,' says Armitage. 'Reckon we've got it covered.'

'Oh, do you? You think you've got it covered? Number one, I don't care. If you want my help getting in to Faerie, Peg goes with you. It's not a discussion. And two, what are you going to do once you get to Faerie? You know where Falias is? You have contacts who can help you?'

Armitage says nothing.

'Exactly. Peg is my tribe. She's the one that goes to Faerie for me when I need . . . items. Items that I don't want anyone else to know about. Understand?'

Armitage just waves her hand in irritation. 'Fair enough. She won't turn on us though, will she?'

'I am standing right here,' says Peg Powler. 'Why do you talk as if I am invisible?'

Armitage looks at her in surprise. 'Fair enough, pet,' she says. 'We'll just ignore all the stories about you pulling little kiddies into the water to drown them. Probably all just made up anyway.'

'No,' says Peg matter-of-factly. 'They are all true. I do not like children. Horrible little bags of disease is what they are. It's their own fault for coming too close to my waters.' She pauses and smiles shyly. 'I like to eat them.'

'Oh.' Armitage takes a moment to readjust. 'Right then. Queenie? Can you take us through?'

'Indeed. And make sure you remind Dagda he owes me a very large favour for this.'

'We will, don't worry.'

Queen Rat leads us back across the footpath and into the trees. She keeps walking until she comes to two trees planted closely together.

'Are you ready?'

I look at the trees. 'Where's the door?'

'You just pass between the trunks.'

'Isn't that a bit inconvenient for people taking a walk through the park?'

'Don't be simple,' says Queen Rat patiently. 'I have to open the doorway for it to work.'

Queen Rat turns to Peg Powler and the two give each other a brief hug. Then Peg walks between the trees . . .

. . . and winks out of existence.

'Off you go, then,' says Queen Rat. 'When you wish to come back, return to the same spot you arrive at. The door will open for you.'

'Thank you,' says Armitage. She looks at me, Winters, and the dog. 'Ready for a trip?'

Winters shrugs.

The dog wags his tail. 'Fuck yeah. Gonna get me a Christmas heist. Shit – wait! We didn't get our mp3 players!'

'Too late.'

'Aw, man. Come on. I wanted to load it up with my Christmas tunes. Can't we go buy one quick?'

'No time,' I snap.

'Jesus, OK. No need to bite my head off.'

'You OK?' asks Armitage.

I nod, but I'm not really. I'm nervous. Terrified. This is a real chance to find Cally, but I can't make the same mistake I made last time. I can't think about her at the expense of the rest of the world. I *know* that, but what if I'm not strong enough? What if it comes down to one or the other again?

Armitage nudges me and we all walk between the trees. There's no sensation of movement. Just a brief moment of darkness and then I'm walking across wooden floorboards in a small, cluttered hut.

I stop moving. The others are by my side and Peg Powler is looking out the window. I can see grey skies and pouring rain.

I look around. There's an old, rickety bed, an ancient-looking closet, a table and chairs that've seen better days, a collection of broken benches and stools against one wall, and an open fire pit in the centre of the room.

'Wow,' says the dog drolly. 'So amaze. Much magical.'

'Yeah, not really what I was picturing when I thought of Tír na nÓg,' says Armitage.

'Do not insult my home,' says Peg without turning around. 'Or I will disembowel you all and let the steam of your freshly opened intestines warm my skin.'

Hearing that kind of thing coming from the mouth of someone that looks like a twelve year old girl is incredibly unsettling. I mean, it would be unsettling hearing it from *anyone*, but from a child? My skin tries to crawl off my body.

The dog laughs. 'She's psychotic. I like her.'

Peg Powler gestures at the closet. 'There are things to disguise your clothes in there.'

I open the doors. There are wooden hangers holding . . . well, what looks like incredibly well-made cosplay costumes. The kind Peter Jackson would stick in his movies. I browse through them and grab the coolest one. Leather jerkin, dark brown cloak. Black boots. There are even those things that go over your forearms, stitched leather covered with intricate designs.

Winters goes for an all-black ensemble, tastefully set off by a red-lined charcoal grey cloak, and Armitage picks what appear to be some kind of priest's robes.

I stare at her. 'Why?'

She gestures at me. I'm busy trying to lace up the trousers and having some trouble pulling them tight enough. 'Look at you. I don't want to have to mess round with all that if I need to take a leak.'

I frown at her. 'Armitage, you're a revenant. Do you even go to the toilet?'

'Well . . . no. But the point remains.'

The dog is sitting there watching us all with an amused look in his eyes. I hold up what appears to be a Robin Hood hat, complete with a feather.

'Yeah. Not gonna happen,' says the dog.

'Come on, man. You want me to wear Christmas hats, you have to wear this.'

The dog narrows his eyes at me.

'I'm serious. No Christmas hats. Even on Christmas day.'

'You wouldn't.'

'Try me.'

He doesn't say anything, so I place the hat on his head. It doesn't really stay in place, so I pull a leather lace from one of the boots in the cupboard and use it to tie the hat on his head.

He sits there looking decidedly unimpressed. 'I hate you so much,' he says. 'Seriously. All those times I said I hated you? I didn't. I realise that now. That hate was nothing. It was a microscopic semen stain on the hotel mattress of life. But this hate I feel now is so much more. It's bukkake-level compared to what came before.'

'Your analogy is incredibly unsettling,' says Armitage. 'And that's saying something coming from me.'

'Whatever.' The dog shakes himself, obviously hoping to dislodge the hat. But it stays in place. 'Right,' he says, attempting to sound like his normal self. 'We have the cleric, the . . .' he looks at me, '. . . rogue?' He looks to Winters. 'And the . . . I don't know . . . What are you? A knight?'

'Don't forget our bard,' I say.

He starts to ask who, but I'm grinning at him so he sighs instead. 'Let's just go.'

Peg leads us out of the cabin and into the forest. The rain is constant, a steady downpour that quickly seeps into my bones. The cloak protects me from the worst of it, but Armitage has no such luck. Two minutes in and she's soaked through. Lucky for her she can't feel the cold anymore.

We push through the fronds of fern that cover the forest floor. A cold mist wraps around the trunks of the ancient, twisted trees. I can tell you this – the novelty of marching through a thick fantasy-type forest wears off in about . . . three minutes. Why the hell couldn't the door just open up inside the city? But, *no*, too easy.

The one thing that keeps me entertained is trying to spot all the Fae creatures attempting to hide from us. They're really bad at it. There are a shit ton of brownies, spriggans, and even a few gnomes. They're all hiding in the undergrowth as if they're posing for a Brian Froud painting.

'You know what all these things are?' I ask Winters.

He glances around. There's movement everywhere. Little

glimpses of black eyes ducking down behind leaves, the shimmer of wings, the rustle of undergrowth.

'Most of them. I mean, we're talking millions of different species. Just like creatures on our world.'

He stops walking and puts a finger to his lips. He lets the others walk ahead. We stand motionless for about thirty seconds, then he points into the trees.

'A ballybog,' he says softly.

I look and see a little creature wading through the mud around a deep puddle. It's ugly as hell and has a nose nearly bigger than its head and a misshapen face. It's entirely covered in mud.

'They protect the peat bogs in Ireland.'

'From what?'

'No one knows. But they get very possessive about their bogs. Try and do anything they don't like and they'll eat your face.'

'Charming.'

Winters points to our right. I see an old man about the height of my shin staring at a bottle of wine that has been tossed to the ground.

'A clurichaun,' says Winters. 'They pick a family and guard their wine cellar. Easiest way to trap one is to toss a bottle of wine in front of it. He won't move till he needs to eat. Then he'll just forage around for worms and stuff. He won't go far.'

There's a flash of movement in a clump of flowers ahead of us.

'That's a heather pixie,' he says. 'They live inside the heather, like Nemo lives in the anemone. They're simple. Not much more than animals.' Winters looks around, then points. I try to follow his gaze but can't see a thing.

'What?'

'There. By the tree root.'

I peer into the gnarled and twisted roots. It takes me a while but then I see it. A little old woman, completely naked, her skin as brown as the tree bark around her. She's just lying there, staring up into the sky.

'What the hell is she doing?'

'She's high. They get addicted to a flower that grows in the forests. It's like LSD to them. All the pixies do it. Makes them very violent though – they're basically a race of junkies and they'll do pretty much anything to get their fix. Think Glasgow on a Friday night after the pubs have closed.'

'Hey!' calls out the dog.

All the Fae creatures around us vanish from sight as the dog appears through the undergrowth. 'There's a road ahead. Come on.'

We start walking again. I pull my hood up and all I can hear is the pattering of rain on my cloak, the rainwater trickling down past my eyes. After a couple of minutes I see Armitage and Peg waiting beneath a copse of trees. I can see a dirt road beyond them, the rain churning it into mud.

'What were you doing?' asks Armitage.

'Sight-seeing. That the road?'

She gives me a look. 'No. That's the *other* big road leading to the city.'

We follow the road for another half an hour before finally cresting a long rise to see the city of Falias spread out below us.

So it turns out Falias is a coastal city. I can see the ocean glinting dully in the distance. But it looks like an earthquake has rocked the area at some point in the past. Spidery, vein-like paths have been gouged through the city, and water has since filled the channels. Some buildings are half-collapsed, while others look like they've had new storeys added on top, the stone a different colour to that beneath. The earthquake must have been worse toward the north, because that part of the city consists of hundreds of small islands, with waterways cutting between buildings and districts, and it looks like barges and canoes are used instead of wagons or ... carts or whatever the hell they use here.

There are two other things vying for my attention. The first, less terrifying thing is the massive wooden ... palace? Temple? Whatever it is, it soars into the sky in the centre of the city, utterly dominating everything around it. It's been designed to look like a tree trunk – shiny and polished, and easily a hundred feet in circumference.

The second, *incredibly* terrifying thing is the vast number of those spider-tree Faeries that are stalking across the city, spindly, segmented legs enabling them to just walk above the buildings and structures, their freaky bodies framed against the grey sky.

I count about thirty of them.

'The Blessed are gaining more power in the city,' says Peg. She spits on the ground. 'They are not nice.'

'And of course that's where we're going,' says Winters.

'You wanted a horrible death, remember?'

As we draw closer to the city, the road changes from a muddy path to a tiled highway about thirty feet wide. I see that the gates set in the high wall are standing open, utterly unguarded. We pass through without any issues, and this makes me very nervous. Any good luck we have now is bound to be offset by terrible luck later on. It's just the way it goes.

We stop walking as we enter the city to get our bearings. Falias is a place of crawling, walking, lumbering chaos. It's every fantasy book you've ever read, every big budget movie you've seen, every cheesy eighties portal fantasy peopled with Jim Henson puppets. The Fae range from tiny sprites flitting through the air, to small spriggans, brownies and gnomes (all using one side of the street), to larger creatures such as elves, giants and dryads (using the other). Fauns and centaurs canter along the cobbles, massive hairy creatures with friendly faces and massive teeth pull wagons and chariots, and dwarves almost buried beneath armour, eyes peering out between helmets and beards, strut around like they own everything they see. There are a thousand other creatures that I have no idea how to identify. Winters looks like a kid on Christmas day, the usual cocky look on his face transformed into utter delight.

'I like this place,' says dog. 'I feel like these guys would be up for a party.'

We start moving again, keeping to the side of the street that the larger creatures use. I nervously watch the skies, wondering if the spider-creatures are some kind of police force, if they'll recognise us as intruders.

'Where are we going?' asks Armitage.

'An inn,' says Peg.

'Yes!' says the dog. 'Do Faeries have sherry? They must do, right? Booze is the first thing any intelligent species invents. Sherry must exist here.'

'Why an inn?' asks Armitage.

'That is where we will find the Queen's contact. He is an awful creature who drinks too much and he falls unconscious every night.'

'Sounds awesome,' says the dog.

Peg eventually leads us down a narrow, muddy lane that borders one of the many river banks that criss-cross Falias. She stops before a sagging, decrepit structure that looks like it's about to collapse in on itself and stares up at a window on the second floor. I follow her gaze. The curtains have been pulled closed, but a lit candle has been placed in the window.

'He is in.'

'He lives here?' asks Winters.

'He likes to be close to his drink.'

'I really like the sound of this guy. London, can't you just quit the Division and buy a pub? That would be amazing. One dog and his man. It would be like an eighties sitcom.'

We all ignore him as Peg leads us along the lane and out into the main street. A mist has started to spread through the city, growing thicker as the afternoon light fades.

Peg pushes open the door to the inn and we follow her into the common room. No one even bothers to look up. It's the Fae equivalent of one of the thousands of faceless pubs dotted around London. Pubs that haven't changed in forty years, with the same fittings, the same scarred tables, and the same nicotine-stained wallpaper. It isn't the kind of place where the curious or even those mildly interested in life come to drink.

We follow after Peg as she climbs the stairs and opens the door to a room. There's a small, wizened man sitting in an armchair, a bottle of booze hugged tightly to his chest. He sits bolt upright when he sees us, his eyes widening in fear.

'It is only me, Scaithe,' says Peg. 'You have nothing to fear.' She pauses. 'Except heart attacks. Or liver damage. Or cancer. What I mean is you have nothing to fear from us.'

'I . . . got the Queen's message.' He struggles out of his chair and moves toward a desk beneath the window. 'It was a . . . difficult request. Four days is not much time . . .'

'Hold on,' I say. 'Four days? She only sent word a few hours ago.'

'Time works differently in Tír na nÓg,' says Peg. 'Now be silent. Scaithe, what did you find?'

The old guy keeps glancing nervously at a closed door off to our right. A bathroom, I assume.

'Scaithe? Did you get the information?'

'I did. Had to grease a lot of palms, but I got it.' He looks to the door again, licks his lips nervously. I don't like the look on his face. It's almost as if—

The door opens suddenly and a tall, regal elf enters the room, wooden sword drawn. He's wearing the same kind of armour as the Marquis had on, covered with elegant sigils and the tree pattern on his chest.

'You will all—'

That's all he gets to say, because Peg Powler launches herself across the room in a blur of speed. Her jaw drops into its terrifying wide maw and her eyes burst to green life as she lands on the elf's chest. He screams, but the sound is quickly cut off as Peg clamps her mouth over his head and jerks back, ripping his head from his body.

We all stand there. Watching in disbelief.

Scaithe stares at the elf in horror as Peg detaches herself from the body. She shakes her head, bringing her mouth back to normal proportions.

'What did you *do*?' Scaithe shouts.

'No,' says Peg in low voice. 'What did *you* do?'

Scaithe pulls his eyes away from the corpse spurting blood all over the wooden floorboards. 'I had no choice,' he says quickly. 'The Queen wanted the information too fast. I got careless. Rushed things. I was caught.' His eyes are pulled back to the body. 'You have to get rid of it. I can't have that in my room!'

'We're not getting rid of anything,' I say.

'You have to. Or . . . or I won't tell you how to get into the bank. Yes. Very tricksy you know. Not just anyone can get in. There are things you have to do first. Get them wrong and alarms go off.'

I look at Armitage. She shrugs. I sigh and gesture at Winters. 'Give me a hand.'

I grab the legs and Winters grabs the arms. We manhandle the body to the window and Armitage opens the curtains to peer out.

'All clear.'

Winters and I half-shove, half-push the body over the sill. It gets stuck halfway over. It looks like the guy is puking over the side.

'Never had to shift a dead body before,' says Winters conversationally. 'You?'

I rack my brains. 'Don't reckon so.'

'Heavier than I thought,' remarks Winters. 'Suppose that's why they call it dead weight.'

'Just get on with it,' snaps Armitage.

We shove the lower half of the body over. It drops straight down and hits the ground with a loud thump.

Armitage picks up the head. 'Coming through,' she says. The head narrowly misses hitting me as it sails out the window.

'Thank the gods,' says Scaithe. 'At least now I . . .'

He trails off, his eyes widening in horror. 'The others.'

'What others?' snaps Armitage.

'There were two more guards. Downstairs.'

As soon as he says it I hear booted feet running up the stairs. I cross the room and grab the sheet from the bed, tossing one end to Armitage. We take it back to the door and I squat down, pulling the sheet low to the ground. Armitage does the same and we pull it tight just as the door bursts inward and two more elves run into the room. The sheet hits them at shin height and they sprawl to the floor, their wooden swords clattering from their hands. Peg is on the move again in an instant, lunging forward, gripping the hair of the elf closest to her. She yanks his head back, then slashes her fingernail across the man's throat.

Blood gushes over her hand and down his chest. She drops him and rushes to the other guard, leaping onto his back as he tries to get to his feet. She bites and tears into the back of his neck, blood spraying out to either side.

I stare in horrified fascination as the first elf thrashes about on the floor, trying desperately to hold the lips of his neck wound together. He stares at me, his eyes wide and beseeching.

Peg is still kneeling on the second one's back. I can hear slurping noises and I realise she's sucking his blood via the massive hole in the back of his neck.

'Uh . . . Peg?' I say.

She turns to stare at me, her green skin now covered in blood.

'We should get out of here. Now, I think.'

There's a little cry of fear behind me. I turn to find Armitage holding a weakly struggling Scaithe at the door.

'Little bastard was trying to do a runner.'

'I'm sorry, OK? I didn't mean to sell you out.' He looks pleadingly at Peg. 'Please don't tell Queen Rat. I've got the intelligence you need. I swear. Let's just get out of here. I'll show you what you need to do.'

17

The Plan

O ne hour later and we've gathered in another hotel room, about three blocks away from the murder inn. (Except for Peg Powler. She slipped into one of the canals as we left the inn, telling us rather ominously that 'she'll be watching us' before vanishing from sight. It's probably better that way. She's too unpredictable.)

This hotel is a lot classier. A proper hotel (I think) and not just a pub. It even has room service.

'First question,' I say. 'Why do you have hotels?'

Scaithe looks at me. 'Well . . . to stay in? Don't you have them over in the Dayside?'

'Yeah, we do. For people who travel.'

'You don't think we travel? There are three other cities within a five-hundred-mile radius. Not to mention towns, hamlets, villages. Where the hell do you think businessmen stay when they come to town?'

'Yeah, London,' says the dog. 'Rein in those preconceived and – frankly – narrow and racist views of Fae society. What's wrong with you?'

'Jesus, fine.' I look at Scaithe. 'Seriously, I just never realised Faerie was like this. It's more . . . advanced than I thought it was. We don't have much intelligence on what goes on here.' I turn to Armitage, 'Right?'

'Sorry, pet. Don't drag me into this.'

I scowl at her and flop onto the couch, folding my arms across my chest.

'Are you sulking?' says the dog in delight.

'Fuck off.'

'You are, aren't you? You're sulking. Like a little baby. Oh, this is brilliant.'

'Dog, I'm going to cut off your booze supply if you don't shut up.'

'Go ahead. I have other sources. You big fucking baby.'

'Nice hat you're wearing,' I say.

The dog's grin vanishes. 'Fuck you.'

Scaithe clears his throat. 'Um . . . would you like to see the wizards who are going to help us?'

'Go on then,' says Armitage. 'You two,' she says, looking at the dog and me. 'Behave yourselves.'

Scaithe approaches a door that opens into the adjoining hotel room. He pulls it open and we're greeted by – I count – seven gnomes having a full-on (but silent) fight. The gnomes are all wearing grubby robes and their faces are twisted with anger as they pummel each other with fists and feet. Some are biting, others are pulling hair, and one of them is kneeling on the chest of another, gripping the trapped gnome's arms and slapping them about his face.

'Stop hitting yourself,' he whispers. 'Stop hitting yourself.'

Scaithe clears his throat.

The gnomes all freeze, staring at us in shock. Then they sheepishly climb to their feet, surreptitiously pushing and shoving each other as they form a line.

'This is the Candlespine family,' says Scaithe. 'They've agreed to help us.'

I can see the family resemblance easily. They all have the same narrow eyes, the same high cheekbones and large noses. They also all have the oversized heads that distinguish gnomes from other Fae. I always think they're going to overbalance, which, I now realise, is also pretty low-key racist. I need to watch that. The Division was talking about doing some courses on inter-species relationships. Reckon I should look into that.

The gnomes all look old, their walnut faces a mass of wrinkles and scars that show a life lived hard. Their eyes reflect the same thing, pain and sadness but also . . . pride? Is that the right word?

Of course this impression is pretty much ruined by the fact that they're all still elbowing each other while trying to stand still and look innocent.

'Stop it,' snaps Scaithe.

The gnomes reluctantly fall into line. The one on the end starts to pick his nose, really getting his finger right up there.

-*Hahahaha, I love these guys,*- says the dog. -*They're going to get us killed.*-

Scaithe points at each of the gnomes in turn. 'This is Dulin, Hulin, Kulin, Vulin, and Sulin. The two ladies over there are Velin and Kelin.'

I glance surreptitiously at Velin and Kelin. They look pretty much the same as the male gnomes, except for a tuft of hair on their chins. I study their faces. I look across at Armitage. She subtly shakes her head and mouths, *Don't*.

Yup. Definitely going to have to take that course.

'The Candlespines have good reason to help us. Their family has been screwed over by the bank and the Blessed. They want their chance for revenge. And don't let appearances deceive you,' says Scaithe. 'Although they look like childish imbeciles – actually, no, even though they *are* childish imbeciles – they're still good at what they do.'

'The best,' says one of the gnomes. The others nod in agreement.

'I wouldn't go *that* far,' says Scaithe. 'You're good. But like . . . *understudy* good, you know? When the main actors are sick, you guys take over.'

'Then who's the main actor?' asks Winters.

'Oh, these three sisters. Amazing at battle magic. They're hired by kings and queens to protect them and take down armies and stuff.'

'So why couldn't we get them?' I ask.

'Hey, we're standing right here,' complains one of the gnomes.

'I think they're over in your world. You guys should watch out for that, actually. Maybe keep your eyes open if you survive this.'

-*Hahahahaha,*- says the dog.

'Actually, now that I think about it, they're the ones who designed the spells for the bank.'

'Seriously?' asks one of the gnomes.

I can't help noticing he suddenly looks worried.

'Yeah.' Scaithe gestures to the table. 'You guys need to read all that.'

I look where he's pointing. The table is covered in rolled up paper, thick files stuffed with documents, and leather bound books.

'What is it?'

'All the information I gathered for you. On the bank, the security, the intruder detectors. Everything you need to break in.' Scaithe pauses. 'Which, I might add, I really don't think you can do. It's impossible.'

'We'll be the judge of that,' says Armitage. 'London? Get to it.'

The planning falls to me because I once mentioned to Armitage that I helped out on a security consult for a bank when I quit the Met. (I was briefly toying with the idea of being a freelance ... something or other, but quickly decided against it when I realised the people I'd have to work for were all rich fuckwits. That was when I moved to L.A. Yeah, I know.

Because you go to L.A. to *get away* from the rich fuckwits, right?)

I take everything into the adjoining room and spend the next three hours reading files. Loads of time, right? When I did it before I had a week to make my report. No such luxury here. I make notes, rub my head, swear, sketch ideas and cross-reference the Faerie magic and spell bibles Scaithe very thoughtfully supplied, read some more, swear some more, drink a thick black herb that is supposed to resemble coffee but really resembles sweet tar, and sink into a dark pit of despair.

Finally, I call the others into the room. Winters is missing in action, so Armitage goes to find him, bringing him back five minutes later.

'Right,' I say, rubbing my head. I have a migraine now. 'Are you all ready to hear this?'

'Not really,' says Winters. 'I was actually having a grand time at the bar. Can we delay it an hour or so? There was a water nymph I think was into me.'

He doesn't seem to be joking. 'No,' I say eventually. 'I can't delay it for an hour or so. We're already down about eight hours.'

'Pity. She looked wild.'

'Keep it in your pants, Winters,' says Armitage. 'That's what got you fired in the first place, remember? And if you're talking about that blue-skinned beauty you were talking to just now, I don't think it was a she.'

'Really?' Winters shrugs. 'Doesn't really bother me.'

'Can we focus here?' I say. Everyone turns their attention back to me. 'Thank you. First things first. Dagda wasn't kidding when he said that this is the most secure bank in Faerie. Hell, I think it's more secure than any of *our* banks.'

'Who would you entrust your porn collection to?' asks Winters. 'If you had to?'

'These guys. Hands down.'

'Respect.'

'First off, there's only one point of access, and that's right at the top of the building, which is itself a hundred feet high. A spell-driven elevator operated by a bank official takes you up to the door. If the bank official breaks contact with a gem stone in the elevator, it stops moving. If the gem stone picks up an increase in heart rate, it stops moving. If the gem stone picks up an increase in perspiration, or panicked breathing, it stops moving.'

'So no distracting the elevator guy,' says Armitage.

'No. Not if you want to get into the bank. Once you get to the top floor there's an enclosed square surrounded by twenty-foot-high walls topped with observation posts. There are wyverns patrolling the top of the wall and the floor is booby trapped. Any unauthorised entry triggers a spell that literally melts the floor away, dropping you into a pit filled with nasty spikes.

'If you're expected, you'll be met by another bank official.' I look over at Armitage and Winters. 'Get this. Your retina is scanned here. *All* eyes in the building are. By tiny invisible sprites that saturate the air. If there's an eye print that's not on the list, the sprites go full Freddy Krueger on the trespasser. No warnings, no slap on the wrist. Full-on ripped apart and eaten.'

'Nasty,' says the dog.

'That's not even the worst of it. Every floor has its own lock, but the locks actually change configuration every hour. The keys are then magically coded to the changed locks.'

'Every hour?' asks Armitage.

'Every hour. Only one key exists for each floor, and they're carried by different officials. So we could get one key, go one floor down, and then we'd be stuck there until we got the key for that floor. And on and on.'

I can see the disappointment on their faces. They're finally realising how impossible this is going to be.

'Hold your tears. I'm not finished yet. Next, there are these . . . magical eyes everywhere. Literally. Big googly eyes positioned all over the bank like cameras. They transfer what they see to a central security room where these live feeds are watched twenty-four seven, and it's this room that controls access to the vaults. If anyone wants to get into their safety deposit box, they're escorted to the vault door where an eye will register their presence. If the bank official is recognised and approved, the vault door will open. If the eye picks up any fear through dilation of the pupil, increased breathing or increased heart rate, the door won't open. This security room is far below ground in a locked off area. There's no access here. And this is where the prisons are, by the way.'

'Prisons?'

'In case anyone is caught trying their luck.'

'Jesus wept,' says Armitage.

'He would if he was trying to break in to this place,' I say.

'How many in this security room?' asks Cal.

'The details are sketchy about that,' I say. 'Obviously the eyes transmit the signals magically, but I don't know how. There must be someone in there monitoring the feeds. Or something.' I shrug. 'That's our main blind spot, the security room.'

'So . . . our little friend here was right?' asks Winters. 'We can't get in?'

I pause and take a sip of my coffee.

'Oh! Oh! Look!' says the dog. 'Wait for it. He thinks he's about to do the clever-dick equivalent of the superhero landing.'

I put my drink down again. 'There might be a way.'

'Boom!' says the dog. 'Look at that smug face. No wonder people hate you.'

'Out with it then,' says Armitage.

'A few years back there was an attempt to break into the bank. The perps were old school. Kidnapped the family of one of the senior partners and threatened to kill them if the guy didn't do what they wanted.'

'Did they make it?' asks the dog.

'Nearly. They got into the vaults but triggered one of the failsafes and ran. They killed the hostage before they legged it. Killed his family too. The owner of the bank spent a month tracking these guys down and then took them to the prison in the bank. He kept them alive for three days, stripping the skin from their bodies and rubbing salt and lemon into the . . . well, the exposed muscles and everything.'

'And how does this help us?' asks Armitage.

'Because after that robbery, the bank overhauled its security protocols. That's when all this new stuff was added. But . . . here's the thing, and this is what might help us. There is one owner of the bank, OK? And beneath him are two senior partners. They're . . . not nice people.'

Scaithe spits on the carpet. 'They are murderers. Horrible people.'

The gnomes grumble and nod.

'The first guy is a priest called Madir. This guy is supposed to be one of the Blessed. Holier than holy, right? Except, this particular priest has a fondness for young Fae children.'

'Jesus,' says Armitage. 'Do all priests have to be such walking fucking clichés?'

'It comes with the robes,' I say. 'You should watch yourself.'

'Fuck off.'

'The second guy is called Dumas. He's a gangster. And *he's* been the point of contact for the Blessed finding their feet in London's streets. He took out rival gang leaders by dipping them in a magma stream that runs beneath the ground somewhere around here. Scaithe? How many did you say?'

'Confirmed? Eighty-seven that he personally had a hand in. Over a thousand that he ordered.'

I let that sink in for a moment. 'He's also how the owner of the bank managed to gain traction in Falias.'

'The owner?' says Armitage. 'That guy who tortured the robbers?'

'Yeah, and get this, he's from our world. Human. His name is Dragoslav Revic. He was a general in the Yugoslav People's Army back in the nineties and was big buddies with Slobodan Milošević. That saying, you can judge a person by the company he keeps? Yeah, that. He stumbled across the hidden world during the war. Made contact with Dumas and helped him take over the city. God knows what treasures are hidden in that bank. Probably Nazi gold.'

Winters raises a hand. 'I'm still waiting to see how this helps us.'

'I'm getting to that – just setting the scene first. See, besides the incredibly thorough security measures I've already described, they've put in a failsafe in case someone targets the senior partners again. A magical kill switch. In the case of their deaths they don't want anyone getting hold of the bank, right? So if one of them dies? Nothing. But if *both* partners die, a lockdown is instantly put in effect. A sort of . . . stasis bubble. No magic works inside the bubble, except for some of the security measures, obviously. The bank staff are all sent home and a team of tactical security personnel are sent in to protect the vaults. These guys are good. Apparently they've fought in a lot of wars and skirmishes here. I mean, if these guys were in the army when it attacked Minas Tirith, the ring would have been in Sauron's hands before the end of Two Towers and they would have rounded up Frodo and Sam and shot them through the back of the head.'

'I'm still not seeing our opening,' says Winters.

I smile at him. 'We're going to kill the two senior partners, Madir and Dumas.'

I wait for a reaction, studying their faces. 'Anybody have any moral objections to that?'

Winters shrugs and looks at Armitage. Armitage shakes her head. 'Sounds like we'd be better off without them.'

'So let me get this straight,' says the dog. 'Your plan is to assassinate the two senior partners of this bank, purposefully triggering the ultra-high-super-duper-anti-robber failsafes put in place to stop the exact thing we're about to attempt?'

'Pretty much.'

The dog wheezes out a laugh. 'We really do need a cool musical score for this, man. This is gonna be epic.'

'Great. But we need some stuff first. And we're going to have to move fast.'

18

The Heist

The Priest

Another four hours later and I'm standing beneath the cold grey sky, studying the outside of a Blessed temple from across the street. It doesn't look very . . . nature-like. I imagined it to be like the temple I saw in the centre of the city. I've seen a couple of the spider-tree Faeries stalking around the city, but managed to duck out of sight every time they came close.

A broad flight of steps leads up to a shaded portico held up by five marble pillars. Wide double doors stand open and two small torches are just visible in the dim interior of the temple. Obviously, the whole nature worship thing doesn't extend to the actual priests of the Blessed. One set of commandments for everyone, and none for them?

Typical priests.

-*So . . . murdering innocent people,*- says the dog. -*You seriously OK with this?*-

-*They're not innocent. You heard. These guys are bad news. And two deaths to prevent an invasion? You don't think that's a good trade?*-

-*The needs of the many outweigh the needs of the few, right?*-

-*What have I told you about quoting Star Trek at me?*-

-*Fine. My point remains, though. If they hadn't been terrible people? If they were saints? Proper religious Fae who just wanted what was best for others?*-

-No religion just wants the best for others.-

-Don't avoid the question.-

-Fine. Yes. I would still do the same. Like I said, two against millions. If I had to sacrifice myself I would.-

-Yeah, but you're insane and have no survival instinct.-

I ignore him and watch the church. A few Blessed monks draped in green-brown robes move up and down the steps, going about their business. The Fae that are walking the streets close to the church all studiously ignore them, looking away as the priests pass. No one wants to be noticed by these guys.

This kind of thing . . . it usually takes weeks of surveillance and planning. Not that I do this kind of thing often, but it's pretty obvious that if you're going to take someone out you have to plan it carefully. There's no room for screw ups.

But no. In typical Delphic Division style we're performing a double hit within an hour of each other, after a couple of hours of planning.

Go us.

Scaithe's intelligence told us that Madir prays at a certain time every day. He's due in half an hour or so, so the dog and I cross the street and walk into the church, nodding respectfully at any priests we pass.

The interior of the church is dimly lit. We're standing in an atrium with a statue of what I assume is Cernunnos staring at me. A massive, muscled figure covered in bristly hair with long, twisted antlers rising up from his head. Even the statue exudes . . . strength. The unstoppable power of nature.

-Scary guy,- says dog.

-Yeah.- I study the statue a moment longer, my stomach dropping. I really don't like the look of this god. Gods in general piss me off, but their motivations are usually pretty basic. They're like children. Jealous. Power hungry. Demanding

attention. Fearing abandonment. But this guy . . . I don't know. I don't think he's going to be easy to figure out, and that scares me.

The dog and I enter the main section of the church. The ceiling arches high above us, held up by intricately carved wooden pillars that travel the length of the room. A second statue of the Horned God has been raised against the far wall, this one about five times larger than the one in the atrium. It towers over everything, the god glowering down on everyone in its presence. The antlers extend outward, forming a branch-like covering over the worshippers that kneel on the hard wooden floor.

I kneel down close to the back of the room, wincing as my knees bump against the floor. The dog lies down and rolls onto his side, closing his eyes.

-What are you doing?-

-Taking a nap.-

-Now?-

-Why not? I'm sure I'll wake up when the shit hits the fan and your ass needs rescuing.-

About ten minutes after the dog and I entered the church, one of the gnomes enters, dragging his ludicrously long robe behind him. I couldn't tell you which one he is. I'm thinking Dulin? Possibly Hulin.

He kneels down on the right side of the room and bows his head. Over the next ten minutes three of his brothers file in, some sitting in plain view, others moving to kneel in the shadow of the pillars.

Not too long after, Madir arrives. He has three bodyguards – huge, burly creatures that look like they could be half-orc, half-human.

Madir kneels down while his bodyguards split up. One stays with him, one moves to the left of me and the other stands by the door.

My heart starts racing and I tense, readying myself.

The signal comes. A phlegmy, coughing fit courtesy of one of the gnomes. It means he's cast a cocoon of silence around the room.

The gnome behind me unleashes a ball of fire directly at Madir.

At the last instant it's deflected. It bounces off some kind of invisible shield and shoots straight up, folding around the antlers and scorching the ceiling.

There's a moment of silence, and then chaos erupts. The worshippers scramble up and flee. The bodyguard standing behind Madir pulls a wand (hah, what a novice) from his jerkin and points it straight at the gnome. Who just happens to be directly behind me. I drop to the floor and a fireball soars over my head. There's a muffled curse behind me. I throw a look over my shoulder and see . . . Vulin? slapping out flames on his arm.

'He's got an invisible shield!' shouts one of the gnomes from behind a pillar.

'No fucking shit, Sulin,' shouts another. 'I was watching that fireball and when it flew up to the ceiling I honestly wondered what was happening. Thank God you're here to show us all how magnificent your powers of observation are.'

'Fuck you!'

'No, fuck you! I hate you, Hulin. You're a dick!'

'Not as big a one as you.'

I listen to this in amazement. Madir is standing up now, staring at Vulin dancing around the church floor behind me, trying to put the fire out. The bodyguard closest to him pulls him back, his wand pointing in the direction of the gnomes hiding behind the pillars. The bodyguard to my left has his wand pointed at Vulin, and the one who was covering the door is now moving toward the pillar where Sulin is hiding.

Before he gets there a fireball erupts from the shadows. The bodyguard tries to duck, but the fireball engulfs the top half of his body, wrapping around him like napalm.

Fuck. I don't like that. I wanted clean deaths.

The bodyguard screams and drops to the ground, writhing around to try and extinguish the flames. The guard standing next to Madir flicks his wand like a whip and a wave of water soars through the air, drenching the fallen guard and extinguishing the flames.

Hulin steps around a pillar and unleashes a sticky, cloying web that drapes across the distracted bodyguard's head. The man tries to rip it away, but Vulin sprints forward from behind me and sticks a massive dagger in the guard's stomach. The gnome pushes and twists. The guard's hands frantically grab at Vulin's head. The gnome pulls away, snarling as he pulls the blade out and stabs again. The guard falls to the floor, blood pumping from his stomach wound.

The bodyguard who had been on fire staggers to his feet and begins firing his wand randomly around the room. I throw myself to the side, rolling behind a pillar. Explosions of dust and marble fly into the air as the guard fires bolts of raw magic in every direction.

'Cast obscure!' shouts Hulin.

'No! Rain!' shouts Sulin.

'Don't be a cretin. Obscure. Do it!'

'Rain is better.'

'Why? We can still see when it rains. You're *such* a moron. Do it now or I swear by Queen Titania's life that I will murder you in your sleep.'

'Shut up!' screams Vulin. 'I'll fucking do it. *Obscuro*. There. I despise you both, and Hulin, I want you to know I pissed in your beer the other night!'

'Bastard!'

'You don't mess with another gnome's beer, Vulin! We've told you this! You are *so* dead.'

'Screw you.'

'Fuck sake!' I shout. 'Can you lot shut up and just do your job?'

One of the two remaining bodyguards zeroes in on my voice. As soon as the words are out of my mouth I feel the pillar I'm hiding behind rumble and shake as magic pounds the other side. I slide to the floor, shielding my head from the debris flying around me.

When I look up again I see a thick mist enveloping the room. I peer around the pillar and catch a glimpse of Madir and his bodyguard ducking behind the statue of Cernunnos. Then the mist grows too thick to see.

Got you.

I reach out and touch the wall, sliding along until I'm behind the massive statue.

A burst of orange fire erupts within the mist, casting a glow like a fiery sunset. It tears through the mist and explodes against the far wall.

No screams, so the gnomes are all right.

I move slowly forward until the huge shadow of the statue looms above me. I stop moving. Is that worried breathing I can hear? I pull my knife out, crouch down, then inch slowly forward.

It's lucky I went in low. A burst of bright blue light explodes into view above me, a continuous stream of raw power that pummels the rear wall. I lunge forward, stabbing out with the knife. A scream, and the lights wink off. A heavy weight collapses on top of me, forcing me to the floor.

I try to struggle out from beneath the body. I see another flare of light and hear a cry of pain. That didn't sound like the gnomes. It sounded like the burned guard. My hand is wet with blood. I try to pull the blade out of the body, but the dead weight is making it difficult. A shadowy figure leaps through the mist above me. Madir, making a break for it.

I hear a curse and a thump. It sounds like Madir has fallen to the floor. I finally manage to pull my arms out from beneath the guard and heave him over. I yank the knife free and stumble into the mist. I can just make out Madir rising to his feet. I'm no more than two feet away.

I move up behind him and stick the knife in the back of his neck. He drops to the ground. Instant. Clean.

That's everyone, isn't it? 'Clear the mist,' I say.

A pause.

'Who said that?'

'Me, you idiot. London.'

'How do we know it's you and not the other side pretending?'

'Good point there, Vulin,' said another voice.

'Thank you, Dulin. I appreciate that. Seriously.'

I sigh. 'Just clear the mist. Please?'

A second later, the mist starts moving, flowing backwards toward an invisible point as if it's film spooling backward.

I look around and take stock. Madir lies at my feet. Off to my right, beneath the statue, is the one I stabbed in the heart. The burned guard lies on the floor surrounded by the gnomes, while the guard Vulin stabbed in the stomach lies in a pool of blood close to the door.

All done. I check my watch.

13:51.

On track.

I catch a movement out of my peripheral vision. I turn quickly and find the dog slowly sitting up. He yawns and shakes himself.

'So when does this guy get here?'

13:35
The Gangster

Armitage isn't happy. Not happy at all.

'I can see a table right there,' she says, pointing through a window into the interior of the restaurant.

'That table is reserved,' says the thin dryad standing in the doorway. 'It is always reserved.'

'Then un-reserve it. We want to eat.'

'Aha-haha,' says the waiter, laughing in an incredibly patronising manner. 'I do not un-reserve tables. And especially not that one.'

Armitage grinds her teeth. 'What *do* you have then?'

'I have a table for two.'

Armitage looks over her shoulder. She's brought the two gnome sisters with her. She points at the closest. She thinks it's Kelin. 'You, come with me. Velin . . .' she glances sideways at the waiter, '. . . just hang back. OK?'

Velin frowns. 'So, no . . .' She mimes an explosion.

'No,' says Armitage hastily. 'Maybe later, OK?'

Armitage turns on the waiter. 'Can we come in *now*?'

'Of course.'

He moves aside and Armitage steps into the restaurant. There's only one other table free. Unfortunately for her and Kelin, it's against the far wall, close to the kitchens.

Armitage slumps into her chair. Kelin sits opposite her and looks around with interest.

A waiter stops at their table. 'What can I get you?' he asks.

'Two specials,' says Armitage, thinking that's a safe enough bet to make him go away.

The waiter nods and goes to the kitchen, leaving them a good view of the empty table in the centre of the restaurant. It's not ideal for an attack. Not ideal at all. Plus, there are four chairs around the table. Armitage hopes they won't all be filled, otherwise they're going to be seriously outnumbered.

'Think that's him,' says Kelin.

Armitage looks up. She saw a sketch of Dumas in the files Scaithe prepared and the man currently walking past the large window is the spitting image. And isn't that just typical? He has three companions with him. *Big* companions.

'What do you think?' she asks. 'Take him out first and deal with the bodyguards after?'

'Dangerous,' says Kelin. 'But it's possible they'll just run once they see Dumas is dead. If they don't, I'll have a ball of fire headed your way. Just . . . make sure you duck.'

'Mmm.' Armitage thinks about it. She isn't one for fancy tricks and magic. Things tend to get messy that way. Especially with spells like fireballs. There's just no controlling them.

She gets up. 'Watch my back. But no fireballs. Use something . . . controllable.'

Armitage heads to the bathroom. She pushes the door open and checks inside. Nothing special. Just a room with walled-off cubicles. Unisex? Uni-species?

Armitage closes the door behind her and heads into one of the stalls. She locks the door and reaches inside her robes, pulling out a small hand-crossbow that Scaithe provided. She pulls the arms up and locks them into place. Then she loads a bolt. It's not amazingly powerful, but it's perfect for what she needs. A shot at Dumas without having to get too close.

Armitage hears the door to the bathroom open and close. She puts an eye to the gap in the door and sees one of Dumas' bodyguards heading for the cubicle next to hers.

Armitage pulls back. An opportunity? Should she kill the bodyguard now and *then* take out Dumas? One less person to worry about. Or should she just head out now and hope the man is occupied long enough for her to do the job? But what if he comes out while she's busy? She doesn't like the idea of an enemy at her back.

So. Kill him now? Her mind immediately says yes, leaping upon the idea of violence. She hesitates as she tries to analyse this feeling. It's something that's been happening a lot since she came back as a revenant, and she's not sure why. She has to be careful when she's angry that she doesn't go full-on Hulk. It's actually starting to worry her. When she gets back she's going to have to ask Parker to research it. See if it's a common trait among revenants, or if it's just her.

But that's for later. Armitage slowly, ever so slowly, eases open the door. Did it creak when she entered the cubicle? She hadn't noticed. She opens it just enough for her to slip out, then moves to stand in front of the bodyguard's cubicle. She points the crossbow and waits.

A *very* unpleasant minute or so later the man finishes his business. As the door starts to open inward Armitage kicks it hard, sending the bodyguard stumbling back against the wall. Armitage uses one hand to stop the door rebounding and fires the crossbow straight at the man's face.

It hits him in the neck, just off-centre. The man tries to scream, but all that comes out is a gurgling gasp. Armitage drops the crossbow and reaches for her knife. The man sees this and lunges forward, blood streaming down his neck and chest.

He barrels into Armitage and they fall to the floor. Armitage tries to push him off, but the man is heavy and unnaturally strong. She should have been able to just toss him aside, but he's actually managing to keep her pinned to the floor. He must have some kind of magically-augmented strength. He grabs Armitage around the neck and squeezes, his face a mixture of pain, fear and fury.

Armitage grabs the man's face, reaching for his eyes. He jerks back, moving out of Armitage's reach. Fair enough. She shifts her reach lower, grabbing the crossbow bolt and yanking it free. Then she rams it straight up under his chin, pushing it deep into his brain.

He stiffens, then slumps over. Armitage pushes him aside and stands up. Well now. That was unpleasant.

She has to move fast, before someone comes in and sees the mess. She retrieves the crossbow and pulls the bolt out of his head.

She reloads the crossbow, then looks at her robes. They're covered in blood. Fuck.

She whips them off and turns them inside out, pulls them back on again. Not *as* bad. They won't hold under scrutiny, but it will do for now.

She leaves the bathroom and pauses in the short corridor beyond. Dumas is sitting at the table, his back to her. She has a clear line of sight.

Armitage raises the crossbow.

She pauses. It's too risky. If she misses she might not get a second chance and she really doesn't want to tell London she messed up. He'd never let her live it down.

She puts the crossbow behind her back, being incredibly careful not to jostle the trigger, then makes her way back into the dining area, weaving around the packed tables. The place is crowded. Not a good spot for an assassination. They should have just waited outside, then attacked Dumas as he came out again.

She almost abandons the plan there and then, thinking she'll do exactly that. But then one of the bodyguards glances her way as she draws closer. The bodyguard's eyes flick over her, taking in her face, then move down to the hand hidden behind her back.

His eyes widen. He starts to rise in his seat. Shit. Armitage lengthens her stride, pulling the crossbow out. The second bodyguard turns to see what his colleague is looking at. Armitage levels the crossbow at the back of Dumas' head and squeezes the trigger.

The bolt slams straight into the back of Dumas' head, disappearing completely into his skull. Dumas jerks forward, his head slamming hard into the table. Armitage drops the crossbow, reaches beneath her robes, and pulls out a long-bladed knife.

She grins at the first bodyguard. 'Come on then, bitch. I've had a rough month and I'm feeling antsy.'

It takes a moment for the other diners to notice. Then the screaming starts. Chairs scrape, cutlery and glasses clatter to the ground, and a press of bodies rushes to the exit.

Something slams into Armitage's back. She stumbles forward, lashing out with her elbow and connecting with the face of the second bodyguard. Bastard crept around and surprised her. He grabs her shoulders and pushes her to the ground. Where the hell is Kelin? She's supposed to be backing her up.

Armitage tries to shove the man off, but he has the same augmented strength as the other guard. He attempts to pin her down, stop her moving, but she manages to squirm around onto her back.

He's plunging a knife down toward her.

His head explodes into a fine mist.

He falls forward. His head is completely gone. All that's left is his neck, blood spurting from the stump and coating her arms, her robes, everything. She groans and rolls to the side, shoving the body away and crawling to her feet. Kelin is standing a few feet away, her wand held in her hand.

'What the hell took you so long?'

'There were people in the way,' she says.

'Jesus, he almost stuck me.'

Kelin looks over Armitage's shoulder. She turns. The last bodyguard is on his feet. She frowns in annoyance. This was supposed to go a lot smoother than this. The guard points his own crossbow at Armitage—

—And the window directly behind him explodes inward and blue lightning wraps around his body. He screams.

Velin is walking slowly across the street, lightning crackling from her fingers and wrapping around the bodyguard. His skin is turning brown, bubbling, peeling from his face. Smoke tendrils rise up into the air.

His scream turns to a shriek. Armitage can see into his mouth. His tongue protrudes, then bursts like a balloon filled with red paint. Velin keeps walking. She pauses outside the restaurant, then claps her hands together. A burst of blue energy erupts and slams into the bodyguard.

Armitage has no idea what is coming. She dives to the ground, pulling a table over as a shield. Kelin throws herself over the table and hunkers down next to her.

Not a second too soon. There is a wet explosion and parts of the bodyguard splatter heavily against the other side of the table. Something slams through the wood inches from Armitage's face. It looks like a piece of skull.

'That,' she says, 'is disgusting.'

They slowly stand up. The restaurant looks as though someone has thrown red paint everywhere. Blood covers the ceiling, the walls, the floor, and all the patrons who were unlucky enough to still be inside.

There's silence in the aftermath.

And then the screams start up again, more hysterical this time, and the mad rush for the exit resumes.

Armitage carefully steps over larger puddles of meat, her feet crunching on broken glass. She ducks through the window frame and steps out into the street.

She nods at Velin. 'Good work, pet. And I don't say that often.'

The gnome nods and gives her a grinning thumbs up.

Armitage checks her watch.

13:57.

They're on track.

19

Xantr Pulhaven approaches the forbidding tower that is the Bank of Falias.

Xantr is fat. Massively so. There's no polite way to put it. He has a colossally rotund stomach that jiggles and ripples as he moves. His double chins have double chins. His head is narrow and balding, with tufts of greasy hair sprouting upwards and wide, pointed ears covered in broken veins. His skin is pale white and covered in mottled patches of yellow.

He is a Balifintere, a race of Fae from across the ocean. The Balifintere are a small community built around ... well ... making money. Making money by giving out loans at exorbitant interest rates to desperate clients. The Balifintere live in a noxious cloud that stops them leaving their smoggy home very often. But when they do, they are required to use magic to assist their breathing.

Make note of this. It will be important.

Xantr stares up at the bank. He seems cowed. Intimidated. And so he should be. The bank is designed to intimidate. A temple raised to the worship of greed and avarice, it takes up multiple blocks, a monstrosity of a building, square and solid and grey.

There is a single black door leading into the bank. Xantr approaches the door and knocks.

The door swings silently inward.

He waits, but nobody appears.

Xantr pushes the door wider and peers into what appears to be some sort of enclosed courtyard. He steps through the door and looks around. Not a courtyard as such. But a cleared space that surrounds a second severe building nestling with the first.

There is a quiet click behind him. The door has closed. He doesn't even turn to look. That would imply nervousness and Xantr does not wish to imply nervousness. He wishes to imply power and stature.

The inner area is lit by floating globes that soar up into the distant heights. The lights are winking on and off.

At least, that's what it looks like. Xantr realises this effect is due to a wide platform descending toward him, blocking off the lights as it drops.

Xantr waits as the platform comes to a gentle stop. There is a figure on board standing with his back to him. His hand is resting on a gem stone mounted on a small pedestal.

Xantr steps aboard. There is a small brass plaque mounted by the entrance. He reads it. '*Do not engage with the lift operator. Any attempts to do so could result in serious harm or death.*'

Xantr glances at the figure as the platform rises upward. He decides it would be wise not to test the veracity of the sign.

It takes about a minute for the platform to reach the top of the building. There's another door here that swings open as he approaches.

Xantr finds himself in a small, empty courtyard. It is about ten foot by ten foot. Towering walls surround him, peppered with rectangular observation posts. He can see movement behind them, and the glint of watchful eyes. There are wyverns. They pace around the top of the wall, glaring down at him with black eyes, trailing smoke behind them. He can smell sulphur in the air.

Xantr waits. After ten seconds or so a section of the wall opposite him fades away to reveal a woman in her early forties wearing an immaculate suit with her hair smoothed back into a tight bun.

She stares at him, her hands clasped before her.

'I made an appointment,' Xantr says.

'Of course,' says the woman in a quiet voice. 'My name is Miss Wording. I will be your bank liaison.'

Xantr frowns. 'You are human?'

'I am,' says Miss Wording as she gestures for him to step through the doorway. 'Mr Revic recruited me many years ago.'

There is a corridor beyond, with marble flooring leading to yet another set of doors. A large, disembodied eye floats in the corner of the passage. It turns to follow Xantr as he passes, blinking owlishly, the pupil dilating and contracting as it studies him.

Miss Wording places her palm against the doors and Xantr feels a brief tingle of magic as they slide open to reveal an elevator with polished wooden walls.

Xantr hesitates. He looks uneasy. 'I was told the elevators were locked with magic keys?'

Miss Wording steps inside the elevator. 'We have upgraded some of our security measures. The keys were burdensome.'

'I see.'

Xantr steps into the elevator. Miss Wording again presses her hand against the inside wall. The doors slide shut and the elevator drops.

Silence. No one talks. Miss Wording stares straight ahead, while Xantr fidgets. He keeps casting glances at the eye attached to the roof of the elevator.

'Do they make you uncomfortable?' asks Miss Wording.

'On the contrary,' says Xantr. He smiles, showing yellow, pointed teeth. 'They make me feel safe. I would actually like them in my bedroom at home.'

Miss Wording arches an eyebrow but says nothing. Xantr clears his throat.

'Obviously, I didn't mean it . . . that way.'

'What way is that, sir?'

'You know . . . for . . . sexy-time.'

'Sexy-time?'

'Never mind.'

The elevator bumps gently to a stop. Miss Wording touches the wall and the doors slide open. They step into a large foyer with red and white marbled tiles, gold trim around the walls, statues placed into recessed wall alcoves and a single, long desk set atop a raised dais.

'Follow me,' says Miss Wording.

She leads Xantr into the room. There is a small gnome sitting on a high chair behind it. Even so, he is only just peering over the top of the desk. Xantr cannot help but notice that the gnome has the most *spectacular* nose. And nostrils that resemble caves filled with stalactites and stalagmites made of thick, coarse hair.

The creature sniffs once, twice, then glances at Miss Wording.

'Magic,' he growls.

Miss Wording turns to Xantr. 'My associate informs me you have active magic about your person.'

'Indeed. My people live amongst clouds that would be noxious to others. We cannot survive away from them. The magic your gnome smells changes the air before it enters my lungs. This is on file, I think. Many of my people bank with you.'

Miss Wording stares at Xantr a moment longer then nods at the gnome. 'Open an account for our guest.'

The gnome heaves open a large ledger. He scribbles away with a feathered quill, then turns the book around so Xantr can sign. Xantr picks up the quill, but the gnome slams his hand down on the page.

'Stop.'

Xantr freezes. The gnome leans forward and pulls on a small ribbon. The left page of the ledger unfolds ... and unfolds more and more, until it bumps up against Xantr's booted foot.

'Terms and conditions,' growls the gnome.

Xantr picks up the quill and signs with a flourish. 'I like to live dangerously,' he says to the gnome.

'You might regret that,' says Miss Wording. 'It states that the bank has the right to claim your soul if you renege on your monthly payments.'

'And his children's souls,' adds the gnome.

Xantr shrugs. 'If I run out of money and can't pay the rent for a safety deposit box, then you're welcome to my soul. My children's too. Annoying little bastards they are. Wish I'd never allowed my wife to spawn them.' He turns to Miss Wording. 'Can we get to the vaults please? I have an appointment with a courtesan in half an hour and I don't like to keep her waiting.'

'Of course. Follow me.'

Miss Wording leads Xantr around the desk toward yet another lone door. Eyes positioned all around the room turn to follow their movement. Miss Wording places a hand over the door and it slides open to reveal yet another elevator. They step inside.

'We are going underground, I take it?' asks Xantr.

'Very far underground.'

'Forgive me for saying, but this whole place seems very ... sparse.'

'Sparse?'

'Not many workers.'

'We do not need them. All our security measure are magical in nature. We find that introducing the human – or Fae – element just increases the chance of things going wrong.'

The elevator opens onto a circular room. Six corridors lead to heavy vault doors. Miss Wording leads Xantr down one on the right-hand side. She places her hand against the vault door.

Nothing happens for a moment, and then a hatch slides open and one of the eyes pops out. Miss Wording leans forward, allowing the eye to study her retina. Then it retreats back into the door.

Xantr hears the clunking of metal, gears and cogs turning and pulling open locks. The vault door slowly swings open and Xantr can see the door is three feet thick.

'Is that steel?' asks Xantr.

'It is. Only the best. Shipped from the Dayside.'

She leads him into the vault. It's thirty feet square, the walls covered from floor to ceiling with safety deposit boxes. Miss Wording gestures.

'Any boxes with the keys in the locks are free. I'll leave you to it.'

She leaves the room. Xantr opens the closest door and pulls out the safety deposit box, laying it on the table. He pulls a square package from his pocket and carefully places it inside. He slides the box back into the wall and locks it, dropping the key into his pocket.

13:45
The Fuck Up

Xantr exits the vault and rejoins Miss Wording in the corridor.

'All done?' she says.

Xantr opens his mouth to speak, but nothing comes out. He frowns and touches his throat. He smiles uncertainly at Miss Wording and tries to speak again. This time a long, drawn-out squeak issues from his mouth.

'Are you unwell?' asks Miss Wording. She is frowning.

Xantr shakes his head and tries to smile. The smile falters. He tries to swallow, but ends up gasping for air. He gestures urgently ahead of them, and starts to walk.

But he doesn't get far before he stumbles to a halt. He straightens up in a jerky movement, spinning around.

Miss Wording takes a step back.

Xantr's face is stretched, eyes wide and staring, a panicky look clear to see.

His mouth opens and closes. His head jerks left then right. Miss Wording locks eyes with him.

'I'm afraid you will have to come with me,' she says, her voice now cold.

Xantr finally finds his voice. 'Shit,' he says. 'No, wait. I've got something for this.'

'Excuse me?'

'Two weeks,' he says.

'I don't understand.'

'Two w ... weeks. Come on. You were from my world. Ah ... fuck it.'

Xantr passes a hand over his face and his head splits into two halves, peeling apart and falling into his hands, where it joins back together once again.

The face of a moderately handsome human man is revealed.

'Catch,' he says, and throws the head at Miss Wording.

Miss Wording does not catch it. Because she's not stupid. Instead, she moves quickly, kicking it straight back so that it smacks directly into the man's forehead.

'Ow!' he says, staggering backward.

Miss Wording sprints straight for him. The man lets out a yelp, turns, and runs. But it's now obvious that the obese body he is wearing is not, in fact, his real body. It is also clear that the disguise is having problems. He staggers and limps, trying to run without bending his right leg, which seems to have seized up.

'Fuck, fuck, fuck,' is all he says as he attempts to make his escape.

He doesn't get far.

Miss Wording tackles him from behind, sending him sprawling to the ground. She rolls him over and slaps him.

'Hey, what the hell? There's no need for that.'

'Tell me your name. Now.'

The man sighs. 'Winters,' he says. 'Cal Winters.' He puts on a smile. 'Stick-em-up,' he says weakly. 'This is a robbery.'

13:57
The Lockdown

Seconds after Armitage kills Dumas, the bank goes into lockdown. The anti-magic field falls across the building in an invisible curtain. Red light pulses through the building and all staff are ordered to leave.

This drill has been practised many times before and the staff manage to exit the building within seven minutes of the alarm sounding.

14:15
The Inside Man

Cal Winters, now waiting in his holding cell, smiles to himself. So far everything is going according to plan. Miss Wording has removed his intentionally-malfunctioning disguise and left him to stew while she is forced to leave the building due to the lockdown.

Except Miss Wording did not do her job entirely success-fully. She failed to check Mr Winters for a second disguise. A second disguise that he is, in fact, already wearing.

A much thinner, closer-fitting one, and one that makes him very nervous. He argued with his former boss about wearing it, but she was very insistent. Mr Winters feels he needs to be more assertive when dealing with his boss, especially when it comes to the potential for extreme bodily harm brought on by disguises that double as explosives.

He takes his clothes off, revealing a curiously hairless body and a freakishly smooth pelvic area, not dissimilar to children's toys. He digs his fingers into his chest and pulls, ripping his skin into two halves. He peels the skin aside, then over one shoulder, and rolls the suit down to his waist. He does the same with the other shoulder, then pushes it down over his legs.

Now Mr Winters is more anatomically correct, and not the smoothly-skinned nightmare fuel of thirty seconds ago.

Mr Winters puts his clothes back on, flips the fake skin over, and starts peeling a red, putty-like material from the inside of the skin. It is not at all magical, unless you find the product invented by a certain Stanislav Brebera to be magical.

And many do. Bank robbers, scoundrels, and lots of military personnel among them.

14:43
The Tactical Security Team

The special security detail summoned upon the death of the two senior partners arrives at the elevator outside the bank. There are five of them. All dressed in black protective masks and body armour very obviously brought to Faerie from the

Dayside. They are armed with rifles, again, not the product of Faerie.

They rise up on the platform and enter the bank through the door at the top of the building and make their way to their designated zones, the elevator locks disabled during the lock-down specifically to allow them free access. Three of them sweep the bank for intruders while two remain by the door of an empty office. Waiting.

14:50
The Big Man

Fifty-three minutes after the two senior partners are killed, Dragoslav Revic arrives at the bank. He locks the rooftop door behind him with a special key. Once the door is closed, it vanishes from sight, becoming one with the wall.

He enters the elevator and descends through the bank, the doors opening again three floors below ground level. He exits and approaches his office. Two members of his tactical team are waiting, as per protocol. There is a bulky backpack sitting on the floor.

'Do we know what happened yet?' he demands.

One of the soldiers takes his mask off. 'Yeah,' he says. 'You got fucked.'

The second officer, who Revic now notices is slightly smaller and plumper, takes off his mask. *Her* mask, he corrects himself.

She smiles at him. 'All right, pet? You know you're wanted for war crimes at The Hague? Great hiding place you've got here, though. A hundred points to Slytherin.'

The backpack shifts and a dog pops its head out. 'Yippee-ki-yay Motherfucker!'

20

Flashback

How it went down

14:15
The Switcheroo

Gideon and Armitage have no choice but to pick a public place to take care of the tactical team.

Scaithe shows them the best location to launch their attack. There is one spot in the city the team has to pass through to reach the bank: a small crossing where four roads meet, with only one carrying on to the bank. It's a tight, enclosed space with high buildings looking down on the street on every side. Buildings they can position themselves on to watch for the mark.

The skies are heavy and grey, a few light flecks of snow swirling through the air, and mist coils around the city. The weather looks like it's going to get worse, which is good for them. It should mean there won't be many Fae out on the streets. Already, the city seems quieter than it was earlier.

London and the dog are positioned on the roof of a building, peering down into the streets below. The rooftop door squeaks open and Armitage appears. She nods a greeting at the gnome brothers who are huddled on the opposite side of the roof quietly arguing about spells.

'All done,' says Armitage, crouching down beside London. 'Any problems?'

'Not really. Just a bit of a mess.'

He checks his watch.

'How long?' asks Armitage.

'Soon.'

'Better get into position then.'

They gather the gnomes and descend down the stairs to the street. The gnome brothers rejoin their sisters and they separate into three small groups, taking up positions between the buildings.

London, the dog, and Armitage step into an alley.

They wait.

Ten minutes later, two coaches trundle into view. London recognises them instantly, as they're exactly as Scaithe described – dark, polished wood, silver trimmings and pulled by what can only be described as demonic horses with glowing red eyes, and sharp, snarling teeth. The horses are massively muscled, steam rising from their flanks and disappearing in the air.

The lead coach trundles over the cobbles toward the centre of the crossroads.

London watches nervously. 'Wait for it,' he mutters. 'Wait for it.'

As soon as the lead coach passes the centre of the crossroads, Dulin triggers his spell. Which, even from a purely objective viewpoint, is pretty impressive.

The coach erupts into the air, propelled upward by the force of the explosion. It flies apart, splinters of wood sending lethal shards in all directions.

The fireball soars high into the sky then dissipates, a black plume of smoke spreading across the square as the twisted frame of the coach smashes back to the ground with a resounding crash.

The second coach has stopped. The horses rear back,

kicking the air and neighing frantically. They pull away, tipping the coach onto its side, and snapping their ropes, and gallop frantically into the mist.

A moment of silence.

A second explosion rips through the cold afternoon. This time the coach simply blows apart, the force of the spell shredding it to pieces where it stands. London feels the heat on his face as he watches the billowing cloud of fire roll upward.

Armitage, London, and the gnomes move in, heading toward the two coaches. Armitage peers into the two wreckages, then straightens up, frowning.

'There are no bodies in here.'

London's eyes widen in alarm. Shit. A decoy. He cups his hands together. 'Scatter!' he shouts.

But it's too late. A bolt of lightning erupts from the thick mist. It sizzles through the air and strikes one of the gnomes, sending him flying through the air to fall motionless on the ground. The other gnomes whirl around and strike back, sending blinding flashes of light rolling through the mist toward the source of the attack.

Their bolts illuminate a small army of guards running into the square, using the mist as cover.

London is not happy. This wasn't in the intelligence reports. They were expecting a small team. Not an army. He reminds himself to have words with Scaithe about this.

The gnomes, Armitage, London and the dog move quickly, sprinting toward the incoming guards, taking the fight to the enemy. Armitage fires off glinting bolts that look like bullets. The gnomes scream and fling fireballs, ice arrows, lightning and any other kind of weapon they can think of. London shoots black lightning that wraps around the guards, draining them of essence and killing them instantly.

Falling snowflakes are melted by the heat of the magical battle. Fireballs and bolts of blue energy burn through the mist, scorching buildings and blackening the cobbled street. A black cloud sprays from one of the gnomes' wands and surges toward a group of guards. Screams erupt from inside the cloud as it moves through them, leaving behind men and women with their skin melting from their faces, pooling at their feet in red and white puddles of blood and muscle.

Another gnome is hit, an arrow punching through his throat. London thinks it's Dulin.

London watches in dismay as the battle unfolds around him. He doesn't understand what's happened. Where are the tactical team? He wonders if they knew an attack was coming, or if this is just a precaution they have always planned on taking.

A second later, a third coach comes speeding into the square, pulled by two of the galloping demon horses. A figure dressed in black tactical gear is driving, whipping the reins to get the horses moving. They careen through the fighters, knocking both friend and foe aside. London sees two more gnomes knocked flying, and three guards trampled underfoot. The coach speeds past the burning wreckage of the decoys and disappears down the street opposite, vanishing into the mist.

London sets off in pursuit. He hears the horses neighing shrilly ahead. He reaches the end of the road and sees the coach disappearing to his left. He pauses for a moment, thinking back to the maps he studied. If the coach is going left, it means it will have to turn right at the end of the street. Which means . . .

London cuts between two buildings to his right.

He can hear the horses coming, their hooves striking the cobbles. He surges out of the alley, then jerks back and spins to the side as he almost careens directly into the coach. He acts quickly, leaping up and grabbing the door. His feet bounce and drag along the cobbles until he pulls himself up.

The door is shoved open and London swings and bangs against the side of the wagon. He shoves off, swinging the door back. The boot is there again, ready to kick out, but London grabs it and yanks. The owner is pulled forward, half-falling from the vehicle. He tries to keep hold of the door but London kicks at his arms and the man falls to the cobbles. The wooden wheels bounce over his neck and he rolls to a dead stop. London quickly shifts position, swinging to the inside of the door, and when it slams shut again he's inside the dim interior of the coach.

And finds himself face to face with a Glock. He is momentarily surprised. But then he grins. This, he knows how to deal with.

He grabs the gun, pushes his thumb hard into the owner's wrist, and reverses the weapon, pulling it out of the figure's hand.

London feels hands grab him. Two more figures in black clothing trying to hold him down.

London fires the gun, emptying the magazine into the Fae inside the coach. Three seconds later they're all dead, slumped in their seats.

London grabs a fresh gun from one of their holsters, climbs out of the coach, pulls himself up, and shoots the driver in the head. He slumps to the side and London grabs the reins of the horses, pulling them to a snorting and steaming stop.

He takes a shaky breath and checks the time.

14:38.

On target.

Now

14:50

Cal carefully applies a tiny amount of Semtex to the door of his cell.

He steps back, studying it critically. How much are you supposed to use? He thinks about it, then adds some more. It still doesn't look like much. He bites his lip.

Fuck it, he thinks, and adds some more. You only live once.

He sticks in the blasting cap then unrolls the wire to the furthest point in the cell and studies the distance.

About ten feet. Not really that far at all.

He sighs. Not much he can do about it, though. He hunkers down into a ball, takes a deep breath, covers his head, and triggers the detonator.

The explosion is not small.

The explosion deafens him. The bottom half of the door rips away, flying out into the corridor beyond, while fragments of the upper half spin and clatter into the cell.

Cal stays curled into a ball for a moment longer, eyes tightly closed, doing a mental checklist of his body. Nothing seems to be hanging off or gushing blood, so that's something. He stands up and wiggles his fingers in his ears, shaking his head sharply in an attempt to stop the shrill ringing.

He waves the smoke away and stares at the door. What the fuck was he thinking strapping this stuff to his body? Is he insane? Why the hell did he draw the short straw? He's going to have words with Armitage about this. He wants danger pay.

And emotional damage pay. And . . . whatever else he can think of.

He ducks into the passage beyond. No security or anything. So at least Scaithe's intelligence on that front was correct. He heads right, moving toward the security room at the far end of the corridor.

He has one more piece of Semtex that he applies to the hinges. He sticks in the blasting cap, then makes sure to move way, way back before detonating it. Like, right to the far end of the passage.

This time the entire door explodes into tiny pieces. Hmm . . . maybe a bit too much of the magic putty there. Cal moves forward and peers through the shattered doorway.

He frowns in confusion. What the hell? He steps into the room, blinking in surprise.

Inside the room is an intricate chair raised up on a high platform. It looks like one of those old barber chairs, all cracked leather and grimy chrome. Inside the chair is what appears to be a sleeping man, morbidly obese, with sores and lesions all over his body. He's twitching non-stop, his limbs jerking, his eyes rolling violently behind the lids as he mutters beneath his breath.

Cal looks up. The ceiling is entirely hidden by what he at first thinks are cables. But they can't be cables, can they? They don't use that kind of thing here.

He steps forward to inspect them.

They're . . . biological. Thousands of twisted umbilical cords that loop down from the ceiling and disappear beneath the chair. Cal bends down. The umbilical cords end in tiny needles of bone that prick into the man's skin. And there's one long, thick needle stuck into the back of his neck.

Cal straightens up and looks around. There's nothing else in the room. This must be what he came here to find.

The umbilical cords . . . they somehow transmit what the eyes see to this poor bastard? That's pretty goddamn sick.

Cal puts his hands on his hips and studies the chair. He doesn't want to sit in that chair. No fucking way. He didn't sign up for this. He stares at the chair. The man jerks violently, his arm reaching up to point at the wall.

'*Empty rooms. Boss is in the building,*' the man slurs.

Cal walks to the empty door. No. He's not doing this. He can't.

He steps into the corridor, then stops. His head drops and he stares at the floor.

Fuck.

He turns back into the room and sets about unplugging the man. There is a wooden lever to each side of him. Cal pulls on them both and the needles slide out of the man's skin. There is a separate lever for the needle in the man's neck. He pulls it and the needle retracts with a wet, sucking sound.

As soon as the man is free of needles, he sits bolt upright in the chair.

Cal takes a step back, but the man doesn't seem to see him. He heaves himself out of the chair and staggers to the wall. He presses on something and a door Cal hadn't even noticed swings outward, revealing a tiny room with a single bed in it. The guy flops face down on it, his bare arse jutting into the air, and starts snoring.

A second hidden door opens to reveal another man. This one isn't *quite* as disgusting as the first. He doesn't have as many sores.

Cal runs forward and slams the door shut before the figure can leave the room. He places his hand to the wall and lets the heat flow out, fusing the door closed.

There's a flurry of movement from the ceiling. Cal looks up and spots half-invisible sprites descend to the chair, busying themselves around the bone needles. Cal moves cautiously forward. The sprites are cleaning the bone needles with long pink snake tongues.

He waits patiently while the sprites finish up, and when they're done he climbs reluctantly into the chair. He doesn't sit back. Not yet. He chews his lip as the sprites vanish into the ceiling.

'Get moving then,' he tells himself.

He waits, leaning forward and hugging his knees. He closes his eyes and sighs. 'Fuck it.'

He lies back, reaches out, and pulls the two levers. He screams as the thousands of tiny pinpricks penetrate his skin. It feels like a million, glowing-hot needles sliding directly into his muscles.

But then a curious numbness spreads through his limbs. He takes a deep, shuddering breath, relaxing slightly.

He reaches up and pulls the lever by his neck.

And then his brain explodes, his consciousness fragmenting in pain and fury, scattering into the aether like a shattered windshield. Each shard of his mind is a part of the whole, each shard a piece of his consciousness that spirals away into blackness.

Callum Winters does not know who he is anymore. He feels his name drifting out of reach, slipping away, leaving him an empty husk.

He spins in nothingness. He *is* nothingness.

A blackness stains his soul and spreads through his whole being, pulling him apart, scattering his consciousness into the night.

And then there is something else. Taking over. Pushing into his mind.

Pictures. Images. One after the other. Appearing all around him, inside him, overlapping, separating, floating together. Shifting imagery, hundreds, thousands of pictures that take over his entire being. He sees them all. Each scene plays out in his mind. Corridors, offices, vaults, exterior shots of the bank, interior shots of the elevators. He is watching the combined feeds of all the magic eyes. All of them at once. Analysing, studying, assessing. He flicks through them all, looking for something, searching. But for what?

He freezes over an image of a large man being led at gunpoint along a corridor.

Something about this triggers an alarm. This is important. *Why* is it important? His attention drifts, looking toward the next image, then the next, flipping through them—

—he comes back to the figures. They're standing before a large door now. There are other people there. Five of them. All dressed in black.

And a dog.

The man is glaring over his shoulder.

It looks like he's arguing.

'I'm telling you, this is pointless!' snaps Revic. 'I can't open the vault door on my own. It has to be approved from the security room, and no one has access to that—'

I butt him in the face with the gun. Not hard. Just enough to shut him up. He doesn't cry out. Doesn't make a sound. He straightens up and looks me directly in the eye.

'You better make sure to kill me,' he says. 'Do you know who I am? How I am feared? In this world and the oth—'

Armitage butts him in the face with *her* gun.

'Sorry, pet. Didn't want him having all the fun.'

One of the gnomes jumps up, trying to hit Revic with the butt of his own gun, but I gesture for him to stop.

'Come on,' he says. 'That's not fair.'

'Just do what you would normally do to open the vault,' I say.

Revic sighs and passes his hand over the wall.

Nothing happens.

'I told you. The security room will have already alerted the authorities that an attempted robbery is taking place. Even if you threaten to kill me, nothing will—'

He's cut off as a panel slides up on the door and an eye wavering on the end of a stalk pokes out. It stares at him, then turns to look at us.

I break into a grin and look at Armitage. She points her gun directly at my face.

'Goddammit, London. I swear to God. If you *dare* make a Star Wars reference right now I will shoot you in the eye.'

I look at the dog instead. His eyes are wide and I can see he's grinning.

The figure in the chair stares at Revic, then at the other two faces. They look familiar to him. He feels he should know them. Why is that? Why are they staring at him like that? What do they want?

He looks down to the floor, where the dog is staring at him, his tongue lolling from his mouth. He . . . knows that dog.

'Do whatever it is you normally do,' says Armitage.

Revic scowls at us both. 'I have contacts in every town and city in Europe. You will be hunted down. I will kill you and your family—'

I grab him by the shirt, pull him close and hiss in his face. 'Don't you *dare* mention my family,' I snarl. 'Do it again and I will make it my personal mission to destroy you. I will find *your* family. Your parents, your brothers and sisters, your cousins, your friends, your high school sweet-heart. I will find them all and I will slit their throats and tell them this is your fault. You think you fucking scare me, you little cunt? You're not scary. You're not the darkness. You're just sitting in the shadow *I* cast. Now open the goddamn door.'

I step back. I can feel Armitage's eyes on me. I look over and she's staring at me with a worried look on her face. No, not just worry. Something else.

Fear?

Revic leans down and peers directly into the eye. He waits there for a moment, muttering something beneath his breath, then straightens up again.

'I told you. It will not open under these circumstances.'

The words the man speaks as he stares at him become solid in the darkness, unfurling like leaves in spring. The words form pictures and sounds that surround him, and he knows he is supposed to do something with them. He feels they are an alarm of some kind. He should activate it.

He stares at the man's face, then shifts focus to the man behind him.

He knows him.

Gideon Tau.

He looks down. And that is the dog.

And he is Cal Winters.

These words are a trigger that brings the shards of his consciousness tumbling back to him. The shattered pieces of his soul reform in glinting fragments, torn pieces of his mind joining together to make a whole again.

Cal Winters grins and focuses his attention on the Revic's eyes, sifting, comparing to records that initiate affirmative responses.

Cal smiles.

The vault door swings silently open.

Revic stares at it in astonishment. 'How did you do this?'

I ignore him and peer into the vault. Everything looks normal.

I sit down with my back against the wall.

'What are you doing?' demands Revic.

'Waiting.'

Cal Winters pulls the handles and screams as the needles slide out of his body. He reaches up with shaking hands and slowly moves the final lever. He can feel the bone slipping out of his neck. He shivers as it pops out, feeling a cold breeze on the wound. He tentatively touches it, expecting to find a gaping hole. But he doesn't. It has closed up already.

He rolls out of the chair and stumbles. His limbs don't want to work properly. He staggers to the door, hits the wall and falls to his knees. His head feels heavy. He crawls into the corridor, pulls himself up the wall and slides along, heading for the elevators.

'Shouldn't he have been here by now?' asks Armitage.

'Maybe,' I say.

'Do you think he's dead?'

'Jesus. Way to jump to the worst conclusion there.'

'It's a possibility.'

Revic is watching us with amusement. He's seriously starting to irritate me.

'Maybe just turn around and Blair Witch the corner there, yeah?'

'Someone is missing?'

I point the gun at him and he turns around to face the wall. As he does so the elevator doors at the end of the passage open to reveal Winters leaning heavily against the wall. He waits a moment, then walks slowly toward us.

'He looks drunk,' says the dog. 'Hey, Winters! If you found booze and didn't share, I am *not* going to be happy with you.'

'No booze,' he says, drawing level with us. 'I'll explain later. And when I do, I want you all to realise how amazing and self-sacrificing I am and give me lots of money and medals.'

Armitage frowns at him. 'You sure you're not drunk?'

'This is all pointless,' says Revic. 'I do not have access to any of the keys. And those safety deposit box doors are absolutely unbreakable.'

'We know that,' I say.

'Then how do you plan to steal from me?'

Winters cracks his knuckles. 'Watch and learn.' He steps carefully into the vault and approaches one of the boxes. He rests his hands on the door and closes his eyes.

At first nothing seems to happen. Then his hands start to turn red, his veins glowing orange and crimson through his skin. The metal of the box door turns orange, then white. The heat spreads out to the boxes around it until the entire wall of safety deposit boxes glows white hot.

But nothing else happens.

'I told you,' says Revic smugly. 'Nothing can break into the vaults.'

'Sure,' says Winters. 'But what about breaking out?'

He keeps his hands in place for ten seconds longer, then turns and sprints back out of the vault, running past us all.

'Not a good idea to stand there,' he shouts.

Armitage and I run after him. After a second, the dog overtakes us. The gnomes come next, with Revic bringing up the rear.

We don't get far before an explosion rips through the vault. A huge fireball bursts into the passage and rolls toward us.

'Drop!' I shout, throwing myself to the floor.

The others all drop to the floor and the fireball soars overhead, heat searing my back. It hits the elevator doors, the flames spreading out along the walls and up the roof. It travels almost all the way back toward us before dissipating into nothing.

I get to my feet and stagger back to the vault, waving the black smoke away.

I peer into the room.

It's utterly destroyed. I don't think there's a single strong-box that has been left untouched. And sitting in the centre of it all is a tiny little dragon that would fit into the palm of my hand. I can feel the heat it's radiating even from here.

Winters pushes past me. He kneels down and holds his hand out to the little creature. It hops onto his hand and he straightens up, studying the surroundings.

It worked. It really did. I hadn't been sure.

When I was reading the files Scaithe had supplied, there was a mention of the last attempted robbery. The thieves had used tame dragons like oxyacetylene torches, harnessing their white hot fire to cut into the boxes. I knew Revic had reme-died that, but I'd wagered this entire operation on the fact that he hadn't bothered with the insides of the boxes. Why would he? Things don't break out of safety deposit boxes.

The little dragon was Winters' idea. They only hatch when activated by heat and they tend to make quite a lot of noise and damage when they did so.

Armitage and the gnomes join us and we spend the next twenty minutes sifting through the wreckage searching for the fragments of the Stone of Fal. While we're doing so I realise that we've let Revic out of our sight. He's gone.

'Let him go,' says Armitage. 'We've got more important things to do.'

We carry on searching until Armitage finally finds them. Small flat pieces of stone with scratchy runes etched into them. She holds them up to Winters.

'You're the expert. What do these say?'

Winters peers at the etchings. 'Well . . . basically . . . they say these belong to Dagda. Hands off or your entire bloodline will be cursed for all eternity.'

'Charming,' says Armitage, shoving them into her pockets. 'Come on. Let's get out of here.'

21

Armitage orders wine and food when we get back to the hotel. It's supposed to be a celebration but I don't really feel we should be happy about what we've accomplished. Sure, we got what we came for, but we lost nearly half the gnomes.

The thing is, they don't really seem to mind. I mean, they *do*, but they consider the cost worth it. Their family got the revenge they wanted.

Winters is another one that isn't filled with the joys of success.

'All I'm saying is, I'm not happy about what I had to do. Kinda feeling like I got the short straw, you know?'

'How's that then?' asks Armitage.

'Who's the one who had to run back to our world to pick up the Semtex?'

'You. But we had other things to plan. And did you have any trouble getting it?'

'No. I mean, there wasn't even anyone at the Ministry, but that's not the point. I was fucking *exhausted*. I don't do exercise. Plus, I had to wear it as a *full-body suit*.'

The dog chuckles. 'You're lucky. If it all went Pete Tong, at least you'd be warm before you blew up.'

'That's not funny.'

'It's not meant to be. We were freezing out there. We had to stand around in mist and rain and snow. What I wouldn't have given to be snug in a cell with Semtex wrapped around me to keep off the chill.'

'Fuck off.'

'Make me,' says the dog happily. Then he goes back to his bowl of booze.

Winters just scowls at the wall.

'Something else on your mind?' I ask.

'You could say that.'

Armitage looks over at him. 'What?'

'Doesn't it bother any of you that these Cuckoos seem to be everywhere?'

I exchange a look with Armitage. It *had* been playing on my mind but I was just trying to get all this over with before having to deal with it.

'No matter how all this goes down – even if we win – we're still going to be stuck with orisha sleeper agents holding positions of power. How do we deal with that?'

I don't have a clue. Neither does Armitage by the look on her face.

'I mean, you guys are OK over the pond. You only had a few of them. But here? They want the UK for themselves. If the Blessed win this, I suppose it doesn't really matter. We're finished anyway. But if *we* win? We've still lost. Or at least, we'll only have won a battle. We'll still have this Cold War scenario going on.'

'We'll deal with that when it comes.'

Winters turns to stare at her. 'No. You don't get it. *I'm* the one who has to deal with it. There's no one left, remember? It's all on me. You guys can go back and sit on your fucking beaches while I'm stuck here trying to deal with black magician cults ruling the country and shape-shifting fundamentalist elves.'

'It's not all rosy for us, pet. We have a potentially unfriendly Oracle on the loose.' She looks at me. 'That's top of your list if we survive the night. Find out where she is and what she's playing at.'

'Jesus, Armitage. You're not asking much, are you?'

'No. I'm actually not. I'm asking you to do your job.' She sighs and looks out the window. 'How long do you think till nightfall?'

Nightfall is when we're going to make our way back to the gateway. 'A few hours,' I say.

'Then we need to pace ourselves. Celebrating is all good and well, but I don't think it's the best time to get pissed.'

I put my drink down and stretch. 'Think I'm going to go stretch my legs. I'll be in the bar if anyone needs me.'

I head to the door.

'Remember!' calls Armitage. 'Pace yourself.'

I nod and leave the room. She doesn't have to worry. Drinking is the absolute last thing on my mind right now.

I've waited.

Nobody can say I've made the same mistake as I did in Durban. I made sure we got the stones. I did my job. I mean, sure, we haven't fixed the lock yet, but sorry, I'm not going to come to the place where my daughter might be held captive and not actually *look* for her. Come on. Anyone who knows me should know that's not going to happen. Armitage most of all. And in an hour or two we should be back in our world.

With Cally. I've vowed that it will be so. If not, then I'll die trying. Because I can't live like this. I can't live the empty life back in our world. There's no point anymore. If I fail here then I've failed Cally for the final time.

I don't tell anyone I'm leaving. I head to the bar, then slip into the passage leading to the kitchen and out the back door. It leads out onto a sidewalk bordering a canal. Rafts and skiffs drift past in the dirty water, pushed by men and women with long poles. I stare suspiciously at the water. I haven't seen Peg Powler since we arrived in the city.

I wait until the coast is clear and pull on the robes. I asked Scaithe to get them for me while I was planning the heist – I knew this moment was coming. He tells me the robes are for the Men of Letters. They usually stay inside the Blessed temple, creating their books and histories, retelling the legends about the Old Ones in illuminated manuscript form. He got these robes specifically because they have huge hoods that I can use to hide my face. I had a very interesting conversation with him, actually. He had a lot to say about the Blessed and the children he has seen among them. None of them ever look happy, he said. All of them are prisoners.

His words woke the pain-beast inside of me, the anger I'd been hiding while we took care of the heist, and it's been close to the surface ever since. I've been trying not to let it out, try not to let it take control, but it's getting harder to resist. It's demanding action. Demanding sacrifice.

I had to leave when I did. Another minute cooped up without doing anything and the pain-beast would have turned on me. This isn't a metaphor. I've started to honestly feel like it's a living beast inside me and that it's trying to take over. The more I fight it, the stronger it gets.

I head through the streets, crossing canals and moving ever deeper into the city. No one stops me. In fact, no one looks at me. They cross the street rather than having to pass me by.

I arrive at the Blessed compound about twenty minutes later. Its walls stand high and forbidding, the temple itself made from living wood. I stand on the street opposite and watch through the open gates. The Blessed come and go, heading inside the temple and out into the streets in groups. I can see soldiers like the one who attacked me in my hotel room, their faces covered with silver masks. There are a lot of elves too. They have their heads uncovered, their pale faces and white eyes glaring at the normal people who call the city their home. Scaithe says it's like a slow invasion. The Blessed move in, start sending patrols out, cracking down on what they call crime or blasphemy, and soon the citizens live in fear and the Blessed are in charge. There is a queen in these parts, someone called Titania, but the Blessed are so powerful, they've even got their people on her council.

I check myself over, making sure I fit in, then I stride across the street and through the gates. No one shouts at me as I do so, which is always a good sign.

I breathe easier and cross the courtyard. As I step inside the temple, the light shifts, turning a warm orange in colour. I reach out and touch the wall. It's warm. It feels like there's a heartbeat there, something pulsing through the wood.

I'm standing in a huge atrium with doorways branching off on all sides and winding staircases spiralling up into the cool darkness.

Scaithe said I need to head toward the rear of the compound. That's where the children are kept.

There are no doors directly ahead of me, so I climb the stairs to the next level and follow a carpeted hallway that seems to be going in the right direction. I pause at the entrance to a warren of cramped corridors. It looks different here. No decorations. Plain. Not at all like anything else I've seen.

I push the first door open. It's a tiny bedroom. There's an unmade bed and twisted sheets lie on the floor. I cross to the window and open the wooden shutters. It looks out into the rear of the compound. There's a massive, cleared space about the size of ten football fields. I can see soldiers training, row upon row of them performing synchronised moves with pikes and swords, watched over by one of the silver-masked fighters.

I can't see any children though.

I lean out the window and look around. The temple and the compound butt up against the wall of the city. There's an open plain on the other side, and I can see a thin cloud of dust visible about a mile away, heading in this direction.

I stare thoughtfully at the cloud. It's big. It looks like a large group of people approaching.

I wait patiently as it draws closer. I can just make out figures in the cloud of dust. Those in the lead are tall. But those behind . . .

. . . I lean farther out the window, my fingers gripping the wooden sill.

Trailing behind them are children. Tied together.

By the time I arrive outside, the cloud of dust is approaching the gate. I stop just outside the door to the temple. The elves leading the soldiers in their drills haven't even looked over at the approaching children. I move to the right of the courtyard and start running. I'm not thinking. A distant part of me is aware of that. This is a stupid move. Stupid. But the pain-beast ignores it. It's come fully awake. I've been trying to control it too long, and it senses my weakness. Senses my fury.

It comes out to play.

I set off at a sprint. I see a few curious looks out of the corner of my eye, but I ignore them. I reach the gates and keep going, running directly for the children.

They're not just tied together. Some are in wooden cages, pulled along by some of the older kids.

I run past the startled guards and pull my knife out to slash the rope tying them together. I hear a shout behind me. I move down the line, slicing the ropes around their wrists, peering into the faces, searching for my daughter.

Hands grab me and I lash out behind me with the knife, feeling it strike flesh. There's a cry of pain. I pull away, reaching the wooden cages. They're locked, the wood heavy and solid. I can't get them open. I peer into each one. Terrified children stare back at me, faces streaked with dirt and tears.

I reach the end.

She's not here. Cally isn't here.

I turn around and see more guards rushing toward me. I cry out in fury and rush the closest, batting his pike away and grabbing his throat.

'Where are the other kids? Where have you put them?'

The guard doesn't answer. I squeeze until his eyes bulge.

'Tell me!' I shout. 'Where's my daughter?'

He doesn't answer. My hand clenches tighter. My fingers dig in. I can feel them curl around his wind pipe. He's gasping for breath. Scrabbling at my face to push me away.

I stab him in the neck with my knife. Blood gushes over me and down his chest. I grab his pike, kick him away and turn. Three more guards are coming. I see the silver-masked Blessed appearing at the gate.

I throw the pike like a javelin. It hits the closest guard in the chest, lifting him from his feet and sending him sailing back through the air.

Another of the guards reaches me. He thrusts with his pike, but I jerk to the side and feel it scrape along my ribs. I grab the shaft, hitting it from beneath so it flies up out of the guard's hands and bring it down on my thigh, snapping it in two. I grab the broken shaft and ram it beneath the guard's chin. It bursts out the top of his head.

I yank it out again and sprint straight for the last guard. He takes one look at my face and runs back to the safety of the compound.

I stand in front of the children. They're all crying now, calling for their mums and dads. Every tear, every sob, adds to my hatred, feeds the beast inside. And this time I let it take me; claim me for its own. *This* is who I am. This is the only way things get done. Destroy those who wrong you. Kill those who hurt innocents. This is what I've been denying all these years. What I argued about on the steps of the museum last month. I feel the pain-beast grow inside, filling out the spaces in my soul. And I welcome it.

I am justice. I am wrath.

The masked guards approach. There are ten of them, with more coming behind. They approach cautiously, eyes on their fallen comrades. I reverse my knife and rest it along my forearm, the bloodied stick in my other hand.

The guards stop about ten feet away. I see my reflection in their masks, twisted, breathing heavily, face covered in blood. My true reflection. The dog was wrong. Armitage was wrong. I don't need to talk this out with shrinks. I don't need to deny who I am, push it down, pretend it doesn't exist. This is the real me.

The other me, the *weaker* one, the one that tries to hide from the rage, he is gone now. Dead.

We stare at each other. I face myself in the silver masks. The children quieten behind me.

I count five seconds.

Then the guards charge.

I scream and launch myself at them. I bat aside a wooden sword, slice my dagger across a throat. Duck down, feel the whistle of air above my head. Punch out with the knife, feel it break through leather and pierce skin. A strangled gasp, a gurgling spray. A thud against my shoulder. I lurch forward, turn around. Someone stands with an empty bow. I throw myself at him, using the broken pike shaft to stab into his ear. He screams and falls.

Another heavy blow. This time against my head. I'm on my knees. I feel hands grabbing me. I look up to see I've fallen next to the kids. They're staring down at me, eyes wide with terror.

And I suddenly realise they're not scared of the Blessed.

They're scared of me.

I reach out to try and reassure them that I'm not the bad one. I'm trying to help them. Another blow to the head. Blood flows into my eyes. I try to pull away, but I'm dragged backward. Away from the kids. Away from my chance to find Cally.

I fight and kick. Another punch, this time to my face. My vision swims. I shake my head and look up into my bloodied reflection.

I recognise the way she moves. My would-be assassin from the hotel.

'I will kill you if you carry on like this,' she says.

'You ...' I say. I reach up and grab her arm. 'Where ... where is my daughter?'

'Shut up.'

'Where is she?' I scream. I try to pull myself up.

Another hit, then another. I feel blackness closing in. My head lolls to the side and then a booted foot connects with my eye.

I come to with my wrists tied together in front of me and a rope tied tight around my neck. I wince and look around.

I'm lying on the floor just inside the entrance to the temple. One of the masked Blessed is watching me.

'About time,' he says. 'Get up.' A man this time. Not the woman who attacked me.

'Where's my daughter?'

'Get up.'

I struggle to my feet. 'Where's my daughter?'

He nods at the door. 'Go.'

I stumble outside into the dim light. Passers-by stare at me. I realise it's not often one of the Blessed themselves get arrested.

'Where are you taking me?' I ask.

'To the Marquis. You can tell him what you were doing here.'

'I just told you what I was doing. Looking for my daughter.'

'Then you can ask him.'

We're walking along one of the sidewalks bordering a canal. My head feels fuzzy, thick. I wonder if it's better to just let him take me to the Marquis and hope I can get my hands on him. I might just have enough time to kill him before I'm taken down.

But no. I can't do that, can I? That's the pain-beast talking. I let it out, but I need to rein it in again. Not completely. Just enough to operate. Just enough so I can get away from this and come back to look again.

Because I know she's here. And I'm not leaving without her.

I see a ripple of movement in the canal. I focus on it and see it move toward me. I frown.

Then Peg Powler erupts from the water. She lands between me and the guard. She grabs the rope attached to my neck and bites though it, then turns and shoves me. I fall, catching a brief glimpse of the guard taking out his wooden sword.

Then I hit the water.

I kick with my feet, pulling myself forward with my tied wrists. I stay under the water for as long as I can, my breath bursting to be released. I aim for a shadow above me, breaking the surface behind a passenger barge.

I peer back the way I came. I can't see the guard or Peg Powler anymore.

I loop the rope binding my wrists over a hook protuding from the back of the barge and let it take me downstream. A few seconds later Peg breaks the surface next to me. She stares at me with her wide eyes, and then winks, ducking below the surface again.

'You did what?' shouts Armitage.

'Does it matter?'

'Fuck yes, it matters. You endangered the mission, London. *Again.*'

'I didn't! That's why I waited till we had the stone. If I got caught you could still take it back.'

'And who's going to take it into the maze? Me?'

'Why not?'

'Because I'm the boss! I delegate that shit to people like you.'

'Fuck, Armitage. Whatever. I'm here now. Let's just go.'

'No. Not until you apologise.'

'Apologise?'

'Yes.'

'For looking for my daughter? For taking the one chance I've had in years to actually search a place where she might be held prisoner? You want me to apologise for that?'

'Yes.'

'Fuck you *and* your high horse.'

I turn back to the door connecting the rooms. I pull it open. The gnomes and Scaithe are sitting inside. 'Guys, ladies. It's been fun. And I'm genuinely sorry for the loss of your brothers.'

'We got our revenge,' says Hulin. 'They died fulfilling their purpose.'

I nod. 'See you round.' Then I leave the room and head along the corridor.

'London, wait up.'

The dog is trotting to catch up.

'You going to bitch at me too?'

'Damn straight.'

'Dog, just don't—'

'What the fuck were you thinking doing that without me?'

I stop walking and look at him. He has a hurt expression on his face.

'What if you found her? Without me? I want to be there, man. I want to meet this kid when you rescue her. She's a part of my life too, you know? How could she not be after everything we've been through? So yeah, fuck you for trying to do this on your own.'

I stare at him, taken aback. I suddenly get a glimpse of how much of a selfish prick I've been. He's my spirit guide. We're connected. On some level he can feel what I feel. He wants her back as much as I do, and I never once considered that. I was too busy feeling sorry for myself. Too busy carrying this pain, determined to shoulder the burden alone. As if that makes me somehow more noble, a better father. Or more deserving to get Cally back. But the dog has been there with me the whole time.

I take a shuddering breath. 'Dog ... I'm sorry, man. Seriously. I didn't think.'

'No, you didn't. I'm so sick of saying this to you. We're partners. You go through life with this cloud of fucking loneliness around you, but you refuse to actually see you're *not alone*. There are people who want to help you.'

My eyes start to prickle. I start walking again, determined not to let him see.

'Promise you won't do it again,' he says.

'I promise.'

'Pinky promise?'

I smile wearily. 'Pinky promise, motherfucker.'

We make our way out of Falias.

It's only when we reach the crest of the hill where we first caught sight of the city that I notice something.

On the opposite side of the city, on the plain where I had seen the kids, the Blessed are massing.

We stare into the distance as row upon row of soldiers leave the temple and form into regiments.

They keep coming. Hundreds, then thousands.

'Where the hell were they hiding?' I mutter.

We watch for a few minutes more. The army (and make no mistake, it is an army) turns to the left and starts marching in orderly lines.

'So where do we all think they're going?' asks the dog.

No one answers.

'Because I think they're getting ready to invade,' he says conversationally.

Again, no one responds.

'The city. *Your* city,' he adds.

'We get it,' says Winters.

'You sure? Because you seem remarkably indifferent to the fact that an army of fanatical, religious Fae are about to invade London. But you know, each to their own.'

'Jesus, but you like to spread the bad news, don't you?' says Winters.

'It's one of the few joys I have in life,' says the dog. 'That and pissing in London's shoes.'

'Let's get these stones back in place,' says Armitage. 'They won't dare to come through if we stop their stupid God from breaking out. No point.'

I hope she's right.

22

We travel back through the gate into Hyde Park and are met by Queen Rat. As soon as we step onto the grass Peg Powler heads off into the darkness.

'Not even a goodbye?' calls Armitage.

'She misses her river,' says Queen Rat. 'Do I take it you were successful?'

'Of course. Was there ever any doubt?' says Armitage.

'Oh yes. Lots.'

'Fair enough.'

'I did Dagda his favour,' says Queen Rat. 'He owes me.'

We don't answer. We're wasting time here. We need to get moving.

'You will tell him?' presses the Queen.

'Sure, sure,' says Armitage. 'We'll tell him. But if you'll excuse us, pet. We have a world to save. Again.'

It's only the four of us now. Me, Armitage, Winters, and the dog. We stop by the Ministry to ammo up before heading to the maze.

By the time I leave again I have two Berettas velcroed to my tactical stab vest, another two in holsters strapped to my legs (plus many, many magazines) and two shotguns over my shoulders (the same ones I used at the Ministry, with magazine extension tubes and side-saddle shell carriers). Plus, I'm carrying the wonderful L119 carbine, with magazines duct-taped together so all I have to do is eject and turn them round.

Two hours after we return from Faerie, we're heading to the Round Church within the Inns of the Court, the location of the opening to this maze.

There's someone waiting for us when we arrive.

Winters raises his gun, but I quickly push the barrel down. The figure before us is shifting in appearance. First an Asian woman, then a white male, then a black child, then a Chinese kid. I've seen this kind of thing before.

'Greetings, Gideon Tau,' says Mother London.

I nod respectfully. 'Mother London.'

She walks toward me. She studies me for a moment, then strokes my jaw. 'You are exactly as my sister described.'

She walks behind me, trailing her finger across my back. Armitage sniggers. Mother London shifts her attention and touches Armitage's neck. She stiffens in surprise.

'The unliving one. I have heard of you also.' She glances dismissively at Cal. 'I don't know who you are.'

'Jesus. I'm the only one who actually *lives* here,' he complains.

Mother London looks him up and down then ignores him and smiles sadly at me. I don't like that look.

'What?'

'Nothing. I just feel sorry for you. I can sense the undulations of your soul across the dreams of my city. You are in for a difficult time.'

'Really?' I say, trying to ignore the sinking feeling in my stomach. 'So nothing's changed then?'

She touches my lips. 'You can pretend. We will see if you come out of this unscathed. I do not think so.'

She steps aside and gestures to the church. 'I would point the way, but I have a feeling you will find it easily enough.' She hesitates. 'I . . . do not normally interfere, but I will tell you that the Marquis is already there with some of his Blessed soldiers. Waiting for his God to return.'

'Is he in the prison yet?'

'No.' Again she hesitates. 'The Marquis will not enter. And I advise you not to either. The prison is ... other. Mortal minds are not meant to experience what the Old Ones have been dreaming.'

'Ominously unhelpful,' says the dog.

'The prison ... brings to life the scars of your psyche. Whatever it is that drives you. It was the only way to keep the Old Ones thinking they were free. To make them think that they were still the gods of old.'

She looks like she wants to say something more, but instead she puts a hand on my arm. She holds it there for a second, then moves away into the cold night.

'Cheerful, isn't she?' says Armitage. She leans the shotgun up against her shoulder. 'Come on then. Let's get this over with.'

She throws me a look as she passes. 'And you, no selling out the human race this time, OK?'

I swing the L119 around and flick the safety off. 'You're never going to let me live that down, are you?'

'Nope.'

'What's she talking about?' asks Winters as we approach the Round Church.

'Nothing.'

'You sure? I kind of feel like it's important.'

'It's nothing,' I say. 'Christ sake, focus, Winters.'

Armitage pushes the door of the church open with her shotgun. She peers inside, checks it out, then straightens up and walks casually inside.

I follow after her into a scene of devastation. Benches have been ripped up, wooden floorboards torn and twisted. Not a single window is intact.

I have no idea how they've managed to keep this from the authorities. Keeping the Covenant secret is one thing, but trying to keep damage to a listed building secret from the National Trust? That's a whole other level of magic.

We file quietly into the room to the left. The damage is even worse in here. The stone floor has been entirely destroyed. Old statues lie broken and shattered. It looks like they used to be knights.

There are black footprints everywhere. I bend down and touch one of them. It's hot and sticky.

Gross. I wipe my hand on my jeans and join the others gathered around a hole in the floor. A set of stairs leads down. There's light somewhere below, a flickering orange glow that dims and brightens. We can hear something at the bottom of the stairs. It sounds like . . . horses' hooves?

'Wait here,' says Armitage softly.

'No—'

She doesn't listen, but moves rapidly down the stairs and vanishes from sight.

There's a brief moment of silence. Then thundering explosions, one after the other. A whinnying scream echoes out. Then the racking click of shotgun shells being loaded.

More explosions.

Then silence.

'You can come down now.'

We descend the stairs and find ourselves in a long, low room. Armitage is standing over the body of a . . . I think at first it's a centaur, but it's not. The thing has no skin, and it's massive. Winters whistles softly.

'Respect, boss.'

'No time for kissing ass.' She jerks her head behind her. 'Not sure, but reckon that's the way in?'

The back wall seems to have vanished. It's just . . . gone. We walk towards it, almost stumbling over a decapitated figure lying on shards of broken glass. I raise my eyebrows at Winters.

'No idea.'

There's an ancient-looking altar in the centre of the room. It's pretty much the only thing left in one piece. It's covered in

something like grey sand. The same stuff is all over the ground
too.

'That must have held the lock,' says Armitage.

'Why don't we just put the stone down here and lock it up
again?' asks Winters. 'That way everyone is stuck in the
maze.'

'The Sins already destroyed one,' I say. 'What if they're
strong enough to break through from the other side?'

'Point.'

We approach the opening. A wide ramp leads down into
the darkness. A cold breeze rises up toward us, ruffling our
hair as we ready our weapons.

'Ready to kick some fairy ass?' says Armitage, as she racks
a shell into the chamber. She looks expectantly at Winters.

'What?'

'Come on. You can't do this kind of thing without a cool
one-liner. If we survive we have to write this up in reports. We
need to sound good.'

'Oh. Um ... Right. Got one.' He racks the slide on his
Beretta. 'Time to send Tinkerbell back to never-never land.'

'Nice,' says the dog.

'Thanks.'

'Aye. Not bad. London?'

'Come on—'

'London, I swear to God I will not go down this ramp unless
you do this,' complains Armitage.

I sigh. 'Prepare to be judged.'

Armitage gives me a pitying look. 'Dog?'

'Watch out, motherfuckers. I'm coming to piss on your
parade. Literally.'

'That's terrible,' I say.

'Fuck you! It's better than yours.' He puts on a stupid-
sounding voice. 'Duh ... Prepare to be judged. Duh.'

'Fuck you.'

I start walking down the ramp. I was half-expecting there to be some kind of moment of magic, an odd feeling to sweep through me. But there isn't. Nothing at all to say we're walking into a maze that hasn't seen a living soul for thousands of years.

Speaking of which. 'Hey, dog. Can you catch their scent and lead the way?'

'I can. Just not sure I want to.'

'Why?'

'Because taking point is never a good survival skill.'

'Just do it. Please.'

The dog trots ahead of us, grumbling darkly under his breath. We follow behind, our guns held at the ready.

We walk down the ramp for about half an hour before it stops at a large hole in the wall.

We step cautiously forward and find ourselves looking out into a cavern of endless space.

Below us, the size of a small city, is the concrete maze, and in the centre of the maze is . . . darkness. A void of nothingness that absorbs the dim light filling the cavern. The maze itself is moving. The walls shift and turn, sliding backwards, forwards, swinging outward and sweeping around to create new pathways while blocking off others.

The ramp carries on down the side of the wall. We run. It feels like time is catching up with us. A pressure is building inside that makes me want to scream.

There's a large, empty space between the bottom of the ramp and the maze itself. We cross it at a sprint. The walls of the maze tower high above us, a hundred feet high, and as we draw closer I see that the entrance to the maze is a stone door covered with iron cogs and gears.

We arrive at the wall and Armitage spins a large wheel nestled amongst the clockwork trappings. Two cogs on either side of the wheel drop into place. Small wheels spin, moving so fast that they're a blur. The larger wheels trundle more slowly, and then the door clunks and groans, slowly opening outward.

There's a collective scream from the other side and the Blessed guards charge us, brandishing their wooden swords. These aren't the ones with the silver masks. These are the elves, like the Marquis.

I bring the rifle up and open fire. The gunfire sounds unnaturally loud, startling everyone. It cuts into the Fae ranks, dropping them to the ground. We move slowly backwards as we shoot, trying to keep distance between us and our attackers. Armitage fires her shotgun, Winters his two Beretta pistols, one in each hand.

They reach us before we can take them all down. A wooden sword swings for my head. I swing the rifle up to block it and kick the elf in the stomach. He stumbles back, then straightens up and tries to thrust the sword into my chest. I twist aside, turn full circle and shoot him in the back of the head.

Another elf comes at me, this one female. She leaps into the air, long-bladed daggers in each hand. She screams, her face a twisted mask of hate.

'Unclean!' she shrieks.

I unload a burst into her before she even lands. What a stupid tactic.

Armitage has dropped her shotgun and is fighting with her bare hands now, her revenant strength coming to the fore. She grabs one of the elves, casually breaks his arm, then kicks out and snaps his leg. He drops, screaming. Armitage steps over him and launches herself at another elf. She soars through the air, lands on his back, grabs his neck, and twists. The head pops off in her hand, spraying blood everywhere.

She lands and looks at the head in surprise. Then tosses it to the ground.

Winters is still having fun with his Berettas, turning in a circle and shooting at every Fae that comes in his direction. There's already a pile of bodies surrounding him.

And he's laughing. His mouth open in a crazy grin. Shooting, killing, laughing maniacally. He's like the dog given human form.

Speaking of the dog, he's having his fun too, but hasn't bothered to change his form. He's content with leaping at throats or ripping away undercarriages, blood and . . . other bits spilling out with wet splashes.

I eject my clip, grab another from my pocket and ram it home again, firing at the final few elves still running toward us.

Twenty seconds after it began, the battle is over.

At least thirty bodies surround us. The smell of hot metal and gunpowder hangs in the air, barely masking the smell of blood and shit and piss.

We enter the maze. The walls tower over us, perspective making it look like they're leaning in, about to collapse on us. The walls themselves . . . they're not just smooth stone. They're segmented, with geometric lines cutting through them. There's a constant noise in the maze, the tick-tick of cogs turning, the grinding sound as the walls of the maze shift and rearrange themselves.

The passage itself is about six feet wide. We spread out to either side as we approach the first intersection. My back is against the right wall and Armitage's against the left, the dog and Winters waiting. I nod and we swing around at the same time, facing opposite directions, guns held level.

Nothing.

The dog trots forward, nose close to the ground. We trail behind him as he leads the way.

After a few minutes he pauses, then backtracks. He moves up and down the same patch of corridor, sniffing the ground, getting more and more annoyed.

I lean against the wall. 'Problem?'

'Old trail, but it just vanishes up against that wall. I—'

The wall I'm leaning against lurches and moves, shoving me forward. I stagger and whirl around to find the wall . . . lifting, separating along the geometric lines I'd noticed earlier. The wall separates to reveal spinning cogs, gears and springs, the clockwork innards that power the entire maze.

The wall slides away from us, opening up a different path. Armitage shoves me. Hard. I stagger forward and glance over my shoulder to find another wall sliding into place where we'd just been standing, blocking off our old path.

The walls stop moving and slide closed again, the clockwork gears inside vanishing from sight.

'I can see this seriously pissing me off,' says Winters.

He's not wrong.

We track back until the dog finds the scent again. This time we manage to follow it for five minutes before the walls move again, once again blocking off our path.

It's slow going.

Half an hour later we turn a corner and walk into another Fae patrol. I bring my rifle up, firing two bursts before they even notice us. Armitage fires off three shells into the closest Faes' legs. They drop, screaming, and the dog leaps on them, tearing out their throats. Winters calmly shoots another four in the head. We're developing quite a smooth system here.

Another Fae comes at me. I squeeze the trigger but my rifle clicks empty. I yank a Beretta from its Velcro holster and pump three rounds into his face and neck. He drops to his knees. Another shot to the head.

Done.

We move on.

As we navigate the ever-shifting maze we come across three more patrols, our ammo diminishing in a worryingly rapid manner each time.

The maze seems to move faster the closer we get to the centre. The walls barely stay still now. The sound of clockwork gears is ever present. I see after-images of spinning gears wherever I look, hear a constant ticking sound that works its way into my brain and tries to distract me from the mission at hand. We're constantly dodging and pressing our backs up against the walls to avoid being crushed by the narrowing passages.

The next time the walls move, the four of us are separated. It was inevitable really. The wall in front of me splits down the centre into two halves. One half swings toward me, shoving me ahead of it. The other half swings in the opposite direction, locking into place and cutting off the others.

'Armitage?'

No answer.

-*Dog? You there?*-

Nothing.

I hesitate for a moment, then decide to keep going. What else can I do?

I walk randomly, because I have no other choice. Whenever the maze changes, I try to head toward the centre, but I have no idea if I'm going in the right direction.

Which makes it something of a surprise when about forty minutes later I stumble into an open space.

I stare around in shock. There's an area of heavy blackness ahead of me. A . . . dome of pure shadow.

That's it. That's the prison.

I sag with relief. I met more patrols along the way, so have hardly any weapons left. Only one shotgun and one handgun that I think might be empty.

I don't move. I wait, listening, for a long moment.

But there's no one else here. Have I beaten them all to it? Even the Marquis and the Sins? Is the lock not even broken yet?

I approach the prison. I'm only now realising that this hasn't been well planned at all. Fine, maybe the Sins haven't destroyed the lock, but how the hell am I supposed to stop them if they turn up now? And deal with the Marquis and his Fae? This isn't a job for a small group of plucky heroes. This is a job for large numbers of tired and grumpy humans and orisha who haven't had their coffee.

All I can do is hope Armitage and the others get here before the Sins turn up.

And that's when I see the small altar up ahead, covered with the same grey powder we found back in the church.

I'm not the first here. The second lock has already been broken.

I look around warily, feeling suddenly exposed. I don't get it. Why hasn't the Horned God come out? Where is the Marquis? Are they *inside* the prison? Are they still in the process of releasing Cernunnos?

I hurry to the altar, shifting my backpack off my shoulder as I do so. Maybe I can still fix this. If I can put the lock back in place, maybe I can trap them all inside the prison. Let them spend eternity locked away with each other. See how they like that.

I wipe the dust away, noting that the altar is covered in odd writing that looks slightly like Scandinavian runes, or perhaps Ogham.

I unzip the bag . . .

. . . And I hear the sound of running feet coming around the dome.

I spin around. Once again, I know immediately that it's the woman from the hotel room, just from the way she moves. She leaps into the air and shoves her legs out, hitting me square in the chest.

I fall backwards, dropping the bag as I do so.

I hit the shadow wall.

There's a surge of electricity. I stiffen, cry out, but then the pain vanishes quickly, replaced by a second feeling, a sudden lurch of . . . nothingness, as if everything has just stopped. I reach out, hoping I can escape, pull myself back out.

But then I'm jerked backwards and the blackness yanks me in, crawling across my body. Into my mouth, over my eyes, down my throat. Into my ears.

A moment of utter, pure panic, a primeval fear that my existence is about to end, and then I'm surrounded by darkness. It's thick and heavy and drapes over me like old velvet, stealing my breath away. I try to move but it's fighting against me, holding me in place. It wants to keep me here forever, like an insect trapped in amber.

I grit my teeth and push forward. I don't know what direction I'm moving in. I just know I can't stay still.

Images appear before me as I make my slow way through the darkness. Images from a past no one has ever seen.

Animals becoming Gods and Gods becoming animals. The Old Ones. The First of All.

There are three of them; towering, eight feet tall. The first two . . . there's something not right about them. They haven't been designed or thought of by anything intelligent. One is a towering creature covered in thick, matted hair. A hollow bone protrudes from the area where its mouth should be. Its eye holes are filled with a black tar-like substance, and the tar drips down over the hair, coating it, making it stick together.

The second looks to be part bird. A massive, twisted being with a huge bone-coloured beak that clacks quietly. Non-stop. The creature's feathers are greasy and muddy, covered in blood and faeces. Wide, empty eyes peer left, then right, up, then down. In constant motion.

And the third I know is Cernunnos.

The Horned God.

He looks more animal than the other two. Steam rises from his heaving flanks. His antlers twist out like the branches of an ancient, winter-dead tree. His body is covered with thick, coarse hair, his eyes black and empty of thought.

This is a creature of instinct. Of animalistic urges and needs. A creature of the hunt.

These are the Old Ones.

I have seen them, as no one else has.

And then I'm suddenly lying on wet mud, blinking the darkness away as if a dark hood has been yanked from my head.

I stare up at the sky and see a multi-coloured galaxy above me, constellations and nebulae in streaks of pink and purple. Brittle stars cold and distant.

I stand up. Directly in front of me are three blocks of crudely carved stone. Two of them are occupied by the gods I've just seen. But the third is empty.

The one where the Horned God is supposed to be sleeping.

I take a step forward and my surroundings shift and change.

The mud and stone disappear and instead I'm faced with a line of people that snakes into the distance. Everyone in the line has belongings clutched to their chests. Money bags, jewellery, children. They shuffle slowly forward, stopping before a thin man dressed in grey robes, who draws a knife across their throats and takes what they're holding.

I frown, not understanding what I'm seeing.

I take another step and the image flickers and winks out, replaced with another. It's dark but I can hear grunting and moaning. Screaming and groaning. I can just make out the movements of body parts; men, women, animal, all of them being mounted and fucked by different versions of the same figure. He looks wasted and pale, his body emaciated, his face twisted with disappointment.

Lust. One of the Seven Sins.

I suddenly realise I'm in the heads of the Sins. The prison has mined their psyches, pulled out what it is that defines them. So what was the first one I'd seen? Envy? Greed?

The picture shifts again. A table, filled with different versions of a figure so putridly fat he is the size of five normal men. He's naked, fat rolls resting on the table, spilling out of his chair to pile up on the floor. Each version of the creature stuffs his face with food. Meat, bones, soup, wine, fruit, even . . . I squint closer, the flesh of babies.

Gluttony.

Another step and another scene. A creature is sitting in a pit full of body parts and gold. Blood swims and bubbles to the surface as the creature shifts around, squirming on his back amidst his treasure.

This is greed. The first must have been envy.

The next sin is more difficult to understand. It seems to be represented by an angel, but the angel's face is ever-shifting, changing from beautiful, sexless features to a twisted, demonic being with its skin melting off its body.

The angel screams in pain as his wings burst into flames.

Then I get it.

Pride. The angel is supposed to be Lucifer.

Another step and another tableau. Figures sleeping on the ground while all around them animals and children die, their bodies withering away from hunger and dehydration.

Sloth.

And finally, all that remains is wrath.

Except, I don't see wrath's vision. Instead I see the Sin as he is now, the same creature I fought back at the Ministry. He's fighting with Cernunnos, and by the flattened landscape around them, the shattered trees and blackened earth, the fight has been going on for a while.

As I watch, wrath grabs hold of the Horned God and forces him to the ground. The Sin grabs his antlers and pulls. The

Horned God screams in fury and pain, but the Sin does not stop. He keeps pulling until with a horrendous crack the antlers snap away from the Horned God's head.

The Sin tosses them aside. Cernunnos falls to his knees and the Sin grabs his face. He bends down and passionately kisses the Horned God, who goes limp, lifeless.

The Sin's body begins to change, the black oil that covers it vibrating and shivering. It flows up and into Cernunnos' mouth. The Horned God chokes and gags, but the Sin does not let go until all the blackness has entered the Horned God's body.

The empty husk of the Sin falls away. As it hits the ground it simply falls apart, dispersing with the wind.

The Horned God lifts his head to the sky and howls.

And it's then I understand what has happened. My stomach lurches with dismay as the events of the past week shift in my mind, taking on new meaning. The Seven Sins were falling apart, too powerful for normal bodies to hold. Even the bodies they were born with in the cavern below Durban were not strong enough. They needed the body of a God to contain them.

The Marquis thought he was using the Sins, using them to free Cernunnos, but all along, the Sins were using *him*. They never intended to release the Horned God. They wanted to *possess* it.

And now that the lock is broken, they can get out.

I feel utterly sick at what is about to happen. They are the Sins of God himself. Which means for all intents and purposes, they *are* God. But without any of his redeeming qualities. (Not that he had many.) The Seven Sins were from the Old Testament God. The righteous fury and anger of a petty child. What stands before me now is partly the God millions believe in, and partly utterly, utterly insane. It's like ... Aleister Crowley being given the powers of an angel.

I can't allow him to leave.

He turns toward me. His eyes widen in recognition.

'You . . .' God says, and his voice is a low whisper that echoes in my head. 'You caused me pain,' he growls.

And God starts to walk toward me. I can't let him get out. If he escapes he'll just . . . destroy. Give in to every base desire he possesses. The Covenant will not hold it in check. Nothing will.

I stare at the creature striding toward me. This is it. This is the end. I'm never going to find Cally. I'm never going to hold her in my arms again. I'm never going to kiss her goodnight. Never see her smile.

And it is at these thoughts that the pain-beast stirs to life. A surge of anger boils through me, terrible and all-consuming. This thing . . . this . . . demented fucking God. It becomes the focus of all my hate. All my anger. The fury sweeps through me with surprising ease. It's like I woke it in Faerie and it was just waiting to come back. To take over.

I let it.

I'm too tired now to fight it anymore. I don't have anything left. It's been trying to do this, constantly wearing me down, since Cally went missing. I've managed to keep it at bay, but now I wonder why I've been fighting so hard. Why I've been pretending I could win. It's not the pain-beast. It's me. More me than anything else. I should just accept myself for what I am.

As I think this, I feel a rush of wind and darkness race through me. I stagger, look up and have the curious sensation of watching me run away from myself.

I don't understand. I straighten up, frowning.

But no, I was right. It's me. Heading straight for God. But at the same time it's . . . not me. The figure I'm watching is larger, bulkier, massive muscles bunching and coiling.

I watch in amazement as I leap into the air and collide with God. I grab him by the throat and pummel his face. Roaring. Swearing. A raw, animal shout of death and fury.

It's the pain-beast. The other me. The thing that has defined me for as long as I can remember. The magic that exists in this prison has given it form.

His face is twisted and grotesque. Me, but not. Features pulled into cruel curves. Dead eyes that no one wants to look into. He wraps his hands around God, squeezing, but God stabs his hands into his sides. The pain-beast screams, letting go. God's fingers slide out of his body. He lunges forward and tears at God's throat with his teeth. God screams and tries to snap the pain-beast's neck.

God looks at me over my shoulder. He screams his fury as he tries to get to me. But the pain-beast stops him, pulling him to the ground. God shoves him off and head-butts him in the chest. Broken antlers pierce his body. God lifts him up, tossing his head and sending the pain-beast flying. He hits the ground hard, but is up in an instant. Running.

Why am I just standing here?

I turn and run toward the black cloud, hearing the fury of God roaring behind me.

I don't look back as I force my way into the blackness.

It feels like I'm walking though time. The years try to hold me back, making my feet sluggish. I look down and my clothes wither and disintegrate. My flesh wrinkles, pulling into the bone. Sores erupt, bones push out through the skin. I hold my hands up and see them putrefy before me, decaying and rotting. I touch my face and I can feel the skull beneath.

I push on. I can see a light up ahead. A tiny white circle of hope. My legs are failing me, rotting away. I fall forward and start to crawl. The light draws closer, but the prison wants to hold me back, tries to devour me.

I reach the light and fall forward . . .

. . . And I hit the ground. Landing on my backpack.

I take a deep, shuddering breath, and I look around. The Fae woman is standing about twenty feet away with the Marquis. They're staring at me. The Marquis looks shocked.

He whispers something to the woman. She comes for me, her sword blade held along her arm, like I've seen in some Japanese movies. I stagger to my feet, stumbling back, and reach up for the shotgun strapped to my back. I grab the barrel and try to point it at her, but she's already on top of me, bringing the sword down to hit the gun. It flies out of my hand. She shifts her balance and kicks it, sending it flying to the side.

I leap forward and wrap my arms around her midriff, pushing her back. She hits the back of my head with the hilt of her sword. Again and again. I shove her away.

I try to pull my Berretta from its holster. She hits my wrist, pulls the gun out of my hand and throws it across the floor.

I stagger back, feeling inside my jacket for my wand. I pull it out and point it, but her wooden blade is already swinging through the air. It hits my wand and slices it into two. I feel a surge of escaping power, and then I'm holding a piece of bone that does absolutely nothing.

I spot the shotgun lying on the ground. I drop the broken wand, dive for the gun, scoop it up and whirl around just as she comes at me, her sword striking down once again.

I bring the shotgun up and the weapons crash together. We stand like that for a moment, both of us trying to push, to gain the upper hand. She's so fucking strong.

I'm just thinking about pulling to the side and letting her overbalance when she does the same thing, spinning to the side and moving behind me as I stumble forward.

Agony erupts in my side. I look down and see the point of her sword jutting out just above my hip. The point vanishes as she pulls the sword out.

I hit the floor, then force myself to roll to the side just as the sword comes down toward me. I force myself to my feet, crying out with the effort and pain.

I see the dropped Beretta out of the corner of my eye. She's standing between me and the gun. I stagger to the right and she moves with me. I try going left but she blocks me again.

I'm losing a lot of blood. The pain is pulsing through my body in agonising waves. I can't keep this up forever.

So I charge. It takes everything I've got left inside me, but I launch myself at her. She straightens up in surprise, then brings her sword around and down, aiming for my side. I throw myself forward, and pain explodes in my arm. I scream, feeling the wooden blade cut deep into my upper shoulder. I feel the wood stick, then she yanks it free. Warm wetness flows down my arm as I hit the ground.

I fumble for the Beretta and roll onto my back. She's coming straight for me.

I fire. Two rounds. That's all that's left. I don't get a chance to aim properly. The rounds hit her in the stomach. She folds in on herself, stumbling.

She uses her sword to steady herself and takes another step. Then another. But then the sword slides from under her and she collapses, hitting the ground hard.

I watch her for a second. By the slight movement of her back I can see she's still alive. But she won't last with wounds like that. I drop the gun. I wince and peel back my shirt, studying my shoulder. The wound is about an inch or so deep and as long as my hand. Blood wells out in a steady stream.

I hear a sigh and turn to see the Marquis approaching. He squats down just out of reach. He stares at me, then at my attacker. He reaches out and prods her.

'Disappointing,' says the Marquis. 'I've been training her for years. Ever since she was a child.'

The Marquis pulls her armour aside. He lifts her shirt to reveal two ugly holes in her stomach. The Marquis clicks his tongue in sympathy.

'Not good that. Gut shot. She might last a while, but it's a slow death. You should put her out of her misery.'

'Fuck . . . off,' I say. It's an effort to speak. I'm exhausted. I have nothing left.

The Marquis smiles. 'You've been quite a thorn in my side, haven't you? And you didn't even know who I was. It is a lesson for me, I think. I should have checked whose child I took.' He taps his head. 'Note to self. Keep that in mind for the future.' He studies me. 'You know that's all it was, right? It's not as if you were particularly clever or anything. Or I needed your child specifically. I was taking children for our army and I took your kid by mistake. You started searching for her, sticking your nose in where it wasn't wanted, so I had to stop you. It was nothing personal.' He laughs. 'Funny story. I thought you and your wife were still living together. That's how she ended up dead.' He leans forward and pats me on the leg. 'So you've got that on your conscience too.'

He sighs and studies the shadowy dome of the prison. 'How long do you think it will take the Sins to release the Old Ones? I mean, you know them better than anyone. I should thank you for that too, by the way. I wouldn't have even known about the Sins if we hadn't been watching you.'

I chuckle painfully. 'Your Gods aren't coming. And Cernunnos is already dead.'

The Marquis frowns. 'What?'

'The Sins . . . they fucked you over. They never planned on releasing the Old Ones. They . . . needed the body of a god to . . . to possess. They've killed your Horned God. They . . .' I wince. 'They have taken his body for themselves.'

His face shows a moment of fear, but then he smiles. 'You're bluffing.'

I shrug, then try to sit up. My side screams at me and I feel more blood flowing over my hip. 'Where . . . is she?'

'Who?' says the Marquis innocently.

'My . . . daughter.'

The Marquis rocks forward slightly on his haunches, then rocks back again. He's grinning now, like a kid with a big secret.

'You really want to know where she is?' he asks.

I stare at him. The sweat is pouring down my face. I'm losing too much blood.

'Fine,' says the Marquis. He stands up. 'Gideon Tau, allow me to introduce you to your daughter.'

I frown. What the hell is he talking about?

The Marquis stares at me, then turns to look at the woman I shot.

'Gideon, Cally. Cally, meet your father.'

I stare at him, uncomprehending.

What . . .

No.

The Marquis gets down on his hands and knees, shuffling toward me like a dog. He has a huge grin on his face. 'Time passes differently in Tír na nÓg,' he says, his voice jittery with excitement. 'Three years out here is . . . oh, about twenty one years over there.'

No, no, no.

'You're lying . . .' I whisper.

'At least you got to see your daughter one last time before she dies.'

He scampers toward her and pulls the mask off. Her head lolls in my direction and we lock eyes.

I stare at the woman in horror. The face . . . I can see Cally there. The daughter I knew. The shape of her eyes, the curve of her nose.

'*No!*' My scream turns into a sob.

Cally is staring at me, eyes wide with horror and pain. She heard everything.

My eyes fill with tears. I choke in terror, in fear. I drag myself toward her.

'Cally,' I whisper. 'Cally.'

Her eyes drift closed.

I reach her. Grab her hand. I stroke her face. 'Cally,' I whisper. 'Wake up, honey. Daddy's here. I've found you, baby. I've got you back.'

A wracking sob tears through me.

'Come on, honey. Don't leave me again. Please. Oh, god . . . Don't leave me again.'

My head falls to her chest. My tears flow across her, trickling down her neck.

I laugh painfully through my tears. 'There are people I need you to meet,' I say brokenly. 'My friends. The dog – he's crazy. You'll love him. He's been waiting to meet you. And Armitage. She's . . . a bit of work, but she's amazing. When you wake up . . .' Another shuddering pulse of fear and pain rampages through my body. '. . . When you wake up, we're going to have a party. A barbecue. By the pool. Perfect weather for it. We'll all get to know each other again. We'll be a big family. You'll see.'

I close my eyes tightly.

'I've got you back now. Everything's going to be all right.'

'I think she's dead,' says the Marquis conversationally.

I lift my head, study her face.

She's not breathing. My daughter is not breathing.

No.

I won't let her die. I put my mouth over hers and blow into her lungs. Then I force myself up, ignoring the pain screaming through my body, and compress her chest.

One. Two. Three. I count to thirty, then breathe into her mouth again.

More chest compressions.

'She's dead, idiot.'

I ignore him.

Something collides with my head. I fall to the side, dizzy. Blood in my eyes. I pull myself up, go back to performing CPR. I can't let her go again.

Something hits me again. I realise the Marquis has kicked me more than five feet across the cavern. I try to get back to Cally, but my head is spinning. My arms give out. I fall onto my back.

The Marquis is standing above me. He's frowning.

'It was funny for a while, but it's just annoying now.'

He puts a booted foot on my chest and holds me down to the ground. He pulls his own sword out and lays it against my neck. I feel the skin part around the wooden blade. Blood bubbles out.

I stare up at his face. He looks more like an animal now than I've ever seen. The casual cruelty of a fox. The hunger of a rabid dog.

His tongue pokes out of his mouth. It's long. He licks his lips . . .

. . . And his mouth opens in a scream. The sword jerks away from my neck. He stumbles back, staring down in horror. I follow his gaze and see the point of another sword sticking out of his stomach.

Cally is standing behind him, staggering, almost falling.

The Marquis looks at her in amazement, then down at the blade protruding from his stomach. 'You . . . bitch!' he snarls.

He takes a step toward her and I'm up on my feet. I don't know how. Ignoring the pain. Ignoring the fresh flow of blood. I seize his shoulders, pulling him away from my daughter. I try to get to her, but he grabs me and pulls me back. I try to shake him off as I watch Cally fall to her knees again. He won't let me go. I spin around. I grab his throat with one hand

and I squeeze with all the hate and loneliness and pain that I've ever felt. I scream into his face, the wordless, primal scream of a parent trying to protect his daughter. My nails dig in, breaking skin.

I push. Push with everything I have. His eyes widen in pain. I feel the skin break, warm blood and meat folding around my fingers. Blood bursts over my hand. My fingers dig deeper, strength I didn't know I had flowing out through me in a wave of black hate. His hands come up and he grabs me by the shoulders. He screams in pain and pulls us together.

Cally's blade, still protruding from the Marquis' stomach, punches into me. I cry out and squeeze even harder. Blood flows over my fingers. I can feel them curling around his oesophagus. He's gasping for breath. Scrabbling at my face to push me away.

I feel something long and sinewy behind my index finger. I curl the top of my finger around it and pull, yanking it from his neck.

The Marquis jerks away, but I'm still holding tight to whatever it is I have in my fingers. His neck rips open and a piece of muscle flops out onto the floor.

Blood gushes over me, down his chest.

The Marquis drops to the ground.

I fall to my knees. I try to push myself up again, to go to Cally, but the pain in my stomach is too much. I fall forward and have to pull myself slowly across the dirt, leaving a trail of blood behind.

When I finally reach her, I take her hand. It's cool and soft.

I stare at it, studying her fingers, remembering when I held her hand as a child, as a baby.

I hear a panicked breath.

My eyes snap up. Cally is staring at me, her eyes clouded with pain.

'I'm going to fix this, baby. I promise.'

'I'm . . . sorry I tried to kill you,' she whispers.

Her eyes flutter closed. I try to stroke her face but pain convulses me, curling me up against her.

My eyes drift closed, and my last thought is, *I've lost her again.*

A sound penetrates the fog of red pain. It's far away, heard through gauze and emptiness and rage.

'London!'

I try to open my eyes. They're stuck together with blood. I force them open and find myself looking into the panicked face of Armitage.

She chokes down a sob when my eyes open.

Then she slaps me.

'What the fuck are you doing? How many times do I have to tell you. You don't do this shit on your own!'

I can't answer. I can feel Cally beneath me. I try to turn over, turn away from Armitage to see my daughter. Hands grab me, pulling me up. I fight them off.

'Stop it,' shouts Armitage. 'Let us take you out of here.'

'No . . .'

I fight them off again. I pull my arms away and drop back to the ground. I reach out and touch Cally.

And I feel something faint. A heartbeat.

A surge of hope burns through me. I turn painfully to Armitage and Winters. 'Take her . . . to the hospital.'

They look confused. The dog bumps his head against my leg.

'Come on, man. You're fucked in the head. What happened? Did you stop them? Are we good?'

'Not . . . yet. The . . . lock.' I look to my backpack.

Winters rushes over and grabs the stone out of the bag and lays it on the altar.

That's it. The lock is back in place. The world is saved.

My world is ending.

I try to stand up, but I fall back again, pain exploding in my stomach. I wince against the pain and I get to my feet. Armitage's arms are around me. I shake her off and I lean down to pick my daughter up. Every movement is pure agony. Every movement brings a fresh welling of blood.

But I do it. I lift my baby in my arms. I turn to the entrance. Take a step. Stop. Almost fall. A deep breath. Another step.

'London,' says Armitage urgently. I can hear by her voice she's freaked out, close to panicking. 'What are you doing?'

'Cally . . .' I say. 'It's . . . Cally.'

'What?' shouts the dog. He sprints around and faces me. He looks at Cally then at me. 'What the fuck are you talking about?'

'It's . . . her. Time . . . different in Faerie.' I stare at him, then a sob erupts from me. The tears come with it. 'I shot her, dog. I fucking shot my baby.'

Arms around me again, this time taking Cally from me. It's Winters, holding her gently. He's looking at Armitage, unsure what to do.

'Take her!' I shout. I fall to my knees again, all my strength falling away. 'Get her to a hospital.'

'London,' says Armitage. 'We can't leave you—'

'*Take her!*' I scream. I take a shuddering breath. 'Please,' I say, softer this time. 'Save her, Armitage. Don't let me kill my daughter.'

Armitage looks at me a moment longer, then straightens up and takes Cally's limp form from Winters. 'Follow me,' she tells him. 'Anything appears, shoot it.'

Then she starts running, Winters hurrying to catch up.

I fall back to the ground. The blood is flowing again. I don't know how much I've lost. Too much, I think. I'm tired. My energy is just . . . gone. I'm not even sore anymore, just . . . empty. And I don't know if that's because I left that part of me in the prison, fighting an eternal battle against God, or if I'm just dying.

My eyes drift closed.

A moment later I feel something on my chest. I manage to move my head and see the dog lying next to me, his head resting on my ribs.

I lift my hand and let it fall onto his fur.

'In it till the end,' I say. And then the darkness folds over me and I feel free for the first time ever.

EPILOGUE

One week after Cal Winters pretty much *single-handedly* saved the world, he wakes up the morning after the night before.

He groans and holds his head. Someone's using a jack-hammer against his skull. 'Fuck me,' he mutters.

'Again?' says a voice.

Cal freezes, frantically hitting rewind on the mental Betamax tape that is the previous night. He remembers lots of whisky. Lots of pubs. Playing pool. Meeting a woman on the freezing streets. Fuck. What was her name again?

Why is he thinking Ribena? That can't be right, can it? Ribena, ribena . . . Rowena! That was it. He remembers thinking it was a weird name.

He opens his eyes and rolls over with a smile.

Only to be confronted by what looks like a seventy-year-old naked woman smiling seductively at him.

Winters leaps from the bed, getting tangled up in the sheets and falling on his arse. 'What the fuck!'

'Good morning to you too, lover,' says the old woman.

Cal looks frantically around his bedroom. 'Uh . . .' he grabs the fallen sheet and wraps it around himself. 'Look, don't take this the wrong way, but . . . who are you? Where's . . . Rowena?'

'Right here, loverboy.'

Cal frowns. 'I don't get it.'

She laughs. 'No? How about now?'

As he watches, the old woman's face changes to that of the woman he stumbled home with last night. Thirty-something. Strawberry blonde hair. Freckles. And gorgeous green eyes.

Fuck, he thinks. Orisha. Shapeshifter? Do the Blessed have a policy of giving their victims one last really good time before murdering them?

'So the pact is sealed,' she says.

Cal blinks. 'Sorry – what's that? Pact?'

'We have performed the rites. I have tasted your seed, you have tasted my juices.'

'Jesus, you don't have to be gross about it.'

'You are mine now.'

Cal winces and rubs his temples. 'I don't know what's going on here,' he complains, 'but I'm getting the feeling it's really not going to be good for me.'

The woman smiles, and as she does so, her face changes. One moment she's Rowena, then she's the old woman, then a black male, then an Asian pensioner, then a young super-model, then a middle-aged man.

'Mother London,' says Cal wearily. The soul of the city manifested. In his bed.

Her face shifts back to Rowena. She winks at him. 'Got it in one, Casanova.'

'And what exactly is happening right now?'

'England is without a Raven King.'

'Right . . .'

'Mother Albion asked me to help appoint a new one.'

'OK . . .' Cal stares at Rowena. She's watching him intently, obviously waiting for a response. 'Do I have a choice?'

'Nope. Think of it as a promotion. You're now the High Protector of Albion, the champion of its people, and the lone magical protector of all who would cause harm to her soul.'

'What's the pay like?'

'Non-existent.'

Cal nods. 'Right then.' He gets to his feet and finds a half empty glass of whisky on his bedside table. He downs it in one and smacks his lips in appreciation.

Mother London stares at Cal quizzically. 'You do know what I'm saying?'

'Yep,' he replies, running a hand over his face. 'That I'm well and truly fucked.'

ACKNOWLEDGEMENTS

First off, a big thank you to my agent extraordinaire, Sandra Sawicka. Your encouragement and truthfulness are an immense help to someone who frequently veers off on random tangents. And thanks to my film and TV agent, Luke Speed. Without your uber agenting skills, we wouldn't be facing the possibility of seeing *Poison City* on the screen.

To my first editor, Anne Perry. Thank you for seeing something in *Poison City* in the first place, and also for your patience while I was going through a hard time during the writing of *Clockwork City*.

And to my new editor, Sam Bradbury. Thank you for your amazing editing on *Clockwork City* and for making the transition utterly painless and effortless. You rock.

And finally, to Erin Maher and Kay Reindl. You're both amazing people and I know whatever you do it's going to be awesome. Fingers crossed for all of us.

In the best books, the ending often comes as a shock.
Not just because of that one last twist in the tale,
but because you have been so absorbed in their world,
that coming back to the harsh light of reality is a jolt.

If that describes you now, then perhaps you should track down
some new leads, and find new suspense in other worlds.

Join us at www.hodder.co.uk, or follow us on
Twitter @hodderbooks, and you can tap in to a
community of fellow thrill-seekers.

Whether you want to find out more about this book,
or a particular author, watch trailers and interviews, have
the chance to win early limited editions, or simply browse
our expert readers' selection of the very best books,
we think you'll find what you're looking for.

And if you don't, that's the place to tell us what's missing.

We love what we do, and we'd love you to be part of it.

www.hodder.co.uk

 @hodderbooks

HodderBooks

HodderBooks